The Mirror

by

P.K. Eden

Cover Art by *The Wild Rose Press, Inc.*

The Wild Rose Press, Inc.
PO Box 708
Adams Basin, NY 14410-0708
Visit us at www.thewildrosepress.com

Publishing History
First Edition, 2024
Trade Paperback ISBN 978-1-5092-5759-1
Digital ISBN 978-1-5092-5760-7

Published in the United States of America

Dedication

For Mom

Thanks to our patient and understanding editor Dianne Rich who helped Patt and me through the process. She certainly earned some Heaven points.

Also thank to Mira Park who helped tremendously with this story.

And much love to my writing partner without whom this story would have never been told.

Prologue

Germany 1945

"Where is the Mirror?"

The SS Commandant's voice sounded like a snake hissing to the bloodied figure tied to a chair in front of him. "Where you and your Fuhrer will never find it," the man said. He smiled through swollen lips, defiance in his tone.

"But you will tell me."

"You are losing the war," the man said swallowing the pain that rose with each word. "It's only a matter of time."

"The Fuhrer needs the Mirror of Snow White so that will not happen."

"I am Primogen. Sworn by legacy to protect all the artifacts. I will not betray my birthright and help you and that madman see what can be and destroy the world."

The SS officer prepared to strike the bound man's face again when a knock at the door stopped him. He lowered his arm. "*Kommen.*"

A young soldier entered. He raised his hand and simultaneously smacked his heels together as he had been trained to do. "*Heil!*"

"Report," the officer ordered.

"The house was empty except for the old woman."

"Did you search thoroughly?"

The soldier let out a frightened breath. "We did and found nothing."

A sneer curled the senior officer's lip. "Bring the woman here."

For a moment, the soldier's exacting stance buckled, but he quickly pulled his shoulders back. "She killed herself before we had a chance to question her."

"Fool!" the commandant spat out before opening a cut on the cheek of the young solder's face with a punishing, black leather-gloved backhanded slap. "Get out!"

The soldier covered his bleeding cheek with one hand and backed away. Once at the door, he saluted and quickly left.

A low snicker filled the room elevating into a guttural, choking laugh.

The Commandant turned slowly.

The captive lifted his battered face. "You see, Herr Schmidt, we will do anything, give anything, even our lives. The search is over for you and your kind. You will never know the future before you live it." He smiled through bloodied teeth. "That is, if you live."

Schmidt felt his rage rise. He grasped the man by his chin so he could not look away. "By now your wife is dead and it is only a matter of time before we find your son. When we do, we will take the treasure from his dying hands."

The prisoner locked his gaze on Schmidt and laughed. "You will never find the Mirror. Even if you do, you will find the Primogens have taken great care to deactivate the magic by taking a small piece and rendering the Mirror dark. The shard is well hidden.

Without it, the Mirror is ineffective, reduced to a useless looking glass." His laugh grew louder. "It's over for you."

Schmidt shook his head. "I beg to differ."

In a movement almost faster than the eye could see, he pulled a black Luger from its holster and shot the prisoner through his right eye. The man's head lolled forward, and blood dripped onto the floor. As the sound of the gunshot faded, the phone jangled on the desk near the window. Schmidt strode across the room, his boots tapping a cadence on the wooden floor. He snatched the receiver from the cradle.

"Was ist das?"

He felt his entire body go cold as he listened to the voice on the other end. Slowly he laid down the receiver and turned to the dead man slumped in the chair. He loaded another round into the chamber of his Luger.

"You were right, old friend. It is all over. The Americans are coming." He shot one more round into the dead man and left.

In the streets, chaos reigned. People ran in all directions, some carrying suitcases or bundles, some fleeing with nothing but the clothes on their backs. Women held crying children and clutched the hands of toddlers. Older children and men who had not been conscripted into the German Army pushed wagons or carts loaded with personal possessions. The screaming of women and crying of frightened children sporadically overlaid the sound of bombs exploding in the distance.

Anger and foreboding clutched at Schmidt's heart. He had to get home. His breath came in short gasps as he wound his way through the panicked crowd. The irony of it all; he should be inheriting the world, not counting the minutes to his end.

He and his family were Taltos. Once loyal members of the Primogens, a secret society possessing some of the most arcane and mystical articles not known to man. Taltoians were a rogue sect bent on eliminating the Primogen protectors and using the objects for profit. For centuries, in the undercurrent of society, Taltoians fought the Primogens to regain the artifacts, but Primogen Sentinels, Council Loyalists, like the one he'd killed only a few minutes before, stood steadfast against them.

The old man wouldn't tell him the whereabouts of the shard from Snow White's Magic Mirror. The shard, a piece broken from the artifact to deactivate it, would lead him to the mirror. Once the mirror was whole, he would control the spirit inside. Depending on what he asked, he could either alter the future or use what he saw to fit into his plan.

As part of the Fuhrer's preoccupation with the mystical, Schmidt had been charged to find out if the stories about the Mirror were true and if so, to bring it to Berlin to help with the war effort. Schmidt had other plans for this magical object, but now the war and the approaching Americans changed everything.

The Sentinel was dead, and his son was surely on his way to Rome or some other Primogen sanctuary. The shard would be hidden once again to ensure it and the mirror were not united unless needed for some noble cause. Though he and Taltoians would not hesitate to use the mystical powers the mirror possessed for unrestricted gain, the Primogens exercised restraint and stayed away from altering the destiny of mankind except in dire circumstances.

After opening the door to his home, Schmidt became acutely aware of the silence. Normally, he would hear the strains of a concerto played on the grand piano by his daughter accompanied by the sweet humming of his wife. Today, however, the quiet was deafening. He closed his eyes, his heartbeat returning to normal. They were gone. Before leaving to interrogate the Primogen Sentinel, he arranged for their safe passage out of the city and made his wife promise she and his daughter would pack and leave. For the first time in days his smile was genuine.

He walked to the bar on the far side of the living room and pulled out a bottle of schnapps. After pouring a healthy portion, he lifted his head and saw his image in the mirror on the wall. The once confident man he saw now looked defeated. Slowly he smiled at the quirk of fate. He saluted and drank the shot in one long gulp.

For the second time that day he pulled the Lugar from its holster and cocked the trigger. He parted the lace curtains on the window with his forefinger. A few people still rushed through the streets as the sound of the war grew closer. There was no way he would sit in an American prison camp until his fate was decided.

His laugh came out like the hysterics of a madman. *I can see the future after all*, he thought, right before he put the Luger to his temple and pulled the trigger.

Chapter One

Present day

Siene Dower turned the corner on Eighth Avenue in time to see her mark moving up in the taxi line outside Penn Station. She took off running toward him. "Wait!" Several people, including her mark, looked her way. She ignored the gawkers and grabbed his arm when she reached him. "You can't get into a taxi today."

He gave her a stern look and pulled his arm free. "Do I know you?"

"Siene Dower," she replied.

"Sorry, never heard of you. Now, if you don't mind." He took a place in the taxi line.

"I do mind." She squeezed in line behind him, ignoring the pinched expression of the woman she cut off. "Better walk today." His annoyed expression told her any convincing would not be easy.

Skilled in the art of quick observation from her duty, as her mark, code name *Catalyst,* inched forward, she quickly evaluated him. He looked to be in his thirties, intelligent and nerdy but in a surprisingly appealing way. His short, cropped dark hair gave him an intellectual air and dark-framed glasses nearly obscured his blue eyes. In contrast to her jeans and black T-shirt, his dark business suit and white shirt with a tie at half-mast made her feel like a student greeting a teacher rather than someone who was about to save a life. Although he stood about six-two in comparison to her average frame, she'd been trained by the best and knew how to stop him if he tried to ignore her. She hoped the situation wouldn't require physical persuasion. She hated being arrested.

She tucked a strand of chestnut hair behind her ear and stepped in front of him. "You have to listen to me." He tried to step around her, but she mirrored his move, planted her feet, and held up a hand.

The Catalyst looked from her hand to her face. "Why?"

"I have to warn you."

"About what?"

"I can't really say." She glanced over her shoulder. The line for a cab was getting shorter, and she was running out of time. She grabbed his arm. "C'mon. Let's get out of here." The angry look in his blue eyes made her take a step backward.

"Look, I don't know who you are or what you're talking about, but you obviously have the wrong person and I'm running late." The Catalyst took a wide step toward a waiting cab.

Siene grabbed onto his arm with both hands and yanked him back. "No, you're the guy. I was sent here to warn you."

He looked from her hands to her eyes. "By whom?"

"I can't tell you."

"For what reason?"

It was a considerable test of her willpower not to blurt out the truth. "I can't tell you that either."

"Are you on some sort of meds?"

Siene shook her head. "I don't do drugs."

He smirked. "Maybe you should."

She returned the smirk. *Okay, that stings a bit.* She didn't want to tell him about the foretelling and sound like the nut job he assumed she was, but she had no choice. She held up her hands in a defensive posture. "Okay. Truth is, if you get into a cab, something terrible is going to happen."

The Catalyst pointed to the sedan he was about to enter. "This cab or any cab?"

"Doesn't matter. Get in a cab today and something awful will happen to you."

A small crowd began to gather around them.

"I think if I stay *here* something awful might happen. Now, excuse me." He put his hand on the cab door.

Siene pulled it off. "No!" Her voice boomed, and she noticed more heads turning toward them. She hated drawing attention to herself, but this guy was not giving her much choice. She positioned herself between him and the waiting taxi. "I can't let you get into a cab."

"What's going on?" A young man in the crowd began jumping up and down to get a closer look.

"I don't know," a woman responded. "I think that man just attacked that woman."

"No," someone else said, "I think she's trying to pick him up. Must be a hooker."

Siene was about to counter the comment but noticed a Transit Authority policeman talking on the small radio attached to his shoulder and working his way toward them. This was not going to end well, she thought. Too much attention.

She grabbed the Catalyst's sleeve with both hands. "We have to go." She glanced at the approaching officer. "Now."

He yanked the material free. "You obviously have mistaken me for someone else. So, if you will excuse me, I am speaking at a very important symposium and now thanks to you, I am definitely going to be late."

"Better late than dead," she said.

A businessman behind them stepped forward. "Are you taking this cab or what?"

"Yes, I am," the Catalyst said. He opened the cab door.

Siene positioned herself in front of the passenger door of the cab. "No, he's not."

The light at the corner turned red and gridlock jammed the intersection.

"I know this is weird," Siene continued, "and there are some things I really can't explain right now. You just have to trust me."

The Catalyst scowled. "Why should I? You are obviously a crazy woman."

"I'm not crazy." She curled her hands around the lapels of his trench coat. "What I am is sorry because there's really nothing I can do to change anything. Whoever gets into that cab is going to die."

The businessman stepped around them. "Hey, buddy, are you using this cab or not?"

"No, he's not," Siene answered.

"She says that whoever gets in the cab is going to die," the Catalyst said.

"Well, you can deal with your nutty friend," the businessman replied, "But I have things to do." He pushed his way forward and got into the taxi's back seat.

The Catalyst threw up his hands. "That's what I said."

With a heavy heart Siene watched the cab pull away. The gridlock had not cleared, so the cab only got as far as the intersection when the light changed to red.

A transit police car moved toward them, its siren chirping intermittently. Grudgingly, the crowd parted. At the curb, one of the officers exited the cruiser and joined the Transit Cop who now stood next to Siene.

"What's the hold up here?" the officer asked.

"I think he tried to steal her purse," a bystander offered.

The Catalyst spun toward the voice. "I did nothing of the sort."

"She jumped him," someone else shouted.

"No, he hit her," a third said.

"I did not," the Catalyst said.

"Can I see some ID?" the officer asked him.

"This is ridiculous." He dug his wallet out of his inside suit coat pocket and handed his driver's license to the officer. "I'm Ben Michaels. Dr. Ben Michaels."

The officer nodded and scanned the driver's license. "A doctor, huh?"

"Scientist," Ben corrected. "PhD in Immuno-Physics."

"Then you should know better," the officer said.

Ben shifted from one foot to the other. "I'm scheduled to give a talk at the medical center near the UN at one, and I'm already late."

"Well, looks like you're going to be even later." The officer nodded to Siene. "And you are?"

Siene's stomach spasmed. This wasn't the first

time her duty had created problems for her. If the officer ran her rap sheet, she'd have a lot of explaining to do. She had been detained a few times when she was caught trespassing during a mission. She forced calm into her voice. "Siene Dower."

Around them the honking of the cars rose and the cab Ben would have taken stopped at the intersection. The officer glanced briefly at the gridlock then held out his hand. "ID?"

She handed her license to the officer as murmurs and conflicting versions of what happened rose from the crowd until the voices blended into one sound, making no sense at all.

Ben pointed to the address on his license. "I live across the river in Jersey."

"I see that, Doc." The officer handed back the IDs. "But I still have to take you and the lady down to the station to sort this all out."

"Sort out what? I was getting into a cab, and she wouldn't let me."

The officer looked him up and down. "You're about a foot taller than the lady and she stopped you."

"That's right."

"So, this is an argument over a cab."

"No, she said if I got into a cab, I was going to die."

The officer turned to Siene. "You threatened to kill him over a cab?"

Siene's shoulders dropped. "No, I am trying to save him."

"From what?" Ben and the officer said in unison.

"It's hard to explain."

"Hey," one of the people in line shouted. "Can you

speed things up?'

The officer took hold of Ben's arm and steered him toward the police cruiser. We need to straighten this out at the station."

"But my talk," Ben protested.

"At the station, you can call and tell them you're going be late." Putting his hand protectively on Ben's head, the officer tucked him into the back seat. He turned. "Now you, miss."

Siene sighed. She couldn't help the businessman in the cab nor the driver, but at least the Catalyst, who now had a name, was safe.

At the intersection, the light turned green, and traffic began to move. As the officer steered Siene toward the cruiser, she watched the doomed cab move forward. A sick feeling encased her stomach. Briefly, she thought about trying to stop what she knew was coming but doing so would only result in more questions. Heavy-hearted, she slid into the back seat of the cruiser.

Ben cut his eyes to her. "Hope you're happy." He set his briefcase on his lap to make room. "I am going to miss my lecture because of this."

Siene closed her eyes. "But you'll be alive."

The officer started to shut the cruiser's door when, at the intersection, the cab Ben was about to take was struck by a delivery truck and exploded. "Holy shit," he shouted. Trying to avoid the collision, several more cars collided nearby. He ducked his head and peered inside the cruiser. "You two, don't move." He pushed the door and ran toward the accident scene.

Siene reacted instantly. She grabbed Ben's briefcase and jammed it between the seat and the car frame. The door banged against the case and shot open.

"What are you doing?"

"Preventing us from getting trapped in this car. The back doors of squad cars don't have handles, and you can't open the windows. Your briefcase was our only chance of getting out. Let's go."

Ben shook his head. "The officer said to wait here."

She held open the door. "You're kidding, right?"

Ben looked straight ahead, his face a stubborn mask. "I will not break the law."

She glanced around. "Listen, you can stay here and wait for whoever wants you dead to finish the job or you can come with me."

Ben swiveled his head to her. "I still doubt someone wants me dead."

"You're about to think I'm a cold bitch but…" She pointed to the intersection. "See that hunk of twisted, burning metal? That's a barbeque you aren't attending thanks to me."

Ben looked toward the chaos. "Good point."

"Then let's go."

The people on the sidewalk no longer cared about them. They ran past the pair, some looking for a safe spot, others taking pictures of the chaos with their cell phones, and others had their phones to their ears, probably connecting to 9-1-1 or fire departments.

Ben exited the cab and grabbed hold of her hand. "I need to know how you knew that would happen."

Siene pulled her hand free. "I can't tell you."

Ben narrowed his eyes. "You can't tell me much, can you?"

Siene shook her head. "Not here and not now."

'You have to tell me something, or I'm not going anywhere with you."

She sighed and her shoulders slumped. "Can't. I need you to trust me."

Ben clutched his briefcase with both hands and glared at her. "You keep saying that. I'm a man of science. I trust what I know and can see. What I know is, I missed my lecture, probably blew my chance at getting a grant to further my research and am about to become a felon for escaping from the back of a police car, all on the word of a madwoman who can't even explain what the hell is going on. Trust you? I wish I never *met* you."

Siene rolled her eyes. Any other person would be grateful. Not this one. She grabbed Ben's arm, turned him toward the intersection, and pointed. "Then trust what you can see. I don't have time to explain right now, so wrap your scientific mega-brain around the fact I just saved your life, Doctor Arrogant." She felt his muscles tense. "All you need to know right now is that the man we let take that cab is burned to a crisp like a marshmallow at a campfire instead of you."

Ben stared silently at the horrific scene. The sickening smell of burning flesh and melting rubber filled the air. Around them the shouts of pedestrians reacting to the horror, the approaching sound of the sirens of emergency vehicles, and the screeching of brakes deepened the shock on his face. Slowly, he turned away.

"Look," Siene continued, softening her tone, "I know you're a doctor and you probably want to help, but you have to come with me."

Ben looked at the flames rising from the vehicles

and could feel the heat on his skin. He turned and looked into Siene's eyes. "Okay. I'm not that kind of doctor. But you're right, let's get out of here."

As they ran in the opposite direction, the distinct feeling she was being watched haunted Siene. Ridiculous, of course; right now, no one cared about anything but the fire at the intersection. However, the feeling felt predatory, and she sensed the threat. She stopped and swept the crowd with her gaze. Tapping into inner senses she was still trying to understand and thinking it could just be a figment of her imagination, she tried to isolate the predator. But there were too many people and soon the sensation faded.

She had to get Ben to Brooklyn. Someone out there was intent on killing him and she couldn't let that happen.

****

The figure standing on the Eighth Avenue post office steps stared at the couple exiting the patrol car and watched them run up 32nd Street toward midtown. He stubbed out an unfinished cigarette with the toe of his pointy cowboy boot and sighed.

The boss isn't going to like this.

He took out his cell phone and hit the speed dial. Good news could wait, but bad news had to be delivered right away. He waited for the call to connect and was glad the boss was thousands of miles away. The last bearer of bad news was still recovering from the hundred or so stitches needed to close a gash extending from lip to brow. He began to sweat as soon as he heard the deep voice on the other end of the line.

"Mr. Davelos, I have some bad news."

Chapter Two

"Did anyone see you?" The voice came from inside of what looked to Ben like a vault in the basement of Siene's brownstone.

"No," Siene replied. She turned to Ben. "Wait here."

"Who's in there?" Ben asked. He tried to look around her, but she stood on tiptoes and blocked him.

"You'll find out in time." She stepped inside.

He started to follow, but she pushed him back and gestured for him to wait. Though he didn't enter, he could hear the conversation.

"There was an incident," she said.

"Is the Catalyst dead?" the owner of the voice asked.

"He has a name. Ben, Dr. Ben Michaels, and he's not dead…just reluctant to believe me," Siene answered.

"They usually are. You probably will need to do a little show and tell."

"The Council will not approve."

"Unless you have another plan, there is no time to get clearance."

She paused before she answered. "I hate this part of my job." She poked her head out of the vault. "How open are you to…" She stopped and blew out a long breath of air.

"Open to what?"

She heard the cynicism in his voice. She closed her eyes. He was going to call her certifiable again. "Open to defying the laws of physics."

Light pulsed from inside the vault in concert with the voice. "Not physics. It is reality. Don't confuse the man."

Siene turned. "Do you want to handle this?"

The light dimmed. "Heavens no. That never goes well."

"Who are you talking to?"

Ben tried to peer into the vault, but Siene raised on tiptoes again and blocked his view. "An old friend."

"You shouldn't have brought him here." Light continued to pulsate from inside the vault.

"Relax, I got this covered," she answered. "I felt eyes on us, so I brought Dr. Michaels here the long way. No biggie."

"A very big biggie," the voice corrected. "You know what's at stake."

"I do, but he doesn't."

Ben took a step forward. "Look, I appreciate your little ventriloquist trick here, but if you don't tell me what's going on and who is in there, I'm leaving." He heard what sounded like a noisy exhale, and then the voice.

"Under the circumstances, I would think a potential dead man should be a bit more grateful."

"That's it. Who is in here?" Ben leaned left then right, trying to look around Siene, but she mirrored each of his moves.

"A friend of sorts."

"What kind of friend lives in a safe in a

basement?"

"Someone who doesn't like humidity and prefers cool places."

"What is he? A troll?"

"Nah, the troll lives by DUMBO," Siene replied.

"Where?" Ben whirled.

"DUMBO—Down under the Manhattan Bridge overpass. Doesn't he know anything, Siene?" the voice asked.

Ben rolled his eyes. "I was joking. I know trolls do not exist."

Siene matched the gesture. "I wasn't, and they do."

Ben raised his hands. "If you're trying to distract me by making up ridiculous stories, it isn't going to work." He suddenly covered his mouth and sneezed.

"*Gesundheit.*"

"Thank you," Ben automatically acknowledged before he realized the reply came from the voice in the vault. "Your mysterious friend is German?"

"Why do you ask?"

"I recognize the accent. Most of the people I have worked with over the past two years were German." He retrieved a handkerchief from his inside jacket pocket and sneezed again.

"*Gesundheit,*" Siene said in unison with the extraordinary voice. "Before the day is over you might discover there is a German bloodline in play here."

She watched Ben blow his nose and then carefully fold the hankie into a perfect square before putting it back inside his jacket pocket. "A neatnik, huh?"

"You have a problem with personal hygiene?"

"Not really. It's just that most of the people I know would have used the back of their hand."

"That's hardly sanitary."

"Relax, Doc," Siene said with a small laugh. "I don't think a sneeze will give us cooties."

"Germs are so easily transmitted by…"

She cut him off with a wave of her hand. "I do know, and I don't need a science lesson right now."

"And I don't have time to give one. I've wasted enough time on this mysterious, and maybe under other circumstances an entertaining detour. But I must find a cab, get back to midtown, and try to salvage my credibility and my career."

Siene grabbed Ben's arm. "No cabs until I can figure this out."

"I already have," Ben said walking toward the stairs. "This is New York, and you are crazy." He shook his head. "People living in safes, exploding cabs. Crazy and dangerous."

"Show him, Siene," the vault voice insisted. "It is the only way."

Siene pushed the vault door closed. "Let's go. There's something you need to see upstairs."

Ben's brows furrowed and he thumbed behind him. "You just locked your friend in the vault."

"He's more like a colleague with whom I have to associate, but really don't want to."

"That's not a reason to lock him in there. Aren't vaults usually airtight?"

"He doesn't need air."

"We all need air." He walked to the vault and pulled on the handle. "I won't be a party to murder. Open it."

"Relax. He'll be fine." Sliding her palm along the wooden banister, she started up the steps. "Ow."

Ben turned. "What happened?"

She looked at her palm. "Splinter."

"Let me see."

"No, I got this." She pinched the tiny sliver of wood with the nails on her thumb and forefinger and removed it with a firm tug, then ran her tongue over the puncture. She held out her palm. "See. All better."

Ben grabbed her hand. "You licked your wound. Interesting."

She laughed. "First of all, it's not a wound. It's a tiny hole." She looked at her palm and could barely make out where the splinter had been. "Secondly, spitting was Grandma's remedy for small cuts. My brother Reed and I did it all the time when we were kids, usually when we'd be doing something we shouldn't and didn't want our parents to know. Spit saved our butts more than a few times."

Ben tipped his head. "Did you know that human saliva contains the most extraordinary antigen that actually promotes healing?"

"No. Should I?"

"It's a medical fact."

"Not one in any First Aid course I ever took."

"But a fact nonetheless." He studied her palm.

Siene pulled free. "You're not going to spit on me, are you?"

Ben's brows drew together. "Think back. Did you or your brother ever get an infection after you used this remedy?"

"No. When something happened, Reed and I would brush off what dirt we could and use good old-fashioned drool for the rest."

Ben nodded. "Fascinating."

Siene snickered.

"What?" Ben asked, furrowing his brow further.

"You sound like Mr. Pointy ears." She forced the smile from her face and clasped her hands behind her back. "Fascinating, Captain, a paste made of spit and dilithium crystals have magically cured your moon pox." It was her best Leonard Nimoy impersonation, but from the look on Ben's face, he had no idea what she was talking about. She held up her right hand, separating her ring and middle fingers, forming a vee. "Mr. Pointy ears—Science Officer." The blank look remained. "Not much of a fan, huh?"

Ben shrugged. "I'm into science not science *fiction.*"

"Okay then." She blew out a long breath of air and started up the steps. "This is going to be a lot harder than I thought."

"But speaking of science," Ben said, closely following her up the steps, "I was about to deliver a paper on this very subject to an array of noted scientists and medical professionals before you kidnapped me and brought me to this dingy, germ-infested cave." He wiped some dust from his sleeve.

Siene emerged from the basement. "I admit Suzy-homemaker I'm not, and maybe it is a tad dusty down there, but I've been busy."

Ben stepped into the kitchen. "With a bit more study, saliva could be the key to supercharging the human immune system. Imagine using our own body to cure terrible diseases."

"And destroy the global Pharma economy in the process."

"There are always consequences," Ben conceded.

"But life is precious."

She snapped up her chin. "I did save yours. At the moment, that should be a little more important to you than spit."

"Saliva," he corrected.

"Whatever."

"It's truly amazing what the body can do naturally," Ben said.

Siene grabbed him by the arm and pulled him away from the doorway. "Yeah, yeah, you can tell me later all about how if you managed to survive that intersection crash, you would have licked your wrist and naturally reattached your severed hand." She pressed a barely perceptible button on the wall and watched as the doorway seemed to disappear. Then she pushed a piece of chair rail back in place before pointing toward the hallway. "But first, there are a few unnatural things you need to know about."

"The last few hours have been unnatural. I doubt if there is anything else you can say or do that would surprise me."

Siene raised an eyebrow. "Hold that thought. We'll circle back to it in a few minutes." With a crooked finger, she motioned him toward the hallway. "This way."

Ben followed her to the library, a room rich in dark wood and leather. At least a few hundred books lined the floor-to-ceiling shelves. Even from a distance he could tell some of the books dated back centuries.

"Sit." Siene motioned to the black sofa next to the door. She walked to the back bookshelf and pulled forward an old book with her forefinger. She skimmed the pages as she walked back to him. About halfway through the book she retrieved a fragile-looking, folded paper with timeworn brown edges.

She sat next to him. "Show me your palm."

Ben held out his hand. "Why? Are you going to read it?"

"Do I look like a fortune teller?"

"You did predict the cab accident," Ben replied.

She rolled her eyes and gently unfolded the paper. Carefully, she dropped three brown, shriveled ovals into his palm.

Ben's brow furrowed. "What are these?"

"Beans."

"I can see that." He looked up. "Is this when I ask you why they were hidden in the book?"

"No, you're supposed to guess."

Ben lifted an eyebrow. "Do you really want to play games, Siene?"

She crossed her arms in front of her. "Actually, yes. You're the hot-shot genius. I'm curious to see if that big brain of yours can think outside the—" She felt a wicked smile form on her lips. "—outside the spit glands."

He shot her an annoyed look and used his forefinger to move the beans around on his palm. They were shrunken but all the same size and shape. Kidney beans, he guessed. Very old kidney beans. He glanced at Siene. "Beans hidden in a book. Did you get them from a prom date instead of flowers and this is your way of telling me that you're still thinking of the prom king?"

She saw amusement replace the annoyance on his face. Okay, maybe inside all the gray matter the man had a sense of humor. She'd try sparring with him later.

Right now, she had to make a seemingly very obtuse point. "Did your mother ever read you fairy tales when you were a child?"

"Yes," Ben replied, still holding the beans in his outstretched hand.

"Which ones?"

"The usual. Hansel and Gretel, Little Red Riding Hood, the Shoemaker and the Elves."

"What about Jack and the Beanstalk?"

Ben glanced down at the beans in his hand and then back at Siene. "Of course, and I suppose you're going to tell me these are magic beans."

Skepticism lit his eyes and Siene knew he wasn't quite there yet. "I know I'm asking a lot, but for a minute, just send all the Einstein stuff to the back of your gray matter and go with it." His expression told her he thought she was nuts and she suspected ninety-nine percent of the world's population would probably agree with him. "I guess laymen might say they are magic."

"Laymen." Ben paused before shooting her a probing stare. "People off their meds like you, you mean."

She held up her finger. "You agreed to go with it."

"No, I did not."

"Let's pretend you did. These beans are the last ones left. It drives my brother, Reed, crazy that I keep them in a book. He thinks it's the first place a Taltoian would look." She held the book up so he could see the title.

"Taltoian?"

"I'll get there in a minute." She lifted her chin. "Look at the book."

White paper showed through the frayed corners of the cover and the embossed lettering worn low by the passing years made the words hard to read. He leaned closer and squinted. *Tales by the Brothers Grimm.* His head snapped up. "Is this an original edition?" He turned the book over and then back. "It looks very old."

Siene nodded. "They are my great-great—maybe another great, maybe not, it really doesn't matter at this point—Uncles Jacob and Wilhelm. The book has been passed down through the generations."

Ben's wide-eyed gaze flared. "You *are* crazy. You expect me to believe these are the magic beans they wrote about? That if you plant them, a stalk will grow as high as the clouds and if we climb it, we will meet a giant who has a goose that lays golden eggs?"

"Yes, and other things. A golden harp..."

Ben stood. "This has been an adventure to say the least, and I will admit you might have a very valuable book that could command millions, but you being related to the Brothers Grimm,"—he looked down at his hand—"And these are magic beans, I don't think so."

"Why not?"

He handed her back the book and held up fingers in a vee. "Two reasons. One, I suspect if there actually was a goose that laid golden eggs, some billionaire would own it and two, a giant, by sheer atomic weight and mass, cannot stand or live on a cloud."

Siene shrugged. "Whether you believe me or not, it's still true."

"Which part?"

"All of it." She slipped her hand under his. "I better take those back now." She carefully placed the beans inside the paper and back into the book.

Ben remained still for several minutes as though processing the information he just heard. "It appears your uncles, if they truly are, are not the only ones who can tell tall tales."

She put the book back on the shelf. "They wrote the stories to protect the artifacts."

"Artifacts. Like those in a museum?"

She looked at him and smiled. "No, the ones in my uncles' stories."

"Which stories?"

"All of them."

Ben blew out a short breath of air. "Hmm. I see."

Siene threw up her hands. "Finally, you believe me!"

Ben tapped his temple with his forefinger. "What I believe is that you are seriously delusional and need help. Help I can't give you, so I'm going to leave now."

He took two steps toward the library door when something heavy crashed to the floor in the hallway and footsteps echoed. They looked in unison as the library door opened and the entry filled with a large man wearing a ski mask, holding a semiautomatic pistol with a thick, stubby silencer pointed right at them.

"Don't move," the gunman ordered.

Ben stepped in front of Siene and reached for the lamp on the end table when a muzzle flash briefly flared as the gunman fired the weapon in his hand. The bullet struck the bookshelf behind them, knocking a porcelain figurine onto the floor.

Siene raised her hands and elbowed Ben to do the same.

"Now that I have your attention, sit and don't do

anything stupid!" With his gun trained on Siene, the intruder walked into the room and pushed her onto the couch. He angled the gun at Ben. "You, Mr. Hero, sit next to her." He kept his aim trained on Ben until he complied, then returned his sights on Siene.

"What do you want?" she asked.

He didn't hesitate. "The mirror."

"There's quite a few in here. Take your pick." She gestured to the one on the far wall while holding the fear and adrenaline inside her at bay. "Take that one."

"Don't play games with me. Snow White's mirror."

Ben stood. "Okay, that's enough." He glared at Siene. "More fairy tales?" He pointed to the gunman. "Is this little antic for my benefit?"

She grabbed Ben's arm. "No and stay out of this."

Ben shook free and took a step toward the gunman.

The gunman countered with a blow with the gun barrel to side of Ben's head.

Ben staggered and dropped onto the sofa.

Siene rushed to Ben and ran her hands across the point of impact. No blood. He hadn't been struck very hard. She turned to the gunman. "You bastard. You could have killed him."

"That's still in play." The intruder pointed the gun at the center of Ben's chest. "I'm only going to ask once more before I shoot Mr. hot-shot hero here. Where. Is. The. Mirror?" He spaced the words evenly for emphasis.

Siene weighed her options. None were good. Someone was going to die if she didn't think of something fast. "It's in France," she lied.

"It's not here. It's in France," the gunman repeated.

For a moment, Siene thought the man was talking to himself, but then she made out the outline of an earpiece under the ski mask and a thin microphone near his mouth.

"Where?" the man demanded, the gun in his gloved hand flicking impatiently.

"Fontblanche."

Through the slits of his mask, she could see his dark eyes narrow. "That property is a maze of buildings. Where exactly on Fontblanche?"

"At the Abbey of Senanque."

"I've been there. It's nothing but a tourist trap with a gift shop." Gun hand still extended, he took a step closer to Ben. "No more lies."

Siene jumped to her feet. "He doesn't know anything, and I'm telling the truth." Panic knotted in her stomach. She couldn't let Ben get killed. She still didn't know what he was meant to do. "The monks have protected the mirror since 1903. It was never moved."

The gunman lifted his weapon in a threatening move. "How do I know you're not making up a fairy tale of your own?"

"You don't," Siene admitted. She gestured toward Ben. "Let him go and I'll go to the abbey with you." Her heart hammered inside her chest as she prayed he'd take the deal.

Ben stood and grabbed Siene's hand. "I go where she goes." His mouth thinned into a determined line.

A snicker came from underneath the gunman's mask. "Fine. I can kill him anytime." He pointed to the door with the pistol. "You first, hero." He grabbed Siene by her upper arm. "You and I are going to get really close until we get the mirror."

"Hey, easy." She jerked in opposition to his hold. "I'm not a ham shank." Pain from his grip shot down her arm to her fingers, but she refused to let it show on her face. Not knowing if the gunman would be able to get off a shot if she made a move on him, she also resisted the impulse to kick him in the balls. She was well versed in the martial arts, having honed her skills in Japan, but that would have to wait until she could be sure the gunman wouldn't hurt Ben. As the Catalyst, he held the key to saving the city, and she needed to find the proverbial lock to set things right.

The gunman shoved Ben out into the hallway and then pushed Siene ahead of him. They had just cleared the doorway when she heard a scuffling sound and then a muffled curse before the grip on her arm released. She whirled around in time to see the gunman stagger backward, his free hand on the back of his head. On instinct, she folded her right leg and drove it forward in a kick to his chest. He flew backward and landed on the floor in a heap. She looked up and saw her brother with his back pressed against the hallway wall, a brightly colored maraca in one hand and a dark brown liquor bottle in the other. Red tassels dangled into his eyes from the sombrero on his head.

She laughed. "I'm glad you used the maraca. It would have been a sin to break a perfectly good bottle of Brazilian cachaça."

Chapter Three

"Is he dead?" Ben blinked twice but otherwise seemed riveted in place.

"No." Siene knelt beside the gunman and pulled off his ski mask. She ripped the earpiece out of his ear and found his cell phone in his back pants pocket. She tossed both to Reed who caught them against his body. "Get what you can before whoever he was talking to dumps the info."

Reed nodded and disappeared into an office. Siene began going through the rest of the gunman's pockets.

Ben reached down and grabbed her arm. "What are you doing?"

"Trying to find out who he is."

"Shouldn't we call the police?"

She shook her head. "That's the last thing we need to do." She found the gunman's wallet in an inside pocket of his jacket and thumbed through it. "Damn. Nothing."

Ben pulled her up. "Who is he?"

"Taltoian, I would guess."

"That's the second time you mentioned a Taltoian. What is that?"

She looked at Ben's confused stare. "Later. I don't have time to explain everything to you right now. Let's just agree he is a very bad man. Grab his legs." She slid her hands under the gunman's shoulders.

Ben did not move.

She jerked the gunman's upper body. "I can't do this by myself. C'mon, grab his legs. We have to lock him in the closet before he comes to."

Ben hesitated for a moment, then complied.

At the pantry door, Siene struggled with the knob, and the gunman slipped from her grasp. He moaned when his head bounced on the floor. "My bad." She kicked the closet door out of the way. "Put him in."

Ben set the man's legs down. "I don't feel right about this. We should call the authorities."

"Don't get all responsible on me."

"Why?"

"Because I don't need the police showing up and asking a thousand questions, and you need my help if you want to stay alive." She struggled to lean the gunman against the wall, but he slid, and his head hit the floor again.

Ben held up his hands. "Why should I listen to you? For all intents and purposes, you kidnapped me, have someone locked in your basement, and showed me beans you want me to believe are magic." He walked to the closet and took a quick look inside. "And let's not forget you have an unconscious man in your closet and won't call the police."

Reed stepped out of the office and into the hallway. "Because our masked man is a killer for hire." He held out a printout of what looked like a rap sheet. "Max Biden. He's an Eraser. Seventeen kills this year alone."

Siene grabbed the paper from him and clenched her jaw. "That bastard sent an Eraser to kill me."

"What bastard?" Ben asked.

"Lucian, Lucian Davelos." She uttered a quiet

curse. "An old friend." Contempt dripped from her words like acid.

Reed shrugged. "Maybe you shouldn't have dumped him."

Siene's glower could have stopped time.

A moan came from inside the closet.

"I think he's waking up," Ben said with a glance inside the closest.

Reed hitched a thumb toward Ben. "By the way, sis. Who's he?"

"That's Ben. He's some kind of brainiac researcher and the Catalyst."

"What's he supposed to do?"

Siene shrugged. "Something with spit I think."

Ben pointed to the closet. "I think one of you should check on this guy."

A groan rose from the gunman and he moved, his right foot kicking a broom into the hallway.

Ben picked up the broom and tossed it back inside. "He's waking up."

"What do you mean something with spit?" Reed asked, ignoring Ben.

Hand on hip, Siene continued to pace. "The mirror activated. It showed me this guy getting into a cab and then the cab near Penn Station exploding when it got to the intersection. Fast forward, I saw New York deserted and in shambles, meaning if Ben died so did the city. So, I intercepted him outside Penn Station and brought him here. He says he's working on a spit project of some sort."

"Saliva," Ben corrected. "And the self-healing enzymes it might contain."

More rustling came from inside the closet. "You

better see this," Ben said more emphatically this time.

Siene and Reed turned to Ben. "In a minute," they said in unison.

"Are you sure he's the Catalyst?" Reed asked.

Siene stopped striding and folded her arms across her chest. "I watched the cab he would have been in get slammed by a city truck, just like the mirror predicted."

Reed pointed to Ben. "With one twist. The professor here didn't die."

Ben took a step forward. "I think you both might be crazy, but just in case some of your story is true, you might want to do something about the guy in the closet."

Reed strode to the closet door and looked inside. "He's right, sis. Max is waking up."

"Not for long." Siene grabbed the maraca from the table in the hallway and whacked Max on the head. He stopped moving.

Reed leaned in. "You didn't have to hit him that hard."

"He's fine," she responded.

"You two *are* insane," Ben knelt and checked Max's neck for a pulse. "Head injuries can be very serious."

"So can gunshot wounds," Siene reminded. She pulled Ben from the closet by his arm before slamming the door and turning the lock.

"That isn't going to hold him for long once he wakes up," Reed said.

"I know. We need the Cleaners," Siene announced.

"Already on it," Reed replied. He angled his watch to his eyes. "I figure we have about ten minutes."

Ben dug in his heels as Siene began shoving him

toward the kitchen. "Stop! Cleaners, Erasers, magic beans?" He gestured toward the closet. "Someone tried to kill us and you're not calling the police. Tell me what is going on."

Siene took a deep breath. "Listen, I promise I will explain everything. You just need to trust me."

"Again, with the trust issue?" Ben exclaimed. "I don't even know you."

Siene extended her hand. "Hello. I'm the stranger who saved your sorry ass from being incinerated in a taxicab. And this—" She pointed to Reed "—is my brother who saved you from a bullet to your closed-minded brain not more than five minutes ago. Now, shut up and follow me unless you want to be looking down the barrel of another gun with no one around to rescue you." She headed down the hallway toward the kitchen.

Ben glanced at Reed and drew down his brows.

Reed folded his arms over his chest. "If I were you, I'd listen to her. You're apparently a few hours past your expiration date and by now Davelos knows it. He never leaves loose ends." He glanced toward Siene. "Correction, maybe once."

Siene spun on her heels. "Reed, isn't there something you're forgetting?"

Reed extended his hands, palms up. "Don't think so."

"Someone you haven't bothered to acknowledge?" she corrected.

"You mean Lina? Well, sis, a funny thing happened while I was in Brazil."

"Reed!" She drew out his name. "Where is Lina?"

He grimaced. "I kinda lost her."

"What do you mean, you kind of lost her?"

"Okay, I actually did lose her."

She shook her head in disbelief. "I told you this would happen sooner or later. You promised you'd be careful. How could you lose her?"

"You know how she likes to get out and shop," Reed protested. "She always turns up sooner or later."

"You better hope she does," Siene warned. "Lucian would like nothing more than to tuck her into one of his pockets and take over the world."

Ben's brow wrinkled. "Who is Lina?"

"Her name is actually Thumbelina. She's kinda into modern day things and…" The sound of a large truck outside caught her attention. Siene glanced over her shoulder toward the front door. "Damn, I don't have time to explain right now." She grabbed Ben's arm and activated the hidden entry. "We've got to move. The Cleaners are here, and they never take very long to mop up messes."

Chapter Four

The fool had failed!

A bead of sweat ran down the side of Lucian Davelos' face. He wiped it away with his thumb, but another followed. His anger wouldn't abate on its own. He needed a distraction. He picked up a remote from his desk and pressed the only button. As the light filtering drapes slid closed, he walked to the office door and flipped the lock. No interruptions.

He walked to the back oak-paneled wall and stared for a moment at the Renoir he bought just last week. The painting was an original, just like everything else he owned or intended to own. He moved his hand under the bottom of the frame and felt for the tiny switch. When he pressed it, the entire wall slid aside, revealing another barrier. In front of him a handprint identification panel turned light green. He placed his hand on the plate and a beam of red scanned his palm from top to bottom. As if satisfied with the results, a small cylinder jutted forward, and Lucian leaned his left eye against the lens. Another scan commenced before a soft ping indicated the recognition process had been completed. The final obstacle slid out of the way.

He looked through the intricate and reinforced glass barrier separating him from his latest prize. "Good morning, Thumbelina."

"It's Lina, you pickle-headed dick wad." Her small

voice was amplified by Bose speakers.

"My, my, is that any way for an icon to speak?"

Lina continued to file her nails. "Drop dead."

"Charming as ever."

She sat on a velvet chaise lounge no bigger than a shoe box. "Just let me out of here, and I can show you how charming I can be."

"Now, now little one, we've been all through this. You know I can't allow that."

"Come on, don't be such a wuss. Crikey, I'm only twelve inches tall. What can I possibly do to you?"

Lucian's smile dropped as the vivid memory of the pain she'd inflicted when he kidnapped her rippled across every nerve ending in his body. Thankfully, he managed to drug her before she could strike again. He wanted her small enough to fit in his pocket and unconscious, so he had to estimate the tranquilizer dosage and mix it with a bit of one side of the mushroom Alice found in Wonderland. Unfortunately, the mushroom diluted the mixture and Lina woke up in his pocket before he could get her to his office. The retaliatory pain inflicted on his manhood was something he'd never forget and something she would pay dearly for when he no longer needed her services.

"So, how's your left one hanging?" Lina shot him a one-sided grin. "Still sore? Not to worry. I only had my pocketknife with me, so the scar won't be big. Oh wait, neither was anything I stabbed either." She slapped her knee and laughed.

"You wouldn't think it so funny if I cut off your air supply or enclosed you completely in darkness."

Lina stood and placed her hands on her hips.

"I've been up against the Ogre of Corinth and I'm

still here." She hated that ogre. Had a scar on her left thigh as a reminder. But she wouldn't let Lucian know. "You don't scare me."

Lucian arched an eyebrow. "Lina, my little angel, we used to be friends. We can be again."

"Not in this lifetime, jerk face. You ruined any chance when you went against the Council."

"The Council is made up of archaic fools. They have no idea the power they hold. Why the Food Horn alone could end world hunger. Rapunzel's tears can cure any and all illnesses."

Lina rose and gave him a cocked hip pose. "It's called the Horn of Plenty, stupid. Do you really think the tears were intended to cure all illnesses? They are living things. The tears choose whom to help, not you."

Lucian's gaze slid away from the reflective glass for a moment before returning to Lina. "Well, I intend to change all that. Only those who can pay and pay well will be allowed to even look upon the marvels I intend to obtain."

"Fat chance, buddy. The second the Council finds out that I'm missing, you're going to be the first person they look for."

"I suspect that, but they can't prove a thing. I'm amazed at how easy it was." Lucian chortled. "There you were sitting atop a palm frond enjoying Carnivale and all I had to do was pluck you up like a ripe cherry. That fool, Reed, probably never knew you were missing until morning."

"You only found me because my screwed-up DNA kicked in and shrank me like wool in hot water." She got up and went to the wall. At least Lucian had cut a tiny window so she could look out at the street. The view, albeit one of warehouses, kept her from going completely mad with her confinement and being at her captor's mercy.

Siene is going to have a major cow when she finds out Reed took me to Carnivale. If I get out of this, I'll never do anything like that again. She almost laughed at the absurdity of her thoughts. *Shit, that's a lie. Of course, I'll do it again.*

Lina turned and saw a muscle tic at the corner of Lucian's jaw. He was a good-looking son of a bitch with dark wavy hair and features of a patrician. She always thought his smile could seduce the panties off a woman from across a crowded room. Once a loyal member of the Primogen Council, he now was every inch the bad guy. Pity someday someone was going to kill him.

"Look, Lucian, I know you. You were a decent man, influential and commanding Primogen. It stunned everyone when you crossed over to the dark side—with apologies to every light saber carrying hero in the sci-fi universe, of course. I can help you. We can fix this."

Lucian shook his head. "There is nothing to fix."

Lina stared at him and then pressed her palms against the glass. "You're making a big mistake."

"The mistake is not mine." The words were deep and powerful as though they'd come out from someone other than the rogue operative he was.

Lina felt fear for the first time since she had been taken. "What are you going to do with me?"

His face relaxed. "Come now, little pip, there is nothing for you to worry about, as long as you do exactly as I say. But first, tomorrow is your birthday, and I have a special surprise. I know how much you like presents, and I promise you are going to love mine." He rubbed his hands gleefully.

She glared at him. "I'm almost two hundred years old. Do you really think you can give me anything I don't already have?"

"Even if it is something a model would walk down a runway?"

"Toy fashion doll clothes again?" She put her hands on her hips. "I have a better body." Fuming, she fought to control her temper. Hissy fits never worked with Lucian. "If you intend to give me something I might like, you can tell me what the hell I'm doing in this glass prison and how long you intend to hold me?"

Lucian leaned closer to the glass. "Forever, since it seems that's how long we'll be living if all goes according to plan."

She could see the pulse throbbing at the base of his throat. "So that's why you snatched me. You want the combination to the vault that holds the water from the Fountain of Youth."

"Among other things."

"There's no way…"

Lucian hit the glass with such force that the entire structure shook, knocking Lina off her feet. "You'll do as I say, when I say, or you'll never see your friends again."

Lina rose, wiped some dust from the bottom of her skirt, and crossed her arms over her chest. "Then I'll stay here forever if I have to."

He snickered. "Forever is a long time, my dear. You'll change your mind."

She glared at him. "You were destined to be a member of the High Council. What happened?"

"History, my dear. History."

"You had history with Siene. We all thought it was a good match." She saw Lucian's eyes darken.

He looked away and then quickly back. "Sometimes history writes a different ending."

"If you think by doing this, you'll win her back, you are sadly mistaken."

Lucian trained his dark gaze on her. "Absolute power is a mighty thing. Once I have the artifacts, I can have anything, and that includes her."

****

Siene looked up from the lock on the vault. "Ben, you have to promise me you'll keep an open mind before I let you in the vault again."

"Are we here to get your friend?"

"No. Reed will take care of that."

"Then is there a back way out through there?" Ben could hear dozens of footsteps on the floor above him.

"Not exactly."

"You said we shouldn't leave through the front, so I would think that if you wanted to get away, you wouldn't come down here unless we could get out through another secret door."

She opened the vault. "We can get out, only we won't be using a door." She stepped inside. "Come in."

The atmosphere was as murky as before, but this time, when Ben stepped into the vault, he found himself staring into a pair of cold gray eyes.

The eyes became larger as though the owner had leaned forward. "Nice to see you again."

It was the same voice Ben had heard before. Trying to see the thing that lived in a vault in a basement in Brooklyn, he squinted, seeing nothing but the eyes.

"And you are?"

The eyes seemed to retreat. "Siene hasn't told you?"

"There wasn't time," she replied.

"Oh my, then this is going to be fun. Hit the lights, Siene."

The overhead LED lights flashed on, and Ben saw his reflection in a large mirror. He looked around. "Where did he go?"

"I'm right in front of you."

Siene nodded. "He is. Look closer."

Ben leaned forward and investigated the mirror. He could see himself and Siene, then, as he continued to stare, the outline of another face began to form. Seconds later he could clearly see eyes, a nose, a grin on a mouth…every detail as though he was looking at a charcoal drawing of a man. He cut his gaze to Siene. "I think I may be hallucinating."

"You aren't." With a nod, she urged him to look even closer. "Mirror, this is Ben. He is the Catalyst."

"Hello, Ben. You can call me TM."

Ben blinked hard and gave his head a shake as the face solidified, taking on dimension and shading. "I *am* hallucinating."

"No, you're not—talk to TM. We are running out of time." Siene pulled the bookshelf in the back corner of the vault away from the wall.

Ben leaned closer, focusing with all his might. "Hel-lo." He said the word slowly, as though he wasn't sure he would be understood.

The face in the mirror retreated. "Personal space, my good man." When Ben stepped back, the face grew larger, centered in the mirror. "And I'm not an alien. I speak English. The proverbial King's English."

Ben turned to Siene. She was busy digging in the exposed dirt of the vault floor. "This can't be happening. It is scientifically impossible to speak to an inanimate object and have the object talk back."

"And yet, you are." she replied.

"This is not real."

She reacted to the disbelief on his face. "You said you would keep an open mind."

He pointed to the mirror and then to Siene. "I must have a slight concussion from when the gunman hit me on the head with his pistol. It has affected the auditory region of my brain." He sat on the floor. "I will be fine in a few moments."

Siene pulled him to his feet. "You are fine now, so get up."

The face in the mirror now took up the entire plane inside the frame. "He's an odd sort. Are you sure he's the Catalyst?"

"Perfectly sure," Siene replied.

Ben put his fingers onto his temples and waggled his forehead. "Must be a bit more serious than I thought. I still hear voices."

Siene sighed. "The mirror is talking, Ben."

The image retreated to the size of a normal human face. "Emerging and talking happens occasionally when I'm needed to help save the world."

Siene folded her arms across her chest. "Modesty isn't one of TM's virtues."

Mouth open, Ben looked from Siene to the Mirror.

TM responded to his stare with slanted eyebrows. "If he is indeed the Catalyst, mankind is in serious trouble this time."

"Be nice, TM."

"I suppose we work with that which we get." The eyes narrowed at Ben. "Well, what's your story?"

Ben remained motionless, mouth agape.

Siene waited, hoping Ben would come around. He just needed some time for his neurons to begin firing again. He slowly took off his glasses, closed his eyes, and inhaled through his nose. When he opened his eyes again, she noticed for the first time how deep blue they were, much like the color of a great expanse of ocean. They were nice eyes, almost beautiful, and in them she could see acceptance rising despite his skepticism.

Ben sighed. "I'm a researcher. What are you?"

"An enigma."

Siene stepped in front of the mirror. "Now, do you believe there is a reason I needed to save you from a death ride in that taxi?"

"I guess I have to," Ben replied. He raked his fingers through his hair before tucking his glasses into his shirt pocket. "Everything I know says this is impossible, incomprehensible…supernatural."

She reached out and touched his arm. "No, I promise you, it's real." She stepped back and opened her arms. "Look around. These are some of the most precious artifacts in the world. We keep most in a main vault, but some are kept in different locations around the world in case Taltos somehow discovers the Sanctuary. Nothing in this world is totally secure. We can't afford to lose them all if that does happen. You already know that the mirror can tell the future. The spinning wheel over there actually does spin straw into gold. The beans I showed you in the library will grow in seconds and take you up to a castle in the clouds."

"Where a giant lives?" Ben asked in a still skeptical-sounding voice.

Siene nodded. "He's pretty harmless actually. Just has had a bad run over the years." She walked around running her hand over several more objects. "Each of these things can impact the world either for good or—" She stopped, remembering. "—for domination depending on who possesses them."

Ben rubbed the back of his head. "What are you? Some sort of conjurer?" He crossed his arms over his chest. "And since I do not believe in magic, it brings me back to the original question—what are you?"

"I'm a Primogen."

"I see. And what's that? Some covert society?"

"Kinda," she confessed.

"Have a secret handshake, too?" He began to pace. "You almost had me for a minute." He gestured to the mirror. "Where's the projector for that thing? He walked to the mirror and felt around the edges. "There must be a mike hidden somewhere."

"Stop! That tickles," TM said.

Ben drew down his brows and pointed at the mirror.

"The premise is not all that easy to explain in the time we have left here." She looked over her shoulder as loud crashes echoed from the floors above. "We have to go. Now!"

"Why?"

She blew out a long sigh. "If you remember, someone tried to kill you?" Her eyes narrowed. "Twice!"

Ben stayed silent for a moment. "Okay. I'll play along. My chances for a grant are all but gone anyway.

What else do I have to do?"

TM's face elongated. "If I had hands, I'd clap."

"Be nice!" Siene scolded. "It is a lot for a Normie to handle."

TM's gray eyes narrowed again. "I suppose. You usually don't let them see us. Something is wrong."

"Big time. Lucian sent an Eraser after us. Reed showed up in the nick of time."

"I assume you've called the Cleaners?" TM asked.

Siene nodded. "They are upstairs now. Afterward, they'll pack things up here. I'm taking Ben to the Compound. We have to tell the Council about this." She opened one of the canning jars she found on the top shelf.

TM sighed. "I guess that means I'm going dark."

"Can't be helped."

Lightning flickered behind the Mirror's face. "I do hate that. No concept of time passing. It drives me mad." TM's ethereal chin lifted, and he shut his now gray-green eyes. "Quickly now."

Siene poured the contents of the canning jar in the dirt she'd loosened. When it touched the ground, the dirt first seemed to liquefy. An eddy formed a swirling tube that started small but then grew large enough to fit a car. Above them, they could hear crashes and thumps. Outside the open vault door, lights flashed.

Siene grabbed Ben's hand. "Time to go."

Ben started walking toward the vault door.

"Not that way." She pointed to the floor and the spiraling ground. "This way."

Ben looked at the pulsating vortex. "You have got to be kidding. I'm not going in there. What is it?"

"Soil from Alice's rabbit hole."

Ben raked a hand through his hair then released it. "Seriously?"

Siene reached to the mirror and broke off one corner. Immediately, TM disappeared, and the mirror went dark. "As serious as a heart attack." She shoved Ben forward and he became engulfed in the spinning murkiness near her feet. Then she took one last look around before jumping in after him.

Chapter Five

In the blazing African sun, Joseph's legs felt like stone. He didn't think he could go much farther without collapsing. He didn't want to be like the others, left for dead by the men who destroyed his village and killed so many.

He'd come to Tanzania to visit his extended family before starting his last year of residency at Massachusetts General in Boston. Once at the village of his grandfather, he'd taken the ancestral name given him. Mosegi. He'd only been in the village a few days before the marauders came. Before he was taken, Grandfather warned him not to reveal his true identity.

Word had come from the neighboring villages that the raiders killed all they thought might challenge them. Although sinewy, Joseph easily passed for a teenager and so he remained quiet and continued the ruse, thinking he could somehow help.

But he was soon forced inside a circle made by the invaders where most of the able-bodied men, women, and older male children gathered, confusion and fear on every face.

A black-clad guard spoke in the native language ordering all to remain quiet and still. When Grandfather reached between two warriors and grabbed Joseph's arms to pull him back, he was assaulted and tossed on his back like a sack of grain. When the last man was dragged from his hut, the raiders left with their captives, leaving only the older women, youngest children, and the sick behind.

That was days ago. The chains around Joseph's wrists reopened wounds from trying to free himself from the jagged metal and sent a fresh wave of blood down his hands and arms. So many times, he prayed for rescue. Instead, every day he faced more endless miles and mindless nights.

"You must walk faster," the man behind him whispered. "You must keep moving. If you fall behind, we will all be punished."

Joseph wanted to move faster but fatigued by the endless walk and weakened by the lack of sufficient food, he couldn't. "Where are they taking us?"

"To the mines." Hoof beats drummed behind them, and the man quickly looked away.

"You swine. Move faster!" a harsh voice shouted. "You need to begin to dig by morning." The horse's hooves thundered against the ground again. Joseph could feel the vibration in his bones.

Just before the raid he had listened to the stories told by the elders around the night fire, stories of a place of despair and evil, filled with men, women, and children who worked day and night. The elders had said no one ever came back to their villages once taken. Strong men were taken in the night and only mindless bodies returned.

For a while the village of his grandfather remained safe, then suddenly men attacked, taking the village without mercy, killing all who tried to escape. The next day, after spending the night eating, drinking, and making use of the women to satisfy their lust, they chose the strongest and put them in chains to begin the walk. For three days now they walked from morning to night without much food or water, the chains never coming off. During the night some of them died. Joseph tried to imagine the evil place the elders spoke of. Now he would witness it firsthand.

As the fourth night approached, they crested a hill and peered down at a pit carved into the earth. They had arrived. Horses circled them, putting the people inside the tight ring they made. Joseph stood rigid as the one who led them stopped his horse only a few feet from him. A thick cloud of dirt torn from the ground by the horses' hooves landed on him, filling his mouth and eyes. His throat closed against the onslaught, increasing his thirst, and further reminding him of the hopelessness that had settled into every part of his body. The ones who died, they were the lucky ones.

"Stop here!" the man shouted.

Joseph did not look up. Looking into the eyes of these men was like looking into the eyes of demons. Part of him wanted to run so they would kill him. It would be easier than facing the mines—only his legs would not move—partly due to fear, partly due to fatigue.

Suddenly the man dismounted, and an underling handed him a bucket. Soon other men came up from the pit, bringing more buckets with them. A hush fell as all the men approached. The male prisoners formed a circle around the women. They were already crying in fear.

The one who led walked to Joseph. "Come here, boy." He set the bucket down and scooped up some of the water inside with a hollowed-out gourd. He held it out. "Thirsty?"

Joseph looked at the guard and nodded.

"Then drink."

With a shaking hand he took the gourd but hesitated, as a nagging feeling pressed him.

"Go on," the man urged. "Drink it."

The water tasted like honey as Joseph slaked his thirst. A second passed and the prisoners rushed for the buckets held by the other men. Joseph was pushed to the rear of the throng where he watched as men and women clawed at the buckets, sucking the liquid greedily down their throats.

Suddenly, Joseph vomited. With no food or water in his stomach for days, yellow bile mixed with some of the water spilled onto the ground from his mouth. A feeling, like a rock forming in his stomach, grew with spreading tendrils of pain. He staggered on wobbly legs, as numbness crept into his limbs and up his neck, spreading like some sort of spirit trying to possess him. He fell to the ground and thrashed, screaming at the increasing pain, feeling as though he was being eaten alive. Slowly, with his last bit of strength flagging, he could no longer fight. He stopped moving and allowed the demon inside him to take over.

Through eyes that now saw only shades of gray, he watched the men reform the prisoners into a line. He rose and joined them as the line staggered into motion and walked into the pit.

****

Lucian didn't bother to wait until the jeep in which he rode came to a complete stop. Grabbing the roll bar with his left hand for balance, he jumped out and strode to the lead guard. "How long until the first shipment is ready?"

"With the addition of the new villagers, about a month."

Lucian cursed. "You obviously don't understand the urgency here."

"Then why don't you tell me," the lead guard replied, holding out his hand for the water bottle his underling offered.

"I need the raw tanzanite shipped in two weeks for sale. The money will hire the mercenaries I need to find the sanctuary."

"What sanctuary?"

Of course he doesn't know, Lucian thought. This man was more concerned with lining his own pockets by brokering blood gems than understanding world politics and finance. No sense telling him about his grandfather, Karl Schmidt. Better to let dead relatives lie. He would never know that a treasure greater than any coming from the earth was out there, just waiting to be claimed.

A second jeep pulled up next to Lucian, the passenger distinctly female. "Africa is so damned hot."

As irritated as Lucian was, a half-smile of amusement lifted his right cheek. "And Brazil is not?"

"Very funny, Lucian. You know I spent most of the time in that damned air-conditioned box you had built."

"It was the box or my pocket, Lina darling. It's much easier to keep track of a full-size woman and not someone the size of a small doll." He was pleased he had managed to obtain one of Alice's mushrooms. It had cost him a small fortune on the black market but mixing a bit of the left side with her food had made Lina grow. He kept her full-size by spiking just about everything she ate. He let his gaze run down her full length, noticing how the heat made her tank top and jeans stick to her five-foot six-inch body. "I do like the new you."

With the back of her hand, Lina dabbed the perspiration forming on her neck. "You tricked me."

"Perspective, my dear. I merely made it more convenient to have you watched."

Lina sighed and blew a stray wisp of hair off her forehead. "How long am I going to be this size?"

"For a while. Full-size or diminutive, you are my insurance policy."

"Insurance, huh? That's a slap in the face."

Lucian smiled. "My dear, the deal was, you help me when needed, and I let you out of the box."

"And just when am I going to be needed?" She *was* worried about making a deal with the devil, but she had to find out what he was planning. "You've been dragging me all over the world and nothing yet."

"You are on a need-to-know basis, and right now, you don't need to know."

Lina bristled. "I told you I'd help you. Are you saying I am not a woman of my word?"

"That remains to be seen." He offered her a perfect smile. "You are a fascinating woman to be sure, but a woman of impeccable candor…hmmm…I'm not sure." He held out a bottle of water to her.

She eyed it suspiciously. "Did you mix something in there, too?"

He twisted off the cap and took a healthy sip before offering it to her again.

"I guess not."

"We are not so different, you and I," Lucian said in

a throaty murmur, leaning closer to her. "I have people who are very concerned about events that could shift the world financial markets and so do you. Using the artifacts to find out these things in advance could help us both. We are the perfect match. Together we can broker a peace between Taltos and the Primogens and rule the world."

She pushed him back with one hand and continued to drink until the bottle was empty. "Not so fast, King of the World. You seem to be ignoring the fact that Taltos and the Council of Seven have been fighting for eons." Her laugh was tight. "You and I, while we may be a match made in heaven for the moment, are not going to get anyone on either side to hug and sing kumbaya just because we say so."

Lucian laughed and arched an eyebrow. "Once inside the sanctuary, the power base will shift and neither side will have a choice. We will have to work together or risk exposing the artifacts to the world."

Lina looked over his shoulder at the line of people walking in and out of the pit, some bringing up full baskets, others returning to have them filled. She didn't know enough about Lucian's plan to derail it just yet.

She blew out a long breath of air. *Crap*. For now, a deal was a deal. She'd have to make good on her part of the bargain until she knew what the hell he was really up to.

****

Siene and Reed watched as the members of the conclave gathered in the meeting chamber beneath Crater Lake in Oregon. She knew this day would change everything; an attempt on the life of a Catalyst had failed and now he had been summoned before the

Primogen Council. They needed to find out more about Ben Michaels to figure out why Taltos wanted him dead.

Two hundred years ago Taltos, the enforcement arm of the Council, came to the sanctuary and made demands of the Primogens. The Primogens had always made the Law of the Protectors, but Taltos wanted to share more in the decisions concerning the artifacts, especially about using them in the new, more contemporary world. Across from each other around a table specifically brought to the Sanctuary by Paz Santos from South America and made from Lignum Vitae, the hardest wood in the world, Taltos and the Primogens met for five days, shouting, slamming fists, as well as swords, axes, and bodies in combat onto the wood with little or no effect until all agreed there was no truce to be had. Taltos then declared itself emancipated from the Council and its laws and left.

While the Primogens moved the sanctuary in secrecy to the bottom of Crater Lake in order to hide it, Taltos found solace across the ocean on the rocky island of Egyptian Semnet. There, slowly, generation by generation, they grew in strength and numbers. But they struck too soon, trying to wrest the location of the Mirror during World War II, and had failed.

Now, they were back. More focused and apparently with a stronger network. More importantly, somehow Taltos knew why Ben needed to die to further their cause, and the Primogens didn't. The Council of Seven would have to meet and try to find an answer.

One by one the members entered the chamber, speaking quietly among themselves, comparing notes on the various and widespread enterprises on which they administered. Kai Soong, the Asian Protector, nodded to Siene and Reed before taking her place next to Caleb Buru, the African warrior who joined the Council after the death of his father. Jon Two-Bear, a great Chief from the Cherokee Tribe of North America, sat alone communing with his spirit guide as he always did before council meetings. Paz Santos, from South America, Quinnock E'ak, Antarctician expert in survival techniques, and Jack Brumboo, an Australian with MacGyver-like abilities to make something from nothing, stood near the bar, waiting.

Siene wondered what this noble council would say when they realized that war with Taltos was inevitable, and that war would probably be fought in the human world. To win, they may even need to use some of the artifacts, a possibility that went against the very grain of their diktat.

Some of the Primogens claimed the time was ripe for an all-out attack on the nation of Taltos. At the last meeting, Quinnock had confronted her. *We are a strong Council, our abilities well honed. Are you afraid to confront Taltos? If so, step aside. I will lead.*

Quinnock had been readying for war in secret. Using Intel gathered by Jack, he planned to strike a blow to the very heart of Taltos in their compound on the Egyptian island. After the initial strike, a private army of soldiers would deploy and eliminate as many of the Taltoian followers around the world as they could find before word got out about the strike. Fortunately, only Jack had found the plan viable. Being the two Primogens living in the more remote areas of the world, they had naturally gravitated to each other and were close. The council had voted against them.

Now, today, Quinnock's plan seemed to have more merit.

Siene and Reed took their places at the table as rumbling whispers arose from the others. Some were concerned about the Catalyst's absence from the meeting and others speculated it would be better to initially talk without him. Siene let her gaze move from one council member to another before taking a deep breath and rising. "I believe Taltos is planning to try to force our hand, hoping to find this sanctuary and then attack it," she said.

"Why?" Jack asked.

"The Mirror activated on its own this time."

Jack stared at Siene a minute before speaking. "You're saying it activated to save the Catalyst?"

"And without anyone summoning the spirit," she confirmed. Whispers rose like the buzzing of bees. She let them continue for a few minutes before raising her hand for silence. "More than that, I believe Lucian is involved."

Jack stood. "How'd ya know that?"

"I thought I saw him a few months ago, but I couldn't be sure." She nodded to Reed who tossed her the cell phone they took from the intruder at the townhouse. "Reed was able to pull a few numbers from the gunman's phone before it began a self-destruct program. He traced one number that led him on a twisting digital path, ending with an old number we had for Lucian."

Jack started to say something, but Reed cut him off. "Relax. I didn't jeopardize protocols. I sanitized the path with a gamma ray flash and then ditched the computer in Central Park."

"Suppose that phone is a homer. It could lead Taltos to us."

"It didn't have a homing device implanted inside. I checked."

Jack pointed to Kai. "I'll feel better if the electronics expert looked at it."

Reed tossed the phone to Kai, who took it apart more quickly than anyone could even follow her movements. She studied it for a few moments before nodding. Reed's face showed his satisfaction.

"This sanctuary is secure, and no one here would ever jeopardize the artifacts," Siene said.

"Maybe not deliberately, but as technology progresses, many opportunities arise. Both to track and to trip us up," Jack pressed, looking directly at Reed. "Kai should have examined the phone, not Reed."

"Reed is quite capable," Kai said.

"To a point," Jack said quickly. "I don't argue with his ability with weapons; designing then, making them from practically nothing and such, but weapons technology is quite different than electronics technology."

"Not so much," Reed defended. "Some weapons use tracers and drones run by computer programs. Besides, there was no time to get the phone to Kai. It would have been wiped clean remotely if we didn't act fast. We did get some information. The electronic trail pointed to Taltos."

"Lucian." Jack growled his name.

"And that's why we have to be even more focused," Siene said. "Together we are a force, our abilities strong. The artifacts have been safe these hundreds of years. Our ancestors used them only in dire emergencies. Taltos has long wished to gain control of them to control the destiny of mankind. We have sworn, like our families before us, to not let that happen. Mankind must make its own future, devoid of any interference that would come with someone using any of the objects. We know Taltos wants the Mirror specifically. Lucian could use it to see the future and manipulate the global economy. Governments would collapse, making them ripe for the taking." She looked at Jack. "We have to set aside any doubts we may have, shut down the counter-operation, and find Lina."

Jon Two-Bear rose. "Then, we must question the Catalyst and try to find answers in what he tells us."

"I'll get him," Siene said.

Chapter Six

Ben looked up when Siene entered the room. She'd changed into some sort of white robe trimmed in red, making her look rather regal. Far cry from the jeans and T-shirt she wore the last time he saw her and definitely more interesting. The attire gave her an aura that was hard to ignore. He tried to stand but halfway up to standing, the room began to spin, and he fell back onto the bed.

"I'm sorry about that. You're feeling the Rabbit Hole aftermath. You get used to it after a while." She disappeared into the adjoining bathroom and returned with a glass of water. "Take deep breaths. It'll pass."

"I feel like hell." He took a sip from the glass she handed him. "But not bad enough to think we teleported somewhere. You must have drugged me and brought me here somehow." He glanced at the glass and set it on the floor next to his foot.

"I didn't drug you and there's nothing in the glass but water." She let out a weary breath. "Teleported? For now, let's say that's what happened. I don't have time to explain. The Council is waiting for us."

He shook his head slowly. "I'm not going anywhere else with you until I have some answers."

Siene knew a discussion was inevitable. She nodded.

"First, what is a Primogen and how are you

connected?"

"I'll have to give you the short version for now. The Council is waiting for us."

"It's a start."

"The Primogens are part of an underground defense society and have been since the mid-1800s when the charge was given from a dying man to his grandson and then to every member of the family, my family, since."

Ben shifted on the bed and rested his forearms on his thighs. "Part of the military and secret like Area 51?"

"No. The government doesn't know about us."

"But you said it was a defense society."

"It's complicated. We don't defend the country; we defend what you would call artifacts."

"Like those from an archeological dig? I thought those were protected by international law."

Siene blew out a long breath of air. She didn't have much practice explaining the concept, but she had no choice. "Here's the deal. You saw some of the artifacts we look after in New York. There are hundreds more scattered over all the seven continents."

Ben's brow furrowed. "You protect fairy tale artifacts? Seriously?"

"Come on, after all that's happened you are still cynical? You saw the Mirror. Heard it talk."

Ben straightened. "Could be all smoke and mirrors." He smirked. "Pun intended."

Her heart sank. Everything that could go wrong, had gone wrong. She thought about her father, her grandfather, and all that she and Reed had given up when the obligation charge was passed to them. She would not be the cause of the fall of the Council.

She paused to collect herself. "Whether you want to believe it or not, these historical objects are among the most powerful artifacts in existence. Some can cure disease, affect time, see the future, and even kill— among other things you cannot even imagine. They must be kept safe and out of the hands of those who would profit from their unique powers at all costs. As long as someone from the bloodline, a true Primogen, has possession of them, none will be exploited. If they remain protected, mankind will move forward and develop without being manipulated."

"And Taltos?" he asked.

"They are Primogens who went rogue and are now our mortal enemies."

Ben looked down then glanced up. "I'm a scientist, Siene. None of this makes sense."

She sat beside him. "I know I'm asking a lot of you, but the next few days are critical. Politics, war. It's all coming together, and we have to try to stop it before the international economy gets all screwed up and sends the world into a global depression." She bit down on her lower lip. "If all that comes to pass, Taltos will declare sovereignty and force the Primogens to challenge them. Conflict could force both sides to use some of the artifacts and, once they are revealed, everything we know would be rocked to its core. Your precious science would seem like a lie. Straw could be spun into gold. Giants would live on clouds. Geese will lay golden eggs for whoever owned them. It would be chaos, anarchy."

Ben stared at her for a moment. "You're serious, aren't you?"

"Deadly. A war is coming and somehow you are a vital part. A catalyst, actually. Whether you choose to believe me or not, what you do in the next few hours or next few days will decide the fate of mankind. The gunman at the townhouse, Max Biden, got away before the Cleaners could contain him. He's probably with Lucian now, planning the next move."

Ben's brows furrowed and released. "Why does this Taltos want *me*? Until yesterday, I didn't know any of this existed."

She shook her head. "I only know TM activated without the call."

Ben's brow furrowed. "What is the call?"

"The mirror doesn't usually activate unless one of the Primogens calls to it." Siene saw confusion on Ben's face. "Like in the story. *Mirror, mirror on the wall.* The one can ask a question. But this time, the mirror called to me. It was an unprecedented warning. I'm guessing somehow the mirror saw a cataclysm and that you can prevent it thus ruining everything for Lucian. That's why he wants you dead."

"But that Max person said he was looking for the Mirror. He never mentioned anything about me. He didn't seem to know who I was. If this mirror could see destruction, why couldn't it show you how to prevent it?"

Siene's shoulders slumped. "Dealing with the mirror and the other artifacts is very complicated. Mirror's visions are not always absolute. But they do foreshadow. We can't discount anything Mirror tells us. We must dissect the warnings to the best of our abilities and pray we are right."

"So, you Primogens are like comic book

superheroes."

Siene bristled. "We are not. We have abilities, not superpowers. For example, I am pretty adept at engineering, and Reed is a weapons expert. The rest of the Primogens have talents that are useful to our cause. That's why we needed the Council together to try to put all the pieces together. We need to figure out the Taltoians' plan. If we fail, the sanctuary could be compromised—making the artifacts vulnerable."

"Okay, let's say for the moment I believe everything you said. Tell me more about this Council I'm meeting."

"The Primogen Council of the Seven Legacies is like an elite senate consisting of a representative from each of the seven continents, each member appointed to protect the artifacts from the folklore of their people." She reacted to the skeptical look she saw on his face. "You've talked to the Mirror. You can't deny the existence of the objects."

Ben nodded. "I can't argue with what I've seen with my own eyes. Go on."

"Each Primogen administers his congress and his contacts in his own way. The how is not important to the Council as a whole. Keeping the artifacts safe is all that matters. Periodically, the Council meets to maintain continuity with emergency sessions called when needed, as one is now. We know Taltos is looking for the Mirror and we know you are pivotal in some manner. In bringing the Primogens together, we hope to figure out why. It could take years to explain it all to you. You just have to trust me for now."

The whole thing was incomprehensible. Supernatural. He was a man of science. He didn't believe in the supernatural, yet here it was right in front of him. He struggled to decide whether he should buy into all this magic talk. What choice did he really have? He had no idea where he was and if Siene was right, his life was in danger. He'd play along. For the moment at least.

He stood. "Okay, let's go."

She took his hand. "Okay."

As they walked through the compound, he could not help but notice the change in her. She seemed more subdued, more serious. It suited her. She appeared majestic.

In the whirlwind of the past few hours, he hadn't noticed just how beautiful she was. But today, in the calm, if you could call it that, he could not help but see it. When they talked, her eyes became so intense. He felt as though one could be swallowed inside them like a sailor on a stormy sea. Her mouth, full and lush, was set below a perfect nose and underscored by a softly curving chin. The robe she wore made it seem as though she slid over the floor instead of walking across it.

"Why are you staring at me?" she asked, breaking into his admiring thoughts.

"Your face," he said without thinking.

She released a little laugh. "What's wrong with my face?"

He grabbed onto the first thought that came into his mind. "It's very balanced."

"Is it?"

"Yes, very unusual. Usually, one eye is slightly bigger than the other, or one cheekbone is a bit more prominent. But not with you." He looked her up and down. "You seem rather symmetrical."

Her smile widened. "I take it you've been assessing me for a while."

"Scientifically speaking, yes."

"Then that explains why every time I walk away, I feel like you're staring at my ass." A thread of humor colored her voice.

"I may be a scientist, but I am also a man." He shrugged.

She angled her head toward him. "Actually, I did notice that back in the library. I never thanked you for stepping up like that."

"You're welcome." He smiled, the corners of his mouth turning up ever so slightly. "By the way, where are we going?"

She stopped at a set of double doors, the only doorway in the long hallway. "Here."

When she turned, he saw a map of Europe emblazoned on the back of her robe, embroidered there in the same deep red that trimmed the edges. She hesitated and then opened the doors and motioned Ben inside. Almost reluctantly, he entered the room.

Inside, he counted seven people, all robed like Siene, seated in brown leather chairs. He let his gaze fall on each one in turn. As a scientist, he always concentrated on the details. To him, this encounter was no different than if he were looking through the eyepiece of a microscope at specimens on a slide.

"Primogens," Siene said. "Welcome Ben Michaels. Dr. Ben Michaels." Some nodded, others did not even try to greet him. She gestured to a woman on her right. "Kai Soong, Asia."

Kai nodded her acknowledgement.

Siene then introduced the remaining. "Caleb Buru, Africa; Jon Two-Bear, North America; Paz Santos, South America; Quinnock E'ak, Antarctica; and Jack Brumboo, Australia. As direct descendants, Reed and I share the council seat for Europe with one vote between us." Siene took her place on the empty chair and gestured to Ben to sit on a chair positioned next to her.

Reed, his robe also trimmed with red, spoke. "Primogens, the Mirror revealed Dr. Michaels is a Catalyst, and his predicted death would have a catastrophic effect on New York City and possibly the world."

"Do you know why or how?" Jack asked in his distinctly Aussie-tinged voice.

Reed shook his head. "As we know from the past, the Mirror can only tell us what *may* happen, not why. After Siene chose to act, there was an attempted attack at the New York townhouse. We know now that Taltos is looking for the Mirror and we have reason to believe the incident at the intersection and the attack on the townhouse are connected. We also now know Lucian is involved."

Whispers rose in the chamber. Jack raised his hand for silence and spoke. "Is it then wise to bring the Catalyst here? Taltos may be tracking him."

"He's been sanitized," Reed replied.

"Sanitized?" Ben's head jerked.

Siene put a hand on Ben's arm. "Just to be sure you couldn't be tracked."

Ben's gaze darted around the room. "Sanitized when? How?"

"Right after you arrived. Before we brought you into the compound," Reed answered. "But don't worry.

It wasn't like you were dipped in bleach or anything." He furrowed his brow. "Feeling nauseous, Doc?"

Ben shook his head. "No."

"Any hair falling out? Any unusual bleeding from an orifice?"

"For pity's sake, he's a scientist," Siene said with a sigh. "Just tell him."

Reed shrugged. "Okay, first we doused you with a mist of methylchlorburanate and then we shot you with gamma rays to be sure Taltos didn't inject you with something organic that could be traced or put a tracker inside you somewhere."

A look of horror settled onto Ben's face. "You used gamma rays on me?"

"You were out cold. You didn't feel a thing." Reed's tone suggested the procedure was commonplace.

Ben began to rise, but Siene put her hand on his shoulder to stop him, "Please, Ben, sit down. I'm sorry but it was necessary. You were treated with a low dose exposure and your DNA is busy repairing itself as we speak."

Her touch seemed to calm him. "I'm not going to turn all green and burly, am I?"

Paz chuckled. "He thinks he's going to turn green."

A warning, but tolerant look from Siene cut the laughter.

"Comic book characters are not real," Paz said. She looked him up and down. "But you could use some muscle. Grow a beard and call me. We'll talk then."

Though smiles rose on the faces of the rest of the Council, none commented aloud.

Quinnock spoke up. "Dr. Michaels, why do you

think you were targeted?"

"I have no idea," Ben replied. He looked around the room. "I have no idea about anything."

"What is your specialty?" Quinnock asked.

"Biomolecular physiology."

"He was working on some spit project," Siene added.

Ben frowned. "Stop calling my work a spit project."

"Excuse me, saliva project." Siene rolled her eyes.

Ben nodded at Quinnock. "I am studying lysozyme and its effect on some infections. It is known to attack the cell walls of many gram-positive bacteria. I think if manipulated correctly, lysozyme could be useful in the treatment of many diseases."

"Exactly what did the Mirror show you, Siene?" Kai Soong asked.

"Besides his death?" Ben glared at her as she continued. "The city was deserted. No one seemed to be left."

"Could be some sort of plague prediction," Quinnock concluded.

Siene shook her head. "I don't think so. The Mirror would have shown sick people if a plague was coming. The city was empty, like everyone just moved out."

"And it is clear Lucian is looking for the Mirror. If he intended to infect people with something, he'd have something ready and be done by now," Reed added.

"Agreed," Siene said.

"Have there been any reports of missing artifacts?" Reed asked.

A low buzz of voices filled the room as the Primogens conferred. Each rose in turn. "None."

"Except for Lina," Siene reminded Reed.

"Lina's missing?" Kai asked.

Reed grimaced. "I sort of lost track of her in Brazil."

"Why was she in Brazil?" Kai asked.

"Lina is an artifact?" Ben interjected.

"When Paz and I left her, she was twelve inches tall. I didn't think at that size she would go out," Reed told Kai.

"Lina is a person, and she's twelve inches tall, *and* she's an artifact?" Ben's voice trailed off.

"Reed, you know better," Kai said. "We all know Lina has been working on sizing at will."

"Lina is twelve inches tall, an artifact, and she's walking around somewhere," Ben repeated in a voice tinged with disbelief.

Reed shook his head. "I know, I shouldn't have taken her away from of the compound."

"Wait. No one in the world has noticed someone a foot tall walking around somewhere?" Ben said, louder this time. He glanced at Siene. "I know you mentioned her in passing, but who or what is this Lina really?"

"Thumbelina," all the Primogens said at once.

Ben looked at the fierce looks on the faces of the seven people staring at him and held up his hands defensively. "I suppose one of you can tell me more about her condition later."

Paz stood. "I have Seekers looking for her day and night."

Reed also rose. "I take full responsibility, and I know that if anyone can find Lina, it will be one of Paz's Seekers."

"My cousins can find anyone or anything," Paz

agreed.

Ben frowned. "I know this is none of my business, to a point anyway, because I have been drawn into all this, but shouldn't more than a few cousins be looking for Lina?"

A few of the Primogens smiled. Jack laughed out loud. "Pazzie here has more than a few cousins, mate," he said.

"What like ten, fifteen?" Ben asked.

This time all the Primogens laughed.

"More like sixty," Jack replied. "And those cousins have cousins. Don't worry, mate. She's got this covered better than the CIA or Interpol. Finding people is her superpower."

Siene rose. "The New York City site has been cleansed and the artifacts transported here. They will be catalogued and inventoried. That report should be ready shortly, but I believe all is secure."

"Since the Mirror is the target, we must safeguard it as we did in the past," Quinnock said.

Siene reached into the pocket of her robe and produced the sliver she removed from the Mirror earlier. "Already done. Also, before we subdued the intruder, I planted some false information with Max about the Mirror's whereabouts which he passed on to Lucian. It should give us time to give us time to figure out what Lucian is planning and how Ben is involved."

Paz stood. "I'll get an update from the Seekers. If something sinister is about to happen, they will find out where and when."

"And I'd like to see the notes on your serum and maybe a sample, Dr. Michaels," Jack said. "Could be an important link."

"My notes are in my briefcase, but I didn't bring a sample of the serum with me to New York," Ben replied. "The only sample I synthesized is in my lab."

"Where's the lab?" Jack asked.

"New Jersey. I'm a principal scientist in Antibody Research at Biosynetrics."

"We can't risk sending someone for it," Kai said. "Undoubtedly, Lucian already knows his mission failed and has sent a team to Dr. Michaels' lab."

"Then, Dr. Michaels can use the lab upstairs to reproduce his serum," Jack said. "Once we know the properties, we can figure out why Lucian wanted him dead."

"You have a lab here?" Ben's voice quickened with excitement.

"I dabble," Jack replied.

"Jack is our resident MacGyver," Reed explained. "Being in the Australian Outback, he's learned to make things from whatever is available. Give him a Bunsen burner and a test tube and you'd be amazed at what he can do."

Jack laughed. "Still can't turn straw into gold like the wheel can, mate, but I'm working on it."

Siene stood. "We all know what we need to do. Let's meet back here in twenty-four hours for an update. Reed and I will take responsibility for Dr. Michaels and his safety."

"So be it," Jack said. The rest of the Primogens nodded in agreement.

Ben held up one hand in protest. "Don't I have a say in this?"

"No," Siene replied.

Chapter Seven

The lab was on the third floor of the complex. Siene and Ben didn't speak as they rode the elevator. At the lab door Siene pressed her hand to a black box mounted on the wall. A blue line scanned back and forth over her palm before the lock released and the door opened. They walked into what looked like a holding area. There, Ben watched Siene press her thumb against another keypad.

"Hello, Siene," a computer voice said as a second set of doors opened. She hit the light switch with her elbow. Ben followed her inside.

"This is the main research lab." She leaned against one of the long countertops lining the walls. "It's fully equipped—Atomic Absorption Spectrometers, Electrophoresis Systems, IR Spectrometers. You know, all the bells and whistles. What do you think?" She could tell Ben was at a loss for words as he turned in a slow circle, seemingly scanning every inch of the lab. "Pretty impressive, huh?"

Ben nodded, eyes as wide open as his mouth. He pointed to the back corner of the lab, "Is that a Particle Accelerator?"

"Will be. Jack's building it."

"I thought he said he just dabbles."

Siene laughed. "That's what he calls it. C'mon. There's more."

The last door on the left had the familiar yellow-triangle biohazard sign in the center along with a system of protected entry scanners on the wall. Through the sheet of thick glass that served as part of the door, a line of white protective suits, along with the necessary gear, hung in cubicles.

"This is our Anatomic Pathology Testing Lab," she said. "A fully automated diagnostic lab that can scan every processed specimen to create a digital image for enhanced analysis."

"You need something like that?"

Siene nodded. "The artifacts are very old, Ben. They don't always mix well with evolving human physiology. The 2007 Bird Flu epidemic? Ours. The Golden Bird didn't adapt well to modern times when it got loose. It infected a few of our Seekers. Before we realized it, the world had itself a full blown H5N1 Avian Flu pandemic."

"I don't recall a fairy tale about a golden bird."

"It's not one of my great uncles' better-known tales. They did write 209 of them."

"Looks like I better make sure my library card is current when this is over," Ben said with a smile. "I have some catching up to do."

Siene smiled with him. "We built this lab soon after the bird flu outbreak to handle anything that may happen again. The Primogens almost released Rapunzel's Tears to atone for the mistake, but fortunately, the CDC developed a vaccine and brought the strain under control."

"I studied H5N1 and the vaccine," Ben said. "That particular vaccine was made from inactivated viruses and did not contain any live viruses. It stimulated the human immune system to make antibodies against the bird flu virus that hypothetically could protect a person. The vaccine was purchased by the federal government for inclusion within the CDC's Strategic National Stockpile and is not available to the general public."

Siene studied his face. "You look like a man who knows more than he's saying."

"In 2011 the CDC found a newly mutated strain. The vaccine did not offer protection against the new H7N9 bird flu, and Biosyn got the contract to adapt the vaccine. I was on the project."

"Were you successful in adapting the vaccine to the new strain?"

Ben shook his head. "Unfortunately, no. But the project did give me a pathway to my current research with the enzyme in saliva. That research is very promising."

"After this mission is over, maybe I can get you a sample of Rapunzel's Tears to analyze. They could help advance your project."

"Does the CDC know about you?" Ben asked.

"Are you kidding me?" Siene replied. "Have you even seen any action hero movies? We can't afford to let them even have a *hint* about the power we protect."

Ben slowly shook his head. "So, you're saying there are 209 magical things here somewhere." Pure skepticism filled his voice.

"209 give or take since we also protect folklore object not written into fairy tales, and they are not all here. Some are stored on each continent in case the sanctuary is compromised. That way, worst case scenario, all are not lost to invading Taltoians. It's not a perfect solution, and we are trying to correct that, but so far all scenarios have anomalies we need to correct."

Ben shook his head. "You seem to have a lot of unresolved issues." He hitched a thumb over his shoulder. "How about I solve one and just leave. Then you can get on with protecting your novelties without having to worry about me getting in the way."

The look in Ben's eyes told Siene that she still had some work to do on him. She walked to one of the metal desks in the lab and slid her backside onto the desktop. She pointed to the chair. "Sit down. Let's talk." Ben complied. "I know you still have a lot of questions, so shoot."

He thought for a moment before speaking. "I don't know where to begin."

Siene held onto the edge of the desk and leaned forward. "Let's agree on some facts first then. There have been a select few objects throughout history that somehow have powers one might deem 'supernatural.' My great uncles started writing about these artifacts in fantastical stories to hide their true existence. Eventually, people started bringing new objects to them so that they could be protected from evil forces. And protect themselves from nefarious lowlifes. You have met the people sworn to protect them—including the person before you now."

"Okay. Magic objects may exist and so do you. I'll cede that." Ben nodded. "First question, then. Where did these artifacts come from?"

"We don't know for certain." She saw suspicion dart around in Ben's eyes. "Accounts of their origin have been lost over the years. We have come to accept that they simply are."

"Why doesn't the world know about any of them? I

would think it would be hard to keep so many a secret for so many years."

"Fair question. Before the Primogens, the artifacts were only protected by those who owned them. For example, the Shoemaker sheltered the elves, Rapunzel collected her tears and told no one of the power they possessed, and the dwarves held onto an apple that could put someone to sleep. Most of the original possessors were not evil, and some witnessed first-hand what happened when an object was misused. They all came to realize what might happen if the objects fell into the wrong hands."

Ben seemed to be processing the information. "So why didn't these possessors, as you call them, just keep the objects hidden?"

"Because they were human, Ben. Not immortal. They knew someday they would die and worried about what would happen after they were gone."

"Sounds like another fairy tale to me."

Siene smiled. "And that is exactly why the Primogens exist. Hear me out, Ben. Please."

He nodded, the skepticism in his eyes softening just a little.

"Rapunzel was the first," she continued. "The Brothers Grimm had already written eleven or so of their fairy tales. She sought them out because of their stories and told them about the healing property of her tears. They didn't believe her at first, so she showed them. I'm told my uncles watched in horror as she cut an artery in her wrist and then looked on in awe as she healed the wound with her tears. The account of how Rapunzel and my uncles united has blurred over the years, but the result was that they wrote her fairy tale to disguise the existence of her tears."

"But wouldn't writing about them bring more attention?"

Siene shook her head. "Back then science was not as advanced as it is today. A story about magical tears was viewed as simply fantasy."

"But what about the good a liquid like that could do for people who were suffering? Why hide something that might, for the sake of argument, have cured cancer or saved Martin Luther King or John F. Kennedy?"

The weight of the life's mission that Siene accepted from her father when she became a Primogen felt like a rock in her chest. Every moment of their lives, the Primogens walked that fine line between knowing the marvels they had could help the world and knowing the same marvels could also destroy mankind if in the wrong hands.

"Rapunzel and my uncles knew that when she died, so did the supply of her curative tears. They also understood that a wondrous gift should be preserved. She and my uncles collected as much of her tears as they could over the course of the time they were together. Only the tears of deep emotion were the tears that could heal. There isn't much of the tears left, and so far, we haven't been able to create something similar. If world leaders knew we had even the smallest drop of something with such great power, wars would undoubtedly be fought to obtain it. Millions upon millions of people could die fighting over this power." She swallowed the anguish that rose in her throat. "I know people die now who could be treated with Rapunzel's tears, but it was a choice that had to be made."

"But think of the good that can be done," Ben protested.

She slid off the table and walked away. This decision was one she, and all the Primogens, struggled with constantly. "It isn't worth the chance. You know the adage about absolute power and how it corrupts absolutely," she said in a voice tinged with regret.

"But there are those who would use it for good. Someone like you for instance. Sure, you may be a little nutty, but why couldn't you or one of the other Primogens dole out the tears and make sure they are only used for good?"

She folded her arms across her chest and dropped her head. "No."

"Why?"

"Because human beings are filled with imperfection." Her whispered words were filled with dread. "Taltos went rogue because a few Primogens wanted world dominance. Think for a moment what would happen if the world economy was predicated on gold coming from straw, or if you could lead your enemies into the sea to drown by playing a flute. It's a balance, Ben. I don't relish the choices we made. I simply understand them, follow the centuries old rules, and accept the cost of what I know, and I've learned to live with that cross."

He noticed that her voice was a sad murmur. "I've upset you. I'm sorry." He stood and walked to her. "It is just the researcher in me coming out and considering the many possibilities for the human race."

Too many times over the years the weight of the decisions she had to make about the great potential of the artifacts grew heavier. It would be easier to endure the great consequences of her fate with someone at her side, someone who would love and understand that her choices were limited, but her destiny was to bear the burden alone. Again, tears came, and she began to cry. Softly at first, but then great sobs came, and she began to shake. Ben put his arms around her and held her held tightly until her tears stopped.

"I'm sorry," she said, pulling back and wiping her cheeks with the back of her right hand. "I don't usually get that out of control."

"It is a lot to handle," he conceded. He took her hand and led her back to the desk and motioned for her to sit in the chair. Then, he slid another opposite her and sat down. "Do you want some water or something?"

Despite everything she was feeling, she laughed. "I'd rather have a shot of vodka, but no, I'll be okay."

"Maybe we should stop."

She sat up straight and rolled her shoulders to ease the tension in her back. "I said I'd answer your questions, and I will."

"You sure?"

She nodded. "I think you are an integral part of a greater mystery. Someone tried to kill you, Ben. We need to know why, and we need your help to do it. But you'll be of no help at all if you don't understand what we are up against." He reached out and took her right hand with both of his. Siene didn't know why, but the gesture comforted her. She curled her fingers around his. "Next question."

"How did your uncles come by all the other objects?"

"Rapunzel knew of the existence of another object.

Leaves. Leaves that can revive the dead. My uncles wrote about it in tale number 16—*The Three Snake Leaves*."

"I've never heard that one," Ben admitted.

"It isn't told much. It's pretty…grim, pardon the obvious pun." She sighed and held Ben's gaze. "This is where it gets complicated."

"How is that possible?" He chortled.

Siene shook her head. "You have no idea. Anyway, Rapunzel met the owner of the leaves and told him of the plan to collect as many enchanted objects as they could and protect them from being used for depraved reasons. He knew of others and sent word. Soon, my uncles had more stories to write. A lot more. Many of the Possessors were old, dying, or simply didn't want the responsibility that came with the gifts they owned, so they left the objects with Uncle Wilhelm and Jacob, and then Taltos was formed."

"You've mentioned Taltos as a group in opposition," Ben commented. "Are you saying Taltos originally had all the objects?"

"That's why this story gets complicated. My uncles named the original society they formed after a Taltos, a figure in Hungarian mythology like a shaman. Most of the descendants of the original Taltoians were honorable men and realized the importance of the charge they accepted. But a few only saw what could be gained from using the artifacts. A battle broke out for control and the council split, giving birth to the Primogens, meaning first ancestor. The Founding Primogens defeated Taltos and carried away the artifacts to a secret place." Siene pulled her hand free, stood, and gestured around her. "So, 209 fairy tales and seven continents later, here we are today. Still protecting the artifacts and still fighting Taltos."

Ben released a long breath of air. "Amazing. It would be hard for anyone to believe that there has been a war raging on the fringes of society about objects in bedtime stories."

"Yet now you know it all to be true." She looked into his eyes. "So, will you help us?"

Instead of Ben's answer, she heard Jack's voice behind her. "Getting the 4-star tour are you, mate?" Jack set the test tubes he brought with him in a tube holder on the lab counter. "Pretty impressive, don'tcha think?"

"It definitely is," Ben agreed. "And seeing everything in this lab, I would say you do more than dabble."

"You're about to find out, mate, cuz I'll be your lab tech while you brew up some of the juice you're working on."

"He's all yours, Jack, just as soon as I show him the rest," Siene replied.

Ben spun to face her. "There's more?"

"A little." She smiled almost sheepishly.

Jack opened the top drawer under the counter and picked up some paper clips and a wrench. He pointed to the Particle Accelerator. "I'll just work on my toy over there. When you're done, bring him over." Whistling, he walked away.

"Paper clips for a Particle Accelerator?" Ben watched as Jack walked to the Accelerator, tossing the wrench in the air with one hand and then catching it with the other.

"Non-corrosive and easily bent. I've seen Jack use

them to replace fuses occasionally," Siene replied.

"Is that safe?"

"No."

"And the wrench?"

She glanced at the Accelerator. "If that thing doesn't start, he may whack it a few times, so I think it would be a good idea to leave this lab before he gets started."

She opened the door at the back, and they entered a room that looked more like mission control at NASA, complete with a version of a world flight tracking system taking up an entire wall. Monitors lined a second wall, each with the name of a major city.

"Wow, this looks like the inside of the mother ship. What is this?" Ben asked.

"Global Monitoring Lab," Siene replied. "It's Kai's. She tracks news stories and monitors key cities around the world. She also has tapped into NOAA's Earth System Research Laboratory to monitor the world's weather."

She pointed to the four technicians sitting at computer consoles. "Those are her Watchers. They determine if the weather or other unusual events around the globe could be related to an artifact being used. Eventually, we'd like to find a way to electronically tag the objects, but so far nothing has worked for very long. Each artifact has peculiar properties. The trackers we tried either get electronically supercharged and then melt, or simply do not adhere." She put her hand on the shoulder of the nearest Watcher. "Everything okay?"

"There's been an energy spike in Central Africa, Ms. Dower," he explained. "Nothing major, just a bit unusual for the area. We're keeping a close eye on the region."

Siene nodded. "Keep Kai posted. She'll decide if she needs to send in Seekers to check it out."

Suddenly, a flash of white erupted on the world map and a red circle encased France. Warning sirens blared and all the wall monitors switched to French cities. The Watchers began a series of pre-planned command activities, and four more men entered the room, taking their places at four computer stations that emerged from the back wall.

"What's happening?" Siene shouted as she leaned over the computer station.

"An explosion in southeast France near Provence. A team of Seekers will be there in ten minutes," the Watcher assigned at the station replied.

Siene leaned closer. "Can you clarify that spike?" She pointed to the blinking red blip on the screen. With lightning speed, the technician's fingers flew over the keys. The pixels waned then cleared. The technician looked at Siene. His blanched expression told her what she immediately knew.

"The Abbey," Siene said in a hoarse whisper. She reached out and pressed a red button, setting off a series of lights and a computerized voice directing all Primogens to the main area.

Ben watched everyone in the room scramble. "This is bad, right?"

Siene grabbed his hand. "Very bad. Let's go."

Chapter Eight

When he reached the edge of the last building in the Abbey, Max peered around the corner and saw the monks running in all directions. He barely had time to pull his head back before one turned and fired a machine gun. Bullets ripped through the air in front of him and then pinged into the stone side of the building as the monk tried to correct his aim. Returning gunfire and the whine of bullets ricocheting off the wall rang in Max's ears.

Farther down, brown-robed monks ran for a white van that had skidded to a stop in front of the rear dormitory. Two armed men slid from the vehicle and began a cover volley. One of the monks stopped, jerked, and fell, sprawling on the ground as arriving bullets found their mark. One of the gunmen attempting the rescue turned his weapon and fired. Max ducked as bullets ripped through the mortar near him.

From the roof above, returning fire answered the attack. Max gripped his gun with both hands and stepped out. His first bullet caught the rescuer near the van in the shoulder as he tried to pull a fallen monk inside. The second shot hit him in the upper chest, and he fell backward. Max emptied his weapon, hitting the side of the van and two more monks before the van bounced forward as the driver hit the gas. The van's tires skidded on the loose stone of the curving driveway before finding traction and speeding toward the exit. It rammed through the Abbey's rear gate, muzzle flashes appearing in sporadic bursts as a hail of bullets followed the van until its taillights disappeared beyond the trees.

Cautiously, Max approached the fallen men at the entrance to the dormitory. Dropping to one knee, he checked the first one he reached for a pulse. None. He moved to the next. Also, dead. The man who came out of the van was dead too, but the monk near him was hanging on. Max motioned to an accomplice with the barrel of the gun in his hand. "This one is still alive. Take him and find out what he knows." Two men grabbed the wounded monk by his arms and dragged him toward one of the armored cars that had pulled up.

A small band of gunmen poured out of the vehicles. "Fan out," Max called. "Search every inch of this place. Bring me any survivors." He pointed to the men nearest him. "You two come with me."

As Max walked into the dormitory, his gut told him that he wouldn't find the Mirror here. The Primogen bitch had lied to him. He almost laughed. But what did he expect her to do? Hand the damn thing over to him like candy to a baby? Still, he'd check the place from top to bottom before he reported back to the boss.

Inside, he stopped at the first door. Gingerly, he turned the doorknob. Locked. Nodding to the men with him, he stepped to one side. The men lifted their machine guns and fired into the lock. The muzzle flashes were lost in the light show as the bullets crunched through the wood and metal. When the shooting stopped, Max kicked open the door and stepped inside.

Just as recon had told him, the room was filled with electronics. Monitors showed pictures of a dozen different rooms, the angles changing every five seconds. Three monks sat at computer keyboards frantically entering what he guessed was a destruct code of some sort.

"Stop!" Max shouted.

But they kept working as if they hadn't heard him. Max shot the monk closest through the head twice. Before the corpse had time to fall, he shot another through the neck and chest. The second monk took a little longer to die, but finally he fell forward onto his keyboard.

The last monk stood and raised his hands high. "I know why you've come. It isn't here."

Two strides later, Max reached him and shoved him back into the chair. After pistol whipping the monk across the face, he waved over one of the gunmen with him. "If he moves or tries to get away, shoot him."

In response, the accomplice put his gun to the monk's head and nodded in agreement.

The second gunman pushed the dead monks out of the way, plugged a flash drive into one of the computer's USB ports, and began uploading the remaining information. Max walked to him and looked over his shoulder at the computer screen. "Are you getting anything?"

"I stopped the eraser worm program, but I don't think I can restore what was deleted." He lifted his chin. "Maybe that monk can undo it."

"Maybe," Max said. "Upload what you can first. I don't trust him." He walked to the monk being held immobile by a gun to his temple and motioned toward the computer. "What were you trying to erase?"

"Last night's sermon," the monk replied with a wry smile.

Max nodded to the gunman, who slapped the monk with the gun butt, opening a gash above his eye. "We both know that's a lie."

Blood ran down the monk's face, dripping from his chin and pooling on the computer keyboard on the desk in front of him. "If you don't like that one, I can tell you another," the monk said in a pain-filled voice.

A sneer curled Max's lip. "I have a better idea." He grabbed the monk's hand and flattened it onto the desktop. From his belt, he pulled out a six-inch, double blade, fighting knife. Without mercy, he plunged the knife into the monk's hand, impaling it into the wood. Pain flashed in the monk's eyes and his body jerked, but to his credit, he never cried out. "If you tell me where the Mirror is, I'll let you go."

The monk's gaze held Max's, challenging. "You are going to kill me whether I tell you or not."

If the monk felt as much pain as Max suspected, his voice never wavered. "You're right of course, but I can make it a less painful process."

The accomplice at the computer removed the flash drive. "I got everything I could." He tossed the drive to Max who caught it in one fluid motion.

Max held it between his thumb and forefinger in front of the monk's eyes. "Wherever the Mirror is, I'll find it." He looked from the monk to the gunman. "Kill him slowly, then burn everything in this room."

****

Lucian sat at the console of the bank of computers and monitors mounted in the back of the modified AM

General Military truck he called home for the past few weeks. Fully equipped as a computer lab, the truck was one of three 2.5-ton vehicles Lucian had shipped to Africa. All were multi-fuel engine vehicles fitted with two 50-gallon fuel tanks to go 500 miles between fill-ups. While his was designed as a mission control vehicle, the others were more support vehicles with a sealed off and lockable sleeping area, roof storage, solar panels to recharge the batteries, as well as racks for cargo and containers, a small kitchen, and an outside shower.

On the computer screen directly in front of him, he could see smoke billowing over Max Biden's right shoulder. "You failed again," Lucian spat out. "If I did not owe your father a great debt, you'd be burning along with the monks."

"I didn't fail entirely," Max countered. He held up the flash drive. "We were able to download some of the information on the hard drive before the eraser worm finished. Get one of your fancy-ass computer geniuses to earn what you pay them and find out what's here."

"Bring it to the base in Greenland on your way," Lucian said.

"Greenland isn't on the way anywhere." The building behind Max exploded, but he did not flinch. "So, I suspect I am going west."

Lucian nodded. "You're going back to New York. I need the Mirror. Siene sent us on this wild goose chase, so I assume the Mirror was there in her townhouse all along. I don't care if you have to rip that place apart brick by brick, you are going to find out where she has taken it." Lucian leaned forward. "And I suggest you do it under the cover of darkness so as not to bring too much attention to your activities. You are aware of the magic of the night. Predators like you thrive there." He didn't wait for Max to respond. He shut off he feed before he could reply.

Just as he did, Lina pulled open the truck's rear door, fanning her face with her right hand. "I know you said to never barge in on you, but I need the air conditioning. It's hotter than hell outside." She laughed. "But you'd know all about that, wouldn't you? Tell Cinderella's stepmother, Lady Tremaine, I said 'hi' when you get back to hell where you came from. Mention that we're taking really good care of that glass slipper."

Lucian frowned and quickly powered down the monitors.

Too late. Lina had noticed. "That wasn't Interpol on one of the screens. What is it? Cable?"

Lucian stood and tried to block her but failed. Lina easily sidestepped him as he lunged for her.

She began punching every control on the keyboard. "Tell me you can get some sort of television feed. I need my shopping channel. I haven't seen Today's Steals and Deals segment in weeks."

Lucian grabbed Lina's chair and wheeled it to the door. Unceremoniously, he tipped it and dumped her onto the ground outside. "Don't *ever* enter this vehicle again," he spat out between clenched teeth.

The short distance she fell only bruised her ego. She quickly stood and dusted off her backside with a few swipes of her left hand. "Relax. I just wanted to order some body lotion. This heat is turning my skin to leather."

Lucian exited the truck and locked the rear door

behind him. He grabbed Lina by her upper arm and dragged her away from the truck. "I suggest you find something else to do."

She yanked her arm free. "Like what? We're miles from civilization and even if I could walk to some town, my clothes are sweat soaked. I haven't had a shower in days." She crossed her arms. "I am really getting bored with this adventure of yours."

Lucian clenched his hands into fists. "If we have to have this discussion again you will be spending the rest of our trip in one of the storage boxes."

Lina bristled. "You'd shrink me?"

"In a heartbeat, darling," he assured. "What did they say about Alice's mushroom in that song?" He feigned thoughtfulness. "Oh yes. Smaller, one side. Larger, the other."

"Jefferson Airplane wasn't really talking about Alice's mushroom."

"But I am." Lucian glared. "You are here because you amuse me, Lina darling. But human size or fashion doll size, you are the same pain in the ass. I suggest you don't push your luck."

Lina tossed her hair. "If I was smaller, I could hide more easily."

"And go where? Out in the jungle you are merely a one-bite appetizer for one of Africa's beautiful cats."

She shot him a look she hoped told Lucian that she wasn't afraid of his threats, but in truth, he was in control now. As she stormed away from him, she vowed to remember to be a bit more careful with her words. Though keeping her mouth shut was not her forte, she didn't doubt for one minute that he would carry out his threat. In fact, she was sure he had every intention of miniaturizing her eventually anyway.

Figuring a way to get out of this mess became her top priority. That, and finding a food taster to make sure Lucian didn't spike her meals with some of the mushroom the next time she pissed him off.

Lord, she thought as she ducked inside her tent. What did Siene ever see in that man anyway?

Chapter Nine

At the compound, hand in a fist poised just above the door ready to knock, Ben stood in the hall outside Siene's living quarters. Along with her and the Primogens, he had watched the horror at the Abbey unfold using high-altitude drones which had high-tech cameras on the scene.

From the two-sided screen that descended from the ceiling over the Council Table, they saw the monks desperately try to send some data to the mainframe at the compound before the attackers could get to the Abbey's computer lab. Security cameras mounted inside the dormitory of the Abbey allowed the Primogens to also watch as Max Biden stopped the transmission that initiated the eraser worm.

Even though the European Watch, the member group assigned to the region, had been alerted, the strike on the Abbey had been too fast, too coordinated, and too deadly for anyone to stop it. All the EW would be able to do was get there as quickly as possible and help the local police assist the survivors, if any.

Siene left the meeting room as Max's henchmen began to slaughter the remaining monks and then set fire to the monastery. He could see the anguish and turmoil on her face as they knew there was nothing they could do to help.

He slipped out as the remaining Primogens began

debating about the appropriate response to the attack, with Jack demanding an eye for an eye, and Reed calling for restraint. He could see by Siene's body language she felt responsible. He had to know she was okay.

He knocked. "Siene, may I come in?" She didn't answer. He flattened his left hand on the door and tried the knob with his right. It wasn't locked. He opened the door slightly. "Siene?"

"Come in." Distress was clear in her voice.

He saw her standing on her balcony, staring down at the courtyard below. As rigid as a statue, face and body in shadowed silhouette, she seemed bathed in moonlight. He knew that could not be possible. They were thousands of feet below the surface of a very large lake.

The closer he got to her, the more beautiful she looked. Her hair swirled around her face in a manufactured breeze, the silver light giving her a soft, ethereal look. Ben knew she was a warrior, a soldier in a war few knew was even being fought. But here, now, she looked vulnerable and sad. His protective instincts roared to life, and at that instant, all he wanted to do was hold her.

Instead, he stood as close as he could without actually touching her. "Hologram?" he asked, looking at the vista that stretched out in front of them.

Siene nodded. "Kai thought that being down here for weeks at a time might be too confining. She, Reed, and Jack redesigned the living quarters with each room having access to holograms. We can program in anything from anywhere around the world." She glanced at him briefly and then looked back into the artificial starry sky. "Me, I like the night. It calms me."

"Are you okay?" he asked her.

She shrugged. "I don't have the luxury of a choice. I have to be okay."

"Would it help if I said I'm not? I mean, as a scientist, I am used to order and control."

A brusque laugh escaped her. "Order and control. That's all that's been drummed into my head for as long as I can remember. Right now, I have neither."

Ben leaned his backside on the railing, turned his head, and looked at her. "I know you think you're responsible…"

Her clipped laugh came again, louder this time, cutting him off. She looked away. "*Think* I'm responsible? I *know* I'm responsible. What I told Max in New York caused all that destruction. I thought I was controlling the situation, but all I did was order the deaths of innocent people."

"What Max Biden did is not your fault."

"But it is." She was aware that her voice cracked and drew in a deep breath to steady herself. "I should have warned them. Some of our best fighters are garrisoned with the monks. I thought that would be enough in case of an attack. I made a mistake and paid with lives."

He straightened and turned her to him. "What you did was save our lives and maybe those of a lot of other people."

"People are dead because of me, people important to this cause."

"Don't you think they knew what they were getting into when they undertook the responsibility? You yourself said, this organization—or whatever you want to call it—is centuries old."

She looked at the serene hologram below and sighed. "You don't understand."

"Maybe scientifically I haven't come to terms with all this yet, but I am beginning to understand just how important those artifacts are." His gaze searched her face before settling on her eyes. "I can see how important they are to you, and I want to help. Tell me what to do."

She shrugged her way out of his hold and walked to the sideboard inside the room. She poured herself a shot of whiskey from a crystal decanter and downed it in one gulp before pouring a second. "Help yourself," she said, saluting him with the glass as she walked to one of the chairs facing the fireplace and plopped down into it. She watched him angle the other chair toward her and then sit.

"Tell me why?" she asked him. "Why do you want to help? This isn't your war."

"Someone tried to kill me, remember? That makes it my war. You think the attack might have something to do with my spit project." He thought he saw her smile. "I would kind of like to know for sure." He leaned forward, forearms resting on his thighs. "And I'd like to know more about you and the Primogens."

"It isn't a very interesting story anymore."

"From what I've already seen, I would disagree." He settled back into the chair intent on taking her mind off what had happened at the Abbey by keeping her talking. "You told me this mission is your birthright, so I get that you have a calling. Growing up couldn't have been easy for you."

A shrug rippled across her shoulders. "Our parents

were very dedicated to their duty. When Reed and I were kids, they were afraid we might accidentally reveal the truth about the artifacts, so they homeschooled us to limit interaction with other children."

"Must have made for a lonely childhood," Ben said.

"At times. But at other times, they let us play with some of the objects and that was really fun." She smiled. "While you were playing with your chemistry set, Reed and I were playing with a spinning wheel that spun straw into gold and mice that helped Cinderella make clothes. That didn't sit well with the other Primogens, so they removed the artifacts from our house and brought them to the compound."

"I'm surprised that they would even allow your family to have some of them in their home. I mean, the situation really could have been dangerous."

"The world wasn't quite as complicated as it is now. But when Taltos stepped up its intent to regain the artifacts, our parents agreed that something had to be done." She took another sip of her drink.

"Letting those things go couldn't have been easy for you."

"There is no comparison between coloring books, clay, and dolls and playing with talking mice and a piece of mirror named Shard that shows you almost anything you ask it to see."

"Shard?"

She chuckled. "It's the piece of the magic mirror that we break off to, in a sense, deactivate it."

"So, this piece is like an off switch."

"With one drawback."

"What would that be?"

Siene stood and walked to one of the drawers in the sideboard. From it she took a rich, cherrywood box, which she set on the end table. Out of the box she took a piece of mirror shaped like an approximately four-inch-long triangle. "This is Shard."

Ben peered at the silver triangle in her hand. Iridescent light began to swirl in the center of the triangle. Soon, a face appeared.

"Babe, WTF? One minute I'm talking to one of the shoemaker's elves about how he wants to hook up with that shoe designer who uses red soles on his heels because he has an idea for a bangin' pair and the next, it goes dark, and I'm shoved inside a freakin' box."

Ben jumped back. "Whoa! What the…"

"Shard, this is Ben."

The teenaged face filled the small mirror fragment. "Dude, you're still alive! Bitchin' cool."

"Watch your language or I'll put you back in the box," Siene warned.

"Who you kiddin'?" Shard retorted. "I'm goin' back in anyway."

"A lot sooner if you don't watch your mouth," Siene said feigning sternness.

"So, where are we?" Shard asked.

"We're at the Compound."

"The old man here, too?" Shard asked.

"He means the rest of the Mirror," she explained. "And to answer your question, Shard, the Mirror is here and in the main vault."

"Bummer. I don't feel like going back to being a thousand years old."

Siene picked up the fragment. "You won't. Not for

a while. But you are going back in the box for now. Say good night, Shard."

"Later, home dog." Shard said.

With that Siene put the fragment back in the box and returned it to the sideboard.

"This Shard, he's a teenager and the mirror guy is an old man. Doesn't seem plausible to me."

Siene sighed. "Nothing about the objects is really rational if you are trying to stuff an explanation into known science. When part of the mirror, Shard, as only a small fraction of the total, completes the circuit and becomes one with the older seer. For lack of a better analogy, it's like removing a fuse from an electrical box. When broken off, as only a piece of the original, he's…younger so to speak. He only ages when activated, and we don't do that very often."

"That just disproved about a hundred scientific conclusions," Ben said.

"Too bad you'll never write about this and win a Nobel Prize."

He furrowed his brow. "You sound sure about that."

"I am."

His instinct was to ask how she planned to stop him but decided against it. "So, what about the origin of the stuffy guy I saw in the mirror?" Ben asked.

"It's sort of a long story."

"We're five thousand feet underground. I'm not going anywhere. I have the time."

They returned to the chairs. "You know the debate about whether or not Hitler was interested in the occult and whether he ran the Nazi party on those principles?" Siene asked.

"Only from what I had to know to pass the history tests in high school and in courses to get the college requirements out of the way."

"I can tell you that he was. The Mirror was in Berlin in the home Uncle Wilhelm lived in with his wife and four children. The Mirror stayed with the home as it passed down through the family, ultimately coming to belong to Uncle Rudolf, who died in 1889. His wife, Aunt Agnes and their daughter, Albertine, continued to live there. About the time Aunt Agnes got sick, Hitler's interest in the occult had peaked. The story goes, Hitler heard tales of the Mirror and ordered the SS to search for it. Agnes knew that if Hitler found the Mirror, he would use its powers to enslave the world. She told Albertine to bring her a hammer. She planned on destroying the Mirror. Albertine begged her mother not to do it, but Agnes would not be stopped. It was said that in her weakened condition, when she swung the hammer and hit the mirror, only a corner broke off. When it did, the Mirror went dark."

"And Shard was born."

"He was," Siene confirmed. "Albertine picked up the broken piece and saw the face of a child in it, which she did not tell Agnes. Instead, she hid the piece. When the SS did come to search the house, all they found was a broken Mirror and a sick woman. The secret remained safe."

"I wouldn't think a broken mirror would have raised suspicions."

"Maybe under other circumstances, but Albertine could not be sure. An hour earlier she met a trusted member of the resistance and arranged to get the shard out of Germany until it was safe for the Mirror to be restored. She had moved the Mirror to Aunt Agnes' bedroom, much like any mirror in any of the boudoirs in any home of any prominent German aristocrat."

"Hide in plain sight."

"Exactly. Besides, I don't think I would want to be the officer who had to tell the Fuhrer that the Mirror was found broken."

Ben nodded in agreement. "Considering the depth of Hitler's cruelty, it would have been better to let him think the Mirror still had not been found."

"Agnes lived long enough to see the fall of the Third Reich. When the Marshall Plan went into effect to help Europe recover after the war, Albertine moved to America to be with relatives and brought the Mirror with her."

"So, she emigrated then?

"Not exactly. She's Primogen. We take care of our own. She settled here in the Northwest until her death in 1973."

"Then, you have family nearby?"

He saw her expression turn sad. "No. Albertine never married. In this line of work, it is kind of hard to develop relationships. They tend fall apart at what you do for a living?" She laughed. "Except for Paz. She has family all over the world. I think that's why Reed likes to spend so much time with her. Her family knows how to party." Siene laughed again. "And how to propagate."

Ben stood and walked to the sideboard. He pointed to a half-full decanter sitting alongside more crystal glasses like the one Siene used. "May I?"

"Help yourself."

He plunked some ice cubes into a glass and looked

over the various bottles. "What's in here?" He held up a crystal decanter.

"It's the Brazilian cachaça that Reed brought back from his trip. Try it. I think you'll like it."

"Wasn't that the same stuff your brother…" Ben made a hammering gesture.

She smiled. "I think he used the wooden maraca on Max, not the bottle."

Ben liked it when Siene smiled. It lit her eyes and removed the tension from her face. He poured a small amount and took a sip of the amber liquid. "It is good." He sat across from her. "This Primogen thing must be hard on your family."

"It's more problematic than difficult. By design, not all the family is called to be a Primogen. Those who aren't know nothing of the calling until it is necessary to replace one of us. That way the bloodline continues for the future. As I said, relationships don't last very long in our line of work, and we have to be sure our legacy will continue."

"That must be awkward during the holidays."

"Not really. We're used to it. But being Primogen does get a little lonely most other times of the year. Our father was afraid that people might find out who we are and what we do, so we weren't allowed many friends. When our parents died in a car crash, we went to live with an aunt and uncle who weren't Primogen. The first thing they did was enroll us in public school. Reed was a senior and I was put in the tenth grade."

"High school. Tough time to be the new kids."

Her smile vanished and her face turned serious. "Very tough. We tried to fit in, but we got bored really fast. Soon Reed started correcting the physics teacher and I finished tests before the teacher had finished passing them out to the rest of the class. It got to be such a problem that the principal had us tested to see if he could classify us and get us out of his school. When the results came back, he told our aunt and uncle that there was nothing the school could do for us, and they should try to get us into some sort of advanced program."

"Sounds like we have something in common," Ben said. "I was an outsider too. You know, horn-rimmed glasses, pocket protector, straight As in the honors classes." As he sipped his drink, over the rim of his glass, he could see a ghost of a smile crease her lips. "So, you and Reed quit school then?"

"No. We went to college. Reed to MIT for Engineering and Elemental Studies, and I did California Institute of Technology for Quantum Physics. We breezed through everything right up to doctorate in record time and eventually came here."

"I'm surprised some government agency didn't take notice. The Feds are always looking for exceptional talent. You know they are always watching. The government would never let one, much less two super intelligent people get far out of their radar range."

"They came. Four different times. Government operatives are a persistent bunch, but you forget we have things."

"What kind of things?"

"After the fourth meeting at a secure location, we said we were thinking of accepting their offer."

"I'd love to find out what that was."

"That story is for another time. Reed and I aren't into trying to make any superheroes like the guy clad in iron."

"He's real too?" Ben asked, eyes widening.

"Not yet," Siene confirmed. "Anyway, we invited the Feds to our turf and let's just say they forgot all about us after that."

"You have the blue flashy thing from that UFO movie too?" Ben leaned forward with interest.

Siene laughed. "You're going to have to learn what is real and what is fiction."

"I may need a flowchart for that."

"We don't have the flashy thing, but what we do have is blue. You ever heard of the *Blue Rose of Forgetfulness?*"

He sat back and smiled at her. "From the Arabian nights."

"It is, and I might have forgotten to mention we not only procure and protect the artifacts, but we also make sure that if someone does discover our secret, they don't remember they did."

"Is that what is going to happen to me?"

She shrugged. "I'm not sure. The Council will decide. I'll tell you when the decision is made so you can prepare. We normally don't do that."

Ben nodded, realizing it was a concession. "So, you and your brother went from teenagers to grad students to Primogen. Didn't your family worry about you socially adjusting or anything?"

"I don't think my aunt and uncle cared very much about anything we did. Once we went away to school, we didn't hear from them except at holidays." She turned her head away.

He waited, hoping she would say more, but the ensuing silence was nearly unbearable. He set his drink on the floor, leaned forward, and put his hand on her arm. "Siene? If I said something wrong, I'm sorry."

She jerked to her feet and spun to face him. "I'm the one who should be sorry. I think I might have told you too much. As I said, this isn't your fight."

Ben rose and reached for her, but she backed away.

"And I told *you* I am making it my fight. Being a murder target isn't a title I want to carry into the future. I'd like to know why someone wants me dead and it seems as though you are the only person who can help me find out. So, my dear girl, for better or for worse, we're a team now." He reached for her again. This time she did not back away. He brushed his hands up and down her arms as he spoke. "The Mirror brought us together for a reason. Let me help you find out what that reason is."

She looked into his eyes and swallowed hard. "One last chance. You don't have to wait until the Council decides your fate. You could walk away from this. Now. Today. You know I can make you forget. Most of it, anyway. You're a smart guy so you might have occasional memory flashes. You'll think you were only dreaming." She bit down on her lip. "Like I wish I was sometimes."

"No deal." His gaze scanned her face. "There just might be something I don't want to forget." His gaze pinned hers.

She heaved a deep sigh as if to gather herself. "Think about what you might have to give up. Your career, your work. Once committed, you can never go back to the life you knew." She wet her lips. "I will not have an opportunity to make this offer again."

Even in her whisper he could hear the seriousness

in her voice, but there was no turning back now. The proverbial die was cast. He would stay at her side until they solved this mystery. "I'm not going anywhere."

"Are you sure?"

"Yes."

She tilted her head and met his gaze. "Why?"

The glistening of unshed tears in her eyes was his undoing. He reached out and wrapped his arms around her and pulled her close. "Because I don't want you to feel alone anymore."

He could feel her melt into him as she wrapped herself around the lines of his body. She leaned her cheek against his. Long moments passed in the comfort of their embrace, and he knew he should move away. But her body felt so good close to his, almost like she belonged there. He felt the stirrings of long buried feelings and struggled to return them to the depths from where they came. As he inched back, he looked into her eyes. "You must be tired. I should go."

She reached up and traced the curve of his cheek with her fingertips. "Or you could stay."

Stay. The word invaded his mind right before his brain jammed. He looked at her face, into her eyes, and saw a silent plea there. As his face lowered toward hers, he knew he shouldn't kiss her. She wasn't ready for any kind of intimacy. Hell, he wasn't ready. He pressed a soft, undemanding kiss on her lips, one intended to only comfort without promising too much, a kiss he hoped would not set free any of the emotion building inside him.

But the moment their lips touched, heat exploded, grabbing him and pulling him into sensations that crashed inside his body. He deepened his kiss and slanted his mouth across hers. He parted his lips and found hers open in return. Their tongues touched and paused, then touched again before beginning a dance that moved with pressure and confidence as the fire inside him grew and reached his heart.

Yes, his brain screamed. *This is good. This is right. This would prove everything that had happened to him was real. Yes, he needed this.* But did she?

He drew back and rested his chin on top of her head. His fingers caressed the small of her back and he took a deep breath, holding it before exhaling. "Must be the cachaça. I don't drink much. Seems like it went right to my head."

She touched his chest with her fingertips and then slid her hands to link up behind his neck, so they were pressed chest to chest, thigh to thigh. "That kiss didn't come from any drink, but just in case, there's more on the sideboard," she whispered right before she pulled his head down and kissed him.

Chapter Ten

Siene felt the change in Ben. She sensed his readiness to toss caution to the wind and submit to the vibrations that raced through them both. It had been so long since she'd been cradled in a man's arms and tasted a man's kisses.

As she stood in the computer-generated moonlight, she recognized that Ben was helping her admit the truth. She didn't know what was right for her, and she may never know for sure. The last man she let break the barriers she set betrayed her as though nothing had ever happened between them. Back then, her actions put people in danger and cost some their lives. If she let go now and let Ben into that carefully guarded part of her, she had no way of knowing if her decision would once again bring misfortune.

She could not deny that she wanted him. His kisses left her breathless. In Ben's arms she felt surprisingly safe, something she had not experienced in a very long time. As the kisses continued, she wanted more than just caresses on her back and more than just his fingers brushing her breasts as his hands roamed her body. She wanted him inside her, deep inside her, making love to her with such abandon that even for a moment she could forget what was at stake. She didn't want to analyze the consequences. They'd deal with them later.

She took a step back and reached for his hand. "I

want you, Ben." She led him back inside the room. "I don't want to think about what tomorrow or next week or next year might bring. Tonight, I need you. Inside me. Now."

"Siene," he whispered.

She didn't need to hear any more to understand he wanted the same. In his eyes she saw desire. Heat and desire filled her center, and she shifted her hips against him, the long, hard ridge of his erection pressed against her. As insane as it might be to give in to temptation, she had no intention of letting him leave the room. Rising on her toes, she kissed him, intent on showing him the invitation was real. Maybe they wouldn't have anything more, but they could have tonight. As her kiss intensified, she felt his embrace tighten. He returned the kiss with fervor, taking handfuls of her hair then cupping her buttocks and pulling her closer so that there would be no confusion about his need.

She wrapped her legs around his waist. "The bed," she whispered.

With long strides he moved to the edge of her bed, but never stopped kissing her. He lowered her onto the lace comforter and sat beside her.

Looking down at her, his voice was low and intense. "Once I start, Siene, I'm not going to stop. I need you to be sure you want this too."

She rose slowly holding his gaze. She opened the buttons on his shirt and pressed her palms against his chest. The fast thump of his heartbeat met her fingertips. She looked into his eyes. "I'm sure, Ben."

Ben dropped his forehead to hers. His hands moved to her breasts, caressing instead of gripping. "I've been fighting it, but God help me, Siene, so do I." They sealed their covenant with a kiss, meeting halfway as equals in their desire.

As she lay back on the bed, inside her a struggle began. She knew she couldn't afford to let this be about romance. Romance didn't do well in her line of work. Love and romance could lead to mistakes, and mistakes could lead to a mission failure or worse. This was about need. Hers. His. She would concentrate on the physical sensations, the heat that grew between them, the feel of his body pressing against hers.

Ben shrugged off his shirt and lay next to her. She placed a kiss on his collarbone and savored the taste of his skin. When she heard the sharp intake of his breath, she swirled her tongue in the hollow of his throat. Her nails scraped his skin as she ran her hands down the ribbed planes of his torso, around his sides, and up the tight muscles of his back.

"Siene." He whispered her name once and then again as if in answer to a question she had not asked.

She sighed with pleasure when his hands moved up her thighs, bunching her dress up to her hips. She first felt the scrape of his pants on her inner thighs and then the emotive feel of his hand on her breast when he reached under her bra and ran a thumb across her nipple. These feelings had nothing to do with the artifacts, or the events in France, or the fact that the Council could remove her as Primogen. It was about her, about him, about now.

Ben growled, the sound coming from deep in his throat. He cupped her bottom where her panties pulled tight across her backside giving way to skin. He slid one hand forward, his fingers finding her wet and hot and wanting. His slow stroking made her wild and she moved with the motion, telling him she wanted more, wanted it all. As if reading her mind, he rose. Their eyes never broke contact as they discarded their clothing.

A small part of her heard the panic filled with warnings. *This is crazy. Irresponsible. You have no idea what you're getting yourself into.* But she willed the voice into the dark recesses of her mind and lifted her gaze. In the play of shadow and light, he stood magnificent in his desire for her.

She slid backward on the bed and made room for him. He placed one knee on the bed, his gaze slowly roaming her body as though he were afraid to touch her. She raised her arms in welcome and opened her legs to invite him inside her body, but not into her heart. She would protect that part of herself at all costs. This was not love. It was sex. It was need.

When Ben positioned over her, he hesitated as though giving her one last chance to protest. She smiled her acceptance, and he reached down and stroked the petals between her legs. She heard a whisper. Her name—his. It didn't matter who said the words, only that they had been spoken. He entered her slowly giving her time to accommodate him. She felt her flesh clench as if to reject his entry. It had been such a long time.

He paused and kissed her. "It's right, Siene."

She softened and accepted the gift he was about to give. She began a low moan, and Ben's movements heightened. Wanting him closer, deeper, she gripped him to make them as one. When he took one of her legs and moved it upward as he pushed ever deeper inside her, she nearly came to satisfy the hunger inside her, a hunger she never felt before.

She tangled her fingers in his hair answering his every move with her own. The dance became a frantic joining, a straining union of bodies sending them toward one possible and inevitable ending.

Her climax came in an explosion, and she screamed out his name not caring who heard her, whether it be the microphone on the security cameras or someone passing by outside in the hall. Her need to feel normal crested along with the physical release, giving her a pleasure she had not felt in much too long a time. She heard Ben say her name in a groan as he followed in a single pounding thrust, releasing him. A shudder rocketed through his body until she felt him nestle against her.

Slowly, the world came back. The dampness of her hair across her forehead, the wetness between her legs, the blinking of a security light that had come on sometime during their fixation on the physical, all the external things she blocked for those precious moments were once again present, reminding her she still had a job to do. Yet, right now, those things meant nothing to her.

She snuggled into his side, curves nestling against him. At this moment, she never felt more normal. The only thing she cared about was the solid weight of Ben's body next to hers, and the rise and fall of his chest in tandem with her own. The regret would come later.

When the intercom chimed again, reality brought back the inner voice she had been ignoring. *What the hell did I just do?*

"Do you have to answer that?" Ben asked. His words were a breath in the crook of her neck where he had rested his head in the aftermath of their lovemaking.

She rose on her elbows. "Yes, the Council has probably agreed on a course of action." She gathered the top sheet around her and picked up her clothes. "I need to be there."

Wordlessly, Ben watched her dress, his eyes, once clouded with desire now returned to a neutral state. "So, that's how it's going to be?" He stood and began to dress with quick movements that held an edge of anger.

Siene did not reply. She stepped into her panties and pulled them on as quickly as she could.

"Wham, bam, thank you, sir?" Ben shrugged on his shirt.

Her gaze met his. "Doesn't sound the same without the rhyme."

Ben didn't smile.

Neither did she.

"Was this—" He pointed to the rumpled bed. "—just a joke to you."

The intercom chimed again.

"Answer it," Ben said. "We can talk about this later."

"If you want." She held her breath, hoping he wouldn't insist.

"You bet I do, and we will, you can count on it," he grumbled.

Chapter Eleven

Max was tired of failed missions. No doubt
Davelos was too. Having to call the boss with bad news
was getting to be a hard pill to swallow. If he didn't
come through this time, he figured he wouldn't have to
worry about a next time. He'd be tagged as useless to
Taltos and especially to Davelos. He might as well kiss
his ass goodbye.

The moon had just risen when Max pulled up to the
New York brownstone. Though most of the adjoining
homes were lit by porch lights or outside accent
lighting, the building he wanted was conspicuously
dark and looked like no one had lived there for a long
time. But he knew better. He still had headaches from
the blow he took to the head inside that place.

How the bitch got the drop on him, he still didn't
know. One minute he was pushing her and her friend
out into the hall and the next, he got coldcocked and
woke up in the back of a van. Luckily for him, none of
the Primogen idiots driving the van bothered to search
him. If they had, they would have found *Lizzie*, the
small, specially revamped derringer he always carried.
They probably had regretted that oversight for the rest
of their short lives, which was only about five minutes.
Tucked away in the small of his back, that 4-barrel with
its rotating firing pin had saved his ass more times than
he cared to count. He imagined one day there would be

more than four guys coming for him and he'd run out of bullets, but for now *Lizzie* was all he needed. That and a sure aim to drop anyone coming at him with one of *Lizzie's* short .32 rounds to the eye. He snickered, picturing the shocked look on their faces. *Enough reminiscing*. Back to the task at hand.

He walked up the stairs and tried the door, though he knew it would be locked. He started to take the tool kit from his pocket when he heard a voice from behind him.

"Moving in?" a female voice asked.

Max turned and nodded, being careful to keep his face in the shadows of the tree next to the steps. "Thinking about it," he said.

He watched two women walk up the stairs to the adjoining brownstone. "It would be nice to have neighbors again," the older of the two said. "That place has been empty for years."

The younger woman rested a bag of groceries on her hip as she fished in her purse. "Mom, seriously? I was just home about a month ago and that woman and her brother lived there." She pulled out a set of keys and turned to Max. "Mom's been having a little trouble with her memory lately."

Max nodded. "I wanted to get a look at the place before I decided whether I would take it or not. The realtor should be here any minute," he added to avoid any questions.

The daughter slid her key into the lock. "It shouldn't be too bad inside. Hasn't been vacant that long."

The girl's mother bristled. "I think you're the one with memory issues, and I hope it isn't from alcohol overload you got from that party college you tricked me into sending you to."

"Go on inside, Mom," the younger woman said before swiveling her head and offering a patient smile. "I apologize. You shouldn't have to listen our mother-daughter disagreements." She gave her mother a will-you-be-quiet look, then turned back to Max. "I hope it doesn't sway your decision to move in. This is a nice neighborhood. It's quiet and the neighbors generally keep to themselves."

"That's good to know," he offered good-naturedly, but hoped they would just go on about their business.

"Well, have a good evening," the young woman said before she walked inside.

Mom poked her head back out. "If you decide to take the place, come over for dinner sometime. My daughter is single and can cook her ass off."

"Mom!" The young woman pulled her mother in and slammed the door.

Interesting, Max thought. Mom here, daughter in college. That would explain the conflicting accounts. He knew for certain that the Primogens would have sent in their Cleaners once security had been compromised. They also would have made sure all traces of Siene and Reed being in the neighborhood were wiped. But with the doll-face next door apparently away at school, she wouldn't have seen anything, and Primogen Cleaners had made sure the mother couldn't remember what she'd seen. Perfect!

He had little chance of finding anything inside the brownstone. The Cleaners were a very thorough bunch. In all his experiences with them, nothing useful was ever left behind. He looked at the neighboring brownstone. Until now.

Doll-face would come out again sometime, and when she did, he'd find an excuse to talk to her in more depth. He pulled out a cigarette and slipped into the shadows of the night. He could wait. All night if he had to. Going back to Davelos without information was not an option.

****

Lina pushed her way through the low-hanging vines, batting them as if they were flies buzzing around her head. Hot and annoyed, she wiped the sweat from her forehead with the back of her hand. "If I ever get out of here, I swear I will never sneak away again," she avowed. "I let my guard down and got made."

She had gotten bored waiting in the small house Paz had disguised as a Brazilian fashion doll dream home. Paz and Reed had left early that day to follow a lead on the missing Morpho Butterfly. Though real morpho butterflies were plentiful in the South American rainforest, this missing butterfly was from an old Brazilian folktale and could transform whomever it alighted upon into anything they desired to be. All the person had to do was use his or her imagination. From rock star to millionaire to movie star, one would only have to think the dream and it would be theirs. Temporarily. Once the butterfly flew away, the dream would be gone, causing often embarrassing and sometimes deadly situations for the unfortunate dreamer.

Though the little playhouse was well equipped with all the modern conveniences thanks to Kai and her technological talents, Lina could only watch reruns of American television for so long. Though she could have ordered from the television shopping network through automated ordering, her tiny voice was barely audible over the phone, and that day was an all-day Food Fest. No way was she interested. Clothes, make-up, and jewelry were more her forte.

So, she had walked out of her miniature double entry doors, gathered all the adrenaline she could summon, and concentrated on that screwed up strand of DNA that allowed her to grow and shrink. She never knew exactly when or if she would change, but that day it worked, and she was elated as she grew to human size. After borrowing some clothes from Paz's closet, she walked out the front door and into the heart of Rio de Janeiro.

She had felt safe in a city of 5.9 million people and knew how to blend in with the locals. In Rio, she was just another beautiful woman among those who called the city their home. She would shop a little, drink some cachaça, and maybe get one of the local hotties to teach her the samba. She did like to dance.

At least that was the plan until she heard someone call her name. She turned, and that's when the lights went out. When she woke up, she was a foot tall and a prisoner behind a clear, plastic panel in Lucian Davelos' penthouse.

That was a week or so ago and she thought things couldn't get any worse. But she had been wrong. Now, she was in Africa, in the goddamned hundred-plus degree, never-ending African heat, sweating like a pig on a spit. Everything she owned felt damp and smelled musty, and she was bored again from being confined to the campsite. That was precisely why every day she ventured a little farther into the lush jungle. She had made such a fuss about the rugged conditions that no one would expect her to go too far. If there was a way out, she'd find it.

She continued through the dense vegetation, hearing nothing but her footsteps and her beating heart. About a half-mile more, another sound joined in. The sound of rushing water. She stopped and listened. "*Yes! Fresh water.*" She tented her hands as if in prayer and looked up at the forest canopy. "Thank you. A bath. Or the closest thing to it in this godforsaken, insect-ridden place."

She picked up her pace and walked toward the sound, realizing she would have to leave the cover of the blanketing branches. She adjusted her path and immediately saw two men with guns coming toward her. She ducked back into the dense brush and crouched behind the large, swollen trunk of a baobab tree.

The men came closer, scanning the area and keeping their guns ready, clearly searching for something or someone. They looked young, tired, and very unfriendly. She didn't recognize either one, so they hadn't come from camp and weren't looking for her. They must be from a nearby village or had been recruited by a warlord to check the area for rivals. She thought about something Reed had said to her back in Brazil, "*It's hard to kill someone. You remember the face forever.*" She only hoped these young men would find it hard to kill her if she was discovered.

The taller man said something in a language Lina did not understand.

"Use common tongue," the other said in broken English. "I do not know your language."

"There is no one here," the taller one said, his

English slightly better. "We can go."

The shorter man raised his hand as the sound of a twig snapping came from his right. "Shh, I hear something."

"Probably an animal."

"I will check. Cover me."

Lina held her breath as the shorter man began walking toward her. Staying perfectly still, she watched as he stopped and looked around for what seemed like an hour.

"Nothing here," she heard him say. "We go back."

Lina peeked around the tree trunk as the jungle appeared to swallow the two men whole as they moved away. She waited until she could no longer hear footsteps moving through the brush. As she started to stand, she felt something move near her calf. She looked down and saw smooth, shiny scales. She felt everything inside her go cold. She began to hyperventilate and felt the beginning panic of a scream bubble up in her throat when a small hand clamped over her mouth. Another hand grabbed the back of her shirt and pulled her deeper into the brush.

Eyes closed, flat on her back, she felt a weight across her pelvis even as the hand stayed across her mouth. Slowly she opened one eye and saw a boy sitting on her.

"No talk," he whispered.

Lina nodded, and he removed the hand from her mouth. He reached behind him and held up a writhing gray snake about fourteen inches long. She felt another scream coming on, but the boy leaned forward and clamped his hand across her mouth once more. Her eyes widened as the thrashing snake in his other hand hit her arm over and over as it twisted to get free.

"Blind snake," the boy said. "No poison, so no noise."

What choice did she have? Scream and get them both shot or stay quiet and try not to throw up. Gathering shreds of her disappearing courage and sure she must have peed all over herself, because her backside felt wet, she nodded. When the boy felt her relax, he removed his hand and tossed the snake into the brush. Then he stood, gesturing for her to stay.

Lina watched him go in the same direction as the two men. Then, remembering the snake, she jumped to her feet and ran a few yards in the opposite direction. Inhaling slowly, she waited until her heartbeat returned to normal before checking herself. She hadn't wet herself. She had landed in mud. She had just finished brushing as much of it from her pants as she could when the boy returned.

He pointed behind them. "They from the camp. They look for me." He picked up a small branch and using it like a spear, poked in the air. "They fight my people. War."

Warring men Lina could understand. It didn't matter where they were. Europe, Asia, the streets of New York City, or here in Africa. Men fought each other for supremacy because that's what men did. It was the nature of the beast. But this time, they were hunting a child. Why? "What did you do?" she asked.

The boy dropped the branch. "I left."

Lina sighed in frustration. She had no time for twenty questions. If she was gone much longer, Lucian would be looking for her. She took the boy's hand and pulled him into the dense brush for cover. She stooped and put her hand on his shoulder. "You left your village?"

He shook his head. "I run from the cave. Where we dig." He turned and began to walk off. He motioned for her to follow.

"What do you mean?"

He covered his lips with a forefinger and kept walking.

The rough footpath was overgrown but not impossible to navigate. Lina stumbled over some growth and remembering the snake had to force herself not to reach out and grab onto the first thing she saw to steady herself. Once this adventure was over, she swore that she would go to a spa and not leave until every bruise and ache and pain was gone.

They walked a few minutes more and she heard rushing water again. A few more steps and she saw the bank. They had doubled back and were near her camp.

The boy waved to her from upstream, standing on a fallen tree near the rapids. She climbed up the boulders and over two more trees until she got to the area beyond the white water near where he stood. Cupping his hands, he stooped and scooped some water. With a toss of his head, he urged her to do the same.

"I could have done that down there," Lina said, sitting on a large rock. As she drank some water from her cupped hands, she heard the boy laugh. "What?"

He pointed downstream. "*Ndovu*."

"What does that mean?"

He pointed to his crotch and then downstream again.

She looked to where he pointed and saw four elephants in the water.

He laughed again and cupped his groin. "More than water there."

Suddenly Lina didn't feel so thirsty. She wiped her mouth with the back of her hand. "I bet there's more than water here, too." She put her hands on the boy's shoulders. "I suppose we should get to know each other. My name is Lina."

He shrugged her hands free. "Mosegi."

"I'm from America."

Mosegi pointed west. "The village of my grandfather is that way."

"And I suppose you're going to try to get there."

He nodded.

Lina turned him around to get a good look at him, then dropped her hands. "You won't be getting very far without food."

"You have food?"

She saw hope in his eyes. "Not with me, but I can get you some."

"No time."

He began to make his way along the bank and away from her. She ran after him and grabbed his arm. "What kind of dig did you leave?"

"We dig for the twilight stones, and no one can leave. Must dig. Dig, dig, dig. Only dig." He pointed at her, his hand forming the shape of a gun. "Bang, bang if you try to leave."

A cold feeling filled Lina, and suddenly she knew. He had been working in the mine. Lucian's tanzanite mine and he wasn't there by choice. Lucian had told her the men working there were recruited from local villages and were well paid. This boy was neither a man, nor, from the looks of him, paid to dig. Lucian was lying about what he was doing in Africa. Lying was something she expected from him, but this boy's condition—hunted by two grown men, and learning that if he were caught, he would probably be shot—made her realize the extent to which Lucian would go to ensure his plan succeeded.

A new sense of urgency replaced the detachment she had settled into after Lucian kidnapped her. Suddenly, discovering why Lucian needed the tanzanite jumped to the top of her to-do list.

"When was the last time you ate something?" The boy was so thin, his ribs were clearly visible, as though he hadn't had enough to eat in a while.

He shook his head.

"You need food." She looked over her shoulder. The camp wasn't far. "If you stay here and stay hidden, I'll bring you some." She had no idea if the boy would trust her enough to do what she asked, but she was counting on his hunger to at least have him consider it.

He nodded and squatted near the trees.

She gestured for him to stay and quickly made her way back to camp.

****

Joseph watched Lina disappear into the brush. His ruse worked. She appeared to believe he was a young villager working the mine. He hoped he could trust her. He did need to eat. She didn't alert the men chasing him to his hideout, so that was a plus. He didn't know what he'd do when she came back. All he knew was that whatever happened, it could never be as bad as working the mines. She could be a friend; she could be a foe. He prayed his pre-med years at Harvard and his residency at Massachusetts General would help him figure out which she would be to him.

****

Hidden in the shadows next to the steps and the trash cans between the Brooklyn brownstones, Max crushed out his sixth cigarette with the toe of his black Italian leather shoe. If Doll-face didn't come out soon, he'd try back in the morning. Feeling antsy, he began to reach for another pack when he heard a car drive up and park.

He heard Doll-face's voice. "Thanks, guys. See you in the a.m."

Damn, he thought, *she must have gone out the back hours earlier*. Still, he had a chance. Timing his move until when he thought she would be at her steps, he walked on to the sidewalk lit only by streetlights and bumped into her. "Sorry, didn't see you," he said at the contact.

When their gazes met, she looked anxious, like a deer in headlights. Her body language screamed alarm and her hand tightened around the strap of her purse. *Good*, Max thought, *she's nervous*. She won't be thinking about anything except getting into her house. Advantage: Biden.

"Hope I didn't frighten you." He took a step away, so he didn't appear threatening. "You probably remember me; I was here earlier looking at the house." He gestured to the brownstone.

She squinted and he could see her visibly relax when she recognized him. "Oh, yeah. What are you doing here at this hour?"

She shifted her purse to her other shoulder and Max almost laughed out loud. If he wanted what was in there, she'd be out cold on the ground, and he'd have it by now.

"I lost my wallet and thought it might have fallen out when I got out of the cab. You didn't see it, did you?"

Doll-face laughed. "If it fell out on to the street, I'd be checking my bank and credit card balances if I were you."

He laughed back to keep up the act and the advantage. "Did that earlier. I wanted to make a last-ditch attempt."

She shrugged and began to walk up the steps.

"Hey," he called out. She turned. "I do have a question, if you don't mind."

"Depends," she answered.

"Who used to live here?"

Doll-face looked at the empty brownstone. "A lady named Siene and her brother. Why?"

"I don't like to rent party houses. After tenants like that, I find that a lot of repairs need to be done to the place and the landlord usually doesn't want to do them."

"You don't have to worry about that. Siene and Reed kept to themselves most of the time. We barely saw them."

That wasn't good, Max thought. "So, you didn't know them, then?"

"I knew her more than him. Like I said, they mostly kept to themselves."

"Do you know where they went?"

Doll-face didn't say any more. Instead, she stared at him as though trying to decide whether to answer. "Why do you want to know?" She moved up one step and took her keys from her purse, making sure she held one of the keys in front of her like a tiny knife.

It took all the control Max had not to backhand her in the mouth. He wasn't used to playing games. He was used to getting the information he wanted quickly, using whatever means he needed. Davelos owed him big time. This back and forth was more grating than anticipating a kick in the nuts, and a lot more painful. One last shot and if he didn't get what he wanted, Doll-face was going to wake up in an alley somewhere with a headache from a little sodium pentothal cocktail to her neck.

"No reason. I was just asking in case they left anything behind." He turned and reached into the inside pocket of his jacket to get the syringe when he heard her call out.

"Wait." She came down the stairs and walked to him. "I don't know where they went, but I do remember overhearing Siene saying she missed home the last time I talked to her."

His fingers unwrapped from around the syringe, and he turned. "Home?"

Doll-face nodded. "She said they were from out West. The Pacific Northwest. Seattle, or Oregon. Some place like that. Does that help at all?"

Helps that you get to walk back up your steps and go home instead of lying in a ditch somewhere, Max thought with a smile. "Not really, but thanks. I'll just give anything I find to the realtor."

As he pulled out his cell Max wondered why a Primogen would tell a college girl about her past. Big mistake, but one he'd exploit. If she asked how he found her, he'd tell her right before he killed her. No sense dying with unanswered questions.

The call connected as he hailed a passing cab, but it went to Lucian's voicemail. "The first-class charge on your credit card will be me taking a trip to Seattle." He laughed. "I always did want to see Puget Sound," he said, sliding into the back seat. "JFK," he told the driver.

"Business or pleasure," the taxi driver asked, resetting his meter.

"If it all works out the way I hope, both."

Chapter Twelve

Siene could see flashing lights through the trees leading to the Abbey. When the Range Rover that Reed rented at the airport turned to the right, about twenty white Renault Megane wagons with blue emergency light bars on the roof were everywhere on the property. Two water cannon trucks that the French National Police apparently used to help douse the fire were parked nearby.

"Wait here," Reed said after stopping the car near the Abbey entrance. "I'll have to clear us." He got out and met the officer coming toward them.

"National Gendarmerie," Siene said before Ben could ask the question. "They are part of the Police Nationale and handle the security of public buildings among other things. We need to wait until Reed gets permission for us to investigate alongside them."

"These National Gendarmerie, they know about you?" Ben asked.

Siene shook her head. "No."

From the back seat of the Range Rover Ben watched Reed continue to speak to the authorities. "From the amount of destruction and number of people out there, I don't see how the French police will let a bunch of Americans walk all over their crime scene."

"Bunch of Americans and one Aussie," Jack said.

"I stand corrected," Ben admitted. "But be that as it

may, I don't see how we are going to be cleared to nose around here."

Out of the car window, Ben saw Reed pull papers from the inside of his jacket and hand them to a second officer who had joined the discussion.

"Ever hear of GIGN?" Jack asked.

"No. What is it?" Ben asked.

"Gendarmerie Intervention Group Nationale. It's kind of a French SWAT team," Siene said. "GIGN is a special operations unit of the French Armed Forces and a part of the National Gendarmerie. Members are trained to perform counterterrorism and hostage rescue missions in France or anywhere else in the world they are needed. You may remember that a few months ago, the media reported on terrorism training exercises at the Oyster Creek Nuclear Generating Station in New Jersey and at Liberty International Airport."

Ben nodded. "The exercise made headline news."

"What you didn't know was the drill was part of a of a top secret, securitized initiative to bring together elite military units from around the world to train together as a greater force to stop the spreading terroristic threat, code name JOLT—Joint Operations Liberation Team. Here in the U.S., the players were GIGN and the U.S. Navy Seals. In one scenario, terrorists took over the nuclear power plant with the intention of shutting down the country's power grid, and in the second, terrorists hijacked an Air France passenger plane with 229 passengers and crew. The Seals and GIGN ran several situations from successful rescues to complete destruction. Both units learned from the operation."

"The media never reported that part," Ben

acknowledged.

"Fortunately, security was not breached, and nothing was leaked. JOLT's ultimate success hinges on terrorists counting on a fractured response by the countries they target." Siene smiled. "Who would think the U.S. and France would form a bond like this?"

Ben drew his brows together. "You're right."

"In the wake of a jihadist group calling for more attacks on France, the French government is very grateful to the U.S. for the opportunity to train with the Seals," Jack added. "The papers Reed handed the officer are from The General Directorate for External Security. Equivalent to your CIA. The Directorate acknowledges our little contingent here as part of the U.S. Navy Irregular Warfare and Counterterrorism Unit and gives us the authority to investigate alongside local French authorities."

"How did you get something like that if the French government knows nothing about the Primogens?" Ben asked.

Jack winked. "A very good forgery compliments of yours truly."

"So, I'm a Navy Seal then?" Ben asked.

Jack laughed. "A skinny one at that."

"What about Siene?"

"Someone has to do the paperwork. She handles the administrative side."

"Rather sexist of you," Siene added.

"If you were more Demi Moore in "G.I. Jane", maybe you could pull off military, but you're more"—Jack tapped his chin with his finger—"let's see, you're more like…"

"Don't bother," Siene said, cutting him off with a

shake of her head. "With all that time you and your flaming imagination spend alone in the Australian Outback, I don't think I want to know."

Jack suddenly straightened in the seat. "Look lively, mates. Reed and his two playmates are on their way here." He leaned back and whistled the notes to *Anchors Aweigh.*

****

Lina broke through the jungle brush, arms packed with food. She was surprised to see Mosegi had waited. He sat cross-legged on the bank of the river just where she had left him. When he saw her, he stood and held her gaze.

When she was right in front of him, she handed him a shiny red apple. "Ever have one of these?"

He studied the fruit and shook his head.

"It's an apple," Lina replied.

"Sand apple?" the boy asked.

"No."

He turned the small fruit over before bringing it to his nose and sniffing. "Not sand apple. Smells good."

Lina laughed. "Not sand apple." She knew the fruit he mentioned came from one of the earth's strangest plants. Considered a tree without a trunk, the branches grew directly out of the ground from the roots. Widely scattered in abundance in the southern part of Africa, the weird shrunken tree bore fruit known as the sand apple. About the size of a plum and dry and smelly, the sand apple was actually quite good to eat once you knew how to handle it. She did not and had no intention of learning. The produce aisle in an upscale supermarket suited her just fine. She found another apple among the food she brought and took a bite.

"Sweet. Try yours."

She watched him examine the apple in his hand before taking a small bite and then slowly starting to chew. He smiled and began to devour what was left.

"Good," he said when he finished. He wiped his mouth with his forearm and eyed the rest of the food in her hand.

"Still hungry?"

He nodded. She handed him the rest of the food she brought. He squatted in a shaded area and began to eat.

Lina walked to a large boulder a few feet from him. After checking it for creeping things, she sat. This boy, Mosegi, was smart. He proved that. And he had escaped from the mines, also it took someone clever to do that. She needed to find out more about this smart, clever boy. He might just be her way out.

****

Siene looked around the underground room. Dank mustiness clogged her nose, making breathing difficult. The only light came from a string of electric bulbs that led to the large basement area. Wooden shelving lined the walls and stood in rows in the center of the room. Whatever had been on the shelves was long gone.

A few people dressed in white coveralls stood to one side, quietly speaking among themselves. She acknowledged them with a nod.

"Not exactly happy to see us," she said to her brother.

Reed tossed his head toward the back. "It's the bodies. The forensic team wants to finish up so they can be removed and released to the Abbot for proper burial."

"The Abbot wasn't in residence when this

happened?" Siene asked.

Reed heard the surprise in her voice. "I'm told he was in Rome for a meeting with the Pope," Reed said. "The authorities have contacted him, and he is on his way back to France." He walked to the first body and knelt. He put on a pair of latex gloves as he visually inspected the corpse before rolling the fallen monk onto his back. "Single shot to the head."

"I count five dead," Jack volunteered. He looked around the dark room. "There's no other way out of here except the door we came through. These monks never had a chance."

"So, they were brought down here and killed?" Ben asked.

Reed stood. "Doubt it. These men were either hiding here or trying to hide something here and were shot when discovered." He pointed. "The bodies are more or less in a line." He looked at Siene. "They were executed."

She closed her eyes and took a deep breath, not caring about the musty odor of dampness or the smell of the beginning stages of decomposition. She exhaled slowly as she opened her eyes. "Biden's signature."

Reed nodded. "I'm not surprised he did this. He's probably really pissed that he didn't get what he wanted in New York, and now he's on a no-holds-barred mission.'

"For the Mirror," Ben said.

Siene nodded. "Whatever Taltos is planning, it has to be big for Biden to take a chance like this. The Mirror must be key. We have to find out what that plan is before any more people get hurt."

Jack stepped around one of the fallen monks.

"These bodies are bad enough—as soon as the coroner confirms these monks were executed, the situation will be getting a lot worse," he said.

Ben stroked his chin. "Why? If the French think this was a terrorist attack, then dead monks can be easily explained."

Jack raked a flashlight over the bodies. "This monk was carrying a weapon. Hard enough to explain that in the face of religious commitment, but it is still holstered. Even harder to explain. It appears he never got a chance to use the gun. That's going to start a whole lot of people asking a whole lot of questions if our friends in white find it. We need to do something about that gun real soon."

Siene nodded to Jack. She put a mini flashlight between her teeth and lifted the digital camera she brought with her. She focused on recording the state of the room, then waited while Jack turned over the closest victim before snapping a shot of the head wound and then took a wider shot of the bodies.

The medical personnel waited patiently until she finished. "*Merci*," she said. "*S'il vous plaît. Convy nos remerciements à Nationale Gendarmerie.*"

Almost immediately the bodies were surrounded by the medical personnel.

"I didn't know you spoke French," Ben whispered, as the foursome walked away from the crime scene and back to the Range Rover.

Jack laughed. "There's a lot you don't know about her, mate."

Siene glared at him. "Not now, Jack. We have work to do."

Ben glanced at a smirking Jack before turning his

attention to Siene. "What did you say in there?"

"I thanked the officer and asked him to extend our gratitude to the authorities."

Ben glanced at Jack once the foursome had passed the last officer on guard and was well out of earshot. "What else don't I know?"

"You two can play twenty questions later," Reed cut in. "We have more pressing matters." He lowered his voice. "Did you get it?"

Jack nodded. "Both the gun and a little DNA for testing." He lifted his shirt slightly so Reed and Siene could see the gray handle of the firearm and pulled the latex gloves from his pocket.

Siene reacted to the look on Ben's face. "Special latex. Treated to pick up trace DNA and capture fingerprints." She gestured to Reed. "He had to be fast getting the gun. The gloves will protect trace evidence."

"I should have guessed," Ben said. He turned to Jack. "Yours?"

"Naw, mate. It's cold and dark in the winter in Antarctica. Quinnock gets bored and invents things sometimes."

Once inside the Range Rover, Reed pulled out two plastic evidence bags. Jack used his shirt to place the gun inside one bag and tucked the gloves into the other. Being careful to keep the bags below the Range Rover's windshield console, he handed the gun to Siene. "Luger LC3."

Siene put the bag into her purse. "He was one of ours? I didn't recognize him."

"Neither did I," Jack volunteered. "But since all our operatives are catalogued, his DNA will tell us the who, what, when, and why."

Reed nodded to Jack and the Range Rover. "I'll drop Siene and Ben at the hotel. You and I will work on ID'ing our mole."

Siene was already dialing out on her cell phone. "And I'll check in with the Compound."

****

Between swallows of food, Lina found out Mosegi had been kidnapped about six months earlier by fighters working for a rival warlord. The warlord, in turn, sold Mosegi and about twenty other men and boys to a second warlord who then brought them to the mines. Mosegi told her six had died on the march to mine the twilight rock, as he called it because of the bluish-purple color. The color of a darkening sky.

"Mosegi, can you tell me how much twilight rock is in the mine?" she asked him.

He shrugged and continued eating.

Lina placed her hand on his to stop him. "Slow down. You'll get sick if you eat so fast," she warned. She sat beside him. "Try to guess. How much twilight?"

"Much more," Mosegi replied. "One man break ground and fall into big hole. Boss man throw torch down the hole and look inside. Then he rolls onto his back and make face like this." Mosegi opened his eyes wide and grinned. "He say to tell *Loose-in*. Then men push diggers to one side and look too. That's when I leave."

Lina suddenly felt sick, barely hearing anything the boy said past the name he mentioned—*Loose-in. Lucian*. She knew Lucian was ruthless but kidnapping and enslaving children was something no civilized human with a conscience would ever do. A sick feeling welled inside her. She had underestimated the depth of his ruthlessness. She would not do that again.

Mosegi stood and stuffed a few pieces of bread into the pocket of his ragged pants. Then he started to leave.

"Wait!" Lina rushed to him. "Where are you going?"

"My village."

As sick as Lina felt from what Mosegi had said, her mind spun with a sudden plan. She only had one chance. "You won't last a day with the warlord's men looking for you."

Mosegi stopped walking and looked at Lina with an expression far beyond his years. "I go get help. Before more are taken."

"I'll help you," she said quickly.

Mosegi smiled and grabbed her hand, pulling her deeper into the jungle.

"No, I'm not going with you." She stood in front of him and held onto his hands. "We can only stop this if you go back."

Chapter Thirteen

Siene held it together until she got to her hotel room, but when Ben opened her door and asked if she was okay, her emotions closed in on her. She turned away and walked inside as panic slammed against frustration and then made way to anger.

She had killed those men. Maybe not with a gun like Max did, but in her attempt to throw Taltos off track, she was as guilty as if she had pulled the trigger. All she ever wanted was to do her job and do it well. She'd wanted a chance to atone for past mistakes. Instead, she was making new ones every day.

Ben's voice came from behind her. "Siene, what's wrong?"

She turned and saw tenderness in his eyes rather than the anger that had simmered there in the basement of the Abbey. She took a step back, unsettled by his nearness and by the hum of her emotions so close to the surface of her soul.

Without another word, she strode to the desk and tossed her room key down. "Nothing's wrong."

Ben closed the door. "Want to talk?"

She shook her head.

"Want me to go then?"

Again, she shook her head.

She watched him walk toward her, his now familiar face, all angles and uncompromising lines, instead of the blurred image she first saw in the Mirror. The way he looked at her conjured a hard, hot ball of wanting in her mid-section. *Bad idea. A really bad idea*, she thought as she pressed a hand to her jittery stomach. But that didn't stop her from gesturing to one of the chairs in the seating area. "Sit down," she whispered.

He waited until she sat before speaking. "Please don't tell me you think this attack was your fault."

"Of course it is. If I hadn't—" She broke off and cursed. "Sometimes there are casualties. I know that. But this was a massacre. Biden didn't want to leave anyone alive to talk to us or didn't want anyone talking to *me*." She frowned, thinking. "Biden found something at the Abbey, something he didn't expect to find, something he didn't want me to find. He had to. Otherwise, killing the monks makes no sense." She looked at Ben and saw a muscle pulse beside his jaw. "I have to find out what that was."

"You don't have to take on this burden alone." The muscle twitched harder, and Ben scowled. "Maybe Reed and Jack will get a lead when they get the DNA results and identify the man undercover."

A chill skittered through Siene. "That's part of what bothers me. None of us recognized the Watcher." She noticed Ben's brows draw down. "We call operatives that we place in a situation like this, the Watchers. Watchers are specially selected and have been thoroughly screened to help the Primogens keep tabs on artifacts that can't be moved to the Compound. They also monitor areas around the world that are deemed sensitive."

"And of what significance was the Abbey?"

"The Abbey is—was—a diversion. When we

moved artifacts from one place to another, we would only use the Abbey as a safe house if we ran into a delay."

"Then why tell Biden the Mirror was at the Abbey?"

Siene closed her eyes. "I screwed up. I thought the Cleaners would confine him until we could find a place to keep him on ice. If I knew Biden had escaped, I would have warned the monks. Watchers have always been assigned to the Abbey, and I felt confident it was secure for that reason." She pressed her lips together. "But everything that could go wrong, did go wrong. Add to that none of us recognized any of these Watchers, and that's even more troubling. I'll feel a whole lot better once we find out who this particular Watcher was."

"So, then we wait," Ben acknowledged.

"We wait," Siene agreed.

"I'll stay with you," Ben said.

She didn't answer, remembering what happened the last time they were alone and feeling a growing desire for it to happen again. Truth was, she didn't want to be alone. But getting more involved with Ben would put his life in greater danger. She couldn't think with him staring at her like he was, like a man who would protect her with his life.

She stood and gestured to the bar. "And while we wait, I could use a drink." She winced when the words came out in a husky voice that didn't sound like hers at all. Probably the stress, she decided. She forced a more practical tone and pointed to the bathroom. "I need to wash the stink of that room off my hands."

She didn't wait for Ben to answer. At the sink, she

flattened her palms against the cool, white ceramic edge and let out a long breath. She stared at herself in the mirror wondering if she knew what she was doing. She pressed her lips together and saw her mouth thin to a determined line. "I'll offer him one drink and then he'll leave, and I can get some rest." But when she filled a glass with water and noticed her hand shaking, she had to stop and take a deep breath to try to slow her racing heartbeat before opening the bathroom door. It was not going to be easy to send him away.

When she stepped into the living area and saw Ben at the bar across the room, her worries were confirmed. His back was to her. He'd taken off his jacket and she could see the muscles in his shoulders ripple beneath the fabric of his shirt as he reached for a bottle of scotch.

She remembered running her fingernails across the broad span of his back, thinking how well-defined he felt, more like a man who worked out at a gym, not a man who worked over a lab bench. He'd turned on the light above the bar and with most of the room still dark, the fluorescent lamp perfectly illuminated him, washing his skin in pearly white, making her think of statues and fine art.

As she silently watched, he reached down and scooped up a half-full glass, tipped it to his lips, and drained the amber liquid. His shoulders shook once in reaction to what she suspected was the scotch trailing a biting path down his throat. Apparently, Ben didn't drink much. Maybe he was as nervous as she was.

He turned and she saw the knowing twitch of his lips when he saw her. "Just making sure we had the good stuff."

She walked to the bar. "And do we?"

He set the glass down with a clink and poured two fingers. "We do." He set a second glass next to his and matched it. He handed one to her and then raised the other in salute. "To the monks."

The smell of scotch permeated the air, working its way into her nostrils. She shuddered at a surge of emotion that blended the strength of desire with the disgust of failure. She emptied the glass in a single gulp.

Empathy gave way to a snap of temper. "And what makes me think it's okay to drink to death when I caused it?" She slammed her glass onto the bar and walked to the sliding door. "Do you have any idea how much those men sacrificed to keep my little secret over the years? And how did I repay them? With a bullet to…" She broke off, knowing her sudden anger had nothing to do with the monks. It was about her, about what she had done, and about Lucian.

Ben walked toward her.

She saw something new in his eyes, a compassion she didn't understand and did not deserve.

He took her hand. "I'm beginning to understand what you are fighting to safeguard. Since my path crossed yours, the world has turned upside down. I found a lot of things I took for granted are actually based in some sort of alternate reality that scientifically should not exist but does."

Siene nodded to the empty glass in his hand. "So that's why you suddenly like scotch?"

Ben's eyes darkened. "Damned if I know." He scrubbed a hand across his face. "It was…" He trailed off as though looking for the right words. "It was a knee jerk reaction in response to something I couldn't control."

Though there was truth in his voice, Siene had heard the very same words from Lucian when he started to question the mission of the Primogens. She ignored the feeling there was an underlying meaning in the words. She wouldn't do it again. She felt suddenly sick. "I can't stay here."

She moved to leave, but he reached out and blocked her path with his arm. "Wait. I didn't mean anything. I was trying to explain."

Siene felt the heat of his body and tasted a hint of his manliness and the scotch in the air. She shifted away. "It's not you. It's just the end of a very long day."

He nodded. "I'll leave and let you get some rest."

She looked into his eyes. A sense of intimacy was created between them when she stopped him from getting in that taxi. She wished she knew why. She tipped down her chin, trying to find the right words. He nudged her face back up with his forefinger, the contact sending a buzz through her system.

He took a deep breath. "Unless you *want* me to stay."

The look in his eyes stripped away her defenses, leaving her with the bare truth. "I do want you to stay, Ben, but if you do, it might be another disaster,"

His eyes darkened and he lowered his arm. "A disaster? I thought the last time we were together was—" His gaze roamed her face like a loving caress. "—rather nice."

"I mean a disaster like the one at the Abbey." She swallowed hard. "Things tend to go wrong when I'm not focused or try to think too much, Ben."

"For me or for you?"

"For both of us," she whispered.

"Maybe you don't have to focus all the time."

She snickered. "Part of my job."

Ben nodded. "I suppose we have done enough thinking for one day. I'll go and let you get some rest."

Despite the disappointment that welled inside her, she nodded and watched him walk toward the door.

He put his hand on the doorknob and stopped. "Wait, I remember something from the last time we were together."

"What?" she asked.

He walked back to her. "This," he said. Then, he kissed her.

Siene gasped at the flare of heat that washed over her. He swallowed the small sound she made and swept his tongue inside her mouth, as she gripped his shoulders, bringing him closer to her. There would be no leaving. Not now. Not when she savored the taste of the scotch in his kiss and felt the strength in his embrace.

She returned his kiss, encouraging more. The heat grew stronger within her, spiraling out from her core until she knew kisses were not going to be enough. She murmured his name, or maybe he whispered hers. She wasn't sure and didn't care.

She dismissed the delight she felt when he moved his mouth to her neck and trailed a path of kisses to her shoulder as simply her need for release. She tried not to listen to the whisper of truth in her ear when he cupped her backside and shifted so she could feel the length of his arousal. But she also couldn't escape the want that roared through her veins and left her dizzy.

Am I falling for him?

She couldn't be. It wouldn't be smart. Ben was the Catalyst. When the mission was over, his memory would be erased, and he'd be returned to the cab line in New York City confused but safe and with a planted explanation of why he couldn't remember the lost days. Primogen Modifiers were experts in controlling delicate situations that could have a butterfly effect on the world in order to protect an artifact. Ben would be no different.

She didn't want to surrender to her rising emotions, especially under the circumstances of their meeting, but the question plaguing her mind made the answer so damned obvious. She *didn't* love him, but she did need and want him, and maybe that could be enough for now. Hell, she'd make it enough.

She twined around him. She wanted him to feel as though he couldn't be sure where she began and he ended. When the last button on his shirt gave up its prize, she pressed her palms against his chest, his skin hot to her touch. She felt her mental barrier give way, and she didn't give a damn.

****

Ben only intended to kiss her once and then give her one last chance to throw him out, but the words caught in his throat from the intensity of her kisses. If she had wavered, he would have stopped. Now he knew damn well they had gone past the point of escaping their desires.

They had come together in a bizarre meeting that shattered everything he knew about the world and its reality. Over the course of the last few days, he had slowly come to accept a world in which science and logic did not exist. He came to realize that reality had no boundaries, and the real fairy tales were possibly being penned by the scientists to explain the theories they could not readily prove. Because of Siene, he could not return to worshipping logic, science, and methodical rules. The reality he wanted was the reality he held in his arms.

He walked her backward to the bed and took her hands in his, aligning palm to palm and allowing their fingers to intertwine. He looked into her eyes, seeking reassurance, but she suddenly stilled and cocked her head.

"Did you hear that?" She tugged on their joined hands until he let her go.

Slowly, the sound of knocking and a voice reached them—small and muffled.

The voice was Reed's. "Siene, are you awake?"

He grabbed his shirt and buttoned it over his chest while Siene smoothed her tousled hair. He walked to the sliding glass door leading to the balcony as Siene reached the door. He raked his fingers through his hair and nodded.

She yanked the door open. Reed and Jack walked in.

"Ben. You're here. Good." Reed set a small laptop on the desk by the dresser. "We got something." He slipped a flash drive into the port and waited as it loaded.

Siene leaned over him. "Where did you get this?"

"From the Abbot. Jack and I met him at the airport," Reed replied. "We thought this whole trip would be all for naught, but the Abbot saved the day."

Jack raised his eyebrows and nodded to Ben. "Should help us button up things here." Subtly, he tugged on the front of the blue shirt he wore.

Ben looked down and saw the buttons askew on his shirt. Fortunately, Reed's gaze was intently watching the laptop as the screen came to life. He turned his back and quickly corrected the problem.

First on the monitor was a picture of the fallen Primogen agent. "John Richards. Third generation Watcher. Recently assigned to the Abbey."

"Why didn't we know about him?" Siene asked.

"He got the assignment about the same time that you headed to New York. I was with Paz, so I turned off my cell." Reed reacted to a look of frustration on Siene's face. "I know, I know. Not a good idea. Lecture me later, sis. Right now, focus on this." Reed turned his attention to the information on the computer screen. "The Monks were monitoring increased activity in Africa." He pointed to the satellite image. "This is an area on the Tanzanian border." He leaned forward and counted. "Seven trucks, five cars, and some sort of hastily built structure. The Abbot said the base wasn't there on the scan the week before, so the monks set the satellite to take pictures every twenty-four hours."

Ben saw a series of pictures scroll across the monitor. He could see trucks appear and disappear over the course of the surveillance. "Do you know what they're doing?"

Jack shook his head. "Not yet."

"Luckily the Abbot took the flash drive with him, otherwise Taltos would have it," Ben replied.

Reed printed out the pictures and ejected the flash drive. "The Abbot knows when to listen to his gut.

Securing vital information is standard operating procedure at our watch points. Surveillance is downloaded every night and secured. In this case, the Abbot took a copy with him. He was going to send it from Italy when the attack happened. That changed his plans. He was afraid his personal computer may have been compromised and was planning a way to deliver the drive personally when we contacted him."

"Is that all we got?" Siene asked.

"It's more than we had twenty-four hours ago," Reed replied. "So, we go to Africa and find out what's going on at the base."

Siene spread the pictures on the desk, took a jeweler's loupe out of her purse, and studied the pictures one by one. "Fuck," she spat out when she got to the last one. "Take a look at this."

"Your Sheila has a potty mouth, mate," Jack said to Ben as Reed bent over the picture.

"She's not my girlfriend," Ben corrected.

"Whatever you say." Jack smacked the back of his knuckles on Ben's chest before pretending to fix the top button of Ben's shirt. He turned to Reed. "What do you see?"

"Lucian," Siene and Reed said in unison.

Chapter Fourteen

It was well past dark when Biden headed back to the hotel in Seattle. He used the computer at the local library to dig into some area records. He made some progress and hit a few dead ends. It had been a very long day.

He concentrated on the one thing he did manage to find out from an old census file. Reed and Siene had lived with relatives until they enrolled in college. After college, he followed their data trail to California, Arizona, and then back to Washington State. Siene eventually moved to New York City, but Reed kept his Washington State address. Real estate transactions recorded in Klamath County, Oregon showed Reed Dower as the owner of close to a hundred acres near Klamath Falls and the Klamath Indian Reservation.

Max set his laptop on the desk in his room and turned it on. Why would Reed Dower buy so much property in the Oregon high desert? The government owned most of the rest of the land in the area, so it would be a good bet to say that he didn't buy it for a potential luxury housing development.

Since records showed Dower had done nothing with the land for years, it was also not logical to assume Dower bought the land to raise livestock, the principal industry of that area. The high desert got only about fifteen inches of rainfall a year. Dower would have had to irrigate the area to grow anything. Add in the Klamath Indian Reservation, the ongoing water rights dispute between the government and the tribe, and it was a good bet there had to be some other reason for the purchase.

Biden pulled out his cell phone and dialed. While he waited for the call to connect, he used the remote to turn on the TV. He paged through the stations and stopped when he got to the national news. A reporter was updating the story on the Sénanque Abbey. A smile grew on Max's face as he listened to the reporter say no group had taken credit for the destruction of the Abbey, and there were no leads in the case.

"Damn, I'm good," Max said when the call connected. "Lucian, turn on the news." He waited. "Like my handiwork?" He laughed. "Relax. The French can dig around for a hundred years. They won't find anything worth investigating. I called to let you know I'll be driving to Oregon in the morning. I'll let you know when I have something. Oh, and I'll need you to make another deposit into my account. I saw a flashy red beauty at the car rental office, and I can't wait to see how it handles on the winding roads of the Cascades."

Satisfied he'd get everything he asked for, he disconnected the call and walked to the laptop. A few keystrokes later, a file photo of Reed and Siene Dower filled the screen.

"Where are you two hiding out, and why is Reed holding on to seemingly worthless land in the high Oregon desert?" A one-sided smile curved his lips. "This is going to be fun."

****

Lina had to be both clever and careful. Lucian was a complicated man. Much like a male version of an evil stepmother, he could be quite neutral at times, working all the angles to advance his position and helping those who would align with him. At other times, when someone or something caused him to deviate from his plan, he could be quite volatile, and no one was spared his wrath. Whatever Lucian was going to do, he obviously needed money to do it. A lot of money. That's why they were spending weeks in this god-awful African heat mining tanzanite.

Tanzanite was considered a semi-precious stone, but one becoming increasingly popular and rare. Lucian would need large quantities of the gem to turn a profit, and profit and must have paid off government officials overseeing the mining to look the other way. She suspected he was using the money to buy alliances. There was only one reason he wanted to lead the counter-organization and that would be to war with the Primogens, to acquire the artifacts, and then use them to influence the global economy on every level.

From what she learned from Mosegi, the workers took the raw tanzanite to a central storage place where it was analyzed, sorted, and then shipped to various markets around the world. Brilliant of Lucian to bypass diamonds and trade in a gem that was both highly coveted and not as closely regulated. With all the attention on making sure Africa's diamonds were mined by licensed enterprises, and then properly laser-etched, it would take some time to notice that the market was being flooded by tanzanite mined by kidnapped men and children.

She took a deep breath and went through a few tai

chi forms to loosen up. When she got back to the Primogen compound, no, *if* she got back to the compound, she would ask Kai to show her a few more. Times like this, when she was at peace and pleasant memories filled her mind, she always promised herself that she would never again take stupid chances. Promises she also knew that she probably wouldn't keep.

She watched Lucian through the jungle growth for a few minutes. He was talking on his cell and didn't look happy. But no matter. She had given Mosegi her word that he would only be spending one more night locked up in the cages built inside the mine to control the workers at night. She had no intention of breaking that vow.

"Hey," she said, breaking through the undergrowth and making sure her voice was light. Despite what she knew was happening, the key to her success would be for her to sound positive.

Lucian held up his hand and finished his phone conversation. "Lina, this is not the best time." His voice sounded more like a growl.

"I take it you didn't enjoy your conversation with whoever called." She walked to the table and poured some water.

"I never enjoy blackmail," he snapped.

Lina feigned surprise. "But you are so good at it."

Lucian gave her a brief scowl then signaled to a burly man holding a rifle. "Bring me the overseer."

The man nodded and then disappeared into the jungle.

"The overseer of what?" Lina asked. She sipped the water, her mind spinning with ways to get Lucian to bring Mosegi to her without putting the boy's life in danger.

Lucian's brow furrowed. "Curiosity can be deadly. You know what happened to the cat."

Lina set her glass on the wooden table and leaned her backside against it. She gripped the table with both hands, partly to channel some of the nervousness, partly to steady herself. "I'm sorry you are having a bad day."

"You didn't come here to find out about my day. What do you want?"

"I want to go home, but what I want and what you'll give me are not quite the same, I'm sure," she replied. She could see Lucian's neck begin to turn red. It was his tell, the first sign that he was getting annoyed. She'd use that. She cautioned herself not to get anxious and inadvertently reveal just how much she did know. "But I do have another request."

"I'm sure you do." Lucian picked up a thick stack of papers from the table and began reading.

"I'm bored," she announced. "You either lock yourself inside that tank-thing with the antennae on the roof, or else the jeep is missing, and you're gone somewhere. You won't hook up something so I can at least cybershop and watch reality TV, and there's nothing for me to do around here."

Lucian didn't look at her. "I have no doubt you have a suggestion of how I can entertain you."

"As a matter of fact, I do.

"I can't wait to hear this," he said.

"Let me go with you next time you go out."

He looked up. "Next time I go where?"

"I dunno. Wherever you go in the jeep."

He began to laugh. "Lina, darling, you know

better."

"Lucian, if I have to face one more day wandering around this god-awful camp, making sure I don't step on a snake and dodging dive-bombing insects, I'm going to go mad." She moved into her best whiney voice. "I can't stand this place. It's hot, it's dirty, and both the men and the animals stink."

"It's Africa. Deal with it."

Lina strode over and grabbed the papers from his hand. "I didn't ask to come here."

Lucian's lips thinned. He held out his hand and waited. After a few seconds, Lina handed him the papers.

"The only reason you are here with me and not locked in a terrarium in my office with someone tossing you food once a day is because we both know you can't be trusted not to escape and try to contact your friends."

Lina crossed her arms over her chest. "No. The only reason I'm here is so you can use me as a bargaining chip to get to Siene."

Lucian shrugged. "Either way I keep you alive because you are useful at the moment."

Lina's mouth formed a perfect 'O'. "I am hurt that you would say such a thing."

"You are a fairy tale anomaly, one that can be very dangerous using that very interesting DNA you have to slip in and out of things," Lucian shot back. "You don't expect me to believe you haven't tried to change size."

"You know I have. But for one thing, I don't know exactly how far anything is from where I am, and for another, the African jungle isn't the place for a twelve-inch snack to wander too far from camp." It was important for Lucian to think she wasn't exploring a way out.

One corner of Lucian's mouth turned up in a nefarious half-smile. "And while I count on you to remember that, mixing a small amount of Alice's mushroom in your food to keep you human-sized helps too."

Lina glanced to the bottles of water on the table.

"Not those," Lucian assured. "We all need to drink water, and I don't need an army of giants that I accidently made peering over the tops of the trees and calling attention to this operation."

"Tainting my food. You are a despicable jerk," Lina shouted.

"And what are you going to do about it? Never eat?"

She crossed her arms over her chest. "Maybe."

"Now that's a thought," Lucian said. "The weaker you get, the easier it will be to keep an eye on you." He laughed. "I don't have time for this. What do you really want?"

Lina took a deep breath. This was the one, and probably the only, chance she would get. She didn't know how to get Lucian to take her to the mines and she had no idea how, once she got there, she would be able to get to Mosegi. But she was a fairy tale character. Surely she could make something up.

"For starters," she said, "I have no one to talk to. The men you hired mostly grunt and walk away when I try to engage them in meaningful conversation. Maybe I can go to the village for a few hours each day and learn the language or find someone to talk to."

Lucian shook his head. "The closest village is eight hours away."

Lina pulled sunglasses out of her back pocket and put them on. "Then, I'm going with you."

"I don't think so." Lucian signaled to a group of men beginning their meal.

The one closest to them set his tray down and walked over. Lucian spoke to him in a tongue Lina didn't understand. The man nodded, walked to one of the jeeps, and drove away.

"What was that all about?" Lina asked.

"I'm finding you a playmate," Lucian said.

****

On the ride to the airport, Ben didn't have much to contribute to the conversation, so he just listened, mentally cataloguing everything so he could be of some help once they got to Africa.

"Caleb will meet you at the rendezvous point," Jack said, double checking their papers and flight plan so personnel at the private airport would let them leave. "I'm going straight to the Compound with the flash drive. Kai will extract everything she can, and then she'll analyze the hell out of the data to try to find out what Lucian is up to."

"Siene, Ben, and I will get as close as we can to the camp we saw on the map," Reed added. "We'll check in every twelve hours."

Jack nodded. He pointed to a group of men standing on the tarmac next to the aircraft. "Best smiles, mates," he said getting out of the car, "and no unnecessary conversation once we get to the plane if we want to be cleared."

At the plane, Ben stood silently as Siene and Jack talked their way through one glitch after another. The pilot Reed hired left a message that he would be thirty minutes late and, because of the attack on the Abbey, the government official was on hand and was checking their papers and being extremely thorough about it. Plus, there was a mechanic working up to his elbows on the left engine of the plane.

The mechanic tugged on the propeller of the Beachcraft King Air 350. It spun a few times and then died. Twenty minutes later, another try with the same result, and then a third. After the fourth try the engine sprang to life.

About the same time, the official seemed to decide he was satisfied with the papers and flight plan and handed the paperwork to Jack who handed it to Reed. "This is where I get off, mates. Safe travels." He saluted and left in the jeep.

Reed began stowing the gear and gestured to Siene's backpack. "Want that in cargo?"

Siene declined. "I'd rather keep it with me."

Ben watched her climb the metal steps leading inside. The more he was with Siene, the more he felt his connection with her strength. She was so very different from other women. Not only was she smart and beautiful, he was pretty sure she could also take a guy down with one punch. He smiled. She could probably bench press a ton of weight, too. That kind of bothered him. He arched his arm and made a muscle. He needed to get into shape. His male instincts kicked in when they made love at the compound, and they had not retreated since. He wanted to impress her, be the strong one, but since he spent more time in the lab than in the gym, improving on his sorry biceps would be an uphill battle. He vowed to make sure he would find more places to be useful before this mission was over. He settled into a seat next to her and buckled in.

"I hope I can help you somehow, Siene," Ben said. "This hero-stuff is all new to me."

Siene stashed her backpack under the seat. "I don't consider this hero-stuff. This is something we do regularly, and you are part of this mission now. I don't know how or why just yet, but you are vital enough for Lucian to try to kill you."

Ben smiled. "Not much of a compliment."

"Once we figure out what you're supposed to do, it will be."

From the seat behind, Reed leaned forward and talked to them from the space between the seats. "This plane was fitted with extra fuel tanks for ferry missions, but we'll still have to stop once to refuel. Ben, I don't suggest you get out and stretch your legs when we land. Once we're refueled and ready to leave, it will be wheels up whether you're in your seat or not. For now, I suggest you get some rest. I don't expect we'll get much sleep once we get to Africa." He settled back, crossed his arms over his chest, and closed his eyes.

Siene reached over and squeezed Ben's hand. "I'm glad you're here."

Ben winked. "Me, too."

A few minutes later they were in the air.

****

Joseph watched the men with rifles gorge themselves with food while the village men and children continued to dig for the twilight stone. He tugged at the thick chain around his ankle. A man with a deep scar on his face put the shackles on him when he came back to camp as Lina said he needed to. He hated the chains. Once a chain went on, it never came off.

159

Many of the men had ankle wounds thickly clustered with fat black flies. He had to be careful if the iron cut him. Men died from the cuts because of the infection. As a doctor, he knew how to help, but under these conditions, he could do nothing but watch them die. He sensed he could trust Lina. Not enough to reveal his true identity yet, but enough to know she might be his only way out. He wouldn't get far in the jungle alone.

He sat and rubbed the reddening skin above the lateral malleolus and laughed. Knowing medical terms was meaningless here.

A guard heard him. Noticing Joseph was not working, he kicked out hard enough to send him to his back. "Work, lazy boy!"

A second guard strode over. "He come back."

The first guard spat. "That one trouble. He go four times. Three times we get him back. Four time he come back." The guard tapped his head. "That one crazy."

"Still good for lion bait," the second man said.

All talking stopped when a heavily armed warlord entered the mine chamber. "I need a boy," he announced. "For boss." He surveyed those working within his view and shook his head. "These near dead. Not good." He started to leave.

"This one." The first guard grabbed Joseph by the arm and yanked him to standing.

The warlord looked at the chain on Joseph's leg. "What he do?"

"He lazy," the guard lied. "Sometime he go sickie and not work."

The warlord circled Joseph. "Free him." When the chain from Joseph's leg was removed, the warlord grabbed his chin. "You coming with me but do something cheaty and out to the jungle you go. Understand?"

Slowly Joseph nodded. "Where we go?" he asked in a small voice.

The warlord signaled to a second pair of guards, each taking one of Joseph's arms.

"Where I take you? You have new job. Get washed. You stink. Then go to boss. After that, no my problem."

****

With darkness falling, Biden stopped the jeep just beyond a large clump of dying western junipers. He'd been returning to the high desert for the past week, waiting, watching. He stood and scanned the area. All he saw was dust and a few stray coyotes looking for mule deer. He grabbed the binoculars from the passenger seat and scanned the vista. It looked even worse up close.

But when he trained the binoculars to the north, he could see a dust cloud rising in the distance. Someone was coming and coming fast. He started the jeep and pulled it behind the brown trees, breaking off some of the brittle branches to cover the front and back. While most of Oregon and Washington considered the conifers an invading pest, Max was grateful for the place to hide.

He leaned over the hood of the jeep and followed the dust trail through the binoculars. In a few minutes he could make out a car with one driver approaching. He scanned the area in a sweeping arc. A remote, rugged terrain, carved by a small creek that paralleled the dirt road, the canyon walls soared to about 800 feet and was broken into pinnacles, fat, flat slabs, and stalagmite shapes. This was no tourist out for a sightseeing trip. This could be the break he needed.

Suddenly the phone in the pocket of his shirt vibrated. He checked the lit screen for the identity of the caller. Davelos. The last thing he needed right now.

"It's six a.m. in Tanzania. You're up awfully early, Lucian."

"Where are you and what are you doing?" Lucian asked.

Max noticed the thread of annoyance in Lucian's voice. He liked that. "Oregon and I'm working. Why?"

"I need you to find that compound," Lucian replied.

"That's why I'm here."

"You need to move faster," Lucian said. "There are some complications."

"There are always complications," Max reminded him. He watched the approaching car through the binoculars as he spoke. "I would think you'd be used to that by now. I am."

"The operation here will be wrapping up in the next week or two. By then I want the location of the Primogen base. If you find it…"

"When I find it," Max corrected.

"When you find it, then," Lucian continued, "do not move on the base until I get there, understand?"

The command in Lucian's voice was clear, and Max thought he knew why. "Do the complications you mentioned involve Siene Dower by any chance?"

"None of your business."

Lucian's tone confirmed it. "You slept with her and the last time Taltos challenged the Primogens, you tried to convince her to switch sides."

"She is not your concern. She is mine. I thought you and everyone else understood that she is my kill if it comes to that. My kill. No one else."

"No one questions your right to kill her and her brother, but I think I know better," Max prodded. "You may kill Reed Dower, but I don't think you'll be able to terminate Siene."

"She is of no importance to me any longer," Lucian countered. "I simply have something to settle with her."

Through the binoculars, Biden saw the car come to a stop next to the creek near the first mud-gray spire. "Look, we can talk about your love life later. I've got company." He disconnected and slipped the phone back into his pocket.

When he looked up, the car and its occupant were gone.

Chapter Fifteen

Reed slept through refueling at an abandoned airbase in southern Italy, and Ben seemed glued to whatever was on his notebook computer. Siene, however, didn't mind the lack of company. She liked the view from the air. The Atlas Mountains of Northern Africa receded to the south, becoming grasslands and shrub land biomes before meeting the Sahara Desert. It seemed like hours before the endless sand vistas began to dot with green as the landscape changed on the flight to Africa's east coast.

When the jungle finally appeared, Siene took out the GPS unit from her backpack to see where they were. She determined they were less than fifty miles from Mount Kilimanjaro. Ten miles past that was the rendezvous point. She let out a short breath. Almost there.

She looked at Ben. He was busy with his laptop, and she began to wonder what made him the Catalyst and, as such, the target of an assassination attempt. How did he fit into the Mirror prophecy? What was he supposed to do? Where and why? She made a mental note to stay close to him with the hope of finding out more by learning about his past through conversation and learning about his current life through observation.

Ever since she had accepted her lot as a Primogen, she'd studied behavior patterns. Wanting to know why people behaved the way they did was an important aspect of her role as a protector. Especially when she was in a situation she wasn't certain she could control. Like this one.

The plane lurched, and she grabbed the armrests as the pilot regained control. Damn, she hated flying.

"Just an air pocket," Ben said.

"I'd rather be on the ground," Siene admitted.

"I don't mind flying," Ben replied. "Being in a plane with nothing to do gives me time to organize my research notes."

"Is that what you were doing?"

He nodded.

"Tell me about your spit project."

"My lysozyme antigen project," he corrected.

"Too complicated a name to remember."

"I guess we'll call it my spit project from now on then."

Siene smiled.

"With the ecosystem of the planet changing, and the threat to rainforests around the world because of human encroachment, my company has been trying to synthesize the antibiotics and antiseptics normally produced with the many species of plants in a tropical forest. The phytochemicals in tropical plants have beneficial effects on long-term health when consumed by humans. Several can be used to effectively treat human diseases. At least 12,000 phytochemicals have been isolated so far, a number estimated to be less than ten percent of the total. My team was working with the secondary metabolites in plants. It is the secondary metabolites and pigments that have the therapeutic actions and can be refined to produce drugs, like dioxin from foxglove used to treat several heart conditions, and morphine and codeine from the poppy used to relieve intensive pain. The Plant Genetic Engineering Team of which I was a part has been studying these herbs with healing properties from around the world."

"Paz always worries about the South American rainforest. When this is over, you may want to talk to her about this."

Ben's smile widened.

She angled her body to him. "Plants, I understand, but how did you progress from herbalism to saliva?"

"An accident actually."

Siene laughed. "Some of the best inventions and discoveries were accidents."

"One of our lab techs dropped a beaker and got a small cut on his finger cleaning up. I told him to go to Medical, but he said we were at a critical moment in our experiments and didn't want to leave. He licked off the blood, put on a bandage, and continued to work. The cut never got infected. That got me thinking. What if someday the rainforests were wiped out either by climate change or the overdevelopment of land or by human greed in overharvesting the medicinal plants? The world could lose some of its most vital medicines. There had to be a backup plan."

"Spit," Siene proclaimed.

"Not as easy as it sounds. There isn't enough antigen in human saliva to cure anything, but I believe that if it was combined with some form of peptide, I could get an overlapping protein chain which might interact with the cellular membrane and trigger immunization activating events within the cell itself."

Siene blew out a long breath of air. "That's a

mouthful. Were you successful?"

"I did prove that the interaction of salivary lysozyme with the surface protein antigen of Streptococcus cures strep throat in mice."

Siene laughed. "If Cinderella's mice get sick, I'll call you." As soon as she said the words, she regretted them. Ben looked disappointed with her reaction. "I'm sorry. I didn't mean to make light of your research. It does sound important."

"I was going to present my findings to Premier Health Investors in Manhattan when you stopped me. Prima Health was considering offering me a grant to do research on my own."

"If you got into that cab, you would have never gotten that grant anyway, right?"

Ben nodded. "Dead men don't do research."

"I'm sorry," Siene said softly. She saw his smile fade.

"I'm not. I like breathing." He reached out and touched her cheek. "I owe you my life. In some cultures, we would be considered engaged, or at the very least, bonded for life."

Siene was about to reply when the plane dipped sharply. Reed sat up in the seat behind her and put his hand on her shoulder. The plane shook and she braced herself in the seat.

"Are we in trouble?" she called to the pilot. She could see him struggling with the stick and watching the gauges.

"Something's wrong with the engine," he yelled back. "There are some parachutes in the back. You better get ready to jump. I'm not sure I can get you all the way to the rendezvous point.

"Don't panic," Siene cautioned Ben as they made their way to the chutes, with hands on anything solid to steady them as the plane continued to bounce. "When you panic, you make mistakes, and it is the mistakes that kill you."

"You've jumped out of planes before?" Ben asked.

Reed handed a parachute to Ben. "We've both been skydiving since we were teenagers."

"I haven't," Ben replied.

"Watch me." Reed donned his chute, explaining each step.

The plane jerked and a stream of smoke billowed past the window. "Are we going to crash?" Ben asked.

"The plane is," Reed answered. "We'll be in the air long before that."

Siene finished fastening her chute and grabbed her backpack. She opened the rear door. The air rushing in forced her to close her eyes for a moment.

"What about the pilot?" Ben asked.

"He'll be fine. He'll bail before he loses control," Reed said. He tugged on the shoulder straps of Ben's chute, making sure it was on him securely, and then patted the container backpack that held the main and reserve chutes. "Skydiving 101," he shouted over the rushing air. "The AAD—automatic activation device— will release the reserve chute at about 750 feet. When it does, grab on to the handles. Pull on the left handle, and you lower the back part of the left side of the chute to slow you down and turn to the left. Same thing with the right; you slow and turn to the right. Pull them both and it's like putting on the brakes. Got it?"

"No," Ben said. "But I will."

Reed patted Ben's chest. "Good. Otherwise, you'll

splat." He turned to Siene. "Ready?"

She nodded.

"I'll go last. We'll try to stay within eyesight, but if we do get separated, we'll meet up with Caleb at the rendezvous point. Twelve hours after any two of us get there, we go and finish the mission with or without the third party. Agreed?"

Again, Siene nodded.

"I guess I'm in, too," Ben said.

Siene gave the thumbs up and stepped to the door.

About that time, the plane began a sharp dive. The motion drove everyone backward. Ben grabbed onto Siene and the back of the small airplane seat to his right to stabilize them. Reed slammed into another seat and fell sidelong onto the floor of the plane. The pilot seemed to recover control and the plane regained altitude.

Reed stood and began walking forward. "You two go. I'll check with the pilot and be right behind you."

"Are you okay?" Siene asked her brother.

He nodded and pointed to the open door. "I'm fine. Now go."

She turned and waved before she jumped.

"Your turn," Reed called out, watching from a small side window as his sister torpedoed her body through the air for a short time before she moved horizontally and waited for the chute to open.

"Are you sure this chute will open?" Ben tugged on the straps of his pack and looked down at the ground through the open airplane door.

Reed shrugged. "If it doesn't, it was nice meeting you." Then he pushed Ben out of the plane.

****

"How are you and your little playmate getting along?" Lucian asked, watching from a chair as Joseph prepared a fresh glass of water for Lina.

"Fine." Lina knew she had to choose her words very carefully. Lucian was a smart man. If he ever got even one tiny inkling that she knew the boy, he would be back in the mines, and she would be in the terrarium Lucian had threatened her with earlier. She hadn't had time to formulate a plan and couldn't believe her luck when one of the guards brought Mosegi to her and told her he was a gift from the boss. "He's a little slow, but I can work with that." She hoped Lucian could not tell she was lying. The boy was smart. She could tell that already from the short time she spent with him in the jungle.

"So then, teach each other things and stay out of my way." With a crooked forefinger, Lucian gestured to Joseph. "Come here."

Joseph cast his eyes down and approached Lucian. He had heard stories about this man and didn't dare look into his eyes. Looking there would be like looking into the eyes of a demon.

"What is your name?" Lucian demanded.

"Mosegi," Joseph whispered.

"And how old are you?"

"Sixteen."

"Found you some real clothing, I see." Lucian snarled. "The tribal shit you wore was falling apart."

"Yes, boss."

Lucian grabbed Joseph's pants and tugged them down. "Are you a man or a boy?"

Joseph stood still. "Been circumcised," he said.

Lucian laughed and let Joseph go. He glared at

Lina. "Another job he can do for you."

As Joseph gathered himself, Lina locked her gaze with his, hoping her expression would tell him that having sex was one job he need not do. "Don't be a pig, Lucian. He's just a boy."

With a barely perceptible nod, Joseph handed Lina the water glass, walked to the far end of the tent, and sat.

Lucian chuckled. "I believe he'll be a fine little pet for you."

"He's not an animal; he's a child. And a scared one at that." Now, she wanted to get as much information from Lucian as she could. "Where did he come from?"

"A village not far from here."

"Was he working the mines?"

"Everyone works the mines, my dear." Lucian gestured for Joseph to bring him water. The boy hurried to comply.

"Good boy," he said when Joseph brought a full glass. "He seems to be a fast learner." He watched Joseph return to his spot at the back of the tent. "But from the look of it, he isn't much of a conversationalist."

"Teaching him some proper English will be my first project."

Lucian stood. "Good luck with that. Trying to get the villagers to do anything needs some persuading." He walked to the tent flap and turned. "Oh, by the way, I've doubled the guards. Don't want you and your pet to wander off."

Lina restrained from commenting as Lucian left.

Joseph joined Lina. He frowned. "He *goffel*."

Lina furrowed her brows. "*Goffel*?"

Joseph squeezed his eyes and mouth together. "Ugly?"

Joseph nodded.

"Do you mean he is not a nice man?"

Joseph nodded even more quickly.

Lina put her arm around his shoulders. "English lessons start now. I have no time to play twenty questions."

****

It was difficult for Joseph to feign ignorance of English. He graduated magna cum laude and had a perfect command of the language, but his well-being, for now, depended on the ruse he had chosen.

Lina did not seem to be part of the invaders, but he still could not be totally sure. He'd wait and stay alive.

****

The parachute swung as Siene drifted to the ground. Nothing she couldn't control. This wasn't her first jump. But she did worry about Ben. When her feet touched the tops of some kapok trees, she pulled on the right parachute cord to steer away, but she was too close to the ground. The first branch she hit knocked her off balance, and she fell through the thick canopy of the jungle, bouncing off branches as she fell.

The fall stopped abruptly when her chute tangled in a large branch, suspending her about four feet above the jungle floor. The momentum of the fall caused her to rock back and forth and her cheek stung from a branch she hit on the way down.

She heard a loud boom and looked toward the sound. She could see smoke billowing into the sky and surmised the plane had crashed. She looked around above her, hoping to see a drifting parachute but saw only smoke and sky through the jungle canopy. Her heart raced and her hands shook, but she finally was able to unbuckle the harness and let herself fall to the ground. Her right leg buckled when she landed, and she rolled a few feet before stopping.

When she got her bearings, she stood and took out her cell phone. This deep in the jungle she was pretty sure it would be useless, but she checked anyway. She held it out and turned in a slow circle. The *No Service* message never left the screen. A shadow fell on her as she finished the circle. Slowly, she dropped her arm and looked up into the painted face of a warrior with the barrel of a gun pointed at her head.

Chapter Sixteen

Siene looked from the gun to the face of the man holding it. She held eye contact, hoping he didn't think her aggressive; yet she didn't want him to think her timid either. The man's eyes held nothing hostile and after a few seconds, he lowered his weapon, but continued watching her.

Siene held still while she quickly assessed her predicament. He was obviously a national—his skin was a deep chocolate color, his eyes just as dark. Though he wore light colored pants and a shirt, his cheeks were painted with two bold stripes of white, his appearance a clear mixture of modern and ancient traditions.

She held her hands at shoulder level as the man continued to watch her, gun in his hand. She noticed he had an old AK-47 rifle slung over his shoulder and wondered why he was so heavily armed.

"I'm looking for Chagga village," she said calmly.

He took a step closer.

She did not back up. She had learned enough martial arts from Kai Soong to disable the man and get away if need be.

"Chagga village at white mountain," he replied, gesturing over his shoulder.

He continued to look at her, still nothing threatening in his gaze. She got the feeling he may be a lookout from a nearby village sent to check the area because of the plane crash. "You speak English?"

He nodded. "From the missionaries."

"My plane had engine trouble."

Two more men appeared from the bushes. All had guns and wore the same face paint.

"Can you show me the way to the village?" Siene asked. She forced calm into her voice. "Do you know the way?"

All three nodded. "But big trouble in Chagga village," the tallest of the three men said. "No one goes there."

"Where is your guide?" another asked. "Jungle dangerous for someone alone."

"I have a guide waiting for me at Chagga village. I was traveling with two others. Have you seen anyone else?"

"We see smoke, no people."

"I have to get to the village. I can pay you."

She began to open her backpack when the tall man grabbed her upper arm and stopped her. "No. No one come back if they go there."

She shook her arm free. "I have to get there."

The men huddled and began to converse in their native tongue. It was useless to try to listen. Even if she could hear clearly what they said, thousands of languages were spoken in Africa. She doubted that even Paz knew all of them.

The first man she encountered turned to her. "You can travel with us as far as our village. From there, it is another day's journey."

She held out her hand. "I'm Siene."

"Apio." He shook her hand and pointed. "Gero and

his son, Kamau."

Siene nodded.

"We will travel in a line to cover our numbers. Gero will lead and you will follow. Kamau and I will walk behind you."

"I can't leave without my friends. We jumped from the plane before it crashed, but we got separated and did not land together. I know they are looking for me."

Kamau said something to his father in their native tongue.

His father nodded.

"I will look for your friends and meet you in the village." Kamau moved off in a fast trot.

Gero began walking. Siene fell in behind him with Apio right behind her. The pace quickened and, in a few minutes, she was breathing heavily. She wasn't used to running like this but surmised in the jungle, speed was an important attribute. The chatter of monkeys filled the air overhead, and the mosses and fungi growing on the jungle floor made their footing slippery. As the ground became more uneven, she lost her footing and put out her hand to try to brace herself against a tree trunk.

Apio grabbed her arm from behind and jerked her backward before she could make contact with the tree. "*Juckbohne*," he said. "Very bad. Can make you blind."

Siene looked over and saw the white-green plant with red inflorescence blossoms creeping up the side of the tree trunk. She'd forgotten the jungle could hold such dangers. She had heard about this plant from Caleb. He had slipped on wet moss and brushed against *juckbohne*. The tiny hairs attached to the plant's pods had broken off and contaminated Caleb's skin and clothes. The hairs of the plant stay active even when dry and must be thoroughly removed wherever they contacted the skin. Caleb was inactive for months because of his run-in with the plant. If not for Apio, she could have been rendered incapacitated and would be no help in trying to find Lucian. She would have to be more careful. She nodded and moved quickly to catch up to Gero, who hadn't stopped running.

The day was hot and humid, and she quickly began to sweat. The rotting leaves and other vegetation provided a cushioned but slippery surface beneath her feet, and she was careful to try to make solid contact with the ground as she ran. No one spoke, so Siene concentrated on the rhythmic beat of her feet as she kept pace.

To keep her mind from dwelling on the plane crash, she thought back to when she was a child and her father first told her about the Legacy. She hadn't understood what he meant, of course; she was only ten. But then every night, he told her a story about the Grimm artifacts and the wonderful things they could do. As she entered her teenage years, her father began to tell her about the terrible things the same artifacts could do if they were misused, and what she thought were just wonderful fairy tales she loved so much became dangerous truths. From then on, the threat of the artifacts being used for personal gain were the only "fairy tales" she heard each night as he sat beside her bed—not the stories told to other children where the prince and princess lived happily ever after. She came to understand and ultimately accept the important obligation her family had assumed as well as the awful burden that came with it.

The three ran for about an hour when Gero suddenly stopped and held up his hand. "Someone's coming."

"Maybe it's…"

Apio covered her mouth and drew his weapon. He pushed her behind him. She could hear the rustle of underbrush and the swish of branches coming toward them. The sounds grew louder and Gero pushed her into a low clump of brush.

Suddenly, Ben burst through the growth. As soon as he saw the men with their guns pointed at him, he held up his hands.

Siene rose from the underbrush. She could see Ben's face relax when he saw her.

"Siene, tell them I'm with you," he said.

She was relieved that he had survived the jump. "He's with me," she said. But the men didn't lower their weapons. Gero said something in his native tongue, and she listened in shock when Ben answered in Swahili. How did he know that dialect? Had he been here before?

Gero nodded and switched to Swahili. A conversation between them went on for a few minutes more before Apio and Gero finally lowered their weapons. "We go on."

Ben followed behind Siene as they walked. "How do you know Swahili?" she asked over her shoulder.

He didn't answer.

"You've been here before." She wondered what else she didn't know about him. First, he was a Taltoian target for a reason she still did not understand and now she heard him fluently speak the national language of Tanzania.

"Not exactly here, but close by."

"Why didn't you tell me?" Apparently, there was more to Ben Michaels than a white lab coat and a petri dish full of spit.

Ben shrugged. "The subject of my past travels never came up."

"And you didn't think you should interject that into the conversation when we were planning this side trip?"

"I thought it might be a nice surprise under the right circumstances."

"I hate surprises. My life has been one big surprise after another, and it's getting a bit redundant. Next time you think there is something you should tell me, please do so."

"I'll keep that in mind."

"You should be happy I don't have the lasso of truth because then you'd have no secrets from me."

"You have that also?"

"We have a lot of things."

"And you'd use it to know my secrets?"

"If I have to. I told you mine, but you seem reluctant to tell me yours." She did want to know. But right now, there was a more pressing issue. "I'd like to know when and why were you in Africa without using anything. I need to trust you completely."

Ben nodded. "A year ago, and for research. I told you I was working for a pharma company. The African rainforest holds many treasures and many secrets, and the company for which I was working wanted to know them."

"When did you leave that company?" His answer might give her another small clue to why he was involved with Taltos.

"My grant was terminated about six months ago. With no money to fund my research, I was terminated too." He tilted his head to one side. "Why do you want to know?"

For now, she didn't see his pharma research as a clear connection to the mission, but she wasn't ruling out some link. She still didn't know why someone at Taltos wanted him dead. "We'll talk about that later, but for now what did you say to Gero? Nothing that would endanger the mission, I hope."

Ben shook his head. "I said we were here to help find out what happened to the villagers."

"It seemed like a lot longer of a conversation," Siene countered.

"He needed some convincing."

She had a lot more questions for him, but for now, she needed to get to Chagga, so she just nodded and kept going.

This little addition to Ben's resume had made him and his role an even bigger mystery. By rights he should have walked away a long time ago after everything she put him through so far, but instead here he was beside her, ready to fight for people he didn't even know despite the danger and the uncertainty. The more she got to know Ben, the more he confused her. Maybe he wasn't the buttoned-up scientist she assumed he was. He was here in Africia before, and he had kept that information from her. This added snippet bothered her. She needed more details to decide whether she should allow him to continue with her on the mission or erase his memory and send him back to New York. The mission was paramount. Her feelings were secondary.

"Apio said Chagga Village is a dangerous place,"

she said over her shoulder. "I want to find out more about what he meant. Could you ask him in Swahili? He may be more open to conversation in a language with which he is comfortable."

"I doubt he would tell me much," Ben replied.

"Why not?"

"Let's just say that when I was here before I was not looked upon as a friend, and the news spread quickly through the villages."

"Why?"

"Right before the grant ran out, I came to Africa to work with some of the more interesting plants of the area, to maybe find a cure for some of the most dangerous diseases in the world. Let's just say the guide I hired when I got here turned out to be shady. I wasn't here all that long. It became too dangerous for me to stay."

The way he said the last sentence sent a shiver up Siene's spine. "In what way?"

"I don't think it would be a very good idea to talk about that right now."

Siene began to wish she had dug a bit more into Ben's past before allowing him to get this involved. He said he spent most of his time in the lab yet failed to mention a little side trip to the African jungle. Trust and a myriad of questions warred inside her, giving rise to the notion that his work was a bit more involved than just a spit project and that's why Lucian wanted him dead. She had more questions than answers and that unsettled her more than she wanted to admit. She needed to find out more so at the very least she could have a defense against the way he made her feel.

She stopped jogging. "Why are you here, Ben?"

"You invited me."

He hadn't answered the question. He was hiding something. "You can leave anytime. I promise, you won't remember a thing."

"But I would still be a marked man. So, maybe I was not exactly invited, but you did tell me that I had to stay close until we found out why someone wanted me killed."

Apio looked at her over Ben's shoulder. "We go faster now." He tossed his chin forward. "Dark coming soon."

Siene kept pace. Like it or not, Ben was right. Until she knew exactly why Lucian wanted him dead, she was not about to let Ben out of her sight. She'd stay close to him until she knew which one or ones they were, and how everything tied into Lucian's plan.

Distracted, she tripped on some buttressed roots and went tumbling to the ground. Ben reached down and pulled her back to her feet. She noticed again how strong he was and recognized that she had someone by her side she could count on for backup as well as for brains if need be.

She wasn't used to counting on anyone besides her brother, especially someone she felt might be hiding something from her. But she was smack dab in the center of a very complicated situation. Reed was missing, Ben was suddenly in covert mode, and she had just put her trust in men who initially had her between the crosshairs of the guns in their hands. Uncertainty began to gnaw at her, and she suddenly didn't know what to believe or who to trust, least of all herself.

Fairy tale enigmas and magic artifacts she could handle. Liars, however, pissed her off.

****

Max began to hate Oregon. He'd walked up and down the riverbank and scanned the canyon walls for hours. Nothing. The jeep had just disappeared. There were tire tracks coming in, but none leaving. He crouched beside the tracks and scanned the ground beyond where they abruptly ended. No footprints either. What was he missing? He stood and looked around at the desolate landscape.

Think. You've been at this for a long time. You know what happened.

He closed his eyes and cleared his mind. Logic did not apply in his line of work. He let his thoughts drift to improbability. After a few minutes his eyes snapped open. Could it be that easy?

He looked at the canyon wall and raised his hands. He smirked. He was used to dealing with fairy tale shit. "Open sesame," he commanded in a loud voice. But nothing happened. He laughed. Of course, it wouldn't be that simple. Why should it? Nothing about this assignment had been simple.

He stood at the end of the tire marks and stared at the face of the canyon for a few moments before running his hand over the striated wall. As the clouds moved away from the sun, the colors of the ancient rock glistened in the light. It was then that Max noticed an anomaly. Some of the colors running along the layers of rock seemed a bit too vivid to be millions of years old.

He pulled out a pocket-knife and scraped through what should have been metamorphic rock and fossil-rich granite. What he found instead appeared to be a high-grade form of concrete, carefully painted to look like part of the rock face.

Sure that some type of hidden door had been built into the landscape, Max sprinted to the rented SUV he had modified and called the number of the contact Lucian had given him. He needed equipment and manpower to get inside without tripping any alarms that may have been set to deter trespassers. It was going to be a long night.

****

"How much farther to your village?" Siene asked.

"Not long," Apio answered. "You will spend the night then go."

Siene was exhausted, so spending the night sounded especially good.

When they arrived at the village about a half hour later, the first thing she saw was a cluster of huts set in a small clearing surrounded by trees. In the center of the shelters was a well, along with a fire being used for cooking by several women. She looked over her shoulder. Ben had disappeared. *Troubling*.

Apio directed her to one of the huts. Inside was a table, chairs, and an area set with cloth over some moss and leaves for sleeping. She used the table to dump out everything in her backpack and searched the contents. She found the Kel-Tec P32 semi-automatic pistol she had packed. The semi was her favorite for concealed carry. It made her feel safe, and she sure needed that feeling now. She tucked it in her belt before taking out the insect repellant and dousing herself and her bag with it. Then, she repacked everything and set the bag under the table.

Once outside she found Apio talking to some of the village men. He looked at her, his gaze concerned.

"Will you send some men to the crash site?" she asked.

When he paused before he answered, she felt her heart sink.

"They have already been there."

"Did they find the pilot or my brother?"

Apio shook his head. "No sign of survivors."

Siene's throat closed. "Any bodies?"

Apio shook his head. "But animals could have dragged any off."

Where was Reed? Her first instinct was to try her cell phone, but there was still no service. She swallowed hard. No survivors. It didn't mean Reed was dead. It meant no one was at the scene of the crash. She closed her eyes, wrapped her arms around her stomach, and took a deep breath. Reed was the smartest man she knew. He'd be okay.

She felt a hand on her shoulder and turned to the touch. *Ben.*

Apio and the others had moved away, probably to give her some privacy to digest the news.

"Where did you go?" she asked him.

"To gather some information on which villages are warring with each other. No sense walking into the middle of a turf war. When we leave, we'll be leaving alone. No one from this village will act as a guide for us. Do you know which way we head to get to Chagga Village?"

Siene nodded. "When I checked the map on the plane, it looked to be due east. I programmed some rough coordinates into the GPS in my watch, so at least we'll have some backup. I suggest we go at sunup."

"Agreed. I don't have enough jungle experience to

get us anywhere at night." He looked around. The well and the cooking fire were deserted. "Seems like the village has pulled up the sidewalk for the night. I'll find Apio and talk about sleeping arrangements."

"Don't bother." Siene pointed to the hut. "I think that's ours for the night." They walked over to the hut and once inside, she gestured to a small area near the table. "Pick a spot. That's where we sleep."

As they settled in, Siene began to feel uneasy. Though she and Ben had talked briefly about his past trip to Africa, she felt he was still hiding something. She would have pressed him until she found out exactly what it was, but she was in the middle of a jungle and would rather not discover that her faith in the only other person she knew at the moment had been a wrong move.

****

Lina settled Joseph in a hammock she hung inside her tent. "Why don't the men try to escape and get back to the village?"

"The men *dwall*," he answered.

"*Dwall*?"

Joseph thought for a moment. "Have evil spirit inside them."

Lina drew down her eyebrows. "All the men?"

Joseph nodded.

"And the boys?"

He nodded again.

"Tell me about this evil spirit."

Joseph swung the hammock back and forth as he spoke. "Bossman does hoodoo, then we get *dwall*. Then, we walk into mine and work. The boys get better. Men no."

This was going to be harder than she thought. "What happens right before you get this evil spirit?"

"We walk and walk and walk. Get fainty and no remember. When we get to mine, boss man stop and give water. Then *dwall* come."

Something in the water, Lina concluded. That had to be how Lucian controlled the villagers. She stopped the motion of the hammock. "Could you get me some of that water?"

Joseph nodded. He tapped his legs and then his head. "Fast and smart."

"I'm counting on it," Lina replied.

Chapter Seventeen

Siene felt restless. The insect spray kept most of the bugs away, but her legs hurt from all the running. Being a light sleeper, she heard every sound Ben made as he slept. She had hoped he talked in his sleep. She needed to find out more about his past.

The new facts Ben had disclosed disturbed her. She knew following the clues would eventually allow her to uncover the mystery that his background had suddenly become, but she still didn't have the major pieces in place. Her doubt complicated the mission. She didn't buy Ben's explanation of why he didn't tell her about his trip to Africa. Now Lucian was in Africa. Considering Lucian wanted Ben dead, there had to be a connection. Was Lucian involved in the disappearance of the villagers? And how did it all tie into the massacre at the Abbey? She still couldn't connect all the dots and it could be that her feelings for Ben had something to do with it. The clock was ticking. If the pieces didn't fall into place soon, she feared the worst.

Through the small window cut into the hut, she could see stars through the trees. She rolled over, kicking her backpack in the process. It hit a chair, rattling the seat against the table.

Ben rose on one elbow. "Can't sleep?"

Siene hoped the reason his voice sounded low and husky was because she woke him and not because she still remembered the feel of his lips on hers. She glanced at him. "No. Sorry to bother you. Not much room in here."

"You should try to get some rest. We have a lot of walking to do tomorrow."

"Don't worry. I won't slow us down."

He sighed. "That's not what I meant. Why are you so defensive?"

She wouldn't respond to that. Self-analysis wasn't something she felt like delving into tonight. "I'm just focused on finding out why Lucian is in Africa. Jungle conditions are a bit out of his comfort zone."

"And you would know because…"

She closed her eyes and let everything she knew and felt about Lucian mingle in her mind so she could pick out the pertinent facts. "He used to be one of us. He isn't a man used to roughing it. He likes luxury and entertainment. Whatever he's doing here, he's doing it for some sort of ultimate gain. It's the only reason he would be in this remote part of the world away from civilization and creature comforts."

"Sounds like you know him pretty well."

"Too well," she conceded.

"You said he used to be part of your group. You mean he used to be a Primogen?"

She nodded.

"What happened?"

"He went rogue a few years back. Killed a few Watchers and convinced some to join him. He went over to Taltos and worked his way up the ranks. He's one of the most powerful Taltoians now. Powerful and dangerous."

"And the Primogens, with all their Watchers and

Seekers and whatever else you have, couldn't bring him in?"

"We tried and lost a lot of good people in the process. The truth is…" she stopped, wondering if she should tell him.

"What?"

"The truth is, I thought I could reason with him. Get him to come back to us. But he betrayed me, and it nearly cost Reed his life." Her heart squeezed with regret thinking this time Lucian may have succeeded. She buried her fear as best she could, but the possibility of carrying on without Reed scared her. She wouldn't let Ben know how worried she was. "Lucian is my mark, my kill if need be. I owe it to my brother."

Ben's eyes widened for a moment, giving away his surprise at her statement. "I don't see you as an assassin."

"I can handle it."

"You've killed someone before?"

She saw emotion run amok in his eyes as he waited for her answer. "I do what I have to do. You don't have a lot of time to analyze consequences when you are facing someone pointing a weapon at your head."

Ben sat up and rested his forearms on his bent knees. "How often has that happened?"

"Too many times." She rolled over, rested her head on her arm, and closed her eyes.

"I'm not the enemy, Siene. I'm just trying to understand all you have to do." He moved to the side of the cot and planted his feet on the dirt floor. "Let me help you."

His voice was a whisper she couldn't ignore. She turned and caught his gaze. "I know you have good intentions, but I have made it a practice to not rely on anyone but myself."

"I don't think the jungle is going to allow either of us to go it alone," he countered. "But you have to let me in. I've come to learn you never do anything without a plan."

He was right. She knew what had to be done. Get to the village. Find Lucian and shut down whatever he was doing. If she had to shoot Lucian to stop him, she would. Maybe. If she could.

"First, we have to find Reed." Her stomach knotted itself when her mind added *or his body.*

"Then get some rest. Tomorrow could be a very long day."

She nodded. "Good night, Ben."

"I'm right here if you need me, Siene."

She heard him settle in and after a few minutes his slow, even breathing told her he'd fallen asleep. He would need his rest. She was not going to stop until she knew what happened to Reed.

The night sounds of the jungle kept her awake, but she knew she wouldn't be able to sleep anyway. So many things about her life filled her mind. The isolation. The duty. The pain of loneliness. She thought she had accepted all the aspects of the Legacy when she accepted the responsibility, but the closer she got to Ben, the more she felt the pain of want. Not just the want of a woman for a man, but more basic wants—a real home, a family, children. As a Primogen, these were things she could never hope to have.

Memories of her childhood flooded her mind, memories of the happy times before she accepted her destiny. She remembered the joy of ignorance, the bedtime stories that ended happily ever after, and the calm of knowing she was the one protected.

Never look back, she reminded herself. It hurt too much—especially lately. She didn't realize she was crying until she felt Ben's arms around her.

"I'm here, Siene," he whispered into her ear. "Don't cry. I won't leave you. Promise."

She reached up and wiped her cheek. She didn't want to, but she rolled over into his embrace. "I'm okay." She shook her head. "Sometimes things get all jumbled up and when my emotions slam into each other, I don't know which to follow. Some days I think I made the right decision and other days I convince myself I need to rethink everything I know before I end up a lonely old lady with ten cats and no family." She expected Ben to laugh, but he stayed still, his gaze locked with hers.

"We're a lot alike," Ben said quietly. "Two of a kind, really. We both are different than most people, and we both know what it's like to wake up in the middle of the night thinking about nothing more than our work. But while you seem to know your purpose in life, I don't. So far, I've wandered through science and medicine, selling my knowledge and expertise to other people instead of working on something I can contribute to the world."

"Research is complicated, Ben. It takes money and is constrained by a whole lot of red tape and legal wrangling."

He nodded. "Precisely why I have decided I need to make some to make some changes."

Siene frowned. "Because of me?"

"Partly. You told me I was a Catalyst. I thank you

for that reveal. To me it means I have the potential to change something."

Siene bit down on her lip. "You are also in danger because of it."

He smiled. "I guess whatever I change is going to be very important."

"I think we are getting closer to finding out what that is, so maybe this isn't the best time to make life-altering decisions, Ben."

"I believe it *is* the best time. It's very easy to give in to what is expected of you, because that way life is easy, but it's also mundane. Then, one day you wake up and realize twenty years have gone by and you have done nothing more than marked time in the same spot like a marching band member waiting for the conductor to tell him the next move. I don't want that, Siene."

"What do you want, Ben?"

"Two things. First, I want to help the Primogens if they will let me. I don't want to have some potion or flashy gadget make me forget everything I've seen and go back to the world I used to know."

"And the second thing?" She saw his smile fade, his gaze focus on her lips.

"This may be my own personal fairy tale, but since I met you, I want us."

"You know that isn't possible, Ben."

"Before a few days ago I'd say neither was a Mirror that can see the future."

It was too soon. She wasn't ready to make that kind of commitment with him—hell, with anyone for that matter. Though one part of her wanted to reach for him, wrap herself around him, and deal with the aftermath later; the other part of her, the part that remembered the duty and the faithfulness to the destiny she had freely chosen wasn't sure a real relationship with anyone would ever be possible.

"This is not the time, Ben."

"A chance at a relationship is not something you schedule."

She smiled. "What is this? Mr. Science giving in to the unknown?"

"I've given in to a lot since you ambushed me outside Penn Station."

"One challenge at a time," Siene said. Then she pressed a soft, undemanding kiss on his cheek, one intended to let him know she was not closing the door but also wasn't promising anything physical now.

At least that was her intention. But the moment their lips touched, the heat reached up and grabbed her, pulling her into the memories of their time together in France, into sensations that crashed inside her body with a combination of what was and what might be. She deepened the kiss almost immediately, slanting her mouth across his, parting her lips and finding his open in return. Their tongues touched, paused, and then touched again with more precision, more confidence.

Yes, this is good, her mind said. *This is exactly what you need.*

She started to lose herself in the moment when other sounds began to filter through the pleasure. Something wasn't right. Trees were rustling, animals were calling out. She felt tension join the sensations around her, and she stiffened and stopped kissing Ben.

"Shh," she cautioned, sitting up. In the next second, she realized she was hearing the sound of machetes ripping through the brush. She stood, dragging Ben with her. "Get what you can. We've got to find someplace to hide."

Ben grabbed his pack. "I thought we *were* hiding."

Siene gestured outside. "We have no idea how many men are out there, if they are armed, or if they are coming for us. Let's have surprise on our side." She pushed him toward the opening in the hut. "Move, but as quietly as possible."

Ben nodded and led the way. At the doorway, he stuck out his head and looked around. He could tell the villagers were beginning to react to the same sounds, but there was no one between him and Siene and an area thick with jungle vegetation. As the sounds grew louder from behind, he nodded and together they ran.

Siene paused just before entering the brush and glanced back at the village. Some of the village men were running with weapons drawn. Suddenly, everything seemed to explode as a torch hit the thatched roof of a hut and instantly flames turned the night red.

Ben grabbed her hand and yanked her into the cover of brush.

Peering through the dense brush, she realized the fire was spreading fast. The hut in which they had been just moments before was engulfed in flames. She gasped as Lucian Davelos appeared and shone a bright light into the blazing shelter.

"She's not in there," she heard him shout.

She didn't want to believe it, but Lucian had just tried to kill her. She gripped her backpack. How did he know she was in Africa? How did he find her?

Lucian turned and, in the firelight, she saw nothing of the man she used to know. This man was dressed in full battle gear, handgun loosely held in his right hand, assault rifle over his shoulder. Webbing around his waist held a knife, grenades, and some spare ammo. Around him were approximately thirty men.

He gestured to the thick brush. "Spread out. Find them. They couldn't have gone far."

Chapter Eighteen

Siene took Ben's arm and pulled him deeper into the brush. Moving around wasn't a great idea but staying could be worse. The pitch-black darkness of night would give them some cover to put a little distance between them and Lucian and his men. Still, they would have to stick to the dense brush.

Siene glanced over her shoulder as Ben began moving away. The moon appeared to center its light over Lucian. By his stance, she could sense his anger and his urgency. This wasn't the Lucian she knew. This man had a look in his eyes that scared her.

Ben grabbed her hand and pulled her forward. "Got any ideas?" he whispered.

"Yes." She pulled the gun from her waistband. "I'm going to shoot him."

Ben snatched the weapon from her hand. "That's your plan? Shoot him?"

"That's the plan."

"Then what's your plan for dealing with the men with him when they open fire on us? Odds are that a few of the bullets won't miss. How does that help the Primogens?"

Siene's shoulders dropped. "You're right." She held out her hand and Ben handed the gun back. After tucking it back into her waistband, she began pushing forward. "Then let's move."

Ben said nothing more until they were some distance from the village. "Could you have killed him?" he asked. Her eyes said yes but she didn't answer. The silence between them grew uncomfortable.

"You said you shot someone before."

She nodded.

"How many?"

"A few. But they were really bad."

"I don't know if I could do something like that."

"I hope you don't ever have to, but the instinct to survive is strong." She caught his gaze. "I hope you do the right thing if you are ever forced to make a choice."

Ben did not reply.

His silence did little to assuage Siene's uncertainty, but she didn't have the time to sort her feelings into neat little pro versus con compartments. Right now she had an escape to plan. She cupped her hand around her watch and turned on the GPS.

"Think there will be a signal here in the jungle?" Ben asked.

"If Caleb is still at the rendezvous point, there will be." After a few moments, she smiled. "And there it is." She pointed. "According to the unit, we need to go that way."

"How confident are you that the signal is coming from Caleb and not from Lucian's camp?"

"Fifty percent," she whispered, as the sound of rustling behind her grew louder.

"I hope you're on the right side of those odds."

Siene ducked under a clump of long-hanging vines. "So do I."

****

Back at the Primogen Compound, bleary eyed and

tired, Jack watched information roll across the computer screen. "What have you gotten yourself involved in, Davelos?" he asked aloud.

He didn't expect an answer. Across the lab, Kai was busy trying to piece together background data from the flash drive he brought back, and Paz was checking in with her myriad of contacts. The remaining Primogens were on high alert waiting for the signal to move and stop Lucian.

He wiped a hand across the back of his neck to try to ease the tightness. The body bags containing the remains of the monks killed in the attack by Taltos were still vivid in his mind. Whatever Lucian was doing in Africa, he needed the Mirror to make it work. Otherwise, the ambush made no sense.

Ignoring the data on the screen for the moment, Jack placed his fingertips on either side of his head, closed his eyes, and started running through some data of his own. The Mirror had activated because someone wanted Ben dead. Lucian's number one henchman had broken into Siene's townhouse looking for the Mirror and the monks died because of it. Davelos was in Africa, and Jack bet his life that it was no coincidence that reports coming in to the Primogens showing villagers were disappearing by the hundreds were also connected to Taltos.

He opened his eyes and blew out a long breath of air. Ben was the key, but he was missing something. Something important. What was it?

He opened another window on the laptop, loaded the data from the flash drive, accessed the files on Lucian and Taltos, and typed in what he knew so far about the current turn of events. He then hit enter to run an algorithm program Reed had written some months ago that would begin automated reasoning. Jack watched as numbers and letters scrolled rapid-fire across the screen, proceeding through a set of successive circumstances, producing output that would list a series of possible conclusions. If there was a link to everything that happened in the last few weeks, this program would find it.

At least he hoped so.

****

Ben and Siene had been walking through the dense jungle for what seemed like days, though it had only been hours. Siene's eyes adjusted as well as they could to the dark, and she wished they had some sort of infrared goggles with them. But no one had anticipated this problem.

Slowly, the light of the dawn began seeping to the jungle floor through the canopy of leaves above them. Suddenly, she stopped. "Quiet. Someone is out there." She pulled her gun and held out her hand. "Give me your shirt."

"Why?" Ben asked.

"I need a silencer. Shots will echo. If Lucian's men are close, they'll find us."

Ben stripped out of his button-down cotton shirt, leaving him clad in a white T-shirt. "How do you want it?"

"Fold it."

Ben nodded and did as he was asked. He saw something feral in Siene's eyes when he handed the shirt to her.

"Keep moving," she said. "I'm going to circle around and get behind whoever is out there."

"Bad idea. We should stay together."

Siene smiled. "Thanks for the concern, but I've been doing this for a long time. If something happens to us, the mission is lost. Separated, there is a better chance of one of us finding Reed and Caleb."

"I don't like that idea."

"It's the only one we have at the moment." She glanced over her shoulder as the crunching footsteps sounded closer. "At times like this, it's more important that both of us recognize the skills we have. I can't find a cure for disease, and you probably don't shoot well enough to hit someone who is probably a practiced marksman."

Ben nodded. "Agreed."

She lowered her voice to barely a whisper. "Trust me on this." She tossed her chin toward the east. "Five minutes and I'll meet you up ahead."

"You're the boss." He glanced over her shoulder in the direction of the footsteps. "But be careful."

"Always am."

He hesitated for a moment and then threw his arms around her neck and kissed her. "For luck."

****

The footsteps had stopped. Siene heard nothing but the sound of her heart beating very loudly as she doubled back. She was careful not to let her mind stray, but when it did, it never went much further than the one hypothesis behind her and the one in front. She was stuck in the jungle with her ex-lover hot on her trail and with a man who was hiding something from her. Not great odds for survival.

Her senses went into hyper-alert as she alternately looked for any sign of movement in the dense brush and listened for the sound of gunshots. When she left Ben, she knew it was highly possible that Lucian's men would catch up to him before she could take them out, but she had to take the chance. The only thing she regretted was not telling Ben.

She adjusted her path and moved west. It wasn't long before she saw two men in the path just ahead. Deciding for the moment not to use the gun, she stayed in the cover of blanketing branches and drew her knife from the sheath at her waist. Two men wouldn't be tracking alone. More were undoubtedly close. She shrugged out of the straps of the backpack she'd taken with her and stashed it in some brush.

The men in front of her scanned the trees, keeping their guns ready. In the filtered morning light, they looked tired. Probably from tracking all night. She thought about what Ben said about it not being easy to kill someone. For her, it wasn't easy as much as it was necessary. She only hoped that the men ahead would find it hard to kill her. She crept close enough to hear them.

"There's no one here. Let's go back," the smaller of the two said.

"Davelos said not to come back without them," the other responded. "Do you want to be the one to tell him we got tired and quit?"

"No. But we've been out here for—"

The second man turned. "Shh. I heard something in the bushes behind us."

"Probably some animal."

"Maybe, maybe not. Cover me."

Feeling the adrenaline beginning to pump through her veins, Siene closed her eyes. Calm was what she needed to do this. Taking a deep breath, she peered through the brush and let her knife fly straight to the man approaching. The knife hit his left shoulder.

He shouted in pain and dropped his gun. The smaller man began running toward her position. She moved quickly, dropping to the ground and rolling just out of the spray of bullets hitting the spot where she had just been. *Damn.* This man wasn't a villager handling a gun for the first time.

Her heart was beating so fast that she got lightheaded from the blood rushing in her veins. She realized she only had a small gun and her wits to get herself out of this situation. *If I live through this,* she promised, *I'll stop acting so superior and let Ben help me.*

The wounded man bled steadily, her knife sticking out of his shoulder. He couldn't appear to raise his arm above his waist. Siene guessed the knife had cut his rotator tendon. Lucky throw. This meant not only would he be in a lot of pain, but he would not be of much help to the other man in a fight.

The wounded man tugged the knife free of his body and tossed it to the ground. He grimaced and began swatting at the jungle brush. "Find them."

His companion began shooting.

If there were two men looking for them, there could be a lot more in the area. Siene realized she had no other choice. She had to protect Ben and possibly give him time to escape. She emerged from the brush behind the wounded man and raised her hands in surrender. "Don't shoot."

Both men turned.

As she walked toward them, she heard a small pop

and then saw blood spurt from a wound on the second man's chest. Eyes wide, he fell backward. She heard more gunfire and saw the man she wounded get hit.

She surmised Ben had ignored her instructions and followed her, coming to her rescue just in time. A rush of uncertainty spread over her just before she realized Ben didn't have a gun and felt something sting her neck. When she touched the area beneath her right ear, instead of an insect barb, she felt a small dart. Pulling it from her skin, she turned in time to see Lucian smiling just before darkness engulfed her.

****

The sound of the gunshots stopped Ben in his tracks. *Siene.* He never should have let her talk him into leaving. He turned and ran. It seemed like an eternity, but when he got back to where they had separated, the only thing he found was trampled brush. *This was bad.* He could feel the adrenaline rush through his body, ramping up his heartbeat and heightening his senses. She wasn't here.

He stooped and scanned the area. A dark spot on some brush caught his attention. He reached over. Blood. But thankfully, not enough to have resulted from the gunshots he heard. Glancing to his right, he saw a glint of metal and found Siene's knife with blood on the blade. She'd wounded someone and the trampled brush meant she'd put up a fight.

He stood and began to track her through the trail of broken branches and flattened vegetation. He shrugged off the thought she might be in danger or wounded. He knew her by now. If anyone was in trouble, it would be those who had her. He would have to catch up to the raiding party before she figured out a way to get the upper hand and either escape or kill all of Lucian's men. He quickened his pace. At least one of her captors needed to stay alive for the Primogens to get the information they needed.

God help those who thought Siene was a delicate flower who would swoon at the first sight of blood. If he had learned anything about her since the time fate allowed their paths to cross, it was that she always had a plan. And once she focused on that plan, there was no stopping her.

Chapter Nineteen

Lina paced in her tent, prowling like a caged lion. Mosegi had been gone for hours. She hoped he had not gotten caught. While she waited for him, she had done a little reconnaissance of her own. Lucian left camp suddenly, taking most of his henchmen with him. Whatever caught his attention must have been critical because he seemed to forget about locking her inside the back of the truck as he normally did whenever he went somewhere. Lucian's rushed exit gave her a chance to snoop around without worrying about security.

Most of the trucks were locked, except for one. The supply truck. She hadn't thought there would be much of anything useful inside, but she had been wrong. Inside, she found what would possibly be the key to her escape and ultimate rescue.

Probably in their haste to obey one of Lucian's commands, one of the men had dropped his handheld radio, an Icom ID-51A, the model like the one Reed always used. When turned on, the display showed the broadcast band, a number Lina memorized. In the few times she used Reed's Icom, she had learned enough to be able to find a sub-frequency far enough down the bandwidth not to be detected. She could use it to locate help and get out of this hellhole.

She fought the urge to try to transmit now. With

Lucian away from camp, she was sure he was broadcasting, and she didn't want to be careless. Plus, now she had a way to listen, a definite plus. She wanted to know more about the mine and how the villagers were controlled. Since she met Mosegi, it was the reason she had put off trying to escape. Leave too soon or too late, and she might not be able to get to the Primogens in time to stop whatever it was Lucian had planned.

Realizing patience was never among her best assets, she tucked the radio deep in the bag with her undies, where it was safe. She laughed. Lucian did like to see his women in push-up bras and thongs, but he had a thing about touching ladies' lingerie—unless he was ripping them from a curvy body. She smirked. The only reason he still breathed was because he hadn't made a move on her. The bitter taste of bile rose from her stomach, and she shook away the thought of Lucian coming at her with arms extended and lust in his eyes.

"Great," she lamented, "not only am I going to have nightmares, now, I'm also going to have to poke out my mind's eye."

****

Max Biden knew he would only have one chance to rip through the artificial canyon wall and maybe only a matter of minutes to find out what was inside. If, as he suspected, he was in front of a concealed door into some sort of hidden secret base, either the American government was going to be awfully pissed when he blew the entrance open or the Primogens would be waiting for him. The former would probably get him twenty-five to life; the latter might get him killed. Either way, he had to roll the dice and take the chance.

Guessing the artificial wall would be no more than about six feet thick or else the mechanism to move the hidden door would be massive and slower than it had been when the jeep disappeared behind it, he attached the military grade C4 about six feet off the ground in the center of the rock face. Into the middle of the thick, gray wad, he set the detonator and held it in place by molding some of the plastic explosive around it.

Satisfied, Max walked away. When he was about 300 yards away, he pulled out his cell phone and entered the code. Behind him, a pillar of fiery smoke and dust rose, boiling upward from the set point like an orange fist of fire punching the sky. In front of him, as if on cue, a line of five military-style jeeps sped forward. The lead jeep slowed, and the driver tossed out a semi-automatic rifle which Max caught with one hand. Vaulting, he jumped into the passenger seat, gun aimed at the center of the blast.

As the debris from the explosion began to settle, Max could make out a gaping hole. His mouth twitched with a smile. His hunch had been right on.

****

As Siene moved closer to consciousness, the voice got louder.

"She's waking up, Boss."

She blinked and heard another voice. Lucian's voice.

"Wait outside."

Her eyes were still heavy, but she forced them open and took stock of her surroundings. She lay on a bed, her head on a pillow. Her temples hammered with a sharp ache, and she felt cold, although sweat beaded over her skin. Nausea churned in her stomach. The substance Lucian put on the dart that hit her neck was something awfully potent. Trying to stave off the pain, she closed her eyes. "Take some deep breaths," she heard Lucian say.

The bed dipped when he sat near her elbow. "You look pale."

She blinked a few times and lifted herself on her elbows. "I'm always pale, Lucian. I don't get out much."

He held out a small plate of food. "I was having dinner. Are you hungry?"

She declined with a shake of her head.

He rose and set the plate on a small table in the center of the room. "Pity. The wild boar is particularly tasty."

She looked past him. She was in a tent. She shifted and swung her legs over the edge of the platform, pushing Lucian away as she did. "Where the hell am I?"

Hands on hips, Lucian frowned. "Ever the lady. Let's just say that you've been my guest for a few hours."

Refusing to let him know just how shaky she felt from the tranquilizer, she stood, squared her shoulders, and lifted her chin. "Okay, then, thanks for the hospitality. I'll be going now." She sprang into motion and made a run for the tent flap.

Lucian grabbed her arm. "I'm afraid you can't leave."

He steered her toward a chair and backed her up until the her legs collided with the seat, leaving her no recourse but to sit. She glowered at him. "You know I won't stop trying."

He laughed. "How far did you think you'd get if you made it out of this tent?"

"Far enough," she countered, hoping he could see the anger in her eyes.

A half-smile rose on his lips. "But, Siene, it's been a while, and we do need to catch up."

"I doubt that you brought me here to reminisce. What do you want, Lucian?" She laughed. "I mean, besides world domination and all the fairy tale artifacts the Primogens are protecting." His expression turned serious.

"That will do for a start."

She crossed her arms. "Sorry. Can't help you."

Lucian circled the chair. "I have to say, you look as good as ever." He let his hand trail across her back before resting his palm on her shoulder. "I like what you've done with your hair." He took a tendril between his fingers and ran his thumb across the strand before bringing the curl to his nose and inhaling deeply. "You've changed your shampoo."

The way he was looking at her sent a shiver down Siene's spine. "We were over a long time ago, Lucian."

"Are you sure of that?"

She glared at him, remembering his forceful grip around her neck, cutting off her air. "You do remember that you tried to kill me right after you were discharged from the Primogens."

Lucian said nothing.

"What was it? Some sort of initiation into Taltos so you could prove your new loyalty?" She felt her stomach clench with pure disgust when she noticed he did not react. "You wanted me to think it was someone else's hands around my neck, but I know it was you."

She laughed, the sound forced and nervous. "The ski mask hid your face, but you should have worn gloves. The scar on the back of your hand gave you away."

Lucian looked at his scar and shrugged.

"You got between me and a scimitar when we were retrieving the Magic Carpet that Taltos tried to steal. You were Primogen then." Her voice softened. "What happened, Lucian? Why did you change?" She stood. "There was nothing I wouldn't have done for you. We…"

Lucian reached out and grabbed her by the back of her neck, his large hand grasping her forcefully, his fingers threading in her hair. "There was never really a *we*, was there, Siene?" He kissed her cheek. "How much do you hate me now?"

Siene didn't answer. She knew a fight between them was coming, and they were evenly matched. But she held a slight edge. She used the emotional pain she had felt when Lucian defected to learn restraint and she chose her battles wisely instead of instinctively reacting. It was a skill she would now use to her advantage. Until she knew exactly what he was doing in Africa and how his plan involved the Mirror, she would wait. Standing her ground, neither resisting nor accepting his hold, she faced him with quiet strength.

"I don't hate you. I pity you." She refused to react to the caustic taste that came up in the back of throat. "What happened to you?"

He stroked her cheek. "Why wouldn't you come with me?"

"Why wouldn't you stay?"

His hold tightened as he brought her closer. He lowered his head, his gaze on her mouth. "Sadly, you were only a delightful amusement in the last few weeks we were together." He brushed his lips over hers.

She sucked in a deep breath of air and hoped it sounded more like anticipation than the disgust she felt. She'd let Lucian think she still had feelings for him even though the very thought of his kiss was heinous. His betrayal of her and the Primogens was unforgiveable treachery. "You told me you loved me, Lucian."

"At one time, perhaps," he replied, his breath hot against her lips. "After I left, I have to admit, I didn't think much about you." His gaze roamed her face. "But now, when confronted by what could be our last days…" He stopped and kissed her again.

His words proclaimed indifference, but his actions said something else. He took her mouth possessively and Siene did everything she could to control the urge to rip his tongue out of his mouth. She had to let him think she still cared.

When Lucian ended the kiss and pulled away, his face showed victory. "You're still mine, aren't you? I bet I could lay you down here and take you and you wouldn't protest."

Siene jerked away, annoyed that perhaps she was playing her part a little too well. "I am Primogen. You are Taltos. There is nothing here for you."

Lucian ran his index finger across Siene's lips, down her chin and throat, pausing in the center of her chest between her breasts. "But there is. I have you, and they'll want you back."

Siene shook her head. "I am expendable."

"Blood calls to blood, Siene. It's true of all mankind and maybe even truer for the Primogens. Your brother hates me more than you do. He will not leave you with me. He'll come and bring others."

"Reed is dead," Siene said with a hard swallow. "Our plane had engine trouble and we had to bail out. I didn't see him in the air before the plane crashed."

Lucian's mouth twisted. "Oh, I doubt he is dead and so do you. You forget how I can read your eyes. They still hold hope." He grabbed her. "We'll fight, you and I. It is inevitable. And one of us will die. That, too, is inevitable. But before, we could reminisce a bit." He placed his cheek on hers. "I know what you like."

His hot breath rolled over her skin, strengthening her resolve. She twisted and tears stung her eyes when she ripped herself out of his grasp.

He responded by grabbing her by her neck. "Don't make me send your body to the Primogen Council."

Tilting her head so she could look into his eyes, she said, "The Council will understand if you do. The Primogens and Taltoians are at war, and there will be casualties. That will not change." She softened her expression. "Unless you come back and make this right."

The laugh that came from Lucian's throat sounded like a cry from hell. "There is no redemption for me."

She knew he would be sentenced to death by the Council. "Then I will kill you, Lucian. Death by my hand will be more merciful than what awaits you at the Primogen Council. The world will be a safer place once I dispatch you from this life."

His free hand roamed her body before settling on her left breast. "Will it bother you much to first have sex with me and then try to kill me, darling Siene?"

"Immensely." She bared her teeth.

"You never protested when we were together."

She struggled against his hold. "You're dead to me, Lucian."

He squeezed her breast until he saw her wince. "Not quite yet. Tomorrow, in a week, or in a year, maybe. One of us will kill the other eventually." His thumb rolled over her nipple. "But not tonight, *mi amore*."

She reached out and ripped his hand from her breast, "So, you're going to rape me?"

"If necessary."

"I can't let that happen."

For a second Lucian's hold on her loosened, giving her a split-second to break free. She made it to the tent flap before a burly guard blocked her escape. With one hand, he grabbed her arm and tossed her rearward before resuming his post. As she stumbled backward, she reached out and broke her fall by grabbing onto the thick pole anchored in the center of the tent. Lucian came up behind her and pressed himself against her back, trapping her between his body and the wood. When she felt his heat, she trembled.

"I won't have to rape you." He forced his knee between her legs, his erection pressing against her backside. He clamped one hand on her breast and pulled her closer. "You will accept me willingly."

Though pinned, she tried to push free. Her backside banged against him in a desperate effort to break the embrace. When he began to thrust against her, she realized he mistook her struggle for arousal. Nausea welled and she stopped moving.

Lucian nuzzled her neck. "See, darling Siene, I haven't touched you, yet you respond." He pinched her nipple hard, and she cried out. "You'll come to like the pain." He swung her around and pushed her against the pole. He pressed his forearm across her throat, grinning as her face reddened.

"Let me go," she rasped.

"Tell me you want me, Siene."

The lust that layered his voice made her feel ill even as she struggled for breath. She needed air but would rather die by strangulation before giving in. "I hate you," she rasped.

"Hate me all you want," he whispered into her ear. "I promise you'll like sex better when on the brink of death." He eased his forearm back to let her breathe before running his hand across her shoulder and down her back to cup her butt.

Siene dodged his searching mouth. "Stop!" she managed to shout between gulps of air. "You don't want me like this. Taking me against my will won't get me back."

"I'll take you any way I want," Lucian promised. "Because, make no mistake, I will have you."

Calling on every bit of strength she could muster, Siene focused on finding some way to overpower him. As he ran his hands over her, his hot breath on her neck, she shifted and brought her knee up hard into his erection. He grunted and doubled over with pain.

Siene raced for the tent flap. On the way, she grabbed a steak knife from atop Lucian's half-eaten supper. A crude weapon, but she knew how to use it thanks to some lessons on elite combat from Kai. Once outside and now on autopilot, she plunged the blade into the guard's neck, twisting it to do more damage before pulling the knife out and running. The guard shrieked in pain, and spurting blood immobilized him. She was ten feet from Lucian's tent when she saw a group of men coming toward her. Skidding to a stop, she scanned the area for a way out.

Lucian's voice boomed from behind. "Stop her!"

Heading toward the jungle, she darted between two tents before one of the men caught her and whirled her around to face him. She raised the knife and plunged it into his shoulder so hard that she felt the blade snap. The man muttered something she didn't understand before backhanding her across her mouth. The strike dropped her to the ground.

She blinked and tasted the coppery tang of blood in her mouth. When she was able to focus, she saw Lucian standing over her, his face hardened with rage. He nodded to the closest man. "Pick her up."

"You bloodied one of my men. He's not happy about it," Lucian said glancing over at the injured man.

"Can't you see the extent I'd go to get away from here?" she asked as she was pulled to her feet. Lucian didn't reply but came at her, determination in his stride. She threw her hands in front of her face.

Lucian grabbed her forearms and pulled her toward his tent.

She tried to dig in her heels, but the ground gave way, and she twisted like a fish on a hook. "You're an animal." She kicked at him but could get no traction on the soft earth and hit his calves and ankles in weak attempts.

Lucian stopped and turned. He grabbed her upper arms and thrust his left knee between her thighs. He grinned when she flinched in pain. He then slid his leg around behind hers and pushed her to the ground.

Siene's head bounced twice. The blow knocked the wind from her, and she gasped for breath.

With a growl, Lucian grabbed her, rolled her onto her stomach, and manacled her hands behind her back before hauling her up. He stood behind her, grasping her hair with one hand, her bound hands with the other. Pushing her in front of him, he forced her back to his tent.

Once inside, he tied her to the chair, giving the rope one last tight tug before he spoke. "I should kill you."

Siene tugged at her trappings. "Why don't you?"

"Because I want you to see something first." He motioned to a guard who nodded and exited. The chair moved as Siene continued her struggle.

Smiling in perceived victory, Lucian tied her chair to the center tent pole.

She was securely anchored in place. She stopped struggling. There was no sense wasting the little energy she had left. She would escape. She just didn't know how at the moment.

She licked the dried blood from the corner of her mouth. The guard had returned. He stood just outside the tent flap. "What did you want me to see?"

"This, darling Siene," Lucian nodded to the sentry.

Siene felt fear for the first time when two other men entered, dragging their prisoner. "Ben," she whispered. "What are you doing here?"

Suspended by the grip on his upper arms, Ben looked at her through swollen eyes. "I'm here to rescue you."

Chapter Twenty

Once inside the cave, Max leapt out of the jeep and shot out two cameras and some overhead lights. He circled his left arm and directed his men inside. "Go! Go!" He waited and watched the men reconnoiter the large room. The sound of rapid gun fire and pings of bullets hitting metal echoed in all directions. "Make sure you get all the lights and cameras," he shouted. "The Primogens already know we're here and are probably on their way. No sense letting them watch, too."

Gun poised, Max scanned the chamber. The jeep he saw outside, and a few other vehicles, were parked inside near the entrance. Most were damaged from the explosion. He looked over the equipment piled on metal shelving—shovels, tools, and some camping gear. Nothing remarkable. Must be a little-used entrance.

"Boss, look at this," one of his men called before tossing him a backpack.

Max caught it easily. He looped the strap of the gun he had been holding over his head. Inside the backpack he found a radio and two handguns. He nodded. "Look around and see if there are any more like this."

As the men scattered, Max hooked the radio on his belt and checked the guns. The clips were full in both. He tucked the weapons behind his back in his belt and started walking down a long tunnel. The cave's odd quiet bothered him. Something didn't feel quite right. The Primogens should have safeguards in place, but so far, nothing. Neither guards nor alarms greeted him.

The men came back with three more backpacks, two of them empty.

"I don't get it," one of them said. "There's nothing here."

Max shook his head. "The Primogens would not have something this structured and this hidden for no reason." He unzipped the cargo pocket on his pants near his right thigh and took out a thermal-based infrared detector. Aiming the sensor at the cavern walls, he kept his gaze focused on the high-resolution screen and watched for any sign of a change in temperature. "There's more here. I can feel it." His gaze held steady through the lens. As the sensor scanned across a section to his right, an area glowed red, contrasting with the blue hue of the rest of the wall clearly indicting a heat source. "There." He pointed. "There's something behind that wall. Let's put some of the tools we found on the shelves to use and find out what it is, shall we?"

He stayed vigilant, gun poised at the ready, as his men lowered their weapons and retrieved the tools. In minutes, they broke through to another chamber with a long corridor lined with an intricate array of pipes. Some were hissing as steam billowed from pressure-releasing escape valves and others appeared moist. A single row of overhead lights illuminated the tunnel in both directions.

"My, my, my," Max said, using the beam mounted on top of the barrel of his gun to follow the path of one of the pipes until it disappeared into the darkness of the right passageway. "Wonder where this leads?" The light caught the shape of a camera attached to a support beam about five yards down the tunnel. He walked toward it, watching as the lens adjusted as he got closer. He smiled and blew the camera to pieces with a single shot. He moved his light back and forth as a signal. "Let's go," he shouted. "I want to get as far inside as I can before we get company."

Single file, with weapons scanning left to right and frontward in wide arcs, Max and his men followed the corridor deep inside the mountain. Darkness grew around them as one by one the overhead lights exploded when they were shot out like targets on a rifle range.

"Switch to infrared," Max shouted as the sound of humming motors got louder. He pulled the night vision goggles down from atop his helmet. "Anything moves in front of you, shoot it."

****

In the Records Center of the Primogen Complex, Jack finished printing out the data from the computer program he ran. He leaned his elbow on the desk and rubbed his forehead with his palm before separating the possible scenarios into five piles. He stood and braced his arms on the desktop for a moment before indiscriminately putting his hand on the top of two. Taking a deep breath, he picked up the first sheet from each and held one piece of paper in both hands. Which one? Guess right, and the world would go back to spinning normally with its inhabitants none the wiser. Guess wrong, and there was a distinct possibility that knowledge of the artifacts would be front page news.

He snickered and his gaze shifted from one sheet to

the other. There was always the eeny, meeny, miny, moe option. Laughing at the stupidity of his thoughts, he heard the door open behind him and turned.

Paz entered and held out a mug of steaming coffee. "Thought you might need this."

Jack took a sip and set the cup on the desk. He opened the bottom drawer and retrieved a silver flask. "Coffee always tastes better flavored." He tossed his head. "Want some?"

Paz held out her cup and lifted her chin. "Why not? Could be my last."

Jack poured until she signaled him to stop.

Paz thumped her cup against his. "Here's to goddamned Taltos. May they rot in hell."

"Without us." Jack lifted his cup in a salute before taking a long drink. "Good cuppa, Paz. You'll make someone a right nice cook someday." He looked at the mug and nodded. "Yeah, a right nice mate for some bloke."

"If I survive this, I'm never getting married." Paz slid her shapely bottom on the desk. "This job of ours doesn't leave much time for romance."

Jack laughed. "What's romance got to do with buffin' the muffin?"

Paz started to answer when the room was suddenly bathed in red lights pulsating in rhythm to the high-pitched shriek of a warning siren. Jack dropped his cup and ran into the hallway with Paz on his heels.

He stopped an armed security team member running by. "What happened?"

Between siren bursts the team member shouted, "Hostiles have broken into tube three. Blue Team is ready to roll." His voice faded as he continued toward the Launch Room.

Jack hit the emergency lock down switch. "Damn it. How'd they find that entrance? I told Reed that tunnel needed to be demolished."

Distant explosions resonated through the air ducts, and Paz took off running. "The passage might have been useful in the forties, but the location was never really defensible," she called over her shoulder. She skidded around the corner, Jack right behind her. "But Reed wouldn't listen. He liked leaving the complex that way when he was here and thought because that entrance was so remote and surrounded by federal land, no one would ever find the way in."

"Taltos did," Jack replied.

"You don't think it could be Federal agents?"

"Nah, the Feds wouldn't be blowin' things up. They'd be takin' it." Jack pressed his palm against the sensor pad to access the elevator to the command center. The double doors swished open. "We can only hope that one of the cameras caught something we can use."

Once inside, Paz slammed the emergency knob and the elevator dropped, speeding quickly through unreadable floor numbers on the pad above the door. The car bounced to a halt at the Command Center level and the doors opened. Inside, a digital sign pulsed with the Intruder-Com 3 warning. Kai was on the control console. Jon Two-Bear and Quinnock were already shouting orders into microphones and cell phones in response to data on the display.

Jack reached around Kai and shut off the siren. "I think better when my eardrums aren't vibrating all the way to the brain." He watched a series of monitors flash shots of various rooms and hallways. "How in the hell did someone find the tunnel?" Jack rested his hand on the back of Kai's chair and leaned in over her shoulder, watching the destruction from the infra-red camera back-up.

Kai tossed her head. "Someone must have left the back door open."

"Who?" Paz asked, donning a headset, and sitting in a chair next to Kai.

"See for yourself." Kai stopped the video display and zoomed in on the shoulder patch of an interloper with his back to the camera.

Paz' eyes narrowed. "A Taltoian battle guard." She spat out the words. "How many?"

Jack peered at the screen. "I count six."

Kai rolled the tape in reverse. "From what I saw before the camera got shot out, looked more like about ten."

Jack straightened. "Not so many. We can clear them out right nice."

Paz saved info to a flash drive. "Only if a team gets there before Taltos finds the material to make a rabbit hole and gets in position to pick us off one by one as we come through."

Jack put his hands on his hips and turned his back. "Damn it, we going through that thing? After steppin' in, I get all buggered and spew for hours."

Kai glanced his way. "Making a rabbit hole is the only way to get there in a hurry. We're ten to twelve hours away by conventional means."

"Another reason why Reed liked the tunnel," Paz added.

"Either we go in the hole or wait here for them to

come to us. Right now, Taltos doesn't have the exact location of this compound, but they will soon enough if we let them through." Kai swiveled her chair to the left. "Any word from Reed and Siene?"

Jon Two-Bear shook his head. "Nothing but static on the com."

"It isn't like Siene not to check in," Quinnock added.

Jon nodded. "I've already dispatched a team of Seekers to their last known position."

Kai keyed coordinates into the console. "Echo Squad and a team of Cleaners are heading to Oregon." She angled his watch. "They'll start moving the artifacts to the alternate location in about two hours."

"Best we hold up our end then." Jack headed for the war room. "I'll get the gear." At the Command Center's rear door, he stopped but didn't turn around. "And add a few chugger bags for me."

Paz laughed. "Planning on vomiting?"

Jack nodded. "Always do using the hole." He moved to the door. "I'll get spare ammo. Meet you on deck 5."

Paz took off her headset and started to move, but Kai stopped her with a hand to her arm.

"There's something you need to see before you go."

Paz settled back in the chair. "Something you didn't want Jack to see?"

Kai nodded. "This part of the video is meant for you." She hit the back button. "This is the camera just outside the stockroom."

Paz watched the stockroom door explode in a flash of brilliant white followed by a hail of bullets showering in from the hallway. When the firing stopped, two men entered. One disappeared behind the rows of shelves while the other started checking the room.

Paz leaned closer. "*Que porra é essa*! Max Biden."

She watched Max scan the room, gun at ready. He smiled when he saw the camera. Reaching up, he adjusted the angle to make sure he could look directly into the lens. Once satisfied at the perspective, he winked, licked his lips, and mouthed a kiss before firing. The screen went black when the bullet hit the lens.

Slowly Paz turned toward Kai. "That son of a bitch better still be alive when I get there." She clenched her teeth. "Make sure Blue Team knows no one kills him but me."

****

In a tent pitched in a clearing surrounded by jungle, Lucian sat at a small table with Ben seated across from him. He nodded to one of the guards. "Untie Ms. Dower so she can join us." Once she was free, he motioned to the empty chair beside him. "Please sit." He turned to Ben. "You don't look much like a hero, Dr. Michaels."

"And what does a hero look like?" Ben asked. He ran his tongue across the cut on his bottom lip. "I hear they come in all shapes and sizes."

"And I hear they look more like James Bond at the end of a mission and not like a man recently beaten to a pulp."

Ben grinned. "Not exactly a pulp. More like a bad trip and fall."

Lucian responded with a hard punch to Ben's right

cheek, opening another cut on Ben's severely bruised skin.

Siene sprang to her feet. "That's enough, Lucian!" She ripped the pocket from her blouse and poured water from a pitcher on it before dabbing at the dried blood on Ben's face. "Haven't you done enough?"

Lucian allowed Siene a few moments before nodding to one of the armed men standing at the tent flap. The man grabbed Siene by her upper arm and hauled her back to her chair. She landed with a thud when he shoved her onto the seat.

"To answer your question, my dear, I haven't begun to do enough. Dr. Michaels made a most unfortunate decision when he turned down my job offer."

Siene straightened. "Ben?"

Ben turned to Lucian. "We've never met."

Lucian simply smiled.

Ben angled his head back to Siene. "I swear I never met this man before today."

Lucian poured some scotch into a glass and watched the amber liquid swirl against the crystal before downing the shot. "You may also be interested to know that Dr. Michaels is also the reason we are here in the African heat."

Siene stared at Ben. "You admitted you came to Africa for business." She tilted her head toward Lucian. "Business for him?"

"I swear, Siene, I never saw this man before the day you pointed him out," Ben declared.

Siene shook her head. "I don't believe either of you."

An armed man dressed in camo suddenly appeared

inside the tent. "Mr. Davelos, you need to come to the communications center."

"Can't it wait?" Lucian scowled. "I have guests."

"I don't think it should," the soldier replied.

Lucian frowned and stood. He signaled to the soldier. "Make sure no one leaves this tent, you understand?" He gestured to the tent flap.

The soldier nodded and took a position just outside.

Lucian walked to Siene. "You two should talk. This may be the last time you can." He cupped her chin with his hand. "I won't be long, *mi amore*. Then, we'll get you cleaned up for dinner and do something about him." He glared at Ben and left.

****

Siene closed her eyes and took two deep breaths. She couldn't let her emotions filter into the line of questioning she would unload in the next few minutes. To get the truth she had to treat Ben like any other suspect she would interrogate. She turned to him. "You speak an African dialect, and you said some warlords weren't too happy with you." She felt everything inside her go cold. "You lied to me."

Ben shook his head. "I didn't lie."

"Are you still working for Lucian?"

"I never worked for him."

Siene glared. "Why didn't you tell me about Africa when you knew we were headed here?"

He let out a short breath of air. "I didn't tell you because I didn't think it necessary."

She closed her eyes. Utter calm was what she needed right now. She opened her eyes and caught Ben's gaze. "A man with nothing to hide would have mentioned that detail, especially considering the circumstances." She clenched her jaw so hard that the muscles in her cheek began to throb. But she wouldn't show weakness. She held his gaze. "What did you do here?"

Ben did not flinch. "I worked in a jungle lab for a few weeks, but I never actually met the man who hired me."

"So, it could have been Lucian."

"Or it could have been the President of the United States. I didn't ask. I was excited that someone felt my work was valuable enough to give me a chance."

Siene hesitated. His explanation seemed plausible, but she was exhausted and in no mood to waste time on considering the logic. She needed answers. She stood and walked closer to Ben. "I don't have time for this."

Ben shook his head. "If I worked for Lucian, I didn't know it. I swear."

"Then why did he say you turned down a job offer." She folded her arms across her chest and walked away. She turned. "He may be Taltos, but he was once Primogen. He wouldn't lie to me."

"You're sure about that?"

She wasn't. "I am," she lied. She sat, making sure she was close enough to look into Ben's eyes but far enough away so he couldn't touch her. "You want me to believe you? Tell me about Africa, and if you lie, I'll know."

Ben licked his dry lips and took a deep breath. "My company was contacted by a philanthropic source and was offered a large grant to study the effect of antimicrobial medications on African Trypanosomiasis, commonly known as Sleeping Sickness. Since I was working on new drug research, I jumped at the chance."

He winced in pain when he shifted on the chair.

"Where does it hurt?" Her tone was softer.

"Everywhere," he said with a pain-filled grin.

She poured a cup of water.

"Unless there is a shit load of aspirin in there, water isn't going to help."

She handed him the cup. "Drink it anyway. To make me feel better and to help you keep talking."

He did both. "African Sleeping Sickness is transmitted by the bite of a tsetse fly infected with a particular protozoa, and if untreated, always leads to death."

"Isn't African Sleeping Sickness rare?"

"It has been present in Africa for thousands of years and was considered rare until an outbreak in 1910 killed more than two-thirds of the population of Uganda. After that, the disease was grouped with other infections caused by protozoa and studied under the Neglected Disease Initiative funded by public sources."

"Simply by the title then, I imagine that funding doesn't come easy."

Ben nodded. "Foundations like to give money to research diseases that can be advertised and marketed. When have you ever seen a sleeping sickness telethon?"

Siene frowned. "That's pretty sad."

"And lethal to many unfortunate enough to contract the illness. Without proper research, drug discovery, vaccines, and diagnostics of the disease itself, there isn't much hope for someone infected to return to a normal life."

"There is no cure?"

Ben shook his head. "Not yet. Treatment is complicated because there are two subspecies of the parasite that are responsible for initiating the disease in humans. The two human forms of the disease also vary greatly in intensity. One, called TBG, causes a chronic condition that can remain in a passive phase for months or years before symptoms emerge."

Siene looked away, her method of absorbing information, before looking back at Ben. She pressed her lips together before continuing. "So TBG is manageable?"

"No. The infection can last about three years before death occurs. The other subspecies, called TBR, is the acute form of the disease and death can occur within months since the symptoms emerge within weeks, with the disease being more virulent and faster developing."

Siene hadn't known Ben for long, but she could see the intensity in his eyes, and hear the conviction in his voice. She began to doubt he had knowingly taken up with Lucian. She moved from interrogator to student, but still needed to learn more before she crossed the line from caution to trust.

"I understand the challenge," she acknowledged. "Since the disease is rare and isolated, I imagine there is little research being done."

"Very little. Funding from high-income countries has been steadily decreasing for kinetoplastid infections."

Siene's eyes narrowed. "Kinetoplastid?"

"Means infected with parasites."

She nodded. "Go on."

"But the downward endowment trend leaves a gap for other funders, such as philanthropic foundations and private pharmaceutical companies to fill."

"This is why the offer was so attractive."

"Yes." Ben looked away and then back. "I thought I could find something to help."

She could see the disappointment in his eyes and knew he was telling the truth. But there was more, and she needed to hear it. "Go on."

"I never met the benefactor. Most of the money was funneled through the pharmaceutical company. I had an email address and phone number I could use if I needed resources quickly. After I accepted the position, I was flown to Cape Town where I thought I would be working with the South African Medical Research Council's Burden of Disease Research Unit, but when I landed, I was met by a man who called himself Dr. Naude, and then was taken to a compound about fifty kilometers north of Tygerberg. The building looked like it belonged to a modern medical research facility, complete with up-to-the-minute labs and living quarters. I noticed that the compound was fenced and guarded."

"Didn't that raise a red flag?"

"It should have, but I was about to find a cure for a rare disease. I think I would have worked on the Titanic knowing it was going to sink if I thought I had a chance to do something remarkable for mankind before it did."

Siene felt a sharp ache fill her heart with his words. How many times had she put herself in danger for the very same reason? Trust line now crossed for the moment at least, she knew Ben could not possibly be part of any covert plot. His work had caught Lucian's attention and that made it more important for her to find out why.

"What did you do there?" she asked.

"Dr. Naude had me get right to work. In a

dormitory wing there were patients in various stages of the disease from disorganized and fragmented twenty-four-hour rhythms of the sleep-wake cycle, to confusion, tremor, general muscle weakness, psychotic reactions, aggressive behavior, coma, systemic organ failure, and death. I took blood samples from all the infected and from cadavers and started my research. For the first few weeks there was nothing remarkable about the cases, and I made no headway. Then as some new patients were brought in, something seemed very wrong."

"How so?"

"Their blood. The samples were suddenly and markedly different."

"How different?"

"The blood had new cells, cells I never saw before. They were…" He stopped and looked at her, brows drawn down.

"Go on," Siene urged. "You can't possibly think I'm going to be all that shocked considering the life I've been living."

"These particular cells had attached themselves to the white blood cells." He paused. "And they were iridescent."

****

Jack cursed, the sound of explosions all around him.

"I can barely hear you." Kai pressed her forefinger deeper into her left ear, cell phone closer to the other. "Don't talk. Shout."

"Tell whoever it is that you're busy and you'll have to call him back," Jack yelled and took a fresh grip on his pistol as shots pinged off the wall behind him. "And watch your ass."

Kai ducked behind a series of thick storage shelves stacked with heavy-duty machine parts.

Max fucking Biden. Jack rolled the name over in his mind, feeling the adrenaline flow freely. *How the hell did he find this place?* He peered over the cover of fallen metal shelving, the Glock in his hand fully loaded, and put two rounds through the belt buckle of an intruder charging him. Another man lifted his weapon, and Jack felt his gun rise through the next four shots. The second man's shirtfront turned red, and he fell backward.

A third man fired from ten feet away. At that range, missing Jack was almost impossible. Two rounds struck Jack's Kevlar vest, slamming into his chest and making him stumble back. From behind him a spray of bullets caught the attacker at the ankles and stitched their way to the top of his head.

"You okay?" Kai ejected the empty magazine and slammed another one home. She took aim at three more men coming at them. She hit the first one between the eyes. Then she dropped two more.

"I'm better than they are," Jack said, looking across the sector and watching as other attackers ran toward the back of the tunnel. He grinned. They weren't getting away. They were running straight for the rest of the Primogens. "Have a nice chat?" He put two bullets into each of the two men Kai had only wounded.

"No," she announced firmly. "That was Caleb. Reed, Siene, and Ben were not at the rendezvous point. Trackers finally found Ben and Siene. You'll never guess where they are?"

"Better tell me then," Jack said checking the Glock.

"Lucian has them."

"Son of a bitch. And Reed?"

Kai just shook her head.

****

Lina paced the small tent. Where was Mosegi? She scanned the area outside the tent flap for the hundredth time with no sign of him. There was nothing but darkness and a few of Lucian's henchmen watching the camp.

He said he could get her some of the water and if Lucian was using something in the water to control the diggers, surely the stash would be heavily guarded. She was almost sure Mosegi hadn't been caught, though. She would know that. One of the guards would have told her. The men hired by Lucian for camp security were damn stupid. Two or three of them thought they were making headway with her. Despite worrying about Mosegi, she smiled. Yeah, as if any of those slime balls would be getting anything from her. But if shaking her booty or showing a little boob got her some valuable information, what was the harm in a little feel now and then?

Her mood suddenly slipped from buoyant to dark. Damn, if only Lucian hadn't kept slipping those wonderland mushrooms into her food or drink or wherever he managed to put it. Try as she may, she still couldn't get back to pint-size and she couldn't stop eating or drinking until the stuff got out of her system. No one knew how long the effects of Alice's mushrooms ever lasted. Besides, doll-sized in Africa, she'd just be an appetizer for some big cat or snake or

234

whatever other animal happened to be hungry. Whatever she was going to do, she'd have to do it full-sized.

She watched the guards' foot patrol and timed her exit when the last one was out of sight. She always thought better when she didn't feel confined. She walked behind her tent and began to pace.

"*Hsst!*"

Lina's head snapped around at the whisper but could make out little in the dimness of the cloudy night. "Who's there?"

"I need to talk to you, but they can't see." The voice was not Mosegi's, but sounded young and male, and filled with stress. "Come by the bushes."

Adrenaline punched her in the gut as she carefully circled around back. "Where are you?"

"Here. Quick, before they see us talking."

The voice came from deep inside the brush edging the camp. Lina hesitated and glanced at two guards talking near a fire. Turning back, she saw a small boy leaning on a makeshift crutch frantically motioning to her with his hands. Making a quick decision, she stepped into the brush. "What are you doing here?"

The boy limped deeper into the shadows, sending a skitter of nerves down her skin. She had never seen this boy before. Had Lucian set some sort of trap? She held her hands away from her sides and kept her weight on the balls of her feet to run or fight if someone pounced at her.

"You said you wanted to talk to me." She kept her voice low and calm, though a sense of danger pulsed around her nerve endings. "Is it about Mosegi?"

The boy nodded.

She was close enough to see the boy clearly now. He was thin, his ribs looking like mountains across his chest. She could see a large wound slashed across his shin, the edges of the skin black and oozing. Her heart clutched in her chest. He needed medical help or he could lose that leg. She'd find a way to help him.

"Mosegi says to meet by the water." His eyes darted from Lina to the camp and back. "The water where you know." He blew out a breath and tried again. "The water where you saw him."

Lina nodded but said nothing. Often, she noticed the longer she waited, the more was said.

The boy fidgeted, then spoke quickly. "He say he has it, but they know and look for him. He say come now. No wait. He give you it, then he has to go away to—"

"Hey! What are you doing over there?" a guard shouted. He began walking toward Lina.

The boy's face twisted with fear.

"I'm puking my guts out. Want to watch?" Lina shouted back.

The guard stopped. "Make it quick and then get back here where I can see you."

She turned and made a vomiting noise before lowering her voice. "Go stay by Mosegi. Tell him to wait for me. I'll be there as soon as I can. You wait, too. I'll get you something for that leg."

"Hurry it up," the guard shouted taking a step closer.

"I'm puking as fast as I can." Lina pretended to wretch again. She turned to the boy. "It may take me a while to get to you but wait for me. Go now."

The boy nodded, and quickly moved deeper into

the brush.

Lina turned and wiped her mouth with the back of her hand as she walked back toward the guard. "All done." She saw skepticism cross the guard's face. She glanced over her shoulder. "But I wouldn't eat much of today's dinner. Guess the meat wasn't quite done."

The guard looked toward the brush.

"You can check if you want, but I tell you, it isn't pretty." Lina counted on the normal human reaction to puke.

The guard grabbed her upper arm. "The animals can clean up that mess. Let's go."

Chapter Twenty-One

"Iridescent blood, you say?" Siene repeated.

"Sparkly as shit," Ben confirmed. He tossed his shoulders. "Well, I know shit doesn't sparkle, but…"

"But…" Siene began, cutting him off and starting to pace. "Some of our stuff does." She spun to face him. "What did you get yourself involved in?" her tone accused.

"Research." Ben straightened his back, stiff from the beating he had received.

"But apparently not entirely for African Sleeping Sickness."

"I know that now. At the time, I thought any research would be good for my career." He looked over his shoulders as a guard passed in front of the tent. "But now I realize getting yourself killed isn't an optimum career choice either."

"We aren't dead yet."

Ben snorted. "Somehow, I think you won't be, but I will. Lucian seems to like you."

"That was in the past."

"So today he doesn't? From what I saw, I think there is still something there for you."

Siene watched another guard pass the tent opening. "Yeah, I suppose."

Ben nodded. "Good, because I don't want to have to worry about you dying when I make my move."

Siene laughed. "You're going to make a move? Your right eye is nearly swollen shut, and I did notice you aren't exactly in the best of shape right now." Still, if she had to admit it, there was something comforting about his presence. They were on the same side, and she knew he wouldn't abandon her. He'd proven that in the jungle. They were bound by whatever Lucian wanted from Ben, and she was distinctly aware that they both knew it. Though neither seemed happy about the situation right now, it was interesting.

Ben snickered. "Lucian will expect you to do some kung fu thing, but not me. Maybe we can use that to our advantage."

"Maybe," Siene admitted. "What do you know about martial arts?"

"Big fan of Jackie Chan."

"So, nothing then?"

Ben shrugged. "That's about right."

Siene tapped her forefinger on her chin and continued to pace. "I guess then it will be up to me to get us out of this."

Ben struggled to stand. "I can fight."

She stopped pacing and put her hands on her hips. "Right. You can barely stand."

Ben huffed. "No need to get persnickety, Siene. I may be hurt, but I can still rescue you."

"You already tried that, and I am not being persnickety."

Ben watched another guard walk by and then turned his attention back to Siene. "You sound like it to me."

"Then maybe you should get your hearing checked."

Ben shuffled forward until he was toe to toe with her. "Why? Everything else is still functioning despite being slapped around a bit."

Siene looked at him like she was interviewing him. "Okay, you may have taken a few steps up from the uptight doctor I saw outside Penn Station, but you are far from a hunky adventurer looking for antiquities in Africa."

Ben straightened as far as the pain let him. "How far?"

She shook her head. "This is no time for analysis, Ben. Let's just say you have improved."

"Damn skippy I've improved," he bristled. "In several areas."

Her laugh came out like a dismayed snort. "Sure."

He came closer. "You sound like you need some show and tell."

"What kind do you mean?" she challenged.

"Like this," he volunteered right before he reached out and slipped his hand across the back of her neck bringing her closer to him.

She pulled back. "This is not the time for romance."

"I may not have another chance."

Instantly his lips meshed with hers, his tongue thrusting inside her mouth, utterly hot and erotic. Why danger always seemed to make temptation that much more forbidden and inviting, she didn't know, but Ben's kiss invaded her senses, deepening her pleasure. Any minute Lucian could come back, but she didn't care. Her hips arched creating a dizzying friction, and she kissed him like she couldn't get enough. He was right. He had improved. She suddenly felt his body tense.

"Siene," he said her name shuddered and broken, "We need to stop."

Stop? No, her mind shouted. *We may not be able to do this for a very long time.* She pressed closer.

"We have to stop." He pushed her away.

She jerked back, panting for breath. "Why?"

She saw him look over her shoulder.

"We have company."

She turned and saw Lucian just inside the tent. He motioned over his shoulder and five of his henchmen appeared.

"How long have you been spying on us?" Siene asked.

Lucian laughed. "Spying is such a harsh word. I was merely allowing one final goodbye kiss."

She crossed her arms, trying not to let him see the fear that rose with his words. "Are we leaving?"

"We are." He confirmed and gestured toward Ben. "He isn't."

Lucian nodded, and one of his men pulled Siene away by her upper arm. The other four surrounded Ben.

Siene struggled to free herself, but the grip on her only tightened. She tried to dig her heels into the ground, but the man dragged her to Lucian and threw her into his arms.

Lucian turned her, one arm across her waist, the other across her neck.

She stopped struggling. "You aren't going to hurt Ben, are you?" She hoped her tone sounded more like a command than a question.

"Not me, my dear," Lucian replied. He tossed his head. "They are." Holding tight onto Siene, he barked his final order. "Take him into the jungle and kill him. Then break down the rest of camp and meet us at the rendezvous point."

"No!" Siene screamed. She pounded on the arm across her stomach with little effect. The time in the jungle weakened her and the blows did nothing.

"For old time's sake, you do not have to watch." He pushed her ahead of him toward a waiting box truck and tossed her inside like a rag doll. "Make yourself comfortable. It's going to be a rather long and bumpy ride."

She scrambled to her feet and lunged at him as the door slammed shut and she hit the metal with both hands. The sound of the lock sliding into place signaled her defeat. As the truck began to move, she squinted into the semi-darkness. Cracks in the truck's thin metal walls allowed enough light for her to take stock of her moving prison. She got down on her hands and knees and prowled. Some of the men Lucian hired were not trained mercenaries. She'd bet her life at least one of them had made a mistake, and that mistake was in here somewhere inside the truck.

****

Lina watched Lucian get into a truck and speed off. "What's up?" she asked the man holding her arm and pulling her back to her tent.

"We're leaving. Pack up what you can in five minutes."

"Leaving? Why?"

"Because we are."

Lina watched four jeeps with machine guns on the rear deck circle the camp. To her left men were carrying military flame throwers and sending streams of liquid fire rolling into empty tents. Smoke poured across the gray sky giving the illusion of rapidly falling blackness. In the distance she could hear gunfire.

"What about the mine workers?" She feared the worst.

"Wouldn't worry too much about them," the guard answered.

Lina heard gunfire and looked in the direction of the dig. *If that bastard is executing people, I swear I'll kill him with my bare hands the next time I see his ass.*

****

The guard held Ben's upper arm in a vise grip as they walked away from the camp. He noticed the jungle around them seemed suddenly quiet. Something was not quite right. The sound of insects and birds chattering just a few minutes ago was now silent. There was a predator close by. *Was that the fate Davelos had in store for him?*

"Where are we going?" Ben asked, as a small branch released by the guardsman leading them whipped by his cheek.

The man didn't answer but kept moving forward using his assault rifle to make way through the dense brushwood.

Ben slowed his steps. "A bit off the path, don't you think?"

His answer was a strong shove to his back, and a head flick telling him to get moving.

As they continued, Ben could see small movements out of the corner of his eye. *Please don't let it be a lion.* A part of him was oddly detached from the situation, and he started to understand how the victims at the Coliseum must have felt as they waited to be delivered to their destiny. Sitting in a taxi and hit by a truck, or becoming lunch for a big cat, either way he never thought that was the way he'd die. Fate might have her due after all.

Just before they emerged into a clearing, something in the bush caught his attention. The movement didn't seem to be animal. Ben tried not to think about a rescue, and though not particularly spiritual, he wouldn't mind a miracle about now.

The group froze when suddenly six soldiers with camouflage paint covering most of their faces stepped into the open with weapons raised. One of the men escorting Ben stepped forward in challenge and the arriving soldiers adjusted their aim. Red dots appeared on Ben's chest and the chests of the men with him. Moments of silence stretched into what seemed like an eternity before Davelos' lead guard issued a command in one of the African dialects. Instantly, the other men surrounding Ben dropped their guns.

Ben had no idea if his situation had improved or had gotten worse until one of the soldiers stepped to the side and lowered his face covering. Ben sighed with relief and his elevated heartbeat returned to normal. "Caleb! You are a sight!" He moved forward and extended his hand.

Caleb grinned and grasped the hand that was offered. "Glad you are safe, my friend."

"Five minutes more and I don't think I would have been. How did you find me?"

Caleb gave his men orders and waited until some of the soldiers had taken away Davelos' men. "I can track anyone, but sometimes, not often mind you, I need a little extra help." He reached into his bag and pulled out a small case. "I think you may recognize this." He unwrapped the contents.

"Man, I thought I'd never get out of there," a familiar voice said.

"Shard!" Ben laughed at the exasperated expression on the face in the piece of the Mirror. "I was wondering how I was going to find you."

"Caleb found me." The blurry face of the mirror fragment frowned, and the background darkened. "You left me in the jungle."

"I had no choice," Ben defended. "I couldn't let you fall into Taltoian hands."

"Do you know what *else* found me before Caleb did?" Tiny lights flashed behind Shard's head. "Bugs, lots of bugs, and a big-ass snake. I hate snakes."

Ben tried not to laugh. "Big snake, huh?"

The lights behind Shard flashed faster. "If I had hands, I'd show you just how big that mother was, right after I…"

"Shard. Enough," Caleb instructed. "There is more to do." He turned to Ben. "Where's Siene?"

Ben took a breath before answering. "Davelos has her."

"Damn! Well, we'll just have to get her back," Caleb said evenly.

"What about Reed. Is he safe?" Ben asked.

Caleb shrugged and shook his head. "Still missing."

Ben reached for assurances. "But he's alive."

"I don't know. I hope so."

"What about Shard? Can't he tell us?"

"I am a mirror, not crystal ball," Shard shot back. "I can suggest. That's all."

"At least try," Ben said.

He watched as the piece of Mirror sparkled, sending rays of light into the air. Shard's face contorted as if he was concentrating very hard. For a few moments, no one spoke. Then, as though someone had turned off a switch the light rays vanished, and the piece of Mirror darkened.

"Nope. Nothing," Shard announced.

Unwilling to settle for that, Ben shook his head. "Try again."

Caleb put a hand on Ben's shoulder. "Maybe a little later, but now, we should go. Davelos may send others to make sure you're dead. He doesn't trust anything he doesn't see with his own eyes, or anything that is not thoroughly checked."

"What about Shard?" Ben asked. "We can't let him fall into Davelos' hands."

"Way ahead of you, my friend. A Seeker will take him to Songwe Airport where he will meet one of our Scribes and they will take Shard the rest of the way to the compound in the US to unite with the Mirror. He will be safe from Taltos."

Ben watched Caleb rewrap the mirror fragment and hand it off to a Seeker who then took off on foot and disappeared into the jungle. "Are you sure the Seeker will make it to the airport? I mean you can't exactly call a cab from here?"

Caleb laughed. "I don't have time to explain about Primogen Seekers. Rest assured that one will protect Shard with his life if necessary."

Ben nodded and walked with Caleb. The soldiers followed in a single file line. "What's the plan to rescue Siene?"

Caleb looked over his shoulder. "We can formulate one at the village."

Ben stopped. "No village. We have to find Siene."

Caleb turned and walked backward. "I agree, but in order to get these men to help me, I promised to deliver food and supplies to their village."

Ben's tempo slowed. "We can't wait. Davelos might kill her." One of the men following behind gave him a gentle poke in the back, and he resumed walking.

"Davelos won't harm Siene," Caleb assured.

"You don't know that. From the little I know about him, I can tell he's crazy and quite willing to do anything to get what he wants, even if that might mean harming Siene."

Caleb shook his head. "He won't hurt her."

Ben's voice rose. "How the hell can you be so sure?"

"Because she almost married him, and as far as I know, he's still in love with her."

Ben stopped, his eyes widening. "What?"

"It's a long story and not mine to tell."

Ben did not move. "Siene was engaged to Davelos?"

"It was a long time ago."

"How long?"

"A while."

"A month? A year? More?"

Caleb splayed a hand out in front of his chest. "I don't have time to play twenty questions, and even if I did, I don't think Siene would want me to rehash the past." He tossed his head toward the west and started walking. "We need to get to the village before dark."

Ben looked over his shoulder in the direction of the

camp and then quickly back. "The thought of leaving Siene with that madman for even a few hours longer is reprehensible." Thoughts of what Lucian might do to harm Siene overlaid with the idea that he loved her warred inside his mind. Both scenarios made anger build inside him.

Caleb picked up the pace. "Many in the village are sick, maybe dying, and I promised to help if the villagers helped me."

Ben looked at Caleb. *Many are dying.* He felt his shoulders drop as a natural feeling to assist rose. "And you're sure Davelos won't hurt Siene."

"Can we be sure of anything?"

Ben frowned. "You're not very comforting."

"A few weeks ago, you thought the Magic Mirror just lived in a fairy tale. Now, you know the Mirror is real. I'm just saying that anything, bad or good, can happen. Nothing is certain but hope."

Ben could not argue. "What kind of sickness?" he asked. "Fevers?"

"No. A strange malady. Some of the men returned to the village one day and acted like a spell had been cast on them. They wandered aimlessly with eyes cast upward."

Once, Ben would have dismissed that description of an illness, but not now. "Like they were in a trance?"

Caleb nodded. "I am told the village shaman tried several times to sweat out the sickness with no success."

"I'm a scientist, not a doctor, but I have seen something similar. And if I am right, sweating wouldn't have worked, but only advanced the progress of the disease like an incubator helps grow samples. To be sure, I will need a microscope, and some slides and needles to take blood. But what I really need is a lab." Ben looked around. "I worked at one somewhere in this jungle, but I have no idea of the location or if the lab is still viable."

"Once we get to the village, I'll send out Seekers. If the lab still exists, they will find it," Caleb assured.

"We don't know how much time we have," Ben cautioned. "We don't know what Davelos has planned."

"Then we should hurry." Caleb waved the group forward.

Caleb and the other men moved at a speed that was more animated than Ben had ever traveled. Soon his sides hurt, and he couldn't speak without gasping for air. The jungle floor was damp, and he narrowly missed slipping on a wet spot that would have caused him to fall. That would have delayed them even longer.

But time was in short supply, and he would keep up with Caleb and the others until they arrived at the village. Once there, he could only give them a few hours. For him, getting to Siene mattered more.

****

Out of the truck and shoved ahead by one of Davelos' two goons shepherding her, Siene emerged from the jungle into the bright sunlight and walked onto the edge of a makeshift airstrip with another large truck parked near a stack of barrels. The sun was high overhead, and she could see a small, rundown building to her right. Her mind whirled. If she was going to get out of this mess, she would have to do something before she was forced inside. Attempting to put some distance between her and the gunmen, she picked up her pace and began counting. On ten she'd try a running escape. She got to seven when she was grabbed from behind and spun around to find a gun aimed at the center of her body.

"Slow down." The larger of the two men with her grabbed her upper arm. "Try anything and I will shoot."

His attempt at English was poor but it was clear enough for her to understand she would need another plan. She held still as a man dressed in army drab fatigues and armed with a pistol emerged from the building and walked toward them. Only three soldiers. Odd. *Where were Davelos and the men from the camp?*

"Get the supplies from the truck," the man holding her ordered.

The soldier with them nodded and walked to a smaller truck parked near the structure.

Her captor pushed her toward the doorway. "When does the plane come?" he asked the approaching man.

The soldier raised his gun hand to shield his eyes against the glare of sun. "Two days," he answered. "Tomorrow boss-man and others will be here with the tanzanite."

Siene walked slowly toward him. Her mind spun. They hadn't searched her after she got out of the truck. Big mistake. She had found a small slice of metal loosely imbedded in the corner on the floor. It took her most of the ride and a few broken fingernails to free the fragment. She managed to conceal the sliver in her bra just before the truck's doors swung open.

"And the villagers?" the goon still holding her asked.

"They will be dead by tomorrow night."

Ice water filled Siene's veins. She could wait no longer. She twisted and buried the piece of steel in the neck of the guard holding her. The makeshift weapon sliced through his carotid artery. He stumbled, blood spurting from the wound. Whirling, she sent the second man sprawling to the ground with a kick to the chest, driving him backward. He hit the building hard and landed in a heap, immobile. She grabbed his rifle and started to run.

Out of the corner of her eye she saw the last man jump from the truck at the side of the building and take aim at her. She sprinted in a zigzag pattern toward the safety of the dense brush surrounding the airstrip. As she cut to the right, a bullet scalded the air close to her cheek. Out of the corner of her eye, she saw the guard getting ready to fire again.

She dove forward, rolling to the side as bullets thudded the ground around her. Jumping to her feet, she raced to the undergrowth and took shelter behind a large tree. Raining bullets shredded the foliage. Moving quickly, she crawled to her left, away from the hail of fire aimed where the shooter believed she was hiding.

The shooter ran to the underbrush next to her, alternately using the barrel of his gun to search the brushwood and fire at movement. She crept silently toward him, watching as he went deeper into the dense growth still searching for her.

When she was a foot from him, she gripped her rifle with both hands and stood. "Hey!" she called out.

The gunman turned and brought his weapon up. He took a step back and set his aim. Angling her body, Siene swung her rifle up, the butt of the weapon catching him in the face. He fell backward and lost his grip on his weapon. She grabbed the gun and brought the backside of her rifle hard against his head as he struggled to get to his feet. He slumped back, unconscious.

Siene stood and scanned the area. More of Lucian's men would surely be coming, but she didn't know when. Her mind whirled with work left undone. She had to help the villagers escape the mines, find Ben and Lina, pray Reed was still alive, and stop Davelos from leaving Africa until she discovered his plan for the tanzanite. Daunting tasks for one person.

Okay. This is my last chance to rethink and prioritize what I must do.

She pictured the last glimpse she had of Reed before she donned her parachute and jumped from the doomed airplane and held onto the knowledge that he knew everything needed to survive. She had heard Lucian order Ben's death. Her heart hitched when she conceded he may already have been killed. Lucian never left loose ends. Sadly, she moved Ben and Reed's providence to the bottom of her priorities.

As concerned as she was with their fate, emotion had to take a back seat to the mission. Her duty, her life, has always been to secure the artifacts and keep them safe. She would act in the way in which she had been trained since the time she could understand the reality of her existence. She had to be logical without allowing family or relationships any weight in her decisions. She'd grieve later.

Then, for the first time in days, Siene smiled. Lina was out there somewhere. Normally a foot-tall ball of hellfire but even harder to control full-sized, Siene pitied the soldiers trying to contain her.

By process of elimination, the villagers moved to the top of her to-do list. She began to sprint to the truck when she heard a vehicle in the distance. Surely it was Davelos or his men, and, by the ominous sound of the racing motor, she was rapidly running out of escape time. She ducked back into the dense brush and waited. One small truck broke from the jungle and headed for the airstrip.

Siene knew she had to act. She stepped out of the brush and into the path of the truck. She held the gun high and fired two shots into the air. The truck headed right for her, and she could see the shadows of the truck's occupants reacting. One man leaned out the passenger window and took aim. Suddenly, the truck jerked to the left and began swerving.

She ran toward the driver's side, matching her speed and her stride with the decelerating vehicle, hoping that staying to the right side would make it more difficult for the gunman on the left to track her. The driver appeared to be both fighting for control of the truck and trying to fend off someone between him and the gunman. As the truck bounded toward her along the uneven dirt, bullets cracked through the air as muzzle flashes appeared in sporadic bursts.

At the last minute, Siene leapt. Calling on her training, she placed one foot on the truck's hood and pushed off again, twisting her body so she flipped and landed on the roof. It was a maneuver she had practiced with Kai during her last training session and was thankful Kai had made her do it over and over until the feat was now almost child's play.

She dropped to one knee and held onto the light panel fastened to the truck's roof as the driver tried evasive action, swinging wildly from left to right while heading for the side of the airstrip building.

The truck gained speed, bullets tearing through the metal roof missing her by inches. Holding tightly onto to the light panel, she pumped three shots through the metal, hoping she'd hit the gunman with at least one. At the building, the driver pulled hard to the right, and she had only seconds to react. She looped the rifle strap over her head, dropped to her stomach, slid backward, and grabbed onto the remnants of a luggage rack with both hands just as the truck slammed into the corner of building and skidded toward the back. Sparks cascaded along the truck, coming in a spray as the vehicle left a scarred wall in its wake. Bullets again ripped along the truck's rooftop, missing her as the van continued forward and began to rock.

Moving quickly, she crawled forward, slid down the windshield on her belly and landed on the hood. On the other side of the cracked glass, she could see the gunman in the passenger's seat slumped to the left, blood coming from a wound near his right ear. The driver was struggling for control of his gun with the center passenger.

Siene fired, shooting through the windshield with her last bullet, shattering the glass. The driver ducked the bullet and pulled hard on the steering wheel. The truck slid to the right, coming up on two wheels before beginning a slow roll as Siene jumped clear. She hurled herself from the path of the out-of-control vehicle and landed in a crouch, allowing her legs to absorb the shock of hitting the ground. The truck careened over on its side and skated along the ground. Even before it stopped, the rear cargo doors opened, and two men rolled free.

Siene ran toward them and caught up with the first

one before he got to his feet. She swung her rifle and brought the butt down on the man's head knocking him unconscious. Before the second man could react and pull up his machine gun, she swept his legs from beneath him. When he fell, she sat on his chest, grabbed his hair, and smashed his head against the ground until he went limp, and his gun clattered harmlessly to the side. Expecting to deal with the remaining passenger, she sprang to her feet and saw Lina climbing out of the vehicle through the broken windshield.

Instantly, she relaxed. She tossed her empty rifle to Lina and picked up the unconscious man's machine gun. "Took you long enough."

Lina shot her a one-fingered salute. "Very funny. Good thing I did come along, or you'd be toast."

Siene gestured to the truck. "Where's the driver?"

"Dead." Lina checked the chamber of the gun she brought out of the truck with her. "Must have reloaded his gun before you popped him." She looked up. "Now what?"

Siene tossed her head toward a vehicle parked next to the airstrip building. "Now we buy some time."

They ran to the vehicle. Siene gestured to an unconscious man lying in the doorway as she unscrewed the gas cap. "Get me his shirt."

Lina stooped next to him and picked up the edge of the prone man's tee shirt with two fingers. "He stinks."

"Don't care." Siene held out her hand. "The shirt, please."

The man started to come around, but Lina banged his head against the side of the building. Quickly she stripped him of his shirt and handed it to Siene.

Siene ripped the shirt into strips and fed them into

the gas tank. "Hope there's enough gas in there to soak the material."

Lina stood. "And where do we get a match in the jungle?"

"Don't need one," Siene replied. She took aim and fired. The side of the truck burst into flame.

Siene and Lina took off running, their victory cries lost in the thunder of small explosions tearing through the walls of the small building. When they reached the vehicle parked at the edge of the airstrip, they turned and saw flames shooting skyward like a curtain going up on an arson scene. One minute there was a building, the next, an inferno.

"Must have been some airplane fuel inside the building," Siene said. She yanked open the driver's side door, jumped inside, and started the engine. "This will slow down Davelos' exit from Africa, but it won't stop him. We have to hurry."

Lina slammed the passenger door shut. "Where to?"

"Back to camp," Siene replied.

"The camp's gone. Davelos torched it before he left."

Siene felt her heart race. Was she already too late? "And the mine?"

Lina shook her head. "I don't know."

Siene jerked the steering wheel to the left and stepped on the gas. "We need to get back to camp and find the villagers at the mine. Davelos never leaves loose ends."

"What about Ben and Reed?" Lina hung onto the window frame as the truck bounced through the brush.

Siene felt her breath catch as a cold fist seemed to

squeeze her heart. "Not on the top of my list right now."

****

At dusk Ben and Caleb arrived at a small village about twenty miles east of the camp where he had been taken by Davelos' men. The village was made up of thatched huts set in a circle around an area near a source of water. The homes were small, and the activity limited since most of the villagers had been stricken with the mysterious illness.

Once settled, Caleb dispatched a few Watchers to search Davelos' discarded camp. He and a small band of Seekers went ahead into the jungle to locate the abandoned laboratory. Ben stayed behind and began to examine some of the sick.

Ben knew he probably could not do much for the villagers until Caleb found the lab. He suspected a possible form of African Sleeping Sickness but, during his examination, he noticed the lethargy exhibited was nothing like the symptoms for the disease. This stupor-like condition was different, presenting more like a zombie state than an actual illness. He put his hands on his hips and shook his head. In a few short weeks, his thinking had moved from science to science fiction. The concern he felt for the sick villagers shifted and took on an added element. What he wouldn't give to argue fact versus fiction with Siene right now. He closed his eyes and for the first time in a long time prayed. Everything was suddenly possible in this new world.

He was about to enter a small hut in which three of the five family members had been stricken with the strange malady when he heard a truck approach. He turned and immediately recognized the vehicle as one belonging to Davelos. Drawing the revolver Caleb gave him, Ben dropped to one knee and aimed at the windshield just as the vehicle skidded to a stop about five yards away. The door opened and he fired.

"Damn it, Ben," Siene shouted, crouching as the bullet passed over her head. "You need to identify the good guys from the bad guys before you fire."

Ben ran to her and held her at arm's length, inspecting her body as he spoke. "Did I hit you?"

She grabbed onto him and kissed him hard. "You could have killed me."

He kissed her back. "I thought Davelos' men found me."

"Good thing you're a lousy shot," Siene whispered against his lips.

"I agree." He kissed her again.

Siene pulled back and scanned his face. "I thought you were dead."

"Not yet." He winked. "But that was the plan."

"How did you get free?"

"Caleb found me."

They were still locked in each other's arms when Lina tapped Siene on the shoulder. "Remember me?"

Siene stepped out of Ben's embrace. "Sorry." She pointed. "Lina, Ben. Ben, Lina."

Lina snickered. "The famous Catalyst." Like an identification laser beam, her gaze scanned him from the tips of his boots to the top of his head. She then spread her arms and waited. "What? No suck-face welcome for me? I am crushed." Her smile widened. "Did Siene ever mention how much I like long hair and beards?"

Ben laughed and ran a hand through his hair then across his chin. "A little hard to find a barber shop in the jungle."

Lina flashed a smile. "All you need now is a brown Fedora and we'll talk about the new look." She looked him up and down. "Maybe more than just talk."

Siene shook her head. "Down, girl. He doesn't usually look like this. He's more brainiac than fortune-hunter."

Lina nodded. "Read a lot of books, Ben?"

Ben's brow furrowed. "I have a Bachelor's in Organic Chemistry, a Molecular Nano Biophotonics Masters, and a Doctorate in Physics, so I think that answers the question."

"So, textbooks mostly, but not a book on firearms."

Ben shook his head. "A bit on laser guided missiles and rockets mostly, but no weaponry."

"I kinda figured." Lina gestured toward the gun in Ben's hand. "Then you might want to take your finger off the trigger and put on the safety."

Siene took the gun from Ben. "Good idea." She set the safety and tucked the revolver into the waistband of her jeans. "I'll hold onto this for a while."

"You don't trust me?" Ben asked.

"Of course, I do." Siene looked at Lina. "She doesn't."

Lina laughed but did not disagree. "I'll check out the food and water supply here while you two get reacquainted. Then we need to get going." She headed into the nearest hut.

Siene's face turned serious. "Was Reed with Caleb when he found you?"

Ben shook his head. He could not help noticing the

fear and disappointment in Siene's eyes. "I'm sure Reed is fine. You told me how resourceful he is."

Siene nodded. "Where is Caleb now?"

"He's headed north to look for the lab I told you about. I want to help these villagers, but I don't know what I'm dealing with. I'll need the lab equipment if it is still there."

"That may have to wait. Davelos is getting ready to leave Africa. I was taken to an airstrip. The men who took me said a plane was coming in two days, and the miners would be dead by then." She began to pace. "Lina and I blew up the airstrip."

Ben furrowed his brows. "You blew up an airstrip?"

She nodded.

"How?"

Siene rolled her eyes. "The usual way. Why?"

Ben shook his head. "There is nothing usual about you."

"I'll tell you how later, but now, we need to get back to the mine. When will Caleb be back?"

"Not sure, but we can contact him with the radio in the truck."

****

Davelos could see the smoke from a mile away. He stomped on the gas pedal and the truck sped forward, sometimes following the dirt trail, sometimes making a new path through the brush.

At the edge of the airstrip, he slammed on the brakes, and the truck skidded to a stop. He jumped out and walked slowly toward what was left of the burning building. The heat generated by the fire slapped him in the face as walls of flame shot upward to one hundred feet. He could see bits and pieces of debris floating in the heat shaft. Davelos' gaze followed the burning fragments as they reached the top of the flame column, paused, and then fell. He knew everything inside the building was gone.

He stared at what was left of the airstrip. Blackened shapes of burnt vehicles lay sprawled on blackened brush. There was no sign of life anywhere. Even if his men had been somehow rendered unconscious or were wounded and down, the air around them would have been too hot to breathe.

He made out the wreckage of two trucks in the flames and surmised he'd lost at least seven men, counting the guard who had stayed in the airstrip building. He also noticed the truck kept at the edge of the strip was not among the burning vehicles. He'd bet all the money he had on him that, when the fire died enough for him to investigate, Siene and Lina would not be among the bodies.

He heard engines approaching. *The rest of my men are here*. He smiled and touched his temple in a salute. *Game on, Siene.*

Chapter Twenty-Three

Caleb's voice crackled over the radio. "We found the lab."

Siene grabbed the radio clipped to her belt and pushed the talk button. "Where?"

"Siene, is that you?" Caleb asked. "I thought you were dead."

She laughed. "Almost, but Ben's a lousy shot."

"Ben shot at you?"

"He thought I was Davelos."

"You're much better looking," Caleb quipped.

Siene laughed. "I hope so." It felt good to laugh, but she could not be distracted. Her voice turned serious. "Listen carefully. We don't have much time. Davelos has packed up shop and is leaving Africa."

"When?" Caleb asked.

"Not as soon as he would like. Lina and I put a few holes in the airstrip."

"Lina's with you? I thought Reed lost her."

Siene swallowed the lump that formed in her throat at the mention of her brother's name. "She's here compliments of Davelos."

"How'd he get her?"

"Long story," Siene replied. She heard Caleb laugh.

"Can't wait to hear it."

Static droned. "Say again," Siene said. She hoped

the batteries weren't failing.

"I asked how you found her," Caleb replied.

"Lina and I ran into each other at the airstrip and teamed up to mess with Davelos' plans although temporarily, I'm sure. He'll have to either fix the runway or clear a new one. I figure we have four, maybe five days. A week tops."

"That's my girl," Caleb called out over the airwaves.

"Don't celebrate too soon," Siene warned. "Davelos is planning on killing the villagers at the mine. We have to stop him somehow."

"We started world surveillance by satellite imaging after the attack on the monastery and have some orbiter shots of an area that was probably his camp," Caleb said. "The mine must be there, too."

Siene's sense of urgency rose. "There's no time to guess. Davelos told me the workers would be dead by morning."

"Hang on," Caleb said.

Siene couldn't hear much. The radio was old and the reception not the greatest, but she could hear Caleb shouting something that sounded like orders. Though his voice was more garbled than clear, she did pick up a few a few words.

Caleb's voice cleared. "Siene, you still there?"

"I am."

"I've sent some Seekers to gather mercenaries and tribesmen to find the mine. I'll keep you updated on their progress."

"Thanks." Siene felt herself relax. Seekers never let her down. She expected this time would be no exception. Now she had a different choice to make—

Davelos or the sickness. Which to handle first? She had slowed Davelos but still knew nothing about the illness. "Caleb, how far is the lab from here?"

"We also found that on the satellite images. Though I can't be sure, but using the GPS in the radio, it looks like a half-day from your position if you hurry."

"Which way?"

"To the river and then north. I can probably get there by sundown. Bring Ben and Lina with you. We shouldn't be separated more than we must be. You were with Davelos long enough to know how reactionary he can get."

She felt a wave of both fear and regret run through her. She often wondered if she was partly the cause of his mutiny. "That I do know." She set down the radio and turned to Ben. "Find Lina and let's go."

Ben fell into step beside her. "What did Caleb mean about you being with Davelos, and what do you know?"

Siene stopped. "Better you don't."

****

The footpath to the river was overgrown but not impassable. Siene, Lina, and Ben followed the sound of rushing water to the bank. The rapids that had formed over rocks and tree trunks were not overly large.

"This must be the Mara," Siene said.

"How do you know?" Ben asked.

"Guessing, really. We were following the river when the plane crashed. Davelos' camp was a few miles south." Siene dipped her chin and rubbed the back of her neck. She pressed her lips together and looked off to the right, hoping against hope to see Reed walk through the heavy brush or pull up to the riverbank on a hand-made raft. She refused to believe he was dead, but too many days had gone by with no word.

Ben did not miss the change in her demeanor. "Something's wrong."

Siene shook her head. "Nothing. Let's go. We've got to get to the lab." She took one last look at the water and headed north along the bank.

Lina got in step with Ben as they followed Siene. "It's Reed," she said. "Siene won't admit it, but she thinks he's dead. If he wasn't, he'd have moved heaven and earth to get to the rendezvous point." She shook her head and looked down. "It's been too long."

Ben ducked under a low-hanging limb. "Maybe Reed is just incapacitated."

"Incapacitated in the jungle is as good as dead," Lina said quickly. "Siene will have to accept that soon or put the mission at risk."

Ahead, Siene maneuvered over a large boulder, scraping her leg on a rough edge. The dull pain forced her to focus. Things could get worse. She would have to put Reed's fate out of her mind and accept that she may never see her brother again. Distractions could put everyone in danger. There were still too many unanswered questions for her to risk grief clouding her decisions. She'd mourn Reed later when she stopped Davelos and found out what was affecting the villagers. Reed deserved more than a failed mission.

For the first time since the Mirror activated and sent her on this quest, she felt ready for the challenge. She would do this without Reed if she had to. Despite her determination not to harbor regret, she wondered if she was partly to blame for what happened to him. She could have insisted he stay behind but deep down she knew nothing would stop him from trying to find Lina. Despite his fascination with Paz, it was Lina whom Reed really loved.

She closed her eyes, picturing the tall, skinny kid who always saved her from the bullies that called her names when they were growing up. Reed was the only one who understood how hard it was, wanting to be smart when other teens were more interested in being popular. She preferred molecules over makeup, science magazines instead of *Vogue* or *Glamour*. Friday nights were spent watching the Science Channel on cable rather than at a movie with a date.

Reed always tried to buffer her from teenage ridicule, telling her that one day, she would understand that her intelligence was a gift to the world. Though she eventually knew he was right, she found the truth to be uncomfortable now without him.

"Please let me find him," she whispered. "Alive."

She turned to make sure that Lina and Ben were close, but when she faced them, Ben's eyes flashed a warning. His gun was drawn, leveled at the dense jungle brush.

Ben ushered Lina behind him and gestured to her. "Get down," he whispered.

Siene pulled her knife from the sheath around her ankle. Before she could move, she heard what had alerted Ben—voices talking in low murmurs and the sound of people moving through the jungle. She dropped into cover.

Five men stepped onto the small path edging the river. Their faces were painted blue and white, and they wore camouflage pants and vests with pockets, but no shirts. Three men had ammo belts draped over their chests, and all five held assault rifles. As soon as they saw Ben, they pointed their weapons point blank at him.

Siene pressed deeper into the undergrowth where she couldn't be seen. Something began crawling up her leg, and she suppressed the urge to swat at it. A poisonous insect or gunshot, it made no difference which killed her if she made any sudden movement, but a sudden fear that Ben might do something stupid like shoot at the men made the decision for her.

She stuck her knife into the back of her pants, got to her feet, and raised her hands to shoulder height. "*Rafiki*," she called. "*Sisi waliopotea.*"

The armed men did not react.

She walked slowly to Ben.

"You didn't say anything that would make them shoot me, did you?" he asked out of the corner of his mouth once she was next to him. "I'm a bit rusty on my Swahili, and how did you know they might understand you?"

Siene smiled at the men. "I said I was a friend and we needed help. Most Tanzanians speak Swahili, so I gave it a shot."

"What else can you say?"

"That was about all."

"Then we're dead."

"Maybe." She saw the men glance at each other. "Do you speak any English? We need help."

The men kept their attention focused on her, but the leader lowered his gun. He pulled out a small radio from his vest pocket. "We found them, Caleb." His accent sounded more Arabic than anything African.

Siene could hear Caleb's voice on the other end of the radio. "Let me talk to Siene."

The leader held out the radio. "We had to be sure it wasn't a trap. We are Seekers. You are safe."

She lowered her hands. "You found us quickly."

"Fortunate for you we were close when Caleb called," the leader replied.

Siene took the radio and pressed the talk button. "I owe you, Caleb." Even with the poor signal she heard him laugh.

"I'll add it to my list."

"Why didn't you radio me about sending Seekers to escort us?"

"I tried but didn't get an answer."

Siene cut her gaze to Ben who mouthed *forgot the radio*. "Technical problems," Siene conveyed.

Caleb reacted immediately. "Then I'll make this quick. Taltos is scouring the jungle looking for you. I'm guessing some Taltoians will probably head to the lab, so what's the plan?"

Siene huffed. "Trying to get there first and secure the place by taking the easy route by the river is definitely out. To avoid Taltos we'll have to cut through the heart of the jungle. That'll take more time."

Caleb uttered what sounded like a muffled curse. "Okay but take the Seekers with you. Davelos probably would not mind if the jungle consumed you."

"I promise you that won't happen. See you at the lab. Out." She handed the radio to the team leader. "You're with us. We head north through the jungle."

He nodded and issued orders in Swahili to his men.

She turned to Ben. "It's getting dark. We need to get moving." She pointed left. "That way."

Lina sauntered to the tallest Seeker and ran her hand slowly down his arm. "Looks like you work out."

The man's brow furrowed.

Lina put her arm around his waist and rested her hand on his chest as she walked with him. "Oh my," she said in a breathless voice. "Tell me, what do you think about women who can—" She bit her lip and winked at Ben and Siene. "—shall we say, adjust to almost anything."

Siene and Ben laughed. It was a good moment's relief from the worry and danger.

After about ten minutes of silence, Ben touched her shoulder. "You look worried."

"I am," Siene replied. "We have to find the lab, secure it, and get it ready for the villagers to start bringing their sick." She bit down on her lower lip. "And Reed's gone." Her voice wavered. "I don't know if I can do this alone."

"You're not alone. I'm here. Besides, you're a warrior, blessed or cursed, depending on how you wish to look at it, to affect changes in the lives of people who are in the middle of a war with Taltos but don't even know they are in danger."

Siene nodded. She had had this kind of talk with her father many times and then, after he died, with Reed equally as many times. But now she was alone. Fatigue ate at her gut and worry took more out of her psyche than the physical exertion of the past few days.

She made a sweeping gesture. "Some say this is where the world began, Ben. Africa. Where humanity started and spread across the world. Maybe we all belong to Africa." She pressed her lips together and looked at him. "I don't want it to be my fault the world might also end here."

Ben slipped an arm around her shoulder. "The world isn't going to end any time soon. I won't let it. I'm here, and I have no intention of letting you do anything by yourself."

Siene placed her hand over Ben's. His hand felt solid. She looked into his eyes and, for the first time in a long time she felt safe.

Chapter Twenty-Four

Siene Dower, Primogen, Guardian of the Balance

The words echoed in her head as she broke through the jungle brush and headed for the building she saw in front of her. Vines climbed up the peeling concrete walls, and vegetation grew over the windows and nearly covered the entrance door.

She turned to Ben. "Is this where you worked for Davelos?" The words brought a seed of doubt back into her mind.

Ben took a step forward and tore some brush from the door. A metal plate revealed the name Hallinger etched into the corroding metal. "This is where I worked."

"For Davelos."

He exhaled through a compressed mouth. "I told you, if I worked for him, I didn't know it."

Siene raised her hands. "Just asking." She walked to the door and drove the push handle forward. It did not move. She angled her right shoulder and slammed it against the door with the same result.

Ben put a hand on her arm. "Let me try."

Her shoulder hurt. She wouldn't try again, nor would she let Ben know how foolish she felt with the failed attempt. She stepped back. "If there's a secret latch or something, you could have told me instead of watching me tear a deltoid."

"No secret lock. Just neglect." He pulled on the plant life covering most of the door then yanked on a thick root partially buried near the bottom until it snapped. The jolt sent him backward.

Siene steadied him before he landed on the ground. "Don't give up your day job for horticulture." She could tell by the look on his face he was not amused.

"Do you want to get inside or not?"

His tone confirmed her conclusion. She swept her hand in a wide arc. "By all means. But the door seems pretty solid so try not to break something being all macho."

"Don't need to be macho." He began pulling more brushwood and undergrowth from around the door. "Just a little gardening will do." After clearing around the frame, he placed a hand on the push bar and one in the center of the door and shoved. The door moved a little.

She signaled to the Seekers behind her. "Help him."

Two of the men positioned themselves against the doorway with Ben. After a few more thrusts, the door fell open.

Siene stepped forward and peered inside. With plant life growing over the windows, she couldn't see much. "Clear a small space in front of each window. We'll need the light, but don't take too much down," she cautioned. "This complex needs to continue to look abandoned for as long as possible. If any light glints from sun on the glass, it could show up in satellite pictures. We have satellites. Taltos has satellites. Davelos will be looking for us. No need to help him get here any sooner than he has to."

The lead Seeker nodded and issued orders to the others.

Siene started to enter the decaying lab, but Ben stopped her with a hand to her arm. "I worked here so let me go first."

She nodded and followed him inside. Not much light came inside through the vine-covered windows, but she could tell they had entered a holding area with what looked like space suits hanging from hooks on the wall. She walked to a window on the far wall and wiped grime from the glass with her palm. She could see a series of showers.

"Decom room." Her suspicion grew. "Serious stuff, Ben. What were you doing here?"

"I told you I thought I was going to save the world, but it didn't quite turn out that way." He grinned. "Maybe this is my second chance, though."

His laughter sounded forced. There was something he was leaving out. She made a mental note to find out what later. For now, however, they needed to find out if this lab was salvageable.

****

For three days Joseph had been waiting by the river for Lina, surviving on the meager rations he'd stolen from camp. Maybe she wasn't coming. Maybe she was dead.

He'd shed his Mosegi guise when he took the small piece of apple and ran from Davelos' men. He was not a very good actor and did not know enough about his grandfather and the village people to be convincing. He knew he could not keep up the ruse and help Lina without making a mistake and being exposed and killed, so reverting to his true identity seemed like the only way to try to survive. Maybe his education in medicine would help along the way.

He pulled the bit of apple from his pants pocket. It seemed benign enough. But his studies in science and medicine in college made him think there was more to this apple's make-up than just carbs and water. There was no refrigeration in caves or the camp, but this bit of apple had not browned. It looked market fresh with no change in color due to oxidation, meaning the phenolic content was possibly very low, blocking the browning. And if the phenolic content was low, so perhaps were the polyphenols in the apple's genetic composition. It was the polyphenols that had the health benefits, yet he could not help but notice the villagers' physical condition failed rapidly after being given water tainted with pieces of this unusual fruit.

He had planned to go into biomedical research after his residency, so he would love to find out more about this specific apple fragment and the theory Lina had about it. He'd wait a few more days. If she did not show up, he'd venture out into the jungle and try to find his way to a large village and ultimately out of the country. His instincts told him this morsel could be important.

****

Ben pointed to the back. "I'll check to see if the generator still works. If not, the trip here was futile. No electricity or running water this far into the jungle." He took two steps then stopped. "But even if the generator is still viable, I'm not sure any fuel left is."

"Don't worry about fuel. Caleb will take care of that. And be careful," Siene cautioned. "There could be booby traps set for trespassers."

"All the more reason for you to stay here and wait until I check the place," Ben said.

She watched the dimness engulf him as he walked away. *Stay here* was a set of instructions she didn't often follow, and there was no time to wait for much of anything. Lucian would come soon. She knew him well enough to know he never left loose ends. They had to both be done with any sample analysis that could be made, and either long gone or ready to fight.

The lab was dark. She could barely make out objects in front of her, so she put a hand on the back wall and followed it until she came to a doorway. Inside, she squinted through the darkness and could see a low workbench in the center of the room. She walked to it and could see a metal box nearly as big as the workbench set alongside the bench. She traced the top with her hand and found a latch. After unhooking the fastener, she opened the lid. The stench coming from inside hit her like a blow to the head. Her eyes watered and it took every ounce of control she had to not vomit. She slammed the lid back down and stepped back.

From what she could tell, it was some sort of chest freezer and, by the emanating smell of decomposition, obviously used to freeze tissue and blood samples. Once Ben got the lights on, if the samples inside were labeled, maybe she would find a clue as to what type of work he was doing in the African jungle away from civilization and way off the grid.

Lucian had given Ben a lab, freezers, a decontamination room, and lab equipment, but not through direct contact. She was cautious by nature but didn't have much time to decide if Ben was telling the truth when he said he had never met Lucian. She may be opening a can of worms if she pushed him, but she'd have to take that chance. Too many lives were at stake.

As she turned to walk back into the front area, she heard the roar of a generator. A minute later, the overhead lights flickered and then came on. She sprinted to the freezer. She took a deep breath, opened the lid, and pulled out a stained package. After laying it on the workbench, she read the label. *Male. African. 35 years old.* She carefully peeled back the paper confirming her suspicion. A blood sample.

"I see you found intake. I told you to stay put."

Ben's voice came from behind her. She turned and held up the package. "What were you testing the blood for?"

"Everything." He took the package from her and returned it to the chest. "You shouldn't be handling anything until we get this lab up and running." He turned and held her gaze. "The blood and everything inside that chest could be infected."

She glanced at the freezer and then to him. "That blood is not viable."

"Not now."

She felt a rush of adrenalin. "What were you supposed to do here, Ben?"

He shook his head. "I wasn't here long enough to do much of anything."

"For now, I have to believe that."

He arched an eyebrow at her. "I'm all you got, so that raises the tolerance bar, I assume."

She nodded. Her heart beat a little faster. For the first time since she became a Primogen, she hesitated in deciding. Could he sense her indecision? Damn, he better not be able to. She still had a lot of things to sort out.

"Tell me what we need to do," she said.

Ben turned in a small circle. "Get this space organized as best we can and set up what equipment we do have, then take inventory to determine what we can actually do here." He ran a forefinger through a layer of grime on the workbench. "It won't be sanitary, but we need to get as close to clean as we can, so we don't cross contaminate once the villagers arrive."

Siene felt her heart clench. "If they aren't already dead."

"Your Seekers will get there in time."

"I have to believe that. We've come so far already." She began gathering glass containers. "I'll clean these now that we have water."

"Returning this to a working lab is going to take time."

"We can have the men here help, and I'll radio Caleb and have him contact the Cleaners. If there are some in Africa, they'll know what to do."

Ben shook his head. "If we get out of this alive, you're going to have to tell me exactly what these Cleaners do among other things."

"You don't want to know." She wrinkled her brow. "And what other things?"

He held her gaze. "This thing you had with Davelos."

She looked away and quickly back. "Not now. Stay alive if you want to know." She saw his jaw clench.

"I guess I'll have to."

She reached around him, picked up a Petri dish from the workbench, and walked to a large sink on the back wall. The faucet sputtered out a rush of brown liquid when she twisted the cold-water faucet. In a few seconds, the brown color gave way to clear liquid. She thrust the small dish under the running water and rinsed the grime away with her hand. She turned and smiled. "Now let's crack this case wide open."

She worked quickly, wanting to make Ben think she was focused on the task at hand. Not letting anyone see that she was afraid was something she mastered, but trying not to let Ben know, no matter how this all ended, his life was never going to be the same was getting harder every day.

****

Lucian cursed. The sound of explosions could be heard over the static of the radio.

"It's done," Biden said.

"How much of the damn plastic explosive did you use?" Lucian demanded.

"Enough. The mine entrance is sealed."

There was no arguing that point. The echo of explosions screamed over the radio airways. "The detonations probably could be heard for miles. Get clear and make it fast. Use your GPS and meet me at the airstrip."

"We're hauling' ass," Biden advised. "Out."

After the transmission ended, Lucian slammed his hand onto the hood of the jeep in which he sat. Damn Biden. He'd been flown to Africa after the fiasco on the west coast. The raid on the Primogen compound had been a failure, taking the lives of ten of Taltos' best and highest-ranking mercenaries without producing anything more than what amounted to a bug bite on the ass of Primogen organization. The Primogens would move operations to another more secure location and not make the same mistakes twice. It would take months, more likely years, to find the new site. Lucian gritted his teeth and felt the vein in his neck begin to throb. Biden would pay for his disrespect. Later. When the mission was finished. For now, Biden was needed, but had moved to the expendable column.

A voice came from behind him. "Sir, I have news."

Lucian turned slowly. He saw two guards holding a village elder and a boy of about nine or ten.

"This man may know about the woman." The soldier forced the old man to his knees.

Lucian looked to the boy. "Who is he?"

"My father."

"Tell me about the woman," Lucian demanded.

Fear strained the old man's face though he tried not to show it when Lucian beckoned for the boy. The second guard threw the child next to his father.

Lucian walked to the boy and put a hand on his head. He turned to the boy's father. "Where is the woman?"

"You and your kind are an abomination," the man declared. His voice was hoarse with emotion. "I will not help you."

Lucian struck the old man in the face with the butt of his pistol.

The man cried out in pain and blood poured from his mouth.

The boy reached for his father but was stopped by one of the soldiers.

"You need some convincing, I see," Lucian said. He dropped his pistol and reached over his shoulder for the machete in the leather sheath across his back. He nodded to the soldiers who then separated father and son. The father's hand was pressed flat to the ground. Lucan freed the sword, and as he did, sunlight glinted along the blade's edge.

The boy's father looked up in time to see Lucian swing the machete. He barely had time to raise his hand and cry out. The blade sliced through the knuckles on his left hand dropping three of his fingers to the ground. He gripped what was left of his hand and writhed in pain.

The boy screamed and tried to get to his father, but Lucian backhanded him to the ground.

Grabbing one of the severed fingers, Lucian held it up to the terrified boy's face.

The boy turned his head and closed his eyes. He began to whimper.

A satisfied smile grew on Lucian's face. Fear. He relished fear. Once someone felt fear, it became a permanent scar. He slapped the boy's face. "Open your eyes or I will kill you and your father."

The boy slowly opened his eyes.

Lucian held the severed finger in from of the boy's eyes, smiling even broader as the boy shook. "I am Lucian Davelos. Tell everyone who did this to your father. Tell them if they know anything of the woman, they must tell me, or I will come and do this to everyone in the village. Do you understand?"

The boy nodded.

"Say my name."

"Lucian Davelos."

"Good. Tell all you talk to that they have five days before I come for them. During those five days I will not attack and will reward those who bring information. After the five days, if no one will help, I will come with fire and burn everything. Say you understand."

"I understand."

"Good. Then you and your father may live." Davelos nodded to the men. They yanked the boy and his father to their feet. "Now go before I change my mind." He watched the two disappear into the jungle. The man might not live to see morning, but the boy would make sure the message was heard.

At the sound of a roaring engine, Lucian picked up his pistol and stood waiting. Four men rode in an approaching jeep. Lucian relaxed. They had come from the nearest town.

"The supplies to rebuild the airstrip will be here in four days," a man with an eye patch reported.

"That's the soonest?"

He nodded. "The material must come in from Tabora."

Lucian waved the men away and processed the news. Four days for the materials and another four days to rebuild. A temporary setback. Nothing more. Confident the villagers would heed his warning, he'd use the time to plan his next move. His work in Tanzania might be over, but there were other opportunities to explore.

He gazed out at the remnants of the airstrip. In the distance, a plume of gray smoke signaled the camp was burning. Soon, nothing of any consequence that could point to him would remain.

But there was one loose end. Siene. She had obviously forgotten with whom she was dealing. He would take great pleasure in reminding her once he found her.

Chapter Twenty-Five

Siene sat at a table in the corner of the lab, slid her elbows on the countertop, and propped her chin in her hands. She went over the events of the last few days and wondered how she let things go so wrong. She thought about Reed and how much she would have to do in the organization without him. He was dead. He had to be. He would never go this long without some sort of contact. She wanted to grieve but knew that would get in the way of decisions she had to make.

She almost laughed out loud. Where did her humanity go? She'd changed so much over the years since she found out about the calling. Not just in the way of accepting her heritage, but also in her spirit. She was older but did not feel wiser. What she felt was tired.

She felt a hand on her shoulder and spun around. Ben. "Where have you been for the last hour or so?"

"Trying to get information on when we can expect some patients."

Siene sighed. "*If* we will get some. Lina Lucian was going to seal the mine with the villagers inside. I haven't heard from Caleb and the Seekers. They could all be dead by now."

"As the adage goes, no news is good news."

"I guess," she said as she saw Ben's eyes darken.

"Hey, you okay?"

"Yes," she said. But she wasn't. She wished she was still in the Primogen Compound where she was in control and Reed was still alive. She turned away from him.

"Your Cleaners did a hell of a job on the lab."

His voice made her pause and collect herself. "Is it functional now?"

"To a degree. It's dirt free, and with the equipment we have here, I can at least take blood samples, centrifuge the sera, and see what the microscope tells me."

"What else do you need?" Focusing on business helped her put her thoughts of Reed aside.

"I could use an autoclave, but I know that's not realistic here in the jungle. I'd settle for giving them a good cleaning and some time under a UV light."

"Will that be enough?"

"It will have to be. I found a bottle of alcohol in a back room, and I have enough laboratory experience to at least control any infection that might occur." He shrugged. "That is, if we get the chance to look into this mystery sickness the villagers have."

Siene nodded but there was something about Ben that made her uneasy. He was hiding something; she could feel it. But she really didn't want to find out on her own in the jungle that her faith in him was totally misplaced. "I'm going to try to reach Caleb on the shortwave. If the villagers are all dead, there's no sense staying here, waiting for Lucian to find us."

"Sure thing. You're the boss."

She walked away ignoring the smart comment. Since he was immersed in this chaos with the Primogens, Ben was changing, too. His skepticism had faded, and he had taken on an agnostic's perspective of caution. It bothered her. She still couldn't completely put him on one side or the other when it came to trust, and she didn't have the luxury of time to find out much more. Sooner or later, she'd have to either take a leap of faith or send him back to the States for the Council to decide.

She spotted one of the Seekers and waved him over.

"Do you need anything?" he asked.

"Could you tell me more about the trouble in this area?"

The Seeker glanced at Ben and then drew her farther away from him. "About six months ago is when the men in the villages began disappearing. I was told some of the elders tried to find the missing men, but they never returned."

"And no one wondered why?"

"Soon the remaining elders refused to speak to anyone who journeyed into their village."

"What do you mean they refused?"

"The elders would not allow the villagers to speak to anyone who came there. The village was then punished by overlords, and no trade happened between village communities. A foreigner gave these orders."

"Did you see this man? Was it Lucian Davelos?"

"No, but perhaps Caleb did."

Siene started to ask another question but saw Ben moving toward them. "Thank you," she said to the Seeker. "If we have to leave here, will someone be available as a guide?"

He nodded. "I can find you a group of men and a guide." Then he closed his eyes, put his hand on her forehead, and muttered some words.

Siene didn't know what he was saying but sensed he had blessed her.

From his neck he took a necklace made of stones and handed it to her. "Be careful in this journey. The way is not always straight and clear, but do not doubt the path."

She nodded.

Ben walked to her. "So, what's the plan?"

"We wait to hear from Caleb."

"I had that feeling," he said. "Why?"

"He's keeping a promise to the villagers. Saving lives is always important."

"This feels personal now."

"It is. I told you, this is my mission." She hoped he'd leave it at that because she didn't know if she understood herself the deeper reasons why she was still in Africa. Was it Reed? Lucian? She only knew the motivation involved being the one to right the past.

Ben moved closer to her. "I think there is more than just your heritage."

"Well, save your brainpower for science. I just like to do my job well." He was more perceptive than she wanted him to be. She motioned for him to walk with her back to the lab. "Tell me more about the strange blood you saw when you worked here."

"Darndest thing. Some of the cells seemed to pulse as though they were alive." He ducked under a low-lying branch. "Never saw anything like it. I would have loved to stay on and find out why."

"Why didn't you?"

"I'm not sure. One day I was documenting research, the next I was told I was no longer needed, escorted to an airstrip, and ushered out of Africa."

Somehow his explanation made her doubts deepen. She was tired of not getting answers from him, and this conversation wasn't helping.

"When we get back to the lab, I'm going to try to contact Caleb and get a status report on the villagers," she said after several minutes of silence. "When you worked for Lucian…"

"When I worked for a research institute," Ben corrected. "I was studying sleeping sickness, not involved in some sort of covert operation."

She ignored the adjustment. "When you were there, did you definitely rule out sleeping sickness?"

"Yes. Why all the questions?"

There was an expression in his eyes she'd only seen once or twice on someone this close to the Primogens: someone about to turn against them. Was he about to put glory above human lives? She knew her misgivings were tied to her past with Lucian. She would not let herself be fooled twice.

She stopped walking and crossed her arms over her chest before turning to him. "Because I must know, Ben. What we're doing here is much too important to worry about loose ends."

He stepped closer to her. "Is that what I am? A loose end?" He wiped his brow with the sleeve of his shirt. "I don't understand you. If I'm some sort of impediment to your great master plan, then why didn't you just let me get in that cab?"

There was something challenging in the way he crowded her. Man-woman challenging. It made her take a step back. She wasn't used to dealing with men who got in her face. She was usually all business. An ice queen in the field. This assignment was like none she had ever received, and it was making her crazy.

"That's not how we work," she finally said. "If we can help without calling too much attention, we do."

Ben nodded. "I guess a crazy woman making a scene at a cab stop in New York isn't all that unusual."

She snickered. "Good thing."

He was still so close to her that she could feel each breath he took as it brushed her face. He smelled of sweat and mint, and, once again, her feminine needs threatened to surface. She hadn't felt this way for a man in a long time. In fact, Lucian had been the last.

It had taken her a long time to get over him. Not because she had been pining away for him, but because she felt Lucian was the one man she could see a future with. He knew what she'd signed up for. The work, the dedication, similar outlooks on life, they meshed. And then there was the passion. At least right up to the time Lucian went rogue.

Ben stared at her, and she realized she was looking at his lips.

"Siene, you okay?" he asked.

"Yes. I'm fine."

He chuckled. "You look like you wanted…" He shook his head. "Never mind."

Shivers spread down her body from the warmth of his breath on her face. He was right about what he thought, though she would never let him know. Maybe it was the fact that he seemed mysterious because she didn't completely know him or maybe it was just some sort of animal magnetism from being in the African jungle. Whatever it was, each time she was alone with him for any length of time, he seemed to make her aware of needs she'd bottled up for too long now.

He had rattled her. She knew it, and he did too. But she'd held her own against hard-ass men her entire life, and though Ben wasn't quite in that category, it would take more than innuendo to get to her.

She straightened her back and stood taller. "What I want is to get that lab as ready as possible so you can show me just what kind of scientist you really are, and why Taltos would be better off if you were dead."

****

Joseph left the river after two more days and made it back to the village of his grandfather. His reunion was welcome, but the situation at the village was grim. Some of the men taken to the dig by Davelos had returned, but they were sick. Very sick. Disoriented and seemingly suffering from some sort of dementia. Joseph felt frustrated. His high-powered, expensive American education seemed worthless against the malady infecting them.

He stood in the doorway of his grandfather's crude cabin trying to draw on what he had learned to help these men. Dawn streaked the eastern sky with purples and reds. As the night disappeared, so did some of the anxiety that hung over him. He knew he might be putting the villagers at risk by returning, but he had nowhere else to go, and could not leave until he discovered the cause of the mysterious illness.

His anxiety grew as he watched a group of men emerge from the jungle and approached them. Most seemed dressed for war, wearing camouflage, and armed with guns. Two carried a litter upon which Joseph could tell lay a man. Beside the litter, a younger man walked.

Grandfather emerged and placed a hand on Joseph's shoulder. "Go back inside. I do not know these men."

"You shouldn't greet them alone. They could be coming for more of our people," Joseph said.

Grandfather shook his head. "There are no more to take. Only the elders, the sick, and women and children are left. Go inside. I will tend to this."

Joseph looked into his grandfather's eyes and saw strength of will. He would not dishonor his grandfather by rebuking him. He nodded. "I will watch from inside. If I am needed, I will be by your side."

Through a small window, Joseph watched his grandfather approach the small contingent. For a few minutes they exchanged words. His grandfather then turned and signaled for Joseph to join them.

"These men are descendants of the Masaai," Grandfather said. "They were on their way to the next village when they came across the man and boy." He gestured to the litter. "The man has a grave injury and may not live to see another morning. They ask for rest and food."

Joseph glanced over to the group. He did not recognize any of them as those who had worked the mine. "Can you trust them?"

Grandfather nodded. "The Masaai are a semi-nomadic people who were forced off their lands when, in the early 1900s, the British government wanted to create wildlife reserves. Since that time, they have moved from place to place until they were allowed to stay in the Ngorongoro Conservation Area. The tribe holds allegiance to no one, but makes trades and treaties as needed. They wish to make one now."

Looking for a reaction, Joseph watched the men carefully.

"The boy says they were forced to work at the camp of those who were mining the Tanzanite, but suddenly the camp was torn down and, in the confusion, they escaped before the mine was sealed. They were questioned about a man and woman who were also prisoners at the camp, and when they refused to cooperate, this man's fingers were cut off."

Joseph looked at the crudely bandaged hand of the man on the litter. The material wrapped around an obvious stump and was soaked with blood. He turned to his grandfather. "Maybe I can help." He started to approach the litter when the leader of the group stepped in front of him.

The leader stood immovable. "You are not from this village."

Joseph shook his head. His gaze remained on the injured man. "No." He turned his gaze to the leader. "But I know the wound needs to be cleaned or infection will come."

"How can you help?" the leader challenged.

Though he knew his identity would be compromised, without help, the man would probably die. Joseph held the leader's gaze. "I was not raised at this village. I am an American doctor visiting my grandfather. My name is Joseph." He saw skepticism rise on the man's face.

"Why were you not taken with the others?" the leader asked.

"I was. Grandfather warned me not to reveal my true calling, and I assumed the role of a native villager. After a while I was able to escape when I was assigned to help a woman who was being held captive by the man called Lucian."

"This woman. Was her name Siene?"

Joseph shook his head. "Lina."

The leader extended his hand. "I am Caleb. I know them both. They are my allies in a terrible fight." He signaled to his men who then holstered their weapons. "After you tend to the injured man, I have questions for you. But for now, tell me what you need."

Joseph turned to his grandfather. "The backpack I brought with me when I arrived here. Is it still hidden? I need the med kit. Depending on the wound, it may be enough."

Grandfather nodded and left to retrieve it.

Joseph pointed. "Take the man there and set the litter on the table inside. I'll get clean water to boil."

Caleb put a hand on Joseph's arm. "I know the man who did this. His name is Lucian Davelos. He doesn't care how many men die while he achieves his purpose. When you are through, you need to tell me everything you know and everything you've seen. Many lives will depend upon what you tell me."

Joseph looked in his eyes and saw the same strength of will he had seen in his grandfather's eyes, and in that instant, he knew he would do whatever he could to stop Lucian Davelos.

Chapter Twenty-Six

"Can you close the wounds?" Caleb watched Joseph push the edges of the gashes at the end of what was the elder man's middle and ring finger together.

"I think I can," Joseph said. "The edges meet perfectly. It was a clean slice. He will have some use of two of the fingers once healed."

Caleb stood behind Joseph, looking over his shoulder. "And the other?"

"Unfortunately, there is not enough of the small finger left to do much more than close the injury." Joseph used some of the hand sanitizer from the tactical trauma kit he brought with him. "If the wounds stay open and get infected, he will have to go to a hospital for treatment. I have some antibiotics in my bag, but not enough. To fully ensure the wounds will not fester, antibiotics need to be reapplied over the next few days."

The man reached out to Joseph. "No. No hospital. The evil one will find out someone has helped." His gaze shifted to his son. "I will not be the cause of more deaths." He attempted to move from the litter, but Joseph restrained him.

"It won't matter anyway," Caleb said. The hospital is hours away and there is no telling how long the wait will be once you get there."

Joseph looked from face to face and knew the man's life was in his hands here. "I need to clean the injuries before I try to close them, but with limited supplies, I don't know what will happen."

"As a boy," Caleb said, "My mother used goat weed. She put the sap on cuts and sores, and then lay on the leaves." He rolled up his shirt sleeve and showed Joseph a scar that reached from his elbow to nearly his wrist. "I was showing off to impress a young girl by exhibiting my prowess with a ceremonial spear and fell. Though the scar is disfiguring, the arm is fine." He rolled his sleeve down. "I saw some at the edge of the jungle."

Joseph nodded and watched Caleb leave to gather the plants. He dug a pair of scissors out of his trauma kit and cut several lengths of the Bleed-stop bandage he thought he would never have to use. He had a small bottle of sanitizer which he used to clean his hands and arms. It was the best he could do for now.

He turned to the boy. "What is your name?"

"Jawara."

"And your father's name?"

"Keyne. It means fighter."

Joseph hoped the man would live up to his name. "I will need your help, Jawara." He looked at the injured man. He lay on the litter, eyes closed. "I have no anesthetic. Closing the wound will hurt. I will need you to hold your father as still as possible."

Jawara swallowed hard. "Father is a warrior. Like his name."

Joseph put his hand on Jawara's shoulder. "Then you must hold him steady for additional strength. Can you do this for me?"

Jawara nodded and walked to his father's side.

Caleb returned with the plants and stripped the

leaves from the stems. Then, carefully breaking the stems into several smaller pieces, he pinched as much sap as he could get onto a section of gauze Joseph had laid out.

"Jawara," Joseph said. "Take your father's other hand and offer your strength." Then, he turned to Caleb. "Hold his shoulders as still as you can."

Caleb took a position behind the litter.

Working quickly, Joseph prepped the wounds, cleaning the wounds with the small alcohol squares he found inside his bag. Keyne's mouth was now in a tight line, and his chest rose and fell in time to the short puffs of air coming from his nostrils. The pain of the alcohol would be nothing compared to the pain of what would come.

"Now, Jawara. Squeeze his hand as tight as you can." Joseph nodded to Caleb who placed his hands on Keyne's shoulders.

Joseph used the curved needle in the trauma kit and quickly put twelve close-set stitches across the wound on Keyne's middle finger. Halfway through tending to the injury on the ring finger, he noticed Keyne's breathing had eased and suspected the man had mercifully passed out from the pain. After closing the injury, he turned his attention to the last wound. There would be no saving any part of the last finger, so he cut away most of what was left with the small scalpel he found in the kit and used the remaining nylon sutures to close the incision.

When he was finished, he washed away the blood and squeezed what he could out of the antibiotic ointment packet, trying to spread it over the areas he closed. With not enough to even cover much, he had no choice but to trust Caleb's rainforest remedy. He spread the goat weed sap over the closures and covered each with some of the leaves. Then he bandaged the hand.

Caleb walked to Joseph and put a hand on his shoulder. "It will work, Joseph. Have faith in the old ways." He walked to the door. "Rest for a few minutes. Then we need to talk about the woman."

****

Siene found Ben with a group of Seekers setting up a holding/quarantine area in a back room for the villagers should they even arrive. She pulled him aside. "How long are we going to wait for Caleb to bring some of the infected villagers before we go to Plan B?"

Ben set up the last cot near the back of the room. "I didn't know we had a Plan B."

"We have to find Lucian and stop whatever he is doing."

"We've been chasing him for weeks, and the only result we have is men dying."

He started to walk away but Siene grabbed his arm. "Ben, the enemy is here somewhere. If he isn't stopped, there will only be more deaths."

Ben put his hand over hers and looked into her eyes but said nothing. She did her best not to look as panicked as she felt. Unless the villagers got here soon, she would have no choice but to abandon the lab. Finding out what Lucian did to them would have to wait. She rubbed the back of her neck with her hand. The intensity of Ben's gaze was almost physical.

He confused her more than any man ever did. There was something hard to pin down about him. She knew he was hiding something, yet she found herself wanting to trust him. She needed him, yet she couldn't allow herself that luxury. Too many lives depended on her.

Momentarily overcome by everything that had happened in the last few weeks, she spun on her heel and walked away. She needed to regain her perspective and find the strength she knew was inside her. Her ex-lover was working against her, and she was mentally broken.

Betrayal was something she was not used to. If the artifacts became public, the result would be a hundred times worse than just dealing with Taltos. The rules would be meaningless then. The fact she worked with a group where everyone was working for the greater good didn't mean everyone was. She had trusted Lucian and he defected. In her mind, Ben was still a question mark, and she was uncertain about too many things.

But even if Ben had nothing to hide, she did. Life for him was never going to be the same after this. She'd always been able to move on after an assignment, but with Ben, she was not as certain, and it frightened her. With Reed gone, she would have to lead alone. She could not afford to let down her guard for any reason. It was important no one saw the chinks she knew were in her armor. She found a spot, checked for insects and snakes, and sat down in the middle of the jungle.

She heard footsteps and turned to see Ben standing there.

He didn't say anything.

"Have you heard from Caleb?" she asked.

He sat next to her. "Not yet. I'm just worried about you." He wrapped her in a hug.

"Don't," she said. "I'm fine. I can take care of myself." His shoulders were more muscular now.

Probably from the time spent away from the creature comforts he was used to. Momentarily distracted by the change, she barely heard his answer.

"I know you can, but I still worry."

"Why?"

"Because I care about you."

She closed her eyes and shook her head. "I can't do this right now, Ben. "I'm not sure I can believe those words anymore."

"Even when someone says they care?"

She thought about the past. "Especially when someone says they care."

"Are you thinking about Lucian?"

She didn't want to admit it. She felt vulnerable when she thought about Lucian and didn't want Ben to know. Vulnerability equaled weakness, and she was determined he'd never see her as weak. But Ben wouldn't let her resist. He pulled her tighter to him in an embrace that left no doubt of his strength. She didn't need strength. She needed emotional energy.

He tilted his head back and loosened his hold. His hands moved up her back. His forefinger caressed the back of her neck and every nerve ending in her body came alive. A part of her knew that anything she did now would not be the wisest course of action, but she was tired. Tired of being a Primogen. Tired of waiting for elusive answers. Tired of wanting to be normal when normal was right in front of her. She was not a superhero. She was human with human needs and wants.

If this assignment went as the others did, Ben wouldn't remember her. He wouldn't remember much of anything. She'd return him to the taxi line in New

York City where she found him. He would have lost some time, but eventually he'd stop trying to find out why. They all did. She made her choice and prayed she would not regret it later.

She tangled her fingers in his hair. "I didn't realize you were thinking about me." She nibbled his jaw and traced a path to his lips until her mouth met his.

"Are you toying with me?" he asked.

"There's no time for that."

She didn't stop to think. Too much had happened in the last few days, and she needed to just let go. So she did, letting her instincts take over.

Each kiss pulled her deeper into the abyss that had beckoned to her since their time in the compound. Doubt and desire combined in a dangerous mix, leaving no room for anything else but surrender. His touch was butterfly light as his hands slipped beneath her shirt, and he kept it that way as he caressed her breasts.

"Are we going to do this in the jungle?" she whispered into his ear.

He smiled against her cheek. "Too late to stop now."

She looked at the ground and grinned. "Then I get the top."

He pulled her down with him, and she straddled his hips. Her core rested on his pelvis, and she could feel his erection through the fabric of his pants. The ground was hard, and a root dug into her knees, but his mouth on hers and his hands on her body blurred the pain.

She shivered as he caressed her breasts. Her entire body was on fire. She writhed against him, trying to find some relief from the ache that grew more intense with each brush of his hands. She looked into his eyes, and she knew she was about to lose something to him that she hadn't been ready to give. But it was too late now.

Reaching between their bodies, she unfastened his pants. When he arched, she shoved them out of the way as much as she could and freed him. She encircled him with her hand and fumbled with her pants with the other. Pulling them down as much as she could, she forced the fabric out of her way and eased him toward her center. She was wet and willing, and he slid into her easily. Bracing her hands on his shoulders, she looked into his eyes as she took him inside her body.

Their position was awkward, but it worked. He gripped her hips and held her as they thrust together. There was not one part of her body he did not reach with each movement. Her body tightened around him as she felt the first tingles of orgasm build. She cried his name as she came and felt the moist heat inside her as he followed.

He fell backward on the ground and pulled her on top of him. She lay there, knees sore and raw from the roots. Her breath came in short gasps as though she had been running, and her heart was beating so hard she was sure he could hear it.

He rubbed his hands up and down her back now that their passion was depleted. Surprisingly, she didn't feel regret. She needed what he offered but knew she could not allow her personal needs to change anything. She shifted and got to her feet. Turning her back, she tugged her shirt down and pulled up her pants. She had no idea what to say.

"Don't put back the barriers, Siene."

She heard his footsteps and felt his body heat for a

second before he put his hand on her shoulder.

"It's too late for that," he said.

She shook her head. The man-woman thing was the one place she was not sure of herself. She could handle a life and death situation. Give her a mystery to solve. Those she could handle. But this…she was lousy at relationships, and she doubted that would change anytime soon.

"I wasn't expecting this either," he said. "We can figure it out later."

"Much later," she said, taking a few steps away from him. "After this operation is over."

She turned around so he wouldn't think he had affected her. Big mistake. He'd hiked up his pants but not fastened the zipper yet. The triangle of flesh leading from his waist downward drew her attention. She watched him shrug his shirt over his shoulders. He didn't bother to button it. A distraction she did not need.

But none of that mattered when she realized his scent still lingered on her skin. She ran her tongue across her lips and could taste him on her lips and tongue. Despite everything she tried to rationalize, she longed for his touch for just a few minutes more.

And that's what started to bother her the most. After Lucian left, she decided that men were temporary. She could not risk the mission by changing that now. She stalked past him, stopping abruptly when she heard rustling coming from the jungle. The approaching footsteps were quickly followed by the jungle brushwood parting.

With forearms crossed in front of her face, Lina broke through the growth like a missile with a purpose.

"Lord, I hate this place." She brushed leaves from her shirt. "There better not be any critters on me." She looked up for the first time since she had entered the small clearing. Her gaze went from Siene to Ben. She watched him zip up before returning her gaze to Siene and pointing. "You got something in your hair."

Siene reached up and pulled out a huge bug with large, pincer-like spiny claws.

Lina recoiled and made a choking sound. "Disgusting. Were you two rolling around naked? Hope it didn't bite anything important." She walked to Ben and tucked her hands under each side of his still unbuttoned shirt. "I'd help you check more places, but you already zipped."

Ben grasped her wrists and removed them from his chest. "Thanks for offering, but I'm fine." He buttoned as quickly as he could. "I remember seeing that bug the last time I was here. It's called a Tailless Whipscorpion, and it is harmless. No venom."

Siene folded her arms across her chest. "So, in addition to your spit project, you studied African bugs while you worked for Lucian?" She forced a smile. "How convenient."

Lina frowned. "Did I miss something?" She looked at Siene and pointed to Ben. "He worked for Taltos?"

"No!" Ben and Siene said in loud unison.

Lina widened her eyes, and her mouth formed a perfect 'O'. "Okay then." She stepped back and raised her hands in a defensive posture.

Siene walked to her. "You were obviously looking for me, otherwise you wouldn't be out in the jungle. Did you hear from Caleb?"

"Yes. A few minutes ago. He said Seekers had left

with some infected villagers and they would arrive in a few hours. He'd join you in the morning."

"Why didn't he leave with them?" Siene asked.

"He said he had something to do."

Siene nodded. She never questioned Caleb during a mission, especially on his home continent. "Did he say how many were coming?"

Lina shook her head. "No."

"Then we better get back to the lab and make sure we are ready. We won't have much time once they arrive. If someone notices the activity here, we could be confronted by mercenaries, the Tanzanian government, or Lucian."

Lina began walking back to the building. "I'd rather take my chances with the mercenaries or the government. Lucian is going to be pissed. We did kinda destroy his airstrip."

Chapter Twenty-six

Joseph stepped out of his grandfather's cabin and saw Caleb by the fire. He glanced up as Joseph got closer.

"Join me please," Caleb said, motioning to him. He broke off a piece of the meat he was cooking and handed it to Joseph.

"You're leaving in the morning?" Joseph asked.

Caleb nodded. "At first light. But before, I need you to tell me about the camp."

"I wasn't at camp much. Mostly I worked the mines alongside the other villagers."

"You never tried to leave and get help?"

Joseph hesitated. "I can't explain why, but I couldn't." He placed his hands on his head. "My mind said to go, but my body wouldn't respond."

Caleb held his gaze. "You feared something inside you."

"There's nothing inside me that I fear. I know myself too well for that." Joseph looked off to the right then back. "I could not make my body move other than what I was told to do. As a doctor, I was lost. I could not begin to help if I could not understand what was happening."

It was embarrassing to try to explain. He was a man of science and education, yet at that time, his body did not respond to reality. Though he was open to other possible explanations, he didn't want to think that he lacked the ability to think with a logical and controlled mind.

He tried to get up, but Caleb held him fast with an iron grip on his arm. "Look at me." He put his hands on Joseph's face, caging his head with the hold. "You are stronger than you think, and you can help."

Joseph stared into Caleb's ebony eyes and saw something he could not define. Caleb looked so confident and in control despite all that had happened. It made him realize how inconsequential he could be in the chasm of time and space if he chose to believe he could do nothing. His concern for his own well-being was trivial as compared to what was happening here and now.

"Tell me," Caleb said. "Lives may depend upon what you say."

"They were a private army," Joseph said. "Not like the local warlords."

"No, they are Taltos," Caleb corrected. "Much worse. They are led by an evil man who uses hired militia to do the dirty work. These men care nothing about life. They only care about money."

Joseph nodded. "They controlled us by rationing food and water." He looked off to the side and then back. "The food was meager, but the water plentiful." He drew down his eyebrows. "Now that I can think clearly, it must have been the water. Now I remember that after drinking it, all reason faded. I saw only in shades of gray and was afraid. The soldiers took care of us. We needed them to live. We did not dare leave the mines."

"If that were true, how did you escape?"

"One day I missed the water ration. After a while, I could see clearly and felt my strength begin to return. I did not drink the water again."

"How did you survive? The jungle is hot, and the mines hotter."

"At night, the soldiers liked to drink and play cards. The more they played, the more they drank. Once they fell asleep, I stole water from their canteens. In the morning, I acted like the others in the trance."

"How long did it take to feel normal?"

"A few days."

"And how long were you there?"

"I don't know. I had no concept of time once I was overcome."

Joseph sat quietly as Caleb appeared to mull over the information presented. Working the mine and seeing the foul conditions under which he was forced to work gave him a thousand reasons not to trust anyone. But he didn't have a choice. He had to trust Caleb.

He took a deep breath and let it out. "Do you believe me?"

Caleb held his gaze for a long while. "Neither of us has much of a choice if we want to stay alive, do we?"

Joseph shook his head. "So, then we can agree there was something in the water helping those you call Taltos control the villagers."

"For now," Caleb answered. "Tell me about Lina. How did you come to work for her?"

"One of the soldiers from camp came to the mine and said he needed someone to work at base camp. I was one of the smallest, so I was chosen. I was told to do whatever the woman wanted, or I'd go back to the mines."

"And none of the soldiers cared about you leaving the mine and not drinking the water you say was tainted?"

"I was told if I tried to escape, I would be shot." Images of what could have happened flashed through Joseph's mind. "Or if I did leave, the big cats would have surely finished me. I had no choice but to stay and work."

"For Lina."

"Yes. She saved my life. I'd do anything for her." He saw Caleb's eyes widen as though his thoughts had solidified.

Caleb slapped his thigh. "That's my girl." His smile widened. "You told her about the water, and she asked you to get some for her."

Joseph nodded.

"Do you still have it here somewhere?"

"I didn't get the water, but..." He stopped. How much should he tell Caleb? Should he reveal what he did get? What appeared to be a small bite of a unique apple piece might be the only bargaining chip he had.

"What did you get?"

Joseph's hands clenched into fists, and he could feel his muscles jumping beneath his skin. Bleary-eyed and exhausted, he was weary of his predicament. What he would do next would end it one way or another.

"I have to show you."

****

Siene hesitated at the door of the room at the back of the lab. The affected villagers, escorted by Seekers, began arriving about an hour earlier. She heard the labored sound of their breathing through the lightweight door. Ben and Lina had gone to check on the lab, and she wished for a moment she didn't feel so alone without Reed. Reed would know what to do. He always did. But now he was gone. It was all up to her to find a solution.

She stepped forward and pushed the door open. The room was shadowy in the late afternoon. The dense jungle let through dappled sunlight, but none streamed through the windows. They were covered with fabric so the activity inside would not be easily noticed. The room was hot, and she could scarcely breathe. But the precautions were necessary.

The villagers the Seekers brought to the lab seemed not to notice her. They lay in makeshift beds either sleeping or staring at the ceiling. The floorboards creaked with each step she took, but none moved. She reached out and took the hand of the nearest man. His skin was warm to the touch but not hot. His eyes were closed and the skin around them sunken and sallow. She did not know if what affected him was airborne, so she went no closer. With no knowledge of the malady affecting them nor how they were infected, this mystery was going to be difficult to solve and they were running out of time. She turned and left the room.

She met Ben in the lab. The refrigerator was old and noisy. It was dusty from disuse, but was apparently working, as was the centrifuge that was spinning in the corner.

"How are the villagers?" Ben asked as she walked in.

He was bent over a microscope checking out a slide. His hair had gotten so long he'd tied it at the back of his neck. He looked rugged, sexy—like a modern-day adventure hero.

"Not great." She sighed. "I don't know how to help them."

"Neither do I—just yet." He looked back into the microscope. "I drew blood from some of them." He looked up. "Come look."

Siene walked to the counter and gripped the barrel of the eyepiece with two fingers before leaning down and setting her eye on the ocular lens. What she saw stunned her into silence for a few moments. She looked up at Ben. "Is this the same iridescence you saw before?"

He nodded. "I took blood samples from a few of the men and what is even stranger is that the irradiated cells range in size and number."

"Meaning?"

He shrugged. "Meaning I have no idea what I am dealing with."

Siene looked around. "Can this lab handle research?"

"I'm not sure. I don't think what we are seeing is a virus, and I don't know how whatever we do have will spread if at all." Ben pushed a small notebook toward the edge of the counter. "But I found this."

She looked over his shoulder and saw a combination of numbers and letters scrawled on paper. "Looks like code."

"No, it's sort of like shorthand for science," Ben said. 'Not exactly like what I'm used to using, but close. I think I can decipher most of it." He began to flip through the pages. "There may be something in here we can use to save time."

The change in his body language told her he was going into work mode. She put her hand on his shoulder. He did not look up. "I'm going to check in with Lina. Maybe she can remember something about the camp that can help."

"Sounds good," Ben replied. "I'll be here if you need me."

She left quietly. Outside she took a few minutes to review what she knew, which she decided amounted to next to nothing. She had villagers in a zombie-like state, glowing blood cells, a missing and possibly dead brother, and a madman trying to kill her. What she didn't have was why.

But she was Primogen. She gave up a normal life to protect humanity and keep safe the secrets that could destroy everything. The fact she'd been able to do so for most of her adult life made her confident she could do it again. Somehow, some way she'd find the answers she needed to make sense of things and return the balance.

But despite all the obstacles she faced and overcame over the years, she knew this one would be the hardest.

****

Joseph returned holding a small bundle clutched tightly in his right hand and stood right in front of Caleb.

Caleb looked up but said nothing.

"I didn't get a water sample, but I believe I got something more."

"Show me." Caleb said.

Joseph sat beside him and began to unwrap the packet. "I think it's a small piece of apple, but I can't be sure. The properties are extraordinary. It should be dead and shriveled, yet it looks fresh." He held it out.

"Remarkable." He saw Caleb's face change as soon as he saw the small bit. "You know what it is, don't you?"

Caleb took the scrap and placed it in his palm. "It is part of an apple. A very special apple."

"Genetically modified?"

"In a manner of speaking," Caleb replied.

"If the make-up of this apple has been altered to allow it to stay fresh, imagine what the process can do to help feed the world." Joseph held out his hand. "We must take this to the scientific community."

Caleb shook his head. "No, my friend." His fingers closed around the apple bite. "Too many already know about this extraordinary artifact."

Joseph drew down his brows. He was not sure he heard correctly. "Artifact?"

"Yes, and one that might just explain why Taltos is here in Africa." Caleb rose and placed a hand on Joseph's shoulder. "Come. We must get some rest. We have a long journey ahead of us, and we need to leave at dawn."

Joseph's thoughts froze. He had no plans to leave with Caleb. "No," he said. "I'm not going anywhere until I have more answers."

"I am oath-bound not to reveal too much to ordinaries. The answers you seek will be found where we are going," Caleb replied. "But by knowing, your life will never be the same."

To Joseph, Caleb's words were more like a riddle than an explanation. His lack of understanding swirled inside him. He was an educated man, a man of medicine and science, yet nothing he experienced over the past few weeks fit into either philosophy or made any sense. He had to know.

"I will go with you," he said. He held out his hand. "But first, give back what you have called an artifact."

Caleb shook his head and gripped the packet tighter. "This does not belong to you. This object belongs to the ages, and I am one of seven honor-bound to protect it."

"How do I know you will not leave in the middle of the night without me?"

"Because I give you my word, and you are also now connected to the seven. I did not witness what you saw in the mines. You will need to tell your story. It may be the only way to stop what is happening here."

Mentally running through everything he knew about the situation, Joseph realized he had little choice. "And there I will find the truth about the mine and the villagers, and the reason they were kept sick to mine the tanzanite in secret?"

"The truth will alter your life path. I hope you can accept what must be." Caleb held Joseph's gaze for a few moments, then walked away.

As Caleb left, apprehension filled Joseph's core, almost changing his mind. But Caleb still had the small bit of apple, and Joseph needed answers. He hoped his trust was not misplaced. He wanted to find out more about the bit of apple, its remarkable durability properties, and why Caleb called it an artifact.

And nothing, not even his own doubts and fears, was going to stand in his way.

Chapter Twenty-Seven

Siene found Lina in the small room off the lab. She was checking the vitals of a group of ten villagers whom Ben had decided were the most seriously affected. Each man had a number attached to his clothing.

Lina glanced up when she heard the door open. "I hope you're here to help. This nursing stuff isn't for me." She handed Siene a blood pressure cuff that looked like it was well past its expiration date, and a stethoscope that didn't look much better. "I'm sure I'm screwing this up. You pump. I'll write."

"After we're done here, I need to talk to you." Siene attached the cuff to the closest man.

"About what?"

"Lucian's camp. I can't quite connect the dots. Maybe you saw something or heard something that could help."

Lina nodded. "Okay, but outside. The smell in here is making me sick."

****

Seated in a jeep with the top down, Lucian waited outside the small town of Arnasic, at an abandoned warehouse and watched a train roll toward a rundown railway station. The building was outside the town's border and was not patrolled by any guards. Outside the town's limits, this part of the country was hostile and dangerous. With his night vision binoculars, he caught glimpses of a man and a woman waiting.

The train was bringing reinforcements. There were still plenty of village warriors he could use, but they were ill-equipped tribesmen. The men coming were trained mercenaries who could track Siene and kill the American and any Primogen trying to protect him.

Gazing through the binoculars, Lucian saw one of his trucks approach. The flame thrower mounted in the back became a ground comet as it spewed red onto the ground. The man and woman waiting began to run as bullets ripped the ground behind them. With the fire turning the night vision into pure white, Lucian could not tell if the man and woman escaped.

"Pity," he said. "Collateral damage." He wanted no witnesses anyway.

"All right," Lucian shouted. "Call them off."

The band of mercenaries on the train would reinforce the small army he had looking for Siene and the doctor. They couldn't hide forever. It was only a matter of time before he found them. When he did, and the doctor was back in his grasp, Ben Michaels would die a very slow, painful death; one that Siene would remember for years.

More satisfying than that, he would have her back, and this time he would not let her go.

****

Once done with taking the villagers' vitals and recording them for Ben, Siene could finally talk to Lina about the camp. They sat outside the lab on the trunk of a fallen tree that Lina covered with two lab coats she found in one of the lockers.

Lina poked at the ground with the tip of her shoe.

"If something crawls up from the ground and bites my ass, I'm outta here. So, make it fast. What do you want to know?"

Siene needed to know anything and everything about the time Lina spent with Lucian, but she'd done enough interrogations to know you can't bombard a person with questions. She'd start slow. "Tell me about the camp."

Lina shrugged. "It was a camp. Dirty, hot, a lot of guards and not much to do."

"There has to be more. Think."

Lina blew out a long breath of air. "Lucian didn't let me see much. He kept feeding me some of Alice's mushroom to keep me large-sized. I couldn't even miniaturize to sneak around."

Siene wondered how Lucian got his hands on that artifact and made a mental note to check the inventory once she got back to the States. For a moment she wondered if anything else was missing, and if there could be a double agent immersed among the Primogens. But that inquiry would have to wait. She couldn't do much from Africa.

"I can't believe you went along with that," Siene said. "I know you better. Keep talking. You saw something. We just have to dig through your memories and bring it to the surface."

Lina handed her a cup of water. "I *am* two hundred years old give or take. "She tapped her temple with a forefinger. "There's a lot of crap in here."

Siene set the cup on the ground. "Let's start with what you did all day."

"Besides try to think of some way to get out of there? I wandered around, trying to find a way to

314

escape."

Siene smiled. "And in doing so, I'm sure you scrutinized every bit of the place."

"I did but there was no way out. If someone wasn't following me to make sure I behaved, I was confined to my tent. Once in a while the guards slipped up and I could wander off for a bit, but I wasn't about to sneak out in the middle of the night and become lion food trying to escape, so I made it my life's work to annoy Lucian every day. I was so good at it that one day he brought me one of the miners to keep me company. He was a teenager. No more than fifteen or sixteen."

Siene nodded. "Now we're getting somewhere. That boy could have seen something useful down in the mines. Was he in a trance like the rest?"

Lina wrinkled her brow. "I never gave it much thought at the time, but no. I was just happy to have someone who wasn't glued to a radio or monitor to talk to."

"Did you talk about the mine?"

"We did."

"What did he tell you?"

"Nothing all that exciting." She shrugged. "They dug, and ate, and dug, and slept. Then in the morning they got up and drank some water." Her eyes widened. "That's how the son of a bitch did it. Stupid, stupid, stupid." Lina smacked her forehead with her palm between words. "I kinda forgot to mention it. The water! Mosegi said he thought there was something in the water."

"Something like what?"

"He wasn't sure."

Siene rose and started to pace. "That makes a little

sense, but a sedative or even a small dose of propofol would wear off. The villagers we examined were more zombie-like than sedated."

Lina joined her. "Plus, they weren't out cold. They followed orders and could work."

"So it wasn't any drug we know."

"However, it was something."

"But what?"

Lina shook her head. "Mosegi was going to go back and get some of the water, and one of the younger miners told me to meet him by the river, but I never saw him again."

Siene stopped pacing. "Seems like we are no closer to an answer than we were before we got here."

"Guess not."

"All we know is we have a bunch of villagers with weird blood who can't seem to fully wake up." Siene began to pace again. "Plus, Lucian is trying to kill Ben, and I don't know why.

"I think he's trying to kill you, too," Lina added.

Siene pressed her lips together in a grimace. "Thanks for the reminder." She pointed at Lina. "And I don't think he's very fond of you right now either."

Lina nodded. "Okay, so I'm on the list. Instead of talking about what we don't know, how about concentrating on what we do know."

"Couldn't hurt." Siene walked back to the tree trunk and sat. "Besides wanting us dead, we know Lucian was mining tanzanite and to do that, he somehow drugged locals to use as miners. We now know he put something in the water to control them."

"We don't know much."

"Not yet, but we will."

"How? The mine is gone. Lucian's gone. Mosegi's gone. We have nothing but…"

Siene held up a hand to stop Lina from talking. "We have Ben, and I believe it's no coincidence Lucian tried to kill Ben at the same time he started his mining operation. There's a connection. I just have to connect the dots."

****

"We found them."

Biden's voice crackled over the radio lying on the passenger seat of the jeep. Lucian jammed on the brakes, the radio sliding onto the floor. He cursed and reached for it. "Where?"

"At the lab you set up a year or so ago. It looks like they've been there for a few days."

Anger clawed at Lucian's stomach. By diverting to pick up the mercenaries, he wasted three days.

Biden's voice broke his thoughts. "Want me to off them?"

"No! Do nothing. Hold your position and do surveillance until I get there. Nothing else. This is my kill." He thought he heard Biden laugh.

"Him or her?"

Tightness grew in Lucian's chest. He didn't have an answer. "You worry about your job. I'll do mine." This time Biden's laugh was unmistakable.

"She's gotten into your head. She played you and now you…"

Lucian curled his right hand into a fist. "Finish that sentence and, when I get there, I'll break your damn jaw."

"Getting soft, are we? There was a time you'd just kill me."

Lucian started to respond but the transmission was cut. He took a silver flask from the glove compartment of the jeep and emptied it in a few gulps. Max Biden was getting much too independent and cocky. Lucian had permanently ended more than a few partnerships that were made of out usefulness rather than a shared belief like the one he made with Biden. The thought he needed Biden for now sent a fresh river of bile into his stomach. Biden was right about one thing, however. Siene had gotten back into his head. To succeed, he just may have to kill her.

And as for Biden, if he became too much of a problem, it would be just as easy to bury him in the jungle along with Siene and Ben Michaels.

Chapter Twenty-Eight

Ben's back was to the door when Siene and Lina entered the lab. He turned when he heard the door open. "I hope you brought some breakfast. I'm starving."

"Been here all night?" Siene asked.

He nodded.

Lina walked to him and put her hands on his shoulders before studying him as though she was trying to read something in his eyes. "You look like hell."

He glanced at his image in the glass window separating the lab from a small office. "Hair's a bit long, I guess."

"That part looks good. Not so much corporate mogul anymore. More action adventurer now." She winked and walked to a chair. "But unless you suddenly discover how to control that thing you have growing from your chin, it's a B-movie action figure."

"You mean my beard?"

"If that's what you call it." Lina snickered. "Looks to me like a first try attempt by a pubescent teenager."

Ben looked back at his reflection in the glass. "I kinda like it. Makes me look rugged."

"You can try some hair growth stuff later if we get out of this, but for now, you need a shave." She sniffed the air. "Perhaps a bath, too."

Ben waved her off and returned his attention to the slides he had clipped to the microscope's stage. "No time. I've been studying the blood samples all night."

Siene leaned her backside against the metal counter. "Find anything useful?"

Ben shook his head. "Afraid not."

"Well, we may have something." Siene lifted her chin. "Tell him, Lina."

Lina nodded. "At the camp, Lucian made one of the young miners my personal butler."

Ben didn't bother to look up. "And?" He fiddled with the lens.

"And we got to talking about the miners," Lina said.

With his eyes still resting on the double eyepiece, he adjusted the focus wheels. He motioned to Siene. "Look at this." He moved backward and let her look at the slides.

"What am I looking at?" Siene asked.

"Two days and the red blood cells are still luminous. With the substandard conditions here, these samples should be degraded and therefore useless, but they look as though the blood was freshly drawn." He shook his head. "That defies all science."

Siene focused on the slide. "How long would it take to find out why?"

"More time than I think we have here," Ben replied.

"It's the only clue we have to what Lucian did to the villagers." Siene glanced up at Ben. "We have to try."

"I've been trying since the blood was drawn," Ben said. He sighed. "I have nothing."

Lina waggled her fingers. "Hello. I'm still here."

"How can that be?" Siene asked Ben. "You told me

you work on rare diseases." She drew away from the microscope. "I would say this one qualifies."

Ben frowned. "What I've seen isn't normal."

"A genetic mutation?" Siene returned her attention to the slides.

"Maybe. But trying to narrow something like that to a specific gene takes years." Ben pulled in and then slowly released a deep breath. "Maybe even decades."

"We don't have decades." Siene's breath caught as a morbid realization washed over her. "And neither do the villagers. You say you have never seen blood samples like the ones we just looked at, so there is also no way to determine the effect the altered blood will have on the men."

"Agreed," Ben said. "I just don't know."

Lina stood and shoved her hands onto her hips. She blew out a long breath of air. "Are you going to listen to me or not?"

Siene looked up from the microscope. "Sorry." She looked at Ben. "You really need to listen to her."

Ben seemed to debate for a second and then leaned against the wall. "What do you have?"

"What I have," Lina said with a touch of sarcasm in her tone, "is how Lucian got whatever it is you are looking at into the bloodstream." She stopped, drew her mouth into a tight line and waited.

After a few long moments, Ben raised his eyebrows. "Are you going to tell me, or do I have to guess."

Lina crossed her arms in front of her. "Do I have your attention now?"

"Yes," Ben said.

"Your *full* attention?"

Ben tilted his head to the ceiling and let out a heavy sigh. "Yes." He watched as Lina walked back to the chair and settled in with exaggerated casualness.

Lina slowly crossed her legs and then checked her fingernails.

Ben opened his mouth to say something, but Siene warned him off with a raised hand. "Tell him, Lina," Siene said.

Lina smiled. "Lucian put something in the water."

****

Lucian's radio squawked for attention. He grabbed it from the dashboard of his jeep and answered. It was Biden. "What have you got for me?"

"In about a minute, a courier should be handing you a flash drive."

Biden's words were barely spoken when Lucian saw a small ATV approach. The men around him sprang into protection mode, and soon the driver's shirt had a dozen red lights clustering the pocket on his left side.

"Relax," Lucian called out. "Biden sent him." He motioned the driver to approach. "But escort him just in case."

With their guns at ready, two gunmen took a position on either side of the driver and walked him to within three feet of Lucian's jeep.

"That's close enough," Lucian said. "I believe you have something for me."

The driver started to reach inside his shirt pocket. As he did, his escorts took aim. The driver raised both hands and stopped moving.

Lucian pointed. "You. Check the pocket."

The selected gunman looped the strap of his AK-47

assault rifle over his head and onto his shoulder before gripping the driver's shirt pocket and ripping it open. He retrieved a USB flash drive and handed it to Lucian.

"Make sure our friend gets safely back to his village," Lucian said.

The gunmen nodded and grabbed the driver by his upper arms.

The radio was still active, and Lucian could hear Biden laugh as the driver was led away. A second later, the sound of automatic gunfire could be heard in the distance.

Biden's voice crackled over the airwaves. "Poor bastard."

Lucian scooped up the radio. "Can't have any witnesses," he confirmed.

"What are you going to do with his ATV?" Biden asked.

"Hadn't thought about it."

"Then save it for me."

Lucian laughed. "Ever the practical man." He held the flash drive with his index finger and thumb. "What's on the drive?"

"Aerial pictures of the lab where your girlfriend and the doctor are probably busy working on finding a cure for your zombie potion, plus some satellite pictures of the area."

Lucian's response was instantaneous. "She's not my girlfriend." Venom laced his voice.

"Right. I forgot. She and the doctor are cozy now."

Lucian curled his left hand into a fist and silently vowed to cut out Biden's vocal cords as soon as this mission was over. For now, he needed the gutter snake. "How long have they been there?"

"A few days."

"How many are with them?"

"Let's see," Biden said with focused disrespect in his voice, "there's those two, Lina…" He stopped and waited for Lucian's reaction.

"I'll kill her, too," Lucian growled. "Along with those who were supposed to watch her."

"My, my, you are having a bad day," Biden said.

Lucian suspected Biden was purposely baiting him. He refused to give that parasite a reaction. Besides, he still needed more information from Biden. He couldn't begin to exact his revenge on the Primogens until he got to Siene and the doctor, so he controlled his anger by sheer force of will. "How many others are with them?"

"A few Primogen Watchers and Seekers. Maybe six or so in total. Nothing I can't handle. The jungle around the lab is thick, so it will be easy to get close unnoticed. I have some men watching the lab and reporting back every two hours. I'll join them late tonight."

"Don't do anything until I get there," Lucian ordered. "I have a few scores to settle." He sneered. "If you would have taken care of the doctor in New York, I wouldn't have to clean up your mess."

"Don't worry. I'd rather watch anyway."

As the radio went dead, Lucian cursed. He shoved the flash drive into the USB port on the laptop on the passenger seat of the jeep. He scanned the first few shots. Biden was right. The jungle growth would give him and his men good cover. With the element of surprise on his side, the next time he saw Siene, it would be through the front sight on his AK-47.

****

Ben glared at Lina. "You couldn't have said something sooner?"

Lina threw her hands in the air. "I didn't think it mattered much. I told you, Mosegi was supposed to get some of the water for me, but we never reconnected."

His shoulders dropped. "Maybe I could have found a clue in that water."

"Do you think he possibly got a sample of the water and just couldn't get to you?" Siene asked.

She gave a half-hearted shrug. "Hell, knowing Lucian, the poor kid's probably dead like Reed."

Siene's head snapped up and she gasped. "We don't know that Reed is dead!"

"Then why haven't we heard from him?" Lina challenged.

Siene did not answer.

"Besides," Lina continued. "You know the drill. If an asset doesn't make contact for forty-eight hours, we assume the asset is compromised and follow appropriate protocols. I've seen it many times before." She jutted her chin toward Siene. "So have you. How do you think you became a Primogen?' She turned to Ben. "Primogens don't quit, and you know too much. There's only one way out, and she knows it."

Ben saw Siene's face turn white and feared she might collapse. He reached out to steady her, but she waved him away.

Siene could see confusion darting around in Ben's eyes. "She's right," Siene said. She closed her eyes for a second to gather herself. "The mission is what is important. Everything else is secondary."

"Including your brother?"

Over the years she tried never to think about a

situation like this. Now she had to do just that. She couldn't let emotions get in the way of the mission. She'd fall apart and cry later when she was alone. For now, she'd have to lead. "Like it or not, Reed and I both knew the potential consequences when we became Primogens. We accepted them. Death is part of the job. When someone is dispatched or killed, we go on and complete the mission no matter what we think or feel."

Ben ran a hand through his hair and wandered a short distance away before returning. "You can't be that cold, Siene."

"It has nothing to do with feelings, Ben. It's what must be done for the mission to succeed."

Ben looked from Siene to Lina. Both stood impassive. "I thought I was beginning to understand you and this thing you do, Siene, but I guess I don't. Not on this level."

Siene closed her eyes, guilt settling heavy inside her chest. She weighed the pros and cons of telling him everything by playing *what if?* so he could understand the repercussions, but there would be too many. It would be better if he took a big step backward and understood she had no choice but to be a Primogen first and a sister later. Too many lives were in the balance for emotion to get in the way.

"Being a Primogen is what I do, Ben. I have no choice but to finish this mission." She was mentally exhausted but could not risk letting him know. And though she needed him too much to let him go, she had to offer him a choice. He could leave on his terms or stay on hers. "If you want out, now's the time to tell me. When Caleb gets here, I'll have some Seekers take you to Dar es Salaam. It's Tanzania's largest city, and home to Dar es Salaam Julius Nyerere International Airport. You can get a flight back to the States there."

Ben took a step toward her.

She held her ground.

"And you'd just let me leave?" he asked.

"It's more complicated than just letting you leave, but yes."

"How complicated?" Ben asked.

Siene felt her insides tighten. "As Lina said, you know too much."

In what seemed like less than the blink of an eye, Lina pushed past her. "And the Primogens *never* allow anyone with that kind of knowledge to…"

Ben moved in front of Lina and stared at Siene. "Is she saying what I think she's saying?"

Siene shook her head. "We don't kill people, Ben."

"Then what is it, Siene?"

Siene hesitated. She looked at Ben and then quickly away. How could she tell him a part of his memory would have to be erased and possibly with it, his life as a scientist. There was never a way to tell how much of him would be gone when Jack got through with the process, but she knew she had to tell him something. Ben would never settle for silence.

"When this is over, you'll be returned to the taxi line in New York as though nothing happened."

"That was weeks ago, Siene," Ben challenged. "That is not going to work."

She knew he was right. "We've done this sort of thing before." She saw Ben smirk. "Trust me."

Ben stood for a long moment staring at her. "I'm all out of trust. That's how I got to this God forsaken place." He caught her gaze and held it. "You're holding something serious back. I need to know what that is."

Siene crossed her arms over her chest and looked at the ground. She couldn't seem to think rationally. Too much had happened. Reed was gone. Lucian was trying to kill her and Ben. The villagers were still trapped in a trance-like state with no remedy in sight. And worst of all, deep down, she knew she loved Ben, but a relationship with him was slipping beyond her reach with each passing moment.

When he held her upper arms, she looked up. "If you stay, you stay on my terms."

"And they are?"

"No more questions until the mission is over." She swallowed hard. "Then I'll tell you everything you want to know."

He heaved a sigh. "I can't do anything with these blood samples here. The lab is crude and most of the equipment outdated. When this is over, it would be best to take them to a state-of-the-art facility in New York."

Lina laughed. "Well, that's not going to happen." When Ben turned to her, she captured his gaze with hers. "Ever!"

He turned back. "Siene?"

A voice from behind them broke the building tension. "Gather round. I have brought the answer to the mystery of the villagers' trance-like state."

Siene shrugged free of Ben's grasp. "Caleb. What? How?"

"I'll let someone else tell you."

He signaled to one of the Seekers standing in the doorway. When the Seeker stepped aside, Joseph walked into the equipment room.

Lina ran to him and threw her arms around his

neck. "Mosegi! I thought you were dead."

He smiled. "Mosegi *is* dead. I'm Joseph."

Lina stepped back. "OMG. You're his twin brother and that bastard Lucian killed him." She held out her hand. "Someone get me a gun. I'm going to return that favor as soon as I see his ugly face."

Caleb laughed. "He deserves a bullet between the eyes, but Mosegi isn't exactly dead."

Lina tilted her head. "Uh?"

Joseph smiled. "I am the person you know as Mosegi. I came to Tanzania to visit my grandfather before I went back to my residency in the states. He gave me the native name, then, when the mercenaries came, he warned me not to reveal my true indemnity for fear I would be killed."

Lina ran and jumped into Joseph's arms. "Good plan! I was so worried about you."

Ben snickered. "You thought he was dead, remember?"

Lina slid from Joseph's arms and glared at Ben. "All a façade."

"You're a doctor?" Siene asked.

"Almost. I'd be a third-year resident if I hadn't been shanghaied," Joseph answered. "I hope I can still continue when I get back to the states."

Lina and Siene exchanged glances. Joseph's future was as much in doubt as was Ben's.

"I'm anxious to begin a career in biomedical research," Joseph continued.

Ben stepped forward. "Virology?"

"Among other things," Joseph replied.

"I may need your help here," Ben said. "I've isolated some unusual blood cells and…"

Siene put her hand on Ben's arm. "Caleb said something about a possible answer to the stupor."

"You have the water?" Lina asked.

Joseph reached into his pocket. "No, but I have this." He opened his hand and unwrapped the contents. "Maybe you can tell what it is?

Siene felt her eyes widen. *A piece of Snow White's apple.* "Damn! That's a bit of the apple." She held out her hand. "May I have it?"

"I'd really like to get this to a modern lab back in the States for study. The properties are most unusual," Joseph said. He closed his fist around the apple.

Siene wrestled with how much to tell Joseph. "It actually belongs to me. I didn't know it was missing. I have the apple from which this piece was taken."

Caleb walked to Joseph. "It's hers."

Joseph locked gazes with Caleb and saw that he had no other choice. Reluctantly, he gave the small piece to Siene. "But I would like to know more about that species of apple. I've never seen anything like it."

"Nor will you," Lina chimed in. "It's one of a kind."

Joseph's brow furrowed. "A new engineered variety?"

Lina laughed. "Sort of."

Siene glared at Lina. Joseph knew too much already. Though she could not be sure Lina wouldn't accidentally disclose too much, she needed to speak to Ben alone. "Lina, why don't you and Caleb take Joseph to the kitchen and get him something to eat." She locked her gaze with Lina's. "He must he hungry, and there are other things to discuss, I'm sure."

Lina sighed heavily. "Not very subtle." She took

Joseph's arm and nodded to Caleb. "C'mon. I think I saw some scotch in one of the cabinets."

Siene waited for them to leave before speaking. "Apparently the apple piece helped Lucian control the villagers." She set the tiny piece on the metal table. Ben reached for it, but she stopped him. "There isn't much left, so we need to be careful. It isn't a renewable resource."

"I'm a bit confused," Ben said. "What do you mean? You said you have the rest of the apple. We can plant the seeds."

She shook her head. "There are no seeds, Ben. This particular apple never had them." Ben's head tilted as though he was weighing what he heard. "I think you better sit."

He leaned his backside against the metal lab table. "I suspect I'm going to hear a fairy tale, right?"

Siene slowly shook her head. "After everything you've seen, you still don't believe?"

"I'm trying."

"I sincerely hope so." She pointed to the apple bit. "It's a small part of what most people would know as Snow White's apple, thanks to my uncles."

He crossed his arms over his chest. "And I suppose, now you are going to tell me what it really is."

She nodded. "It was brought to my uncles by a woman who claimed it had been passed down in her family for generations. She was old and losing her faculties and could not remember much about it. At that time, they called it madness; now we know the condition as Alzheimer's Disease. She knew she didn't have much time and had heard about my uncles from the woman who had brought them her healing tears."

"Rapunzel, I suppose."

Siene did not miss the mockery in his voice. "No. Gretchen. A farmer's wife. Rapunzel was for the story."

Ben looked at the floor and shook his head.

"Just listen," Siene said.

He looked up and nodded.

"The woman told my uncles the apple was centuries old and had properties that, if used one way could help, such as putting desperately ill people into a coma until a cure could be found for their illness and used another way could kill if too much was ingested. She did not know how to use it but begged them to keep it safe until which time someone could unlock its secrets. Even to them, her story sounded implausible, and they turned her away. In desperation, she took a bite of the apple and immediately fell at their feet."

Ben stood. "She died with just one bite?"

"That's what my uncles thought. They could feel no heartbeat nor feel her chest rise. They tried everything they could to help her but failed. As Uncle Wilhelm carried the woman to his carriage to take her to the local undertaker, he jostled her slightly as he went through the door and the apple bit fell from her mouth. He nearly dropped her when he heard her deep intake of breath."

Ben's eyes widened. "A trance. Like the villagers, only deeper."

She nodded. "They knew they had to keep the apple safely away from anyone who might accidentally try to eat it for fear the person could be buried alive, as in those days bodies were quickly interred."

"So, you're theorizing a controlled amount of whatever is in this apple is what Lucian used on the villagers."

"It's the only explanation."

"How did he know how much to use?"

"I don't know. Who knows how many villagers were his lab rats until he found the right proportion. He must have tested the combinations on…" She closed her eyes and then snapped them open. "Oh my God!" She grabbed onto the table to keep from falling.

Ben ran to her. "What is it?"

Slowly she looked at him. "It's you, Ben. I finally think I know why Lucian wanted you dead."

****

Lucian trained the binoculars on the doorway of the lab. He could see no movement. "Are you sure they are in there?"

"They're there," Biden said. He raised his AR-16 and scanned the lab through the targeting sight. "Buru brought someone in about an hour ago. No one's left since." He lowered the weapon. "Ready to rock and roll?"

"Not yet," Lucian replied.

"How long are you going to wait?"

Lucian could hear irritation in Biden's voice. He lowered the binoculars and slowly turned. "Until I'm ready." He held Biden's gaze and said nothing more until Biden blinked.

Biden poked his tongue into his cheek and inhaled a long breath. He blew air out slowly and hooked the AR over his shoulder. "I need to take a piss. Maybe you'll be ready when I get back."

As Biden walked away Lucian lined the center of Biden's head in the rear sight notch of his Glock-19. He would have liked nothing better than to pull the trigger and watch Biden's head explode, but that would only alert Siene. She had no idea he had the lab surrounded. The element of surprise would work in his favor. Slowly, he lowered the gun. Biden's end would come soon enough.

Chapter Twenty-Nine

Ben stared at Siene for an overlong moment before asking, "How can you know why Lucian wants me dead?"

"I don't actually know, but I have a theory," she replied.

"Since when?"

"Since Caleb brought Joseph here with that piece of Snow White's apple. I think it has something to do with your spit project."

After the unexpected revelation, it took Ben a moment to find his voice. "First of all, stop calling it my spit project. My research is serious science. And second, I think you're guessing just to connect some dots."

Siene laughed at him. "Guessing? Is that the best you can come up with after all we've been through?" She threw her hands in the air and turned a quick circle. "Why in the world would you think I'm only guessing about someone trying to kill you?"

"To get my attention?"

Siene rubbed her brow trying to stave off a developing headache. "Seriously?"

Ben held up a hand. "Okay, maybe it's a little more than trying to get my attention. But jumping out of a plane and parachuting into the African jungle, getting captured by your crazy ex-lover, and being threatened with death has left me a bit unnerved and a whole lot scared."

"People who try to kill people generally leave a bad feeling." She folded her arms across her breasts. "Do you want to hear what I think or not?"

He swept his hand in front of him. "By all means. Tell me another fairy tale."

Siene glared at him. "Will you get over that already?"

"I'm trying."

Siene didn't care for the demeaning tone of Ben's words. She'd deal with that later. She took a deep breath and began. "Remember when I told you the woman who brought the apple to my uncles took a bite of it to prove a point?"

Ben nodded. "And they thought she had died."

"Yes, but then when the apple bit was dislodged from her mouth, she woke up."

"Lucky for her."

Siene shook her head. "Not luck. Spit."

Ben laughed. "Seriously?"

"Yes. It all makes sense. Your spit project is the reason I had to rescue you, the reason we're here in Africa, and the reason Lucian wants you dead." She paused to let her theory gel. She knew her reasoning was solid, but Ben looked irritated.

"That's the best you can come up with for me having a target on my back?"

Ben sounded more annoyed than open to the possibility. It took her a moment to find her voice. "You don't believe me?"

He shook his head. "I think you're weaving more of your uncles' stories."

Siene put her hands on her hips and glared. "I'm telling stories?" She glared. "After all we've been through. Why would I do that?"

"As I said, to get my attention." He paused. "After all, we haven't been very…" He paused again. "Close lately."

She threw up her hands then folded her arms across her chest. "You are thinking about sex at a time like this."

"A momentary lapse of judgment."

Siene didn't like the turn the conversation had taken. She'd get it back on track. "Do you want to hear about my theory or not?"

"Actually, I do," Ben admitted.

"Good. As I was saying—" She raised her eyebrows and shot Ben a tight-jaw look she knew he would understand. "—You told me all about some enzyme that, if extracted and manipulated, could possibly help find cures for some diseases."

Ben nodded.

"So is it that far-fetched to think that your spit project…"

"Research project," Ben corrected.

"Research project," Siene repeated, spacing the words for emphasis, "could impact Lucian's plan for world domination because what you found could alter the effect the component in Snow White's apple, whatever it is, or possibly even negate the trance-like state."

Ben seemed to be considering her conclusion.

The mental restraint she needed as she waited for him to react was in danger of snapping. "Well?"

He stood silent for a while and then said, "It's

possible."

"Glad you agree." She began pulling him toward the small specimen refrigerator.

He grabbed her shoulders to stop her. "What are you doing?"

She shrugged herself free, opened the refrigerator door and grabbed a few test tubes of blood. "We have to test the idea." She placed the tubes in the holder on the counter and handed one to Ben. "Here."

He looked from her hand to her face. "What do you want me to do with that?"

"Spit in it."

"You're kidding."

"No. If we are going to restore the balance between good and evil, you have to spit in this." She shoved the test tube closer to him.

Ben scowled. "That's not how these things work."

"But you agreed it was possible."

He nodded. "Far-fetched, but possible."

She held up the test tube. "So, spit in this and find out."

He pushed the tube away. "I don't work in your fairy tale world, Siene. I live and work in reality, and in reality, cures aren't found by simply spitting into test tubes. It takes time. Lots of it."

He started to walk away but Siene stopped him by grabbing his arm. "Ben, time is also the enemy here. If Lucian gets his way, he might possibly carve up the apple to accomplish whatever it is he is planning, and its medicinal uses could be lost forever. Now to mention a distinct possibility of more outsiders knowing about us."

Ben put his hand over hers and looked into her

eyes. "Let me work, Siene. I promise I'll get you an answer."

She nodded and did her best not to look panicked because she was beginning to believe that unless Ben threw out his cerebral beliefs and let her lead him to what she knew was an alternate reality, Lucian might just succeed. She pulled her hand free, spit into the test tube, and handed it to him. "Here, in case you decide I'm right."

Ben looked down at her hand and nodded. He took the sample and walked to the counter.

Overcome by everything that had happened in the last few days, she spun on her heels and stalked out of the lab. She needed to regain her perspective. The mission first, then her feelings for Ben and what to do with them. She needed to find the strength deep inside herself. She'd always been able to move on. Complete the mission, win the day, and send the nonessentials back to their lives minus a few memories. She longed for no man because she decided long ago that men were temporary and wanting one would hurt a lot more than living without one. Lucian had helped underscore that.

She hardly noticed the path she had taken after leaving the lab, but realized she was too far from the buildings to feel safe. She turned back and began walking but stopped abruptly when she saw Lucian standing a few feet away with a gun trained on her.

"Hello, Siene," he said.

She noticed he was alone. "What are you doing here?" Damn, she had let herself be so distracted by Ben that she hadn't taken a weapon with her when she left the lab. Maybe she didn't have a gun, but she vowed it would take more than Lucian alone to capture her again.

"I'm here to take you back," he answered.

"I don't understand." *Back where? The camp was gone, the airstrip destroyed. What did he mean?*

"Back to where you belong, Siene. With me." He held out his hand. "Why did you run from me?"

"You held me hostage, tried to kill Ben, and made zombies out of a lot of villagers, Lucian. I decided not to sit around and chat with you until something happened to me."

He shrugged. "All that doesn't matter now." He gestured behind her. "Once I destroy the lab and everyone in it and take you back to the Taltoian stronghold, I'll have everything in place."

Anger began to build and spread through her body. By trying to stop him, she'd endured more than she ever thought was possible, and now he thought she was going to give in and go quietly along with his demented plot. He must be out of his mind.

"How did you find me?" she asked. Deep inside she knew the answer. He bankrolled Ben's past research project. The lab was Lucian's.

"You mean the good doctor didn't tell you?" He lowered his outstretched hand.

She knew she had to keep him talking until either Ben or Caleb noticed she was missing and came after her. Once one or the other did, they should be able to make a move on Lucian. She'd have a better chance fighting with Caleb, but Ben was better at the cerebral side of combat. She'd just have to be ready to move on Lucian with either one. "I know you were the anonymous backer Ben worked briefly for. I know he was here, so this must be your lab."

"Correct," he confirmed.

"And Ben's new project is why you wanted him dead."

"Also correct."

"How did you get the apple piece?" Suddenly she realized there was a serious security breach in the Primogen compound. No one knew that an artifact was missing. There was a traitor among the Primogens. If she somehow survived this mission, she'd find out who.

He grinned. "Money and the promise of power are strong motivators, Siene."

She didn't know how long she could keep Lucian talking without him taking some kind of action or some of his mercenaries joining him. Where the hell were Ben and Caleb? One of them would do. Both would be better.

"It doesn't have to be this way, Lucian. You were a Primogen. You can be one again. Let's work together to figure out how."

"We can't, Siene."

"Why not?" she asked. But in her gut she already knew the answer.

"The Taltoian faction has grown. We're ready to act. The Primogens have hogged the glory for too long. It's our time now. There's nothing left for you to do but either choose to join us or choose to meet your end." He stepped forward and brushed her cheek with the back of his hand. "I don't want to hurt you, Siene, but I made it clear you are my kill."

"You'd shoot me, Lucian?"

He ran a thumb across her lips. "I hope I don't have to."

The anger boiling inside her nearly exploded. She

clenched her fists to keep from beating the crap out of him. She only waited because she couldn't be sure he wouldn't shoot her.

"I'm not going to lie, Lucian. I'm not going down without a fight," she warned him.

"I would expect nothing less. I've always admired your spirit, Siene."

"Is that what you admired? I thought it was my ass."

He threw his head back and laughed. "Lord, I missed you. You always were a feisty one."

She was getting sick of waiting to be saved. Time to cut to the chase. "You've turned another Primogen, haven't you?" The smirk on Lucian's face answered for him.

"Everyone has his or her price, Siene."

No longer able to control her rage, she doubled her fist and punched him right in the jaw. His head snapped backward, and he dropped the gun. Blood spurted from his nose. Both lunged for the gun, but Siene managed to kick it away and into the underbrush. Lucian cursed and advanced on her, but she stood her ground ready for whatever he would do.

Lucian slashed out with his hand in a chopping motion aiming for her neck. She ducked but he still connected with her shoulder. The sharp pain made her cry out. She turned, and for a moment, she remembered another Lucian, the man with whom she once thought she would share the rest of her life defending a noble cause. But that man was gone. The man standing before her now would kill her to get what he wanted.

"I'm not your enemy, Lucian," she said.

He sneered. "You have been since the day you

chose the wrong side."

She tried to ease away from him, but he attacked and kicked her in the side. She groaned and twisted out of his way. Her retaliation kick connected solidly with his groin.

Cursing, he fell to one knee, then staggered to his feet. "You always thought you were better than the rest of us, Siene."

"Then why did you want me?" The affair they had seemed to be taking on a new meaning.

"To show your brother and the rest of the Primogens that by sleeping with you, you could be controlled, and I could move up the hierarchy."

She held a neutral expression. What a fool she'd been. She thought Lucian had been interested in her because they had a moral goal in common. "You would have anyway. Reed and I spoke about needing someone as second in command. It could have been you." Her words were not truthful. Lucin had always been on the fringes of being a dissenter. He was put on the watch list right before he went rogue.

"It doesn't matter now, does it?" Lucian asked. "I made sure Reed knew I was screwing you. I knew he hated that, and I hated Reed."

She hesitated. She let herself be used by this man just to have someone close. That would not happen again. "Reed's dead," she said. "We can work to bring everyone together for the benefit of mankind."

Lucian laughed out loud. "Mankind will benefit once they are brought under control and herded in the right direction like sheep."

"You don't mean that."

"Oh, my dear, I do. I have set myself on a path

from which there is no turning back."

"Lucian, there is always a way back."

"Not this time." He punched her hard in the stomach and she dropped to her knees.

She couldn't breathe. When she looked up at him there was a lunacy in his eyes she'd never seen before. She struggled to her feet. Tears of pain blurred her eyes. "So, it's you or me," she said.

"Afraid so. Once I'm done with you, we'll take the lab and kill everyone inside."

She couldn't let that happen. Her ears were buzzing, probably from the lack of air, but slowly it became easier to breathe. He was still talking, but she turned to him and just reacted. Her kick connected with his solar plexus with as much accuracy as her battered body could produce. She felt a small victory as he grabbed his side and groaned.

"Bitch."

"I told you I wasn't going down without a fight." She began backing up toward the lab.

He rose in a fighting stance. "The next time I hit you, you won't be getting back up."

He advanced on her, and Siene kept moving backward, searching for something to use as a weapon. There was nothing. She took a deep breath and tried to remember what Kai had taught her about using an attacker's momentum against him.

Lucian swung his leg in a side kick. She grabbed his ankle and brought her foot up to trip him to the ground. Using a grip on his shoulder, she pushed him down. Then, still holding his leg, she brought the heel of her foot down hard on his groin again. He curled into a ball and lay on the ground. About then, she heard rustling to her right and spun.

Ben stepped out of the tall brush. "Siene, I'm glad I found you. I tested the spit in the test tube on the apple piece—"

She motioned to the ground.

He saw Lucian still motionless on the jungle floor. "How did he get here?" He saw her cut lip. "And what the hell happened?"

"I'll tell you on the way back to the lab."

Lucian started to sit up.

Siene grabbed Ben's arm and began to run. "And now would be the best time to get moving."

Ben looked back over his shoulder. "What about him? Shouldn't we take him to use as bait?"

"We can't. Bringing Lucian with us is more dangerous than leaving him here. He will do everything he can to slow us down until Taltos gets here."

Ben swallowed hard. "And you are not going to do anything but leave him here?"

"Yes."

"For a moment, I was afraid I'd have to watch you kill him."

"I was tempted but I'll let Taltos handled that," Siene shouted over the sound of their footsteps. "Lucian has failed in his mission, and Taltos considers everyone expendable. We have got to get out of here now if we are going to have any chance of surviving to fight another day."

Once back inside the lab, Siene gathered Caleb and the few men he brought with him and briefed them. "I doubt Lucian was here alone, but I also think he would have attacked us by now, unless something is stopping him. What that is, I have no idea, nor do I care right now, and I'm not going to try to guess. He obviously has made a serious mistake by waiting, and we have to use that slip-up to try to get away and regroup somewhere safer."

"How and where?" Caleb asked. "The lab is most likely being watched by some of his mercenaries," Caleb said. "And if so, we are outnumbered and outgunned."

Siene nodded. "Probably, but for the moment, the mercenaries don't know I cold-cocked Lucian. We grab what we can and go in different directions."

Ben stepped forward, watching Caleb begin to gather equipment and supplies. "That's your plan? We simply walk out the front and back door and hope no one notices?"

Caleb checked the chamber on his semiautomatic and shoved it into the back of his pants. "You have a better idea?"

Ben didn't answer.

Siene shrugged on a vest and walked to the door. "Ben. Caleb, Lina, and I have been in situations like this before. Trust me." She gestured to Lina. "You go with Caleb. Ben and I will head in the opposite direction. Take as many of the stronger villagers as you can." She tossed him one of the radios. "If you don't hear from me in twenty-four hours, we're dead. Finish the mission without us."

Caleb nodded. He gestured to his men and headed with Lina to the back room that held ten villagers.

Siene watched him go and wondered if she would ever see him again.

Ben grabbed her arm. "What about the villagers Caleb can't take?"

Siene swallowed hard. "They'll stay here." Ben started to protest, but Siene held up a hand to stop him. "It is the way it has to be. For now." She held his gaze. "I don't like it, but I have no choice. This is much like the choice you had to make in New York when we met; stay and do nothing or go and try to stop the madness." She touched his hand. "We are in too deep to do nothing. You've seen how Lucian works."

"We could have made him come with us and turned him over to the authorities, Siene."

She shook her head. "You don't know him. He's very dangerous. Even if we did manage to stop him, Taltos has dozens of others just like him. We stop this here and now or the world as we know it is over." She looked away then back. "Lucian will never let you live, Ben. Help me finish this."

She saw the indecision run wildly in Ben's eyes. She didn't have much more time to convince him to leave with her. She'd go without him if need be. Then, as though everything seemed to gel within him, she felt his hand take hers.

"Let's go before I change my mind."

Chapter Thirty

Hours later Siene and Ben saw the edge of a village in the distance. It bothered Siene that their escape from the lab had been so easy. She sensed something was wrong. She dropped to her belly. "Get down," she said to Ben. "This could be a trap. It's too quiet."

"Too late," Ben said. He pointed to a group of four men coming toward them. The men wore camouflage pants and vests with pockets. Two had ammunition belts draped across their chest, and all held assault rifles. "Can you tell if they are friend or foe?"

Siene shook her head. The men kept their guns trained on Ben. They apparently hadn't seen her yet. She had a moment's fear that Ben would do something stupid like try to shoot one. She was not going to hide like some sort of coward. She had to try something. She got to her feet and raised her hands to shoulder height.

The tallest of the four men pointed his assault rifle at her and stepped forward.

"We are looking for the village of Lushoto," Siene said to him.

He said nothing.

Siene remembered the talisman Joseph had given her. "I wish to show you something."

Still no reaction from the man.

"I wear it close." Slowly she began to move her hand toward her neck.

The man in front of her took a step closer.

She stopped moving her hand. "I am looking for the tribal chieftain of that village. He is called grandfather by one of my friends. That friend gave me a talisman to show to him to prove that I am not an enemy." She dropped her chin. "I wear it around my neck."

He nodded to one of the men around Ben who then pointed his rifle at Siene. After the cohort's aim was reset to her, he lowered his weapon and reached toward Siene.

"Don't touch her," Ben called out. He began to move toward her, but one of the men guarding him turned his rifle and jammed the buttstock into his stomach, driving him to the ground and taking his breath from him. He wrapped his arms across his midsection and could do no more than utter disjointed sounds.

Siene took a step toward Ben but was held back. For a moment she stiffened but quickly shook away her apprehension. She held the gaze of the man restraining her. He had to see the amulet if they had any chance of continuing. She leaned forward and let him fumble for the necklace. Once he found it, he ripped it from her neck—she refused to flinch at the quick shot of pain when the cord broke.

He held out the talisman to those with him.

They nodded and lowered their weapons.

"This is a gift of protection," he said. "Now I need to know if you stole it, or if it was truly given."

His accent was different than any she had heard before, but she had no trouble understanding him. "It was given to me by Mosegi, the grandson of the village chief. I wish to be taken to him."

The man shook his head. "That is not possible."

Siene looked over his shoulder. "Is that not his village?"

"Lushoto now belongs to a warlord."

Siene's stomach clenched. *Lucian.* She had spent days battling him physically and emotionally. She and Ben were close to filling in the missing puzzle pieces. She ran from Lucian back at the lab to protect the sick villagers, Joseph, and Shard. Hopefully, they were safe. She would not run again. It would end here.

"Take me to him," she said.

"No."

"Why not?"

"The warlord has ordered everyone away."

Siene gestured to the weapons. "Why didn't you fight him?"

"More of his men joined him last night and searched neighboring villages. Some were burned, others spared for now." He glanced at his companions. "We killed a few of his men and took their guns. We barely escaped. We carry all we have and were hunting for survivors to join us when we found you."

She speculated that Lucian had called on reinforcements after his confrontation with her. Now, he would not stop until he found her—even if it meant killing everyone in his way. She couldn't let anyone else die because of her. She'd find him, one way or another, and stop him. Even if it meant Lucian had to die.

"I know the man who has taken the village and can help you get rid of him." There was no way she was turning around now. She was too close. "And I know the villagers are sick and dying." She glanced at Ben. "He can help you treat them."

He raised his gun again, and his eyes narrowed. "How do you know these things?"

She knew he may not understand what she was about to say but had to try to get him to understand that she came because the villagers were dying. "I am a Protector, and as one, I am sent to help when and wherever needed." She looked over his shoulder at the village. "Take me to the village and let me speak to the one I know as Grandfather. He will know why I have come."

"He is a prisoner in his hut. Guarded by soldiers of the warlord."

Siene stiffened. "I will find a way to save him and hopefully help you." She held out her hand. "I need the necklace back." The request was met with silence. She lowered her hand. "I am Siene." She pointed to Ben. "He is Ben. A doctor. He also wants to help the villagers. Men are looking for us. We believe that the same warlord who now controls the village sent them. If they find us, we are dead. If we are dead, we cannot help free this region from the grip of evil."

The warrior took her chin in his hand and lifted it until her eyes were level with his. He watched her carefully as she spoke.

"We have a common enemy," she said. "Many lives depend on what Ben and I do now. I have no time to debate you. You can help us, or you can go, but we will make sure to free Grandfather and take him to safety."

He scanned her face before speaking. "I am Erevu," he finally said. "It means clever and capable."

"You will help me?" she asked.

Erevu nodded. He handed her back the talisman. "We will help. But we wait until dark. For now, we hide."

Siene retied the necklace around her neck. "Erevu, I look forward to seeing how clever and capable you are."

Erevu trilled sharply in a sound that perfectly mimicked a local bird. His cohorts lowered their weapons and reassembled into a line.

Siene and Ben found their place in the group as they all moved out. As they walked, she thought about Ben's reaction to all that had happened over the last few weeks. Though he had tried to accept what was in conflict to everything he knew as a man of science and had actually come a long way in accepting some of what he'd seen, he might never be able to understand her allegiance to the artifacts. Science was methodical, a certainty that was either black or white. She asked him to see the shades in between, and just as he was about to cross from his world of absolutes into her world of endless probability, he seemed to pull back and question what he had seen and experienced as though accepting the objects as real would negate everything in the scientific world. He was an academic, an intellectual who could never fully accept the inexplicable world in which she was destined to live out her life. In a way she knew more than he ever could imagine. *A Primogen.* That was who she was and forever would be. Though she wanted to be able to share her life with someone in whom she could find respite, she could not compromise any more of herself for anyone. Too much depended upon keeping the

Legacy strong.

Ben walked next to her just as the sun set. His arm was pressed against his midsection. "I'm not feeling all that well," he said.

"You took quite a shot," Siene said. "Let me take a look." She pushed his shirt up and saw the skin just above his belly button was red and well on its way to bruising. After gently palpating the area, she concluded there was no internal injury, and he would just be sore for a few days. "I think it would be best if you didn't try to save me for a while. It's not working out all that well for you."

"I suppose I could use more practice in that area," Ben said.

Siene was about to agree when they heard gunfire from up ahead.

Erevu signaled for the group to stop. "Can you shoot?" he asked, tossing a handgun to Siene.

She nodded.

Erevu gestured to Ben. "What about him?"

"I can hold my own," he replied.

Erevu checked the magazine of a 9mm and handed it to Ben. "Don't waste the bullets. There are no more."

Siene took up a position between Erevu and Ben and waited to see who would come out of the jungle. If they were Lucian's men, they were responsible for the deaths of many innocents and were now headed for the village. She straightened her spine, raised her weapon, and vowed there would not be any more loss of life.

"Those men heading toward us, they are the enemy, right?" Ben whispered.

Siene glanced at him. She did not really expect him to know what to do, but he stood next to her, rigid, with the gun in his hand aimed at the jungle. "Probably," she whispered back. She thought she saw fear in his eyes. She had asked so much of him since that day in the city. Instinct told her this time was going to be worse than any other. She wasn't sure how much more he could take.

"Shouldn't we hide or something?" he asked. "I feel like bait."

"The tribesmen know what they are doing."

Ben moved closer to her. "Are you sure we won't get caught in some sort of tribal war?"

"We have to trust them," Siene answered. She had no choice. Someone was moving closer.

She heard the footsteps rustling though the brush, but more significant was the lack of jungle sounds again. No birds chirping, no monkey chatter. The tribe members with them began to chant. The rhythm of their voices crept into her body, and she knew whatever it took, she would be a part of this fight to the end.

She thought of her father's advice when he first taught her to shoot. She leaned toward Ben. "Keep your eye on the target and don't put too much of your finger on the trigger…otherwise, it will pull to the left."

He nodded and braced his left hand under his right.

In the next second three men entered the clearing, each with their hands above their head.

It took Siene a second to react. "Hold your fire," she screamed out as she dropped her gun and ran toward the tall man in the center. "Reed!"

Chapter Thirty-One

Ben, Siene, and Reed sat on the trunk of a fallen tree while Erevu and the men who had accompanied Reed sat around a small campfire a few feet away.

"Glad you didn't kill me, Sis," Reed joked.

"It was close. And now that I know you're okay…" Siene reared back and punched Reed in the arm.

He laughed and rubbed his bicep. "I expected as much."

"Where have you been?" She glanced at Ben.

"It's a long story, Sis."

"For now, give me the Cliffs Notes version. As you can tell, we have a situation here and don't have a lot of time to hear your normal, embellished version."

Reed grinned. "I missed you, too."

Siene could not wait much longer. The relief in seeing her brother was rapidly turning into a combination of anger and the need to get moving. "Where were you? Why didn't you try to contact me? What happened?" She asked the questions rapid-fire. "I didn't see you parachute out of the plane. I thought you were…" Her breath caught and she closed her eyes. When she opened them, Reed was grinning. "Stop it. Don't laugh."

"I'm not laughing. I'm picturing you selling my stuff on eBay after you completely take over the Primogens."

She knew he was trying to get her to calm down through humor and had to admit it was slightly working. "I know we talked about what would happen if one of us…"

"Died," Reed finished for her. "Say it."

Siene glared at him.

"You never could fully handle the concept."

"We'll talk about that later after we fix the mess we're in with Lucian."

Reed lifted his eyebrows. "Ah, the old boyfriend. He always swore he'd get you back."

Ben snapped up his head. "What?"

"Lucian never could fully let go of Siene. As he was escorted from the Primogen compound, he promised he'd come back for Siene."

Ben frowned. "You never mentioned anything like that, Siene."

"Lucian and I weren't that close," she countered.

"The hell you were," Reed said.

"No, we weren't."

"Then why did you decide to marry him?"

Ben sprang to his feet. "You were going to marry Lucian?"

Siene looked away and then back. "Kinda, sort of." She stared at Ben. "Now is not the time to go into that."

"But we will," Ben insisted.

"If we get out of this jungle alive." She waited for Ben to say something, but he stayed silent. She angled toward her brother. "Right now, I need to know what happened to you."

"Nice save, Sis," Reed acknowledged.

Siene glared at him. And gestured for him to start talking.

"I went into the cockpit to see if the pilot knew what was wrong, but he had bailed. I tried to steady the plane, but it was in a graveyard spiral. Not getting out of that one. By the time I got to the back, the plane was about two thousand feet from the ground. It was jump or die in a fiery crash. So, I jumped." He saw the disbelief on Siene's face. "I knew my parachute might not open properly, so I also prayed as I hit every tree in sight on the way down. The chute opened just enough, and the trees broke my fall a little, but I still slammed into the jungle floor. Next thing I know, it's days later and I wake up on a litter in a remote village with moss and something really smelly wrapped around my head and a Babu tending to me."

Siene turned to Ben. "A Babu is a healer who possess a vast knowledge of local plants and herbs, but the basis of the healing is grounded in the supernatural."

"You're telling me Reed fell out of a plane and got saved by fairy tale magic?" Ben said. "This adventure I'm on gets better and better."

"Not exactly," Siene replied. "It's more folklore than fairy tale. Babus often report being visited in dreams by ancestors or spirits who reveal how to treat those who are injured."

"So, a ghost saved Reed."

Siene shook her head. "No, physics and luck saved Reed, along with his excellent physical condition. The recommended minimum altitude for a chute to open is about one thousand feet, but daredevils and stuntmen have deployed at lower altitudes. Plus, the trees slowed his speed. Add in that Reed is in great shape, and we have a miracle with an asterisk." She turned to her brother. "I am glad you're here. I need all the help I can get to stop Lucian."

"Fill me in, Sis." Reed rose and stretched. "All that lying around has made me feel lazy. I need a good adventure right about now."

Erevu walked over and joined them on the fallen log. "My scout tells me the village has only a few mercenaries left. If you are to rescue the one you call Grandfather, we go at first light. The rest of those who listen to the warlord will surely return soon."

Siene nodded. "We'll be ready."

"We sleep here," Everu said. "The men need rest. I suggest you rest also. Check the brush for night animals before you settle in. There will be bats overhead, but leopards like to wander in the night. Make sure your gun is loaded and by your side."

****

The men fell asleep as soon as they had eaten, but Siene was wide awake. She'd used the radio to check in with Caleb. They were resting at a village to the north and would soon be out of radio range, but they were safe for the moment. Though she had never been particularly spiritual because of her vocation, she closed her eyes and wished them Godspeed. After all, the artifacts existed, Lina was a living mystery, and Rapunzel was once alive. She had no way of knowing if other miraculous objects were scattered across the world, and if they did exist, perhaps they would help Lina, Caleb, and Joseph stay safe.

She sat on the ground and leaned against a tree. Ben was lying on his side, his back to her. She couldn't tell if he was asleep or just quiet. She felt a weight press down on her as she ran through all the possible outcomes of this mission and knew no matter how it ended, this operation would have no victors. Joseph's memory would have to be erased to a point before he was taken by Davelos to protect both him and the Primogens. And Ben...she closed her eyes. He could never remember that they even met.

Her breath hitched when she heard a low-flying helicopter. Ben was at her side in an instant.

He watched the helicopter pass overhead. "Guess someone is looking for us."

She nodded.

"Davelos?"

"Probably."

"Well, that sucks."

Siene smiled. "Is that your professional opinion, Doctor?"

"Who else could it be?" Ben snapped. "It's obvious your boyfriend misses you. He's probably moving heaven and earth to find you."

"He's not my boyfriend," Siene snapped back. "And believe me, Lucian doesn't believe in heaven. It could be someone sent by the Primogens looking for us." But the more she thought about it, she doubted any of those remaining at the compound would send a chopper. Too noisy. It would alert any Taltoians in the area that they were close.

"Wouldn't you know?" Ben challenged. "Don't you have the gift of telepathy or something, along with all those fairy tale things?"

She glared at him. "Of course not. I told you; we aren't mutants or anything like that. We are just humans who have been given an inviolate charge."

Ben sighed. "I'm sorry. But you must admit, it has

been a bit much for someone like me to swallow."

"Some like you?"

"A man of science who, for his whole life, believed in absolutes. A plus B always equaled C, and now…"

She nodded. "Now A plus B takes a right turn, a few lefts, a couple twists, and equals Z instead." She waited. He said nothing more. "I appreciate that you are at least trying to understand that when you mix black and white, you get gray." She forced a smile. "Gray is where I live."

He stood and extended his hand. "Be careful, Siene."

She took the hand he offered and rose. "It's not always possible. I have to take care of things."

"But who takes care of you?" he asked so softly that she had to strain to hear him.

"I do," she answered. She pulled her hand free. Hadn't she already proven to him that she could take care of herself? She had gotten them through a few harrowing incidents, and before this was over, she was sure there would be a few more.

"I'd like you around when we get out of this jungle," he said. "Don't put yourself last anymore."

"Why?" she asked.

"You're smart. You'll figure it out." He pulled her toward him, tipped her head back and kissed her as if there was no tomorrow.

She tunneled her fingers in his hair and cupped his head to try to take control of the embrace, but when his tongue brushed hers, she shivered with an awareness that had nothing to do with fairy tales or artifacts. She never felt this bewildered before. *Why now? Why this man?* She pulled away.

He rubbed his thumb across her bottom lip. "Think about what I said." Then he walked away.

She watched him go. Overcome by everything that happened, she sat back down and once again leaned against the tree. She needed to regain her perspective. Morning would be here shortly, and with it, the beginning of the end. She needed to find her inner strength and could not afford to be distracted. No matter how pleasant the distraction might be.

****

Siene awoke to gunshots coming from the village. She sprang to her feet.

Erevu tossed her another small firearm. "Big trouble. We go."

She grabbed his arm as he began to sprint into the jungle in the opposite direction of the village. "What about the villagers?"

He shrugged free. "If they are not dead, they will be. The warlord will kill them all. There are only a few of us. We cannot change their fate."

She watched Erevu and his men leave. She knew the warlord was Lucian and guilt weighed heavily on her. She was responsible for what was happening to the village. Lucian was fixated on her and Ben. She would not abandon the people even if she had to try and rescue them herself.

"You can do what you choose," she said, already staring toward the village. "I have to help them."

Ben matched her stride by stride as they joined up with Reed. "We're going to die, aren't we?"

"I certainly hope not," she replied. "I think it best if we fan out and go into the village from several directions."

"Wouldn't it be better if we stayed together?" Ben asked. "Like safety in numbers."

"If we have the numbers," Reed said. "In situations like this, Siene and I found that if we separate, there's a better chance of one of us getting through."

"Ben isn't familiar with guerilla methods."

Reed tossed his head. "Guess he'll have to learn on the fly."

"No," Ben protested. "I'll go with Siene."

"You can't." she said. "With Lucian gunning for us, if we are together, we might both be killed. We have to separate to ensure one of us can relay what we've discovered to the Council."

"Can't Caleb and Lina do that?"

She shook her head. "We don't know if they'll make it."

Reed put a hand on Ben's shoulder. "We do what we have to do to ensure the success of the mission."

Ben looked from Reed to Siene. "Well, I don't like it."

"That doesn't matter, and we are wasting time," Siene said. "We'll meet up in the village and look for Joseph's grandfather." She turned to Ben. "It will be all right. I've done this dozens of times."

Reluctantly Ben nodded. "Maybe it's time you didn't have to do so much alone."

Reed checked his gun and gestured to Ben. "Let's go." He ducked into some thick brush.

"You'd better catch up to him," Siene said. "There's a big jungle out there and not a street sign in sight."

Ben leaned forward and gave her a quick kiss. "For luck."

Siene kissed him back. "Now go."

"I don't like leaving you," Ben said.

She heard reluctance in his voice. "There is a greater chance of both of us dying if we stay together,"

"That makes no sense."

"Neither do all the fairy tale objects you've seen. This isn't a normal situation, and Lucian doesn't play by Geneva Convention rules." She kissed him again. "If you want to see me again, you'll go. I promise we'll meet up in a much safer place if you do." She couldn't let him know she wasn't sure.

Ben enveloped her in a long hug. "I'm going to hold you to that." Then he kissed the top of her head and headed into the jungle.

Siene did not move until she lost sight of him. "We'll need more than luck," she whispered. "We may need a miracle."

She could hear gunshots and surmised Reed had fired at movement coming from the jungle cover. She had bet it was one of Lucian's men. Lucian never did the dirty work himself. He liked his marks delivered. The sound of more gunfire confirmed her suspicion.

The firefight began to die out at the edge of the clearing surrounding the village. Siene eased her way around the trunk of a large kilgelia tree. A soldier in khakis about one hundred yards away saw her and fired directly at her. She fell to the ground trying to stay as low as possible. There was little cover now, and she wondered if she made a mistake in trying to approach the village too soon.

She lifted her head and saw the soldier striding toward her. But before he had a chance to fire, she heard a shot and he fell to the ground in front of her.

She looked beyond him and saw Reed raise his gun in a salute. He had circled back to make sure she was okay. Despite his calm pronouncement of the Primogen rules of engagement, she knew he worried about her.

Continuing forward on her belly took a long, agonizing time. She would have rather run but keeping low seemed to be the key to staying alive. She continued straight to the first hut, knowing every second she took might be a second out of Grandfather's life. When she got close, she half-ran, half-walked toward the first building. Standing, she leaned against the thatched walls and heard movement inside. She uttered a quick prayer and then ran for the doorway, knowing she would be exposed for a few seconds.

The air near her cheek stirred as a bullet whizzed past her face. She ducked and rolled into the doorway, not knowing what she would find—but the hut was empty. The bullet that nearly hit her had not come from inside. She quickly looked over the interior and left. Outside, she scanned the area, but could not see Ben nor her brother. This was not good.

Suddenly, she heard footsteps behind her and turned. *Lucian.* She ran but he caught up with her in two steps and took her to the ground. She arched her back and tried to twist away, but he held her in an iron grip that did not allow much movement. Suddenly, he moved his hands and put them around her neck. She clawed at his hands in a desperate attempt for air.

"Stop," she managed to choke out.

"You have to die," he said. "There is no other way."

There was madness in his eyes, and she knew nothing she could say would stop him. She tried to pull his hands away but the adrenaline surging through his body from his rage gave him a strength she could not match. But it was not her nature to give up without a fight.

She crossed her arms and slammed them against his arms. The blow buckled his elbows, but it wasn't enough. She then bridged her legs and arched her hips for momentum before delivering another blow to his forearms, breaking his hold. At the same time, she locked her left leg outside his right foot, swung her hip, and pushed him from her.

She tried to get to her feet, but Lucian tackled her at the back of her legs and brought her back to the ground. She struggled to get out of his grip, but he held on. Drawing her leg back, she kicked him in the chin. As the heel of her boot connected, his head snapped back, and he groaned. But he refused to let go. He clawed at her legs and began dragging himself up her body until he was on top of her. Then he reached out and slammed her head into the ground.

Her head spun and she willed herself to stay alert. Gunshots echoed in the distance, but she had no idea if they were from friend or foe. If she were going to live, she would have to do it on her own.

She realized that physically she didn't stand a chance against him. Normally, he was stronger than she was, and his rage only pushed that strength higher. She had to try to connect to the man he once was, the lover he'd been.

"Please, Lucian, don't kill me." Perhaps she could gain the upper hand by appearing frightened.

He relaxed.

For a second, she thought she saw a tenderness in

his eyes.

"I don't want to hurt you, Siene," he said. "But what else can I do?" He moved back.

She sat up. "We can work together. Isn't that what you always wanted us to do?"

He knelt beside her and ran his forefinger down her cheek. "I thought so at one time."

"We still can."

He shook his head. "I don't trust you, Siene."

"But you can. Let's find a place away from here where we can talk." She wasn't sure he would listen, but if they were both still alive, she had a chance.

Lucian shook his head.

She saw him glance over her shoulder. His face changed and anger rose again in his eyes. She looked back. Ben was coming at them, gun drawn and with an expression she had never seen on his face. "Take cover, Ben!" she shouted. But he just kept coming.

Lucian jumped to his feet. He reached behind his back and pulled out a semi-automatic handgun and fired. He hit Ben in the arm and the leg. Her ears rang from the nearness of the shots. She could do no more than watch the blood flow down Ben's arm and leg as he fell to the ground.

Ben still managed to fire off two shots. One hit Lucian's side, the other grazed his temple. Lucian dropped to his knees.

He raised the handgun and aimed at the center of Siene's chest. "It's over, darling. I win."

"No, I do," a voice from behind her said right before a shot rang out, catching Lucian right between the eyes. He fell to the ground and lay still.

Siene rolled to her feet and turned to come face to

face with Max Biden. "I suppose I'm next."

"Not today," Max said, firing two more shots into Lucian's body. "I feel generous." He holstered his weapon.

This is insane. I was taught to never leave an enemy alive under circumstances like this. "You aren't going to kill me?"

"No. Consider this a freebie."

"Why?"

"Killing you doesn't fit into my plan right now." He fired another shot into Lucian. "Killing him does." He looked her dead in the eyes, "But the next time we meet will be a different story." He saluted and bolted out the hut.

Siene hurried to Ben's side. She pressed her hand to the wound on his leg.

"Ouch," Ben said flinching. "That hurts more."

She closed her eyes and rested her forehead against his. "You crazy man. What were you thinking?"

"I was thinking I'd finally rescue you," he said with a rasp.

She shook her head. "It hasn't worked yet. Besides, I can take care of myself."

"I know, but you aren't invincible. I don't like that you constantly think you have to put yourself in danger for a higher cause."

She noticed each word he spoke was strained. He was putting on a show for her, but he was hurting. The coppery scent of blood confirmed her fears. She took off his shirt and ripped it into pieces.

"Where's Reed?" she asked as she wrapped his wounds.

"The men we met in the jungle came back and

joined us. As we were walking toward the village, we ran into a pair of Primogen Seekers looking for us and then a few of Davelos' men. We got into a scuffle but quickly overpowered them. When we realized they had been heading this way, Reed sent me on ahead to find you and warn you while he wrapped up business there.

"I need to get you to a hospital," she said. "The leg wound is a through-and-through, but I can't tell if the bullet is still in your arm. Can you stand?" She didn't wait for an answer and helped him to his feet.

"Damn, that hurts."

"Now, can you walk?"

"Yes," he said in a voice filled with resolve.

"Here we go."

Ben cursed when he took a step forward. He swayed and nearly fell to his knees. "This is going to be a lot tougher than I thought."

"You've done worse," Siene said, forcing herself to sound upbeat.

"Hell, I didn't have two holes in me at the time. You're kinda rough on a guy."

"Annoyances of the job." She held him up, taking all his weight and wrapping her arms around him.

They took a few steps and saw Reed coming toward them. "Lucian's dead," she told him.

He took Ben from her. "You finally killed him. I knew you would someday, Sis."

"I never got the chance," Siene replied. "Max Biden beat me to it."

Reed stiffened. "And you are alive. That makes no sense."

"I know," Siene said. "Biden said killing me didn't fit into his plans."

Reed grimaced. "Now *that* scares me."

"Me too," Siene agreed.

Ben began to sag against Reed. To prevent him from hitting the ground, Reed hoisted him up by his arm. Ben groaned with the sudden shift and slumped against Reed.

Siene cradled Ben's face in her hands. "He's out."

Two Primogen Seekers took Ben from Reed. Ben was still unconscious when they loaded him onto a litter and took him away.

"What happened?" Reed asked.

Siene crossed her arms in front of her. "Lucian came up from behind me and tried to choke me. We were locked in hand-to-hand combat for a while, and I knew I couldn't beat him that way, so I tried to reason with him."

Reed laughed. "That's rich. Who blinked? You or Davelos?"

"It wasn't anything like that. Ben came charging in on his white horse and Lucian shot him. He was about to pull the trigger on me when Biden shot him."

"Just like that."

"Just like that," she confirmed.

Reed shook his head. "And he let you live."

She nodded. "I couldn't believe it myself."

"Where's Biden now?"

"He ran off into the jungle." She hugged her stomach and shook her head. "I wonder what he meant by killing Lucian was a freebie."

Reed put his arm around his sister. "I'm sure it won't be long before we find out. For right now, I suggest we search the village for Joseph's grandfather. He is a wise and cunning man who has survived despite decades of dealing with warlords and local civil wars. I have no doubt he found a safe place to hide."

Chapter Thirty-Two

The small settlement of Alert in the northernmost region of the Qikiqtaaluk Region, Nunavut, Canada was a perfect place for the temporary Primogen compound. Just 500 miles from the North Pole, the Canadian census showed Alert's permanent population to be zero. All Alert's residents were temporary, serving a six-month tour of duty staffing a military signals intelligence radio receiving facility at Canadian Forces Station Alert (CFS Alert), as well as a Global Atmosphere Watch (GAW) atmosphere monitoring observatory. And because the region was targeted as an emergency alternate headquarters site since the end of World War II, the Primogens also made sure that those assigned to this station were Primogen Watchers.

Alert would have also been the perfect place for Siene to emotionally heal if she could stop thinking about Ben. She stood on the veranda of her room in the multiplex buried deep beneath the ice and wondered how she would move on now that the mission was over. She knew guns, how to get a fake ID, and how to disarm an enemy agent in under three seconds. But those skills would not help her forget Ben. Once his memory was erased, he would never know she existed. She wished she could do the same, but that was not a choice she could make. She heard a knock and then his voice.

"Can I talk to you?"

She turned from the railing and her breath caught. He hadn't cut his hair, and his beard was neatly trimmed. Hardly the man she rescued from a taxicab what seemed like a lifetime ago. "Sure."

He walked to her and leaned his backside against the railing. "I'm going back, aren't I? That's why I'm meeting with the Council today."

"We have our rules, Ben. We've had them for centuries."

"Why?"

He had that tone. The one he always had when he quizzed her on a point or when he questioned his scientific beliefs.

"Why what?" she asked.

"Why do I have to leave? I want to understand all I've seen. I want to try to help."

She shook her head. She knew as a scientist he would want to finish exploring all that could be done with the artifacts, but that was too dangerous to the overall legacy. Someone other than those born to be Primogens could not be trusted to understand why the artifacts should not be used to help humanity except under extreme circumstances, and even then, with only the highest degree of debate and with the maximum number of potential alternatives considered beforehand. The temptation and lure of power was just too great. Even if Ben wanted to stay, the vote to include him had to be unanimous. What was called "A Decision to Become" had never happened. Besides, he was a dangerous distraction for her now. She had changed. She no longer wanted to be alone, and that could jeopardize future missions.

"You have to leave for the common good." She looked into his eyes and couldn't give him any more than that.

He put his arm around her and hugged her close. "We can do this, Siene. Together."

She gave him a half-hearted smile. "Are you trying to be my hero again? You know how that's worked out in the past." She tipped her head back and looked up. "Whatever is going on in that supercomputer brain of yours, don't worry about me."

"I can't help it," he said.

She held his gaze. She banished the worries and fear that had been her constant companion since they had left Africa to the back of her mind and pretended she was just another woman standing in the arms of her man. "How did we get here?" she asked him.

"I think it had something to do with a mirror," he replied.

She slipped out of his arms and turned away so he would not see the tears well in her eyes. What if he asked her to go with him? What if Jack did erase her memory of this charge she was given and everything that went with it. *What if...?* Her heart beat faster. No, Ben wouldn't ask her, and she wouldn't go. Their fates were separately written. There was no turning back for either of them.

****

Ben paced outside the door leading to the room the Primogens now used as the council chamber. He knew this sanctuary was temporary. The Primogens would move somewhere more secure. He also realized he knew too much. He had moved from target to liability. He heard the door open and turned. It was Jack.

"C'mon in, mate."

"Before I do," Ben said, "can you answer a few questions?"

"Very few," Jack hedged.

Ben gestured to the door. "What's going to happen in there?"

Jack laughed. "Haven't you heard the adage 'ignorance is bliss'?"

"How about the one that says, 'knowledge is power'?" Ben shot back.

Jack thought for a moment. "I can tell you this much. You're going back."

Ben rubbed the back of his neck. "Aren't you afraid I'll let it slip about all of you?"

"Nope."

Caught off guard by the flippant tone of Jack's voice, Ben pressed him. "I'm a scientist, and scientists are both curious and relentless. I can't simply turn off what I've seen."

Jack crossed his arms and stared. He pursed his lips in thought, then threw his hands up. "What can it hurt to tell ya?" He slapped a hand on Ben's shoulder. "You're gonna kinda do the Harry, mate."

Ben's forehead furrowed. "Do what?"

Jack stepped back. "In the '60s our prime minister went swimming one day and didn't come back."

"So the Primogens are going to kill me."

"Naw, nothing like that, and sorta like that." He tapped Ben's temple with his forefinger. "You may lose a few brain cells, though, like Joseph."

"What happened to Joseph?"

"He's getting returned."

Ben saw a sly smile rise across Jack's mouth.

"Exactly what do you mean by returned?"

"He'll be going back to current conditions minus a few weeks."

"How?"

"We had him take a sickie, but he'll be apples in a few days."

Ben shook his head and sighed. "In English, not Aussie, please."

"Yeah, right. We set it up so that when he goes back, he won't remember anything about the mine, Taltos, or us. We adjusted his memory to before he was taken by Davelos. He's at his grandfather's village now in an induced coma. All he'll know when he wakes up is that he hit his head."

"You mean his memory was erased."

Jack nodded.

"How can you be sure his grandfather won't tell him what happened? Isn't he a loose end?"

"No, mate. He's one of ours."

****

Siene sat at her place at the council table. This would be the last time she saw Ben. It hurt, but it was necessary. When he entered, her breath caught. She thought she was ready. She wasn't.

Reed rose as Ben approached. He gestured to an empty seat at the table. "Please, sit."

Ben scanned the room. "There's one of you missing."

Reed sat. "Quinnock E'ak has been removed from the Council and returned to Antarctica. He will be replaced."

"Why was he removed?" Ben asked.

"When confronted, he broke down and confessed

his part in what happened. He wanted the Primogens to deal with Taltos once and for all. He was the one who gave Davelos some of Alice's mushroom and the piece of Snow White's apple. He hoped to force a confrontation when Davelos used the objects, so he is no longer considered viable."

Ben nodded. If the Council did that to one of their own, surely there was no hope for him.

"And now we need to conclude our business with you, Dr. Michaels," Reed continued.

Ben looked at Siene.

She looked away.

"How so?" Ben asked.

"You'll be returned to New York with our thanks."

"But without some of my memory."

Reed shot Jack a cold stare.

Jack just saluted.

"It can't be helped, Dr. Michaels," Reed said. "The success of the Primogens in keeping the artifacts safe from humanity lies in our ability to operate in the gray areas of normal life. While we appreciate your contributions to the Legacy, we can't trust your silence."

Ben stood. "Then let me join you."

A gasp arose from a few of the Primogens.

"Impossible," Kai said.

"He's kidding, right?' Jon Two-Bear shouted. "If you think I'm going to let a stranger into the Legacy…" His voice trailed off.

Siene rose. "He's not exactly a stranger. Technically, he could be considered 'Primogen blood', and as such, quasi-family."

Silence encased the room, and the Primogens

looked from one to the other.

"How so?" Reed asked.

Siene continued. "The Flu Pandemic of 1918 was one of the deadliest in the United States. While the 1918 H1N1 virus had been synthesized and evaluated, the properties that made it so devastating were not well understood. With no vaccine to protect against influenza infection and no antibiotics to treat secondary bacterial infections that can be associated with influenza infections, control efforts worldwide were limited to non-pharmaceutical interventions such as isolation, quarantine, good personal hygiene, use of disinfectants, and limitations of public gatherings. As the Public Health Agencies organized, they needed someone to take charge and coordinate the efforts." She looked at Ben. "That person was your great-grandfather, Ben."

Ben dropped into the chair. "What are you saying, Siene?"

"The Council considered using Rapunzel's tears to stop the spread by strategically curing areas of infection. They brought in your great-grandfather under the guise of a summit with the World Health Organization. The Council told him about the tears and suggested a vaccine could be forthcoming." She smiled at Ben. "It took a lot of convincing for him to believe the tears were real."

"Guess it runs in the family," Ben said.

Siene nodded and continued. "But with 500 million people affected worldwide, and only a finite amount of tears remaining, the Council and Ben's great-grandfather finally acknowledged there was not a sufficient quantity to make enough vaccine to treat everyone. After much talk and consideration, it was decided that the measures already being taken were the only way to stop the spread. For the good of mankind, Ben's great-grandfather willingly allowed the Primogens to erase any memory he might have had of the Council and its heartbreaking decision to let the virus run its course."

Ben sat stunned for a while before finding his voice. "How could the Council and my great-grandfather have condemned over 500 million people to die? That goes against the Hippocratic Oath every doctor takes."

"I cannot speak for your great-grandfather, but it is one of the decisions we as Primogens must make in dealing with the charge we have been given," Reed said.

"The pandemic did die out," Siene continued. "The end of any pandemic or epidemic occurs because the virus circulates the globe, infecting enough people that the population no longer has enough susceptible people for the strain to flare. When you get enough people who achieve immunity, the infection will slowly die out because it's harder for the virus to find new susceptible hosts."

"But it can mutate," Ben cut in. "I can help with that if an outbreak occurs in the future."

Reed shook his head. "We, as Primogens, cannot afford to speculate on what may or may not happen. The world is large with too many variables. We can only try to handle what happens in the here and now."

Jon rose. "Why is it none of the rest of us knew this?"

"For security reasons, I suppose, "Jack said.

"But there was an account written in a secret journal." She looked at Reed. "Our parents had it hidden in the attic. I suppose they would have given it to us eventually, but one day, I was bored and found it. I knew I could not tell anyone, even Reed. If the Council found out our parents had a written record of a Primogen decision, we might have all faced being returned."

Jon nodded and sat. "But how does that all relate to Dr. Michaels being considered as Primogen 'blood'?"

"It's a stretch, I know, but Ben's great-grandfather helped make a heart-wrenching decision then, and Ben can help now if needed. He is a research scientist and a doctor. Science and technology have made great strides since 1918. He might be able to find a way to synthesize Rapunzel's Tears so in the case of another pandemic, we can help save lives." She walked around the conference table as she spoke, making sure she caught the gaze of the remaining Primogens. "We no longer can count on the past to protect our secrecy. This is an age of the Internet, search engines, and brilliant minds who, with enough time and money, can find us. We must have others join us if we want to survive and protect mankind from itself. Don't erase his memory. Let him use his knowledge and skill to keep us safe."

****

Siene packed the last box of her stuff and moved it to the doorway. It had been three months since she had left Africa. Taltos had been quiet. Joseph was making great strides as a Research Physician at the Texas Medical Center. Quinnock E'ak was doing well in Antarctica, though his reprogramming needed updating as memories sometimes returned. He was carefully tended to by his wife; he was unaware that she was a Primogen Scribe he had met while getting supplies at McMurdo Station.

Caleb had stayed in Africa. The villagers were slowly recovering from the effects of Snow White's apple. Ben had succeeded in using the antigens in saliva as a partial antidote to the poison in the apple, but it was necessary to use some of Rapunzel's tears as a catalyst. The amount of tears was dangerously low, and now his mission was to try to synthesize a hybrid of the antigens and the tears to use in future pandemics.

"Hurry up or we'll miss our flight."

Siene hurried out the door to find Ben waiting for her. She was slowly getting used to having him in her life. She handed him the carry-on. "I'm going to miss this place."

"Our first home." Ben quipped.

Siene smiled. They had been living together, if you could call sharing a suite next to her brother as home.

"Before we go," she said. "There's a call for you."

Ben cocked his head. "No one knows I'm here."

Siene walked to the library table against the wall and pressed a button on the underside. A center section of the wall retracted and revealed a large monitor.

"How come I never knew it was there?" Ben asked. He smiled. "I've spent a lot on time in this room."

"You were otherwise occupied." She connected the call.

Ben's smile widened. "Lina! I wasn't sure I'd see you again."

"Humm." Her voice sounded like a contented purr. "Look at you. A lot less Albert Einstein these days."

Ben raised his hands and turned in a slow circle.

"You like?"

Lina laughed. "I dare not say with Siene in the room, but it is an improvement."

"Where are you?" Ben asked.

"Back in Brazil. My vacation was interrupted by a kidnapping, so I thought I'd finish it before I got my next assignment. And look." She stepped back, snapped her fingers, and miniaturized. The next instant she was back full-sized. "Gives me a headache, but I'm getting the hang of my talent."

Siene stepped up to the monitor. "I hate to cut this off, but the helicopter is waiting, and I have one more surprise for Ben."

Lina waggled her fingers. "No prob. See you, Ben. I'm going to the market later. Maybe I'll get you that nice fedora we talked about to complement your new look." She winked and the screen went dark.

Siene gestured to the door. "We should hurry, but there's one more old friend who wants to say goodbye." She led him to a room next to the elevator and swung open the door. Immediately Snow White's Mirror illuminated.

"My good man, nice to see you. I thought you'd be dead by now," TM said.

Ben grinned at the face staring at him from the center of the Mirror. "Thanks to you, no."

The smile of satisfaction on Mirror's face widened. "Another job well done. If I had hands, I'd pat myself on the back."

"You sound a little like Shard," Ben said. "How is he?"

Behind Mirror, the vista darkened. "Annoying as ever. He keeps talking about a snake and how you left him in the jungle." Mirror sighed. "Teenagers. So annoying. Because he ages so slowly since he is not used much, I'd say in a hundred years or so he may become tolerable."

Ben laughed. "Thank you for saving my life." He encircled Siene's shoulders in an embrace. "Because of it, I met Siene." He briefly glanced at her. She placed a hand over his and smiled.

Mirror's eyes narrowed. "I sense he isn't going to be returned."

"He's one of us now," Siene said.

"Oh, jolly good," Mirror returned.

"Sarcasm?" Siene asked.

"I'd rather not say."

"I'd love to stay and continue this chat, but we really have to be going. Ben's lab is being set up and I know he is eager to begin his new research."

"Well then, run along and save the world." Mirror rolled his eyes. "Someone has to do it."

As Ben and Siene walked to the elevator that would take them top side to a waiting helicopter, Ben slipped his hand in hers. "I know the new compound is ready, but you never told me where it was. I really am anxious to get started."

She stopped, turned to him, and grinned. "I wanted it to be a surprise. How do you feel about the Bermuda Triangle?"

His eyes widened. "It is a step up from the African jungle. And no snakes."

His laughter echoed in her heart. She didn't know what the future held for them. Even the Mirror couldn't tell her that. But she did know, no matter what happened, she would never be alone again.

A word about the authors...

P.K. Eden is the alter ego of multi-published and award winning authors Patt Milhailff and Kathye Quick whose debut novel *Firebrand* was lauded as comparable to the Harry Potter series, garnered 5-Star reviews, and won numerous Reviewer's Choice Awards

Patt Mihailoff is a multi-published author who writes in a wide range of genre's including, paranormal, erotica and short stories, but she has a particular affection for historical westerns, medieval stories with a twist and short stories.

In 2009 Patt received the prestigious *Author of the Year* award from the Romance Writers Of America New York City chapter, followed by *Mentor of the Year* award in 2010.

****

Born long, long ago in a place not so far away, Shenandoah, Pennsylvania, Kathryn Quick has been writing since the Sisters in St. Casmir's Grammar School gave her the ruled yellow paper and a number two pencil.

Kathye is a best-selling, multi-published, and international author who writes in several genres including contemporary and career romances, romantic comedies, historical romances as well as urban fantasy.

Kathye's previous books with the Wild Rose Press include her Bachelors Three series (*Bachelor.com* – *Solid Gold Bachelor* – *The Bachelor's Agenda*) which follow three very eligible bachelors as they find their soulmates, as well as *Cynthia and Constantine*, a medieval historical romance. She is thrilled to be writing again for the Wild Rose Press.

Milton Keynes UK
Ingram Content Group UK Ltd.
UKHW020738071024
449371UK00014B/928